ONE OF *THE NEW YORK TIMES BOOK REVIEW*'S
BEST ROMANCE NOVELS OF THE YEAR

ONE OF GOODREADS'S RISING STARS
OF SCI-FI AND FANTASY TO DISCOVER NOW

ONE OF *PASTE*'S BEST NEW
FANTASY BOOKS OF THE MONTH

ONE OF *BOOK RIOT*'S GREAT NEW BOOKS TO READ

"Set in the same universe as author Everina Maxwell's
fantastic arranged-marriage space opera *Winter's Orbit, Ocean's
Echo* features new characters, a new setting, and a new trope at its
center. (Fake dating versus marriage of convenience, but let's
be real, both options are A+ great.)"
—*PASTE*

"Lush and poetic. There are moments that gesture toward
the crystalline beauty of *This Is How You Lose the Time War* by
Amal El-Mohtar and Max Gladstone, or the character-forward
complexity of Lois McMaster Bujold's beloved Vorkosigan Saga."
—*THE NEW YORK TIMES BOOK REVIEW*

"A slow burn that eventually blazes into a supernova."
—*BOOKPAGE*

★ ★ With starred reviews from *BO*
PUBLISHERS WEEKLY. and *LIBRA*

T0051398

Praise for

OCEAN'S ECHO

"One of the rare books that deliver at every level on every page."
—*The New York Times Book Review*

"This earns a space on shelves alongside the very best of the genre."
—*Publishers Weekly* (starred review)

"Truly original . . . Writing fantastically memorable characters, Maxwell masterfully draws out a rich and complicated story that explores military incursions, familial ties, and the impact of secrets revealed."
—*Booklist* (starred review)

"This standalone set in the same universe as *Winter's Orbit* is an exciting, fast-paced sci-fi adventure with great world-building and complex characters. Fans of Jessie Mihalik and J. S. Dewes will enjoy."
—*Library Journal* (starred review)

"*Ocean's Echo* is a slow burn that eventually blazes into a supernova, a novel constrained in its location but massive in its ambition."
—*BookPage*

"Compassionate, queer, slightly horrifying, and wildly inventive—*Ocean's Echo* whisked me into a faraway world of spacefaring outcasts and rogues, teased me with the promise of not-quite-human romance, and vaulted me into a transcendent meditation on identity, truth, and the meaning of existence itself. What a glorious read!"
—Ryka Aoki, author of *Light from Uncommon Stars*

"*Ocean's Echo* digs its teeth into the psychic-soulbond trope and gives it a good, hard, gleeful shake—and what falls out is a fast-paced and gorgeously written tapestry of exciting space adventure, heart-clenching romance, and deft examination of the duties we owe to one another and what it means to be human in a vast universe. I was hoping that it would give me the same feelings of awe and delight that *Winter's Orbit* did, and instead it delivered them on an *even higher level*. This is space opera at its best."
—Freya Marske, author of *A Marvellous Light*

Tor Publishing Group Books by Everina Maxwell

Winter's Orbit

EVERINA MAXWELL

OCEAN'S ECHO

BRAMBLE
TOR PUBLISHING GROUP
NEW YORK

OCEAN'S ECHO

Copyright © 2022 by Everina Maxwell

A Bramble Book
Published by Tom Doherty Associates / Tor Publishing Group
120 Broadway
New York, NY 10271

www.brambleromance.com

Bramble™ is a trademark of Macmillan Publishing Group, LLC.

The Library of Congress has cataloged the hardcover edition as follows:

Names: Maxwell, Everina, author.
Title: Ocean's echo / Everina Maxwell.
Description: First edition. | New York : Tor, 2022. | "A Tom
    Doherty Associates book."
Identifiers: LCCN 2022034338 (print) | LCCN 2022034339 (ebook) |
    ISBN 9781250758866 (hardcover) | ISBN 9781250758880 (ebook)
Subjects: LCGFT: Science fiction. | Novels.
Classification: LCC PR6113.A9823 O73 2022 (print) |
    LCC PR6113.A9823 (ebook) | DDC 823/.92—dc23/eng/20220721
LC record available at https://lccn.loc.gov/2022034338
LC ebook record available at https://lccn.loc.gov/2022034339

ISBN 978-1-250-75887-3 (trade paperback)

Our books may be purchased in bulk for promotional, educational, or business use. Please contact your local bookseller or the Macmillan Corporate and Premium Sales Department at 1-800-221-7945, extension 5442, or by email at MacmillanSpecialMarkets@macmillan.com.

First Bramble Edition: 2023

Printed in the United States of America

0 9 8 7 6 5 4 3 2 1

TO ELEANOR

THANK YOU FOR THE JELLYFISH. I LOVE YOU.

PART ONE

CHAPTER 1

Tennalhin Halkana arrived at the party fashionably late, which might have meant something if he'd been invited in the first place. Tennal often set out to make trouble, it was true, but this evening, he was genuinely here for a drink and a good time.

That was a lie. He also wanted an architect, and this party would be full of architects.

The party was in the penthouse of the most exclusive hotel in the city. It was a glittering front for an underground gambling ring, so it was full of dangerous people, but Tennal had stopped caring who he mingled with some time ago. Tennal floated from one gambling meetup to another these days, always just interesting enough to be kept around, never involved enough to get in serious trouble. As a lifestyle, it had its ups and downs. As an escape plan, it was an amateur one, but he could keep it going as long as he had to. He just needed the right architect.

He didn't risk the private drone service ferrying people up to the balcony. Instead Tennal flirted his way past security in the hotel lobby and walked into the elevator as if he belonged there. There was no security at the penthouse door. People didn't go to this kind of party uninvited, but Tennal had found there were very few things you couldn't do if you didn't care about fucking up. Tennal was low on money, low on options, and didn't have a lot left to lose.

The penthouse was a dark fug of noise and low-level sensory vibrations. It was dimly lit by colored glows under tables and light filaments like sprays of vivid flowers in the corners. Dozens of people gathered around various games, or the bar, or smaller tables where more serious business was being done. Under the talking and the music, there was the low, vibrating drone that people on certain chemical substances found enjoyably hypnotic. Some people were obviously high already. Tennal was envious.

But he'd been right. There were architects.

That woman over there, with the flint-and-gold necklace and the weapon at her belt, was an architect. So was the gray-haired tough picking over the buffet. So—interestingly—was the ethereally beautiful twentysomething waif who looked like someone's trophy boyfriend. Tennal didn't often meet architects his own age.

None of them were that good. They weren't slinging around mental commands at the bar or anything, but Tennal could see it: architects gave off an aura, if you knew how to look for it, like light radiating from a star. The ones he was watching were pretty faint. They might be able to take over someone's mind for a split second, but only if they really tried. Tennal was looking for someone else. Someone better.

Of course, every architect in here would be careful what they used their mental influence for. Using it on the wrong person in the street might get you a warning from law enforcement, but in here, it might get you shot. And architects had the *acceptable* kind of power.

Tennal was too sober for this.

He slid into a seat at the bar and smiled glitteringly at the bar-tender. "What's free?"

There was usually something free at these things. The bartender paused and squinted at him suspiciously, as if Tennal didn't look quite wealthy enough or dangerous enough to be here. Tennal didn't show any signs of backing off, though, and eventually a shot glass came sliding across the bar.

Might as well ask. Tennal tilted his head at the dozens of conversations behind him and said, "So, which one's the boss?" *The boss* might refer to any number of people in the city of Sanura, but in here, it meant the leader of this gambling ring, the one who owned this hotel. "I was told he's an architect."

The bartender's hand stopped on the table. Tennal felt a sudden spike of wariness from them. They met Tennal's eyes and shrugged.

At that point, someone tapped Tennal on the shoulder, and he flinched.

He tried to cover up the twitch as he turned. He had to get that kind of reaction under control. If the legislator had really found him, it wasn't as if her people were going to gently tap him on the shoulder and start a conversation.

This wasn't much better, though. A young woman in an armored vest stared down at him, her hand resting on a holster at her hip. This was somebody's bodyguard.

There was no security at the door for this kind of thing because everyone brought their own security. If you turned out to be law enforcement, it was very simple: you left, or somebody's bodyguard would shoot you. Tennal wasn't law enforcement, though if they'd known exactly who he was, he wouldn't have totally blamed them for shooting him.

"I don't think you were invited," the bodyguard said.

Tennal raised his hands in front of him, fingers spread. "I'm unarmed. Promise. Unless you count three tissues and a pack of soothers—and honestly, I'd have to get very inventive."

She gave him a thin, unimpressed stare. Flint ear studs glinted under her short hair. "I've seen you before."

A jolt went through Tennal. *She couldn't know.* Could she?

Tennal's mind was always a little too open to the universe. He wasn't an architect, because that would have made life too easy. No, he'd ended up with the *un*acceptable kind of powers. He nudged his senses further open, just a fraction, and read her mind.

The instant he opened himself up, a dozen minds flared in his perception. The party was crowded; each person moved in a haze of their own moods like a shimmer of light. And if architects were faint stars, pulsing with intention and influence, Tennal was the opposite. Nobody had ever told him what his mind looked like from the outside, but he had his suspicions: an unsettling void, a black hole.

As far back as he could remember, Tennal had always been aware of a low-level drone from the minds around him. It was like an indecent form of tinnitus. Random impressions drifted in his direction, and if he actively tried, he could read them: vague emotions, nonspecific intentions, nothing particularly helpful. People's surface thoughts were seldom interesting, in any case—right now, from the crowd in the room, Tennal could feel hunger, irritation, interest, boredom. All standard.

Reading that kind of background mental drone wasn't illegal. Not quite. After all, it was only a step above watching people's body language; he wasn't going any deeper. Tennal focused on the bodyguard, looking for *threat*.

Nothing. She wasn't interested in threatening him, and there was none of the prurient interest that would suggest she knew who his family was. She was just fed up with her long shift, overdue for a break, and Tennal was paranoid.

"I'm just here to ask a favor from the boss," Tennal said, leaning back against the bar. "Is that a crime?"

He could have tried announcing the reader thing, but he needed to save that for when it would make an impact. Being a reader—they were rarities—made him just scandalous enough to be interesting, and Lights knew nobody was inviting him anywhere because of his delightful personality.

She gave him one of the most unimpressed looks he'd seen in his life, and Tennal was a connoisseur of unimpressed looks. "Ask the boss for what? Three square meals and a job?" She slapped a hand on the bar to get the bartender's attention. "You should clean up and get out of here. I hate the ones who get in over their heads."

The bartender, who obviously knew her, slid her a plate of food. Tennal paused in the act of popping out a mild soother from the pack in his pocket. Yes, he was coming off a days-long hangover, and yes, his meals and sleep were all over the place because the concept of scheduling was fatally dull, but surely he didn't look like that much of a mess. "I'm doing fine, but I appreciate the concern."

She took the food without looking at Tennal. "I'm back on duty in an hour. You should be gone before then."

"Or I could get your boss to invite me to stay," Tennal suggested. He got a flash of irritation and knew his guess was right: she worked for the host of this party. He could use that.

"Lights," the woman said to the ceiling, as if a divine Guidance might come to her aid and throw Tennal out a window. She jerked her head at the bartender. "Get him some food. Put it on the party tab; fuck knows these nights cost thousands. Maybe he'll sober up and leave."

Tennal was thrown. He opened his mouth to say he didn't need charity—or at least not this kind, not *pity*—but she'd taken her sandwich and gone.

Tennal vindictively ordered the most expensive plate on the menu, the one that came with gold leaf scattered around artistic constructions of pastries and fruit. He ate the pastries while he watched the crowd and scanned for clues to the boss.

As he watched the bodyguard leave for her break, he made one more attempt to read her. He had to be careful. Reading was draining, and if he went any deeper than the surface layer, she would feel it. And if she felt it, he would be in a *lot* of trouble.

All he got when he tried was a pulse of vague awareness from her toward one corner of the room, where a small knot of older people had gathered to play cards.

Tennal examined the corner. The gamblers there looked like military veterans; most people with any kind of power on Orshan had been in the army at some point. Their clothes were dark, but most of them wore colored division paraphernalia: pins, medals, colored bands. They had their own private drinks cart. When Tennal casually moved across the room and opened his mind—he had to be close to read someone's aura with any certainty—they pulsed like a cluster of suns. Tennal breathed out. *It's one of you.*

Tennal was out of options. Time for his plan of last resort.

Nobody stopped Tennal from walking up to the game. This corner of the party was quieter and more private. Hanging lights shed a dim amber glow over the card game, the only other illumination the night skyline through the windows. Silver jewelry glinted in the darkness on wrists and chests. Tennal would bet money that these were the leaders of *all* Sanura's gambling rings.

He could feel himself being watched. He glanced at the armed bodyguards casually standing not too far from the table, which just confirmed it.

Tennal was fine with being watched. He smiled back at the hostile stares and surface-read the bodyguards until he found the one who was at slightly heightened stress levels, the sort that might indicate you'd been a two-person team, until your partner took their break, and now you were covering the post alone. Tennal paused and zeroed in on the gambler that bodyguard was watching.

Found the boss.

Not all the ringleaders had been playing this round. One was at the drinks cart. He was pale, well-built, and expensively dressed, with a wooden gender-mark on his bracelet like the one on a casual silver chain around Tennal's neck. Tennal would have given him the time of day even if he hadn't been an architect. When Tennal looked through his reader senses, though, there wasn't any doubt about the architect bit.

Tennal slipped in beside him and leaned over the selection of drinks.

He should be careful. If he had the right person, this man owned the underground racing market, half the financial district, and the weapons trade. Tennal should be polite and circumspect. But Tennal had never been careful, and he only knew a few ways to get someone's attention.

He reached out and jostled the man's arm so he dropped his glass.

"Whoops," Tennal said insincerely. "Let me get that for you."

The man grabbed his wrist without changing expression. Tennal felt a flash of anger from him.

Time for the party trick. Tennal passed a hand over the lavish collection of imported drinks and picked the one most prominent in the man's thoughts: a small blue bottle of distilled silverberry, which had embossing from some galactic backwater and was probably worth its weight in gold. Tennal thought it tasted like neat oil. Bad choice for a favorite; his opinion of the man's taste went down.

Tennal carefully poured it into a new glass without dislodging the man's grip on his wrist. "I heard you do favors for readers."

The man released his wrist. He smiled faintly. "Direct. I do favors for readers who do favors for me."

Tennal opened his mind and focused on him. The man wasn't giving much away on the surface—mild interest, a condescending sense of being in control of the room. He had met readers before, so maybe he thought he knew what Tennal could do.

Readers were scattered and rare. Most reading didn't actually tell you that much about what someone was thinking. Tennal, like any reader, could focus on someone and read them on a shallow level whenever he wanted, though he would only pick up a vague outline of their feelings and intentions, and if he left his mind open for too long it gave him a headache. Even that shallow reading was illegal, but it could be useful if you were discreet about it.

Readers who could go deep, beyond surface emotions, were even more of an anomaly—so much so that many people didn't

believe they existed. Tennal might have appreciated being an aberration more if it hadn't nearly gotten him arrested several times
when he was growing up. But hiring out his deep-reading skills
wasn't an option because people had a habit of noticing you were
doing it. And he didn't want to get *too* far into a criminal operation. He'd have to pretend to be good, but not too good. "I might
be able to help you out."

"I work with readers now and then," the man said, watching
him. "Before we go any further, though, tell me—how good are
you at defending yourself? You're not much use to me if the first
architect you meet can make you spill your guts."

Tennal let a lazy smile creep onto his face. He twirled the em-
bossed bottle. "I'm hard for architects to get to," he said. "You
want me to prove it? How about a bet?"

The boss cleared a table for them with a look. His bodyguard
didn't even have to step closer. He waved a hand for Tennal to sit
opposite him.

At the back of his mind, Tennal knew this was further than he'd
ever gone. He was taking risks he wouldn't have imagined a few
months ago—but it was fine. It was all fine. It had to be fine, because Tennal had run out his welcome everywhere else. He'd be
out on the streets if he didn't find something. Going home wasn't
an option. "Let's make this easy," Tennal said. He held out his
glass for a refill. "I bet you I can go three minutes without drinking that. Start the clock."

The boss laughed. "If I don't write you, you mean."

Writing was the informal term for the way architects bent your
mind into compliance. It was more accepted than reading, since
at least you knew it was happening—and there were so many
bloody architects, you couldn't turn a street corner in Exana
without tripping over one. Tennal had never seen why that was
so much better for society than reading. "How good are you?"
Tennal asked, with enough skepticism to sound like a challenge.
This man was obviously an architect, since he glowed bright to

Tennal's reader senses, but Tennal had seen better architects. "Try me."

The boss gave him a second look, eyes flicking up and down. "All right, then." He looked over at his bodyguard and tapped his wristband.

After a few moments, the bodyguard silently laid a display case on the table. He flipped up the lid and stepped back.

Tennal tried not to react. It was totally innocuous: a display set of liquor glasses, the high, flared type common in this part of the world. They were emblazoned with the full set of military divisions. Red for Cavalry, charcoal for Infantry, Archer gold, Vanguard blue . . . the full dozen was there, even the smaller divisions with no political influence.

"Pick your poison," the boss said, watching his face.

This was a test. The first architects and readers had been created by the military, twenty years ago, so anyone Tennal's age must have got the reader gene from a veteran parent. That meant Tennal's family was tied to one of the divisions: if not Cavalry, which was currently in charge of the legislature, then maybe Infantry, or Navy, or one of the others. Military politics mattered everywhere on this bloody planet. You couldn't escape it. The man wanted to know if Tennal would admit who he was connected to.

Tennal ignored the vivid red of the Cavalry glass and picked one of the others at random. Yellow glinted between his fingers as he slid it over to be filled. "Three minutes," he said. "Try writing me."

"And what do you want if you win?" the man said.

"You own this hotel," Tennal said. "The people I've been rooming with want me out. I need a place to stay for a while." He tried to sound casual. He'd been kicked out this morning, not to put too fine a point on it, but that was an unnecessary detail. Tennal didn't like the word *desperate* and saw no reason to apply it to himself.

"That's all?"

Tennal felt it. The first touch of an architect command, like a solar flare in his peripheral vision. He didn't react. "I'm buying time," Tennal said. He leaned back in his chair, the liquor glass between his fingers. "Why, can't you afford to let me have a room? Business not doing well?"

The boss struck.

Being written by an architect felt like unshielding your eyes in front of a furnace. A bright mental light flooded Tennal's eyes, his whole brain, a dazzle that shoved out every other thought. If Tennal found an architect strong enough—or took one of the small neuro-enhancer pills currently nestled in his pocket—he could sink into that white blaze and turn his brain off. As unnerving as it was, it was always a break from the never-ending, relentlessly dull business of existing as himself.

Of course, Tennal was almost sober, and this didn't cut it. The architect's command glanced off his mental walls like sunlight off a mirror. Raising an ironic eyebrow would probably have been suicidal, so Tennal inspected the glass in his fingers instead.

The man tried again. The timer ticked down.

A little pool of silence grew around the table as people realized what they were doing. The mental battle took place in complete silence, the boss staring at Tennal as though he could bore a hole in his head through sheer willpower. Tennal slung one ankle over the other and tapped his fingers on the glass. Light beat vainly on the walls of his mind.

The timer beeped softly.

Tennal met the boss's eyes over the table. "My win." There was a dangerous moment when the man leaned forward, a sudden twist of anger radiating from him like a sour note. A shot of adrenaline went down Tennal's spine. He lived for this kind of high, even as he knew it was a bad idea. But if he had fucked up—if he'd finally gone too far—

Then the boss relented. He shrugged and clicked his fingers at one of the hangers-on nearby. "Get him a room. Long-term stay."

He kicked his chair back from the table and rose. "We'll talk another day." He paused. "Your accent is from Exana?"

It was a question. Not to get information but to see what Tennal would say when prodded. Tennal had a reaction ready. "Left it behind, obviously," he said. "Why would I want to be around the politicians? I'm here to have fun—party capital of the planet, what's not to love?"

The man smiled without warmth. "I hope you have fun, then. Enjoy your night."

It was a dismissal. Tennal's moment in the spotlight was over. It was time for him to dissolve back into the crowd and be safely anonymous.

Instead Tennal knocked back his horrible drink, looked up, and said, "Have you got anything better?"

CHAPTER 2

Tennal didn't go back to his new room that night. The noise of the party swallowed him, and later, the drones moved across the windows like stars. His head was mercifully quiet for a few hours.

The next day, Tennal found himself waking up in a mostly deserted penthouse with a hangover and an architect. Again.

The bed moved as the architect from last night climbed out. Tennal made a wordless noise and unstuck his eyelids. The man didn't say anything to him but started to pull on a set of clothes folded beside the bed: expensive cuts and fabrics, plus an encrypted pod comm on a flashy lace-gold chain. Tennal should probably have memorized his name.

"You look like shit, sweetie," the boss said. "I've got a call to take care of. You go have a shower." He put an architect's command behind *shower*, a mental flare of light, but it brushed past Tennal like a breeze sliding against glass.

A familiar disappointment settled over Tennal. He'd popped some neuro-enhancer tablets last night to bring down his defenses, but the effect had worn off. "Yeah, yeah. You going to bring me breakfast first?"

The boss chuckled. "Y'know, most readers who do jobs for me have more tact. I wouldn't even believe you were one if I hadn't seen you party. Later."

Tennal levered himself up on his elbows as the architect disappeared. The sun was well above the horizon. Light stabbed in through the penthouse's glass roof: it looked like nobody had remembered to set it to opaque the night before. Sanura's morning skyline gleamed.

Tennal felt like death. There was a tab of soothers on the bedside table that had survived the night; he absently popped one of them out. Soothers didn't interfere with your thinking, only provided a mild buzz that took the edge off the world. Tennal wondered what time it was.

A few moments' searching located his wristband under the bed. It blinked error lights as he fished it out; he'd had someone butcher it a few months ago to take out any function the legislator might use to locate him. Not that Tennal was the legislator's top concern, of course, but the more effort required to retrieve him, the less likely she'd bother. It made his wristband into more of a glorified timepiece than anything useful for—

The wristband pinged. Tennal dropped it.

He stared at it as it continued to ping softly on the floor. It shouldn't be able to do that. All the comm functions were cut off. A thread of terror coursed down his spine, setting off a wave of adrenaline. He crouched beside the wristband and picked it up.

The projection that spilled out of it wasn't a comm. Tennal suppressed the adrenaline-fueled part of him that had perversely *wanted* it to be a comm and investigated further. It looked like he hadn't totally disabled the scheduling functions, even though he hadn't used them for months. A spinning graphic was trying to remind him that his sibling had some sort of event scheduled. He'd set a reminder for it back when he was still taking comms. Her commencement ceremony for Legal academy.

Tennal's crouch gave way, and he sat on the floor.

The nausea he'd been suppressing came back full force. He wanted to go back to bed and preferably never get up. But that wouldn't solve this. All the other students would have family supporting them at the ceremony, or at least on comm. Zin and

Tennal weren't close to many members of their own family, and it wasn't as if their gen-parent would be there unless science had made some serious advances in posthumous communication. He hadn't even remembered Zin was coming up to the start of her course, after she'd spent years working for it. He hadn't wanted to think about it, in case he had to make some sort of decision.

He grabbed his wristband, pulled on some clothes, and stumbled out of the penthouse.

The upper floors of the hotel were littered with detritus from last night's party, but there were very few people. A few floors down, Tennal found an empty lounge. He threw himself in a leather chair, told his wristband to project over the table, and painstakingly set out to reengineer the damage.

It was tricky work because Tennal only knew what he'd gleaned from the programmer who'd disabled it in the first place. The one thing he didn't want to do was reactivate any of the location functions. It took him a good twenty minutes, stuck in the mess of number trees that underpinned the program, before he could resurrect some semblance of the voice chat and contact a single person.

Finally his wristband projected a swirling gray pool in the air at head height, waiting for Zin to answer her comm. The delay gave him just enough time to consider finding another soother.

Then the gray faded out, and a projection coalesced above the table: a sixteen-year-old with a short black bob, a gray lawyer's tunic, and a startled look. A pit opened in Tennal's stomach. He pushed his hair out of his face, wished to the Lights he'd showered, and said, "Hey, Zin." There was a moment's horrible silence. Tennal's best smile wasn't having the effect he wanted. "All turned out, look at you."

"*Tennal,*" Zin said. "Light of Guidance, *where are y—*" She visibly stopped herself. Tennal saw her swallow. "I won't ask," she said. "Your business. Glad you, um. Glad your comm's working now."

That made Tennal feel worse. He could see her glance around his projection, as if for any clues to his whereabouts he'd accidentally included. She caught herself and looked determinedly back at him. They'd had arguments about coming home before. "Yeah," Tennal said. "Just thought I'd—well. You all right?"

"I'm fine, thanks." Zin ducked her head slightly and added, "I'm entering second in my year," in the tone of someone who didn't want to boast but also desperately wanted to boast.

"Well, of course," Tennal said. "You just said hello, didn't you, and they waved you on in. 'Quick, give her a high mark, or she might pick another career track.'"

That won him a flicker of a smile, though she tried to look solemn. "That was completely and truthfully how it went."

"But, hey, congratulations." Tennal took a breath. He had to say something sincere, or there'd have been no point in sending her a comm. He wasn't good at sincere. "It's a, you know. It's a huge achievement. Very proud of you." It sounded wrong when it came out, but from the surprised shift in her face, the way she held herself when she was pleased and trying not to show it, he'd obviously gotten something right. In the glow of success, Tennal carried on. "Nice job, especially for a reader."

And he'd ruined it. Her expression froze.

"You know what I mean," Tennal said, in a quick attempt to paper over it. "I just mean, not as an architect. You know you didn't get it through the family, or—or reputation or anything." He was digging a hole for himself. He stopped before he got any deeper.

"I know," Zin said, her voice brittle. "I know you're hung up on it. I don't really want to define myself like that."

It was her commencement day. The least Tennal could do was force out the word. "Sorry."

She swallowed and tugged at one of her earlobes, making the earring chime. "No, I'm sorry. I know it's not been—such an issue for me." Her voice strengthened. "You look terrible, by the way."

Tennal flicked his hair theatrically. "Oh, *thanks,* sis. Let me tell you, that's not what the last five people who hit on me thought." He aimed for the needling tone he'd always used at home. It fell flat.

Usually she'd make an exaggeratedly disgusted face and tell him he was awful, maybe shout over him to get him to stop. But she was eight months older than he'd last seen her, and all she did was look at him steadily.

"You've lost weight," she said. "I'm not going to—don't take this the wrong way, Tenn, but you look *haggard.*"

"Yeah? What's the right way to take that?" Tennal said. "Can't believe I called you just to get insulted. Worst family."

Zin didn't rise to the bait. "You can take it how you like," she said quietly. Her expression was grave above her green-and-gray pre-Legal uniform. "Tenn—"

"I have to go," Tennal said. "Someone's coming. Too many fans, too little time. You know how it is. Speak later."

Zin's image winked out as he cut the projection. His smile fell off his face as he tried to settle his heartbeat. He hadn't meant to worry her. He'd talked to her, though, he'd done it; wasn't that something to be proud of? He scrubbed a hand across his forehead and decided it might not count.

He didn't move for a long time. There was a buzzing noise in his head. That was a new and exciting hangover symptom. He should probably eat something.

"You're still around?"

Tennal jerked up from his slump as a shadow fell across him. It was the bodyguard from last night. In the morning light, it was obvious she hadn't been drinking like the rest of them: her clean, sharp-angled face was alert and guarded. "Your room's not on this floor."

"Gotta recharge the batteries," Tennal said. "It's a reader thing." She snorted. "It's not."

Her absolute certainty was as good as an admission. Tennal

paused as a puzzle piece fell into place. He couldn't tell from looking at her, but: "You're a reader."

"Full marks," she said, turning away to draw some water from the cooler. "Why do you think I left you alone last night? You weren't a threat." She didn't seem fazed that Tennal had publicly read someone last night. The advantage of this crowd was that nobody ever involved law enforcement.

An unexpected silence settled over the room, broken only by the hangover buzzing in Tennal's head. He felt himself skate over a lot of things he normally tried not to think about. This bodyguard wasn't in the army, so she hadn't been directly neuromodified herself. Either her gen-parent or a gene donor must have been a military architect or a reader. Just like Tennal's gen-parent. "How good are you?" At her expression, he broke off. "Oh. Army strength."

"Not as far as the regulators know," the woman said. She finished her water. "I was going to ask you how you got out of conscription, but on second thought, this was a fucking stupid conversation to start. You're just hiding, aren't you?"

"I'm not on the conscription list," Tennal said. The legislator had never outright threatened that. A family member who was a reader was bad enough. A *conscripted* reader would be worse.

"Of course you're not," the woman said. "Or you'd be there already."

Tennal tapped his fingers on his sorry-looking wristband. "Technically it's not conscription anyway, is it?" he said. "Technically you have to break the law first, if you don't volunteer." The army officially disapproved of readers but still found the strong ones useful. If you were strong enough, it was amazing the minor technicalities that counted as breaking the law. Readers made good pilots, apparently. They synced you to an architect to keep you reliable—because, after all, you'd broken the law.

The woman snorted. "Like fuck anyone volunteers." She moved her head. "What's that noise?"

Tennal realized two things at the same time. The buzzing wasn't part of his hangover, and disabling locators wasn't nearly as easy as he'd thought it was.

The spike of realization made all his muscles coil up. He should have known what that buzzing noise was because he'd grown up with it in the background. He hadn't recognized it—he hadn't been listening out for it—because Sanura didn't have its own military base.

"Shit," he said. "That's a Swift-47 engine."

"What?" the woman said sharply.

Tennal had already shot out of his chair and was hammering at the room control panel by the door. "You need to get out. *You*, specifically, need to get out. Warn any other strong readers. Where the fuck is the fire code on this thing?"

The woman reached over his shoulder and jabbed a sensor. "Police?"

"Worse," Tennal said. "Army." He gave it confirmation for the highest-priority alarm: fire in the room. "They must have scrambled, so they won't have all the exits blocked off yet. Take a fire chute from the service stairs. They'll be following the location of my wristband, so I bet they'll come in at one of the top floors." He slipped it out of his pocket. "I'm going to—" He broke off. *Dump my wristband in the penthouse* was on the tip of his tongue. That was the next logical step. He could blend in with the crowd on the way out, and they'd waste time finding his abandoned wristband.

Sprinklers started to lower from the ceiling. The woman backed up a couple of steps and paused in the doorway. "So I need to find a new city?"

Tennal's thoughts were already going down the same track. The army would go through Sanura's underworld like a dirt grinder, sifting for info on where Tennal had run to, because they'd have to justify losing the objective of their scramble. She might get detained. Tennal mostly didn't care about the people he met here because they were just as shitty as himself, but he had an unwelcome surge of fellow feeling for another reader. She'd made some bad choices to end up in this job. What Tennal was about to bring down on her head was worse.

This was why Tennal shouldn't hang around decent people.

Fuck. He turned on his wristband's communications then jammed his fist in his pocket. "Maybe not," he said. "Just stay away from me."

They split up outside. A section of the wall outside had opened to show the mouth of a rapid-fall chute, glowing red. Tennal bypassed it, hammered at the button to call the lift, then remembered fire alarms turned off lifts at the same time as he heard the corridor sprinklers start. He ducked into a stairwell with damp hair and shoulders, coming up with new and inventive names for the prat who had decided to set off the fire alarm, and took the stairs up three at a time.

He was only five floors from the top, but it felt like twenty. He was nauseous by halfway up. Underneath the seething panic he thought, *I used to have more stamina than this.*

The penthouse was still empty when he staggered into it. Discarded bottles and cups lay scattered around. Tennal caught himself on the back of an uncomfortable designer chair and watched as the gray silhouette of a hoverplane grew larger and larger, circling down toward the building. It looked like it was going to come through the balcony. The door was locked, but it wasn't as if that would hold them up for more than ten seconds.

Tennal found himself moving automatically toward the cooler in the corner of the room. When he realized what he was doing, he shrugged and grabbed another handful of glasses by their stems.

He had his back to the balcony. That was fine. He poured himself a glass of champagne, letting the pounding of blood in his body blend in with the enormous, world-encompassing noise of a Swift's four turbo engines drawing up within ten meters of him.

There was a lower rumble as it cut back on power and hovered level with the balcony, nearly kissing the rail. This was good champagne.

The shattering of bulletproof glass made him turn.

"Twenty seconds just to break some glass," he said. "A bit slow, officers. Care for a drink?"

CHAPTER 3

Three uniformed soldiers had dropped from the plane to the balcony. Once the soldier with the impact drill had shattered the door, they released their harnesses and stepped over the broken window glass into the penthouse. Tennal barely registered the two armed rankers. They were just background to the third figure.

He was an army officer, stocky, with a bald head and an evidently lofty rank—Tennal couldn't read rank tabs, but he felt a stab of apprehension from the miles of gold braid encrusting his uniform. But the officer's nominal rank didn't matter. The moment he stepped in the room, a vivid glare of light flooded Tennal's head, drowning out even the pounding of the engines. Tennal couldn't see. He couldn't think.

There were very few Rank One architects on the planet. The legislator had scrambled one to get him.

The mental light of the command battered Tennal with the impulse to *stay where he was;* Tennal winced against the glare, like an industrial flashlight shining a foot from his face, and couldn't move his feet at all. He had techniques to deflect that kind of threat, but he couldn't concentrate on them under the pulsing headache. "I'll take that as a no on the drink," he said. "You don't think you could turn that down, could—"

"That's him," the architect said. "Secure the exits." He jabbed a finger at the doors to the corridor and the bathroom. The rankers were already moving, one to cover each door. They pointed their incapacitator guns outward, against intruders, rather than in, but this was only a slight improvement.

"No? No, I suppose not," Tennal said. He'd finished his glass. He set it down, leaned on the edge of the table, and picked up the bottle. "How about—"

The architect turned his entire attention on him, and Tennal's vocal cords locked up.

"No," the architect said. The command filled Tennal's mind with an unbearable white heat. His headache worsened. Tennal had played around with being written for fun, but he'd forgotten what a Rank One could do to him. He'd forgotten what it was like to be written by someone with no positive intent, no attempt to be considerate, just a searing pain as the command coruscated across the pathways of his brain and stripped them clean. The edges of Tennal's vision blurred. The only thing he could hear was the architect's voice, thin and scratchy, filling his whole mind. "Put that down and step away from the desk, Sen Tennalhin."

Tennal's arm moved before he'd even consciously registered the instruction. His muscles made him step jerkily into the middle of the room. *Shut him out,* he thought desperately. *It's not real. You don't have to do it.* But to convince himself of that, he had to use defensive tricks, which meant holding several thoughts in his head at the same time, and he had no hope of doing that with a hangover and the lingering effects of last night's enhancers.

"All right, now what?" he made himself say. It was a struggle to speak—the full glare of the architect's attention made him want to stay very still and hope to pass unnoticed—but that was just the architect mutation trying to hijack his reactions. But if Tennal had one talent, it was sliding out of things. No architect he'd met could put a compulsion on him that lasted more than a few minutes, and even this Rank One would have to stop paying attention at some point. "Can't you just give my aunt my regards?"

The architect snorted. "Turn around." Tennal's mouth snapped shut as a renewed flash of light tore his thoughts away from him. He turned and felt the sharp edges of handcuffs around his wrists.

"Not taking any chances?" Tennal said. It was easier to talk if he told himself he wasn't going to move just now. "Where do you think I'm hiding the burn gun, in my sock?"

The architect put a hand on his shoulder and spun him around. "You're a strong reader," he said. "I know your abilities. I've been briefed on you. If I get a single hint that you've tried to deep-read me or anyone we encounter, I will sedate you for the journey. Understand?"

It didn't have a command behind it, which meant he wasn't lying about his briefing and knew compulsions wouldn't last long on Tennal. Tennal swallowed a flash of resentment at the accusation. He might shallow-read on a regular basis, but cracking open people's brains for a deep read wasn't something he made a habit of, and besides, it was extremely illegal. Writing people was also technically illegal, though that didn't seem to be stopping this architect. "Of course," Tennal said. "I'll leave the brainwashing to you."

It was a deliberate insult. Architect commands were temporary and nobody, architect or reader, could change someone's brain completely—though architects had done a better propaganda job of reassuring the public. But if Tennal had been hoping for a reaction, the architect disappointed him. The clang of a command came back into his voice. "Get on the plane and shut up. I got pulled from region command for this, and I'm not in the mood for bullshit." Tennal was already stumbling toward the Swift's landing ramp by the time he finished speaking.

The architect gestured for the rankers to move out. One of them put her foot in someone's discarded shirt, soaked from being used to mop up a spill, and nearly stumbled. "For fuck's sake," she muttered. "This isn't army work."

"More like the planet's most expensive taxi service," Tennal said over his shoulder. "Where do I sit?"

They put him in one of the rows of carrier seats in the dim, bare-bones interior of the plane. One ranker took the adjoining seat to guard him, though there wasn't exactly anywhere he could go. Tennal managed bravado for all of a few minutes before slumping uncomfortably forward and shutting his eyes. The architect was up front with the pilot and, thank Guidance, had stopped writing.

"Sen Tennalhin," the other ranker said. "There's a medic detailed to receive you at the other end. I need to take some blood for tests."

Tennal extended his arm without opening his eyes. "To make me presentable?"

"Not information I have, sir," the ranker said, but the tone of his voice said *probably*.

It was going to be a long journey back. Tennal had made hops on commercial flights to get to Sanura, a couple of hours here and there. "Hey," he said. "I suppose there's no chance you could drop me off at a . . . family event? If we really floor it, we might make the last hour of my sibling's commencement."

"No, sir, we have orders for your movements."

Tennal rolled his arm as the ranker released it. "Course you do."

The ranker read the results to the medic through a low-resolution comm, nearly inaudible under the drone of the engines. Tennal didn't understand most of what the medic said, but he heard *alcohol withdrawal shot* and *enhancer withdrawal* and winced. You could take withdrawal shots to get functional again in a short period of time, if you didn't mind spending an hour or so retching, but they weren't pleasant. "Two at once?" he said. That was going to be miserable.

He could see the medic looking at him through the projection. They frowned down at their notes as if something had surprised them. "From the results here," the medic's crackly voice said, "it looks like you've had this coming for a while."

Tennal dragged his hands down his face. "Oh," he said, "I know that."

It was four hours before they roared into the capital. The city of Exana, low-rise and picturesque, rolled out far beneath them like a sack of mosaic tiles. Other cities on Orshan's three planets might be older, or richer, or more impressive, but Exana was the seat of government and, more viscerally, Tennal's home: its winding streets and bright gardens were a sight so familiar that they might as well be traced across his skin like the web of his own veins.

The plane landed in the old army barracks behind the sprawling wings and domes of the Codifier Halls. It was another two hours before Tennal was done with the medical fun and games. He had experience being treated by army medics—his aunt trusted them more than civilians—and at least they didn't try to offer sympathy. When the withdrawal shots were out of his system, they cleaned him up, put him in hospital civvies, and passed him over to an unsmiling low-grade ranker who escorted him between the barracks and the halls.

The Legislator's Residence was tucked into a small walled garden attached to the Codifier Halls, the whole enclave overshadowed by the great dome next door. A narrow path wound through the garden between tall bushes thick with dark, glossy leaves. The residence itself was a low house of yellowing stone. The lintels had once been covered with carved patterns, but weathering had softened the edges, and now sprays of late-spring flowers climbed over them and threw suckers into the stone. The air was heavy and close.

Tennal was shown in by a security guard he didn't recognize and told to wait. He used to be on first-name terms with the entire guard rotation. It was just starting to sink in, like water creeping between rocks, that eight months was a long stretch of time.

He stood blinking in the dimness of the reception room. The legislator wasn't here.

The walls of the reception room were covered with darkened screens. The only light came from the room's centerpiece: a map disc set into the floor that projected astral bodies above itself. Orshan's three precious planets shimmered in the air, magnified many times but still the size of marbles: Orshan Two, covered with sprawling megacities; Orshan Three, green and rural; and Orshan Central, where Tennal stood now in Exana's spring evening. Not far beyond their orbit was the great bulk of the galactic link—disturbed space that funneled ships to unimaginably far destinations. Their gateway to the rest of the universe. The galactic link spun around itself slowly, like an enormous tangle of thread. Clouds of disturbed space drifted through the air of the room. Tennal ran his fingers through one just to see it flicker.

As he did, one of the screens lit up with an incoming call.

It might be Zin. Tennal instinctively waved a hand to answer it before he remembered he didn't live here anymore.

A face flashed on the screen before he could cancel it. The caller was some military high-up: she had a close-shaved head, an air of serenity, and an emblem in the golden colors of Archer Division. A flint pin on her wrist cuff showed her gender reference. The text underneath the screen said GOVERNOR-GENERAL OMA, ARCHER LINK STATION.

She surveyed Tennal with some surprise. "The legislator has junior aides handling her calls, does she?"

"I'm a maintenance technician," Tennal said blandly. "This comms point is broken, sorry." He raised his hand to kill the connection.

"Wait," the governor said. There was no architect spin under it—that would be impossible, over a comm—but something in her voice made Tennal pause. She gave him a surveying look. "You must be the nephew."

"No relation," Tennal said. "I'm here to steal the silver."

The governor smiled. When she smiled, it was like taking the cover off a fusion reactor; an edge in her voice somehow reminded Tennal of the distant rumble of an alarm. "You can pass on a message to our darling legislator for me."

Tennal had admittedly not tried that hard to be convincing. "Can I?"

"Tell her I'm up to my neck in mopping up rebels," the governor said, "and Archer Link Station is only stable because of my troops. And if she sends me one more order to demobilize my soldiers, I'll resign."

"I'll tell her," Tennal said, since it seemed the only way to end the call.

"My gratitude," the governor said. The screen winked out.

Tennal stepped back from the screens, uneasy, as if the web of politics his aunt moved in had left some clinging residue on his hands. He left the map and carried on into the house. He was only here until he could escape again.

The inner study was empty and quiet when Tennal stepped into it. Clematis flowers tumbled around the arches that led to the legislator's private garden, their fragrance scenting the early evening air and drifting in through the gaps in the latticed wooden screens. It was dim: the only light was a guttering oil lamp under his aunt's patron Guidance shrine that had nearly gone out. Tennal crossed the room, his tread swallowed by the soft patterned carpets. She'd let the lamps run out of oil again—she always forgot, and the household staff wouldn't touch a shrine that didn't belong to their own families. He added more oil to the guttering one and refilled the two lamps that flanked it. When he carefully lit them with one of the tapers in the jar beside the shrine, the red glass took the flame and fractally reflected it, glowing softly, until there were a dozen lights flickering around the Guidance icons above.

Tennal snuffed the taper and slumped down in one of the chairs. He felt drained, like a piece of clothing put through the wash. His thoughts were clearer than they'd been for a while, sharp-edged and crowding into his head. There was an itch in the back of his mind like someone had scrubbed it. It wasn't fun.

He didn't move when the light switched on in the corridor,

throwing a harsh white rectangle through the open door. A silhouette strode through the doorway and gestured at the room panel. Tennal squinted in protest as all the lights in the room blazed to life.

They illuminated a small figure with a sharply angled face and a presence like a blast of freezing air. She'd clearly come straight from political business, probably Convocation, because her civilian-style jacket and her wrap skirt were more colorful than her taste usually ran to. Her earrings were half-formal, diamonds winking in the light. A flint bracelet glinted at her wrist. She'd only started wearing jewelry to reassure people she was civilian enough to hold office.

"Of all the shitty new rankers I have ever had the pleasure of commanding through their first fuckups," the legislator said, propping her hand on the mahogany table, "you have reached deeper and more inventive pits than I ever dreamed possible."

Tennal stretched out his legs in front of him. "Hello to you too, Auntie dearest."

"You've got some fucking nerve," she said. "Stand up."

It wasn't an architect command—though the legislator was powerful, she famously didn't use her abilities to govern—but it was still an order. For a moment Tennal contemplated disobeying. He knew she could make him, though, and the thought of being written any more today made everything in him revolt. He slowly unfolded himself from the chair.

The legislator looked him up and down. "The shaking's from the withdrawal shots, is it?"

"I'm trembling in reverence," Tennal said. "New to the big city, you see. Never thought I'd meet the legislator in person. Should I bow?"

Before he'd left, he would have gotten a *don't fucking push it* and a gesture to sit. This time she just turned away, activating the holofield in a frame on the back wall. The lack of reaction left Tennal more unsettled than if she'd shouted.

Tennal sat again slowly, trying to control the shivers. He made his voice light and unconcerned. "Did you see Zin's commencement? I wanted to catch the last bit, but your people wouldn't let me out of Medical."

The legislator didn't even look at him. "Your ability to give me complete horseshit while looking like butter wouldn't melt in your mouth never ceases to amaze." The holofield turned milky white as it retrieved a file. "I can see you wanted to go to Zinyary's commencement. You wanted it so much, you lost yourself on the other side of the fucking planet and had to be dragged out by an armed retrieval team."

The holofield now showed a map: a projection of a familiar coastline slowly zooming in on the urban sprawl around Sanura. Other files started appearing around it.

They were projections of people's faces. Tennal had drifted with various party crowds; they were all here. Gamblers, fixers, people who hung around for the thrill of association—in the eight hours since the first ping of Tennal's locator, someone on the legislator's payroll had thrown together a comprehensive file on what Tennal had been doing for the past eight months.

"Recognize any of these?" the legislator asked.

Tennal shrugged noncommittally. She obviously knew a lot already, but that didn't mean he had to give her anyone's identity. "Vaguely."

The legislator waved a hand. A red glow highlighted about half the faces. "These ones are wanted by local regulator forces. Did you know that?" Tennal swallowed, his throat suddenly dry, and didn't say anything. The faces all faded except six, which enlarged and started to rotate, floating against a white background. "They're small fry, though. These six are wanted by global agencies for crimes against the Orshan state. High up in the internal structure of some of our worst criminal rings. We've seized four of them on the back of this report."

Text spilled out on the screen below each face. *Extortion. Money laundering. Blackmail.* "I wasn't friends with these ones." It was half-true. Tennal hadn't been close to any of them, but he'd spent long evenings with people who were close to *them.* And he knew the faces. The last one was the pale architect he'd slept with the night before.

"Don't tell me you don't recognize them," the legislator said softly. "You've spent the past few months helping them stuff their pockets."

"I didn't—"

The legislator slammed her hand on the table and Tennal jumped. "You *performed* for them," she said. "Like a monkey on a string. I know you've been trading on your reading abilities. I'm sure it was fun, getting favors out of criminals, but all that *fun* was built on Sanura's criminal economy. Do you know where those gambling profits go? Shall I give you a rundown of the hits these scum put out? The law-abiding traders they've squeezed out of business? The weapons and drugs and spyware those gains bought them?"

Tennal was no longer trying to answer her. He'd propped his elbows on the arms of his chair and rested his head in his hands.

"And that's before going into the rest of it," the legislator continued relentlessly. "The cleanup team registered over a dozen readers—"

Tennal's head came up sharply. "Did you bring them in?"

"You will shut the *fuck* up," the legislator said, with such viciousness that Tennal fell into a sullen silence. She watched him for a moment then carried on. "Accept you've lost all right to be trusted. You let criminals write you. You have natural defenses and have been extensively drilled in deflection techniques; nobody should be able to write you. That means you were taking drugs to let them." She leaned over the desk slightly, and Tennal found himself shrinking back even though he was several feet away. "Was that fun? Did it bring you a fucking *thrill,* that some fifth-rate architect might write you so that group of thugs and wastrels could use you better? Is that what you wanted?"

Tennal shut his eyes. He could claim he hadn't realized, but he knew deep down that wasn't an excuse. He knew what kind of circles he'd been running in, even if he'd thought he was keeping his hands clean. All the other facts would have fallen into place if he'd taken a moment to consider where the money was coming from and going to. "All right," he said. "I'm a fuckup. Is that what you wanted to hear? We knew that already." He bit the bullet. "What are you going to do about it?"

The unspoken words were *this time*. He'd been sent to various elite institutions for difficult teenagers back when he was young enough, he'd had lectures, he'd had therapy—he'd gone through everything the legislator could think of to get him back on track. This was why he shouldn't have come home. He was going nowhere from here. She could try any counseling intervention she wanted, but neither of them could get away from the facts: Tennal was a nightmare, his aunt hated it, and that would be their dynamic until one of them died. Tennal braced himself for the latest psychocorrection technique.

"I've put you on the conscription list," the legislator said. It was short and brutal. "A Cavalry research fleet is leaving for a mission into disturbed space, and I've found a junior lieutenant strong enough to sync you. As of twenty-two hundred hours tonight, I wash my hands of you. You'll be the responsibility of the fleet's commanding officer."

At first Tennal couldn't process it. It was like a blow to the back of the head, sending all his thoughts spinning wildly. Conscripted into the army. *Syncing.*

"You can't sync me with someone," Tennal heard himself say. The words came out in a voice that didn't sound like his own. "Not a random lieutenant. Not someone you haven't even vetted. That's *permanent*—Guidance Lights, that's giving someone write access to me for life!"

Syncing was the last resort to neutralize a strong reader who had gone rogue. Tennal had never read up on the details, because why think about the worst-case scenario, but he knew the basics. An architect could link their mind irrevocably with a reader's. Once they'd done that to you, that was it: no more defenses, not even your own natural walls. The architect could write you as easily as lifting a finger. You'd lost.

That was why the army took rogue readers. They couldn't cause trouble after that.

"Doesn't that cause you problems as well?" Tennal said. He was trying to be reasonable, but he could hear the desperate edge in his voice. "What if they order me to spy on you or work against you? I won't be able to stop myself from being written."

"You won't be anywhere near me," the legislator said. "You'll be under military movement orders. And when it comes down to trusting you or trusting a junior lieutenant with a clean track record—why the fuck do you think this is difficult?"

Despair surged inside Tennal like a wave. The army chewed up readers. He knew they made great assistants to pilots—something about the sensitivity to fluctuations in space—but he'd never heard of a *retired* synced reader. What would the army do, just let them go? He was going to be tethered to a console, using his powers by the command of an architect, for the rest of his life. "Just send me into the army," he said, though even saying it left a bitter taste in his mouth. He could recognize when he was fighting a last-ditch retreat. "You want me out of the way, I'll enlist. Don't make me sync with an architect." *Leave me a way out.*

She didn't respond immediately. Tennal took a breath and continued, "I won't let them, anyway. You must know that. Not even your Rank Ones are strong enough to force me into synci—"

He broke off. She knew that. Whatever Tennal thought of his aunt, he had an ingrained respect for her ability to track all the threads of her plans. She would have factored in that Tennal was strong enough and stubborn enough to mentally refuse a sync, even with all the pressure she could bring to bear. So—"You've primed me," Tennal said. It came out as a monotone that barely hid the spike of horror. He knew it was true because logically it *had* to be true, but a split second later, he connected it with the scrubbed-clean itch in his head. "You chewed me out for taking enhancers, and you've had your medics *artificially prime me to sync.*"

"Of course I have," the legislator said, as if this weren't horrific. "What did you think I was going to do? You're a stubborn ass."

"This is illegal," Tennal said through his teeth, "even if it's you doing it." The military had used abandoned xenotechnology to make the first generation of architects and readers. A sliver of those alien remnants could mess up anyone's brain; they could almost certainly prime his mind to sync. But Orshan's remnants should have been locked up decades ago. They shouldn't be able to hand them out to medics. "I could go to—" He had to stop there and think. He didn't know who could enforce the law on the legislator herself. The regulators already knew Tennal had slithered out of consequences he shouldn't have. She was probably covered under some national security loophole.

"I can't put you into the army without syncing you," the legislator said flatly. "You've squandered or abused your reader abilities in every way you could think of. No division would trust you without someone in charge of you. You've given everyone enough proof of what you do when you're left to yourself." She switched off the holofield, and the images sank back into gray mist. "Report to the duty officer in the Cavalry barracks once we're done. I've told a ranker to escort you back to the base."

She'd already made the arrangements. Tennal dropped his itching head back into his hands, finally recognizing there had never been any other outcome on the table. He'd burned through every chance he'd had.

It briefly flashed through his head that if he pushed himself out of his chair and ran right now, the security guard at the door probably wouldn't be expecting it. He could sprint down the back streets to the transit lines, hop on one of the rush-hour shuttles.

He still had people he could call in Sanura, people who might lend him money—and face-field masks were easy to find. He could get on a commercial ship off-planet . . .

The spinning wheels in his mind ran to a halt. It was a laughably bad plan. And even if it worked, even if he somehow managed to escape the Orshan sector, he would be cutting off everyone he'd ever known. He would never get back in touch with any old friends. He'd never see Zin.

He pressed the heels of his hands into his eyes until he saw stars. "Fuck this," he said, but it was an admission of defeat. Part of him wanted to say, *You're going to regret doing this,* but that was melodramatic, and more important, he didn't think he could deliver on it.

"This wasn't a choice I wanted to make," the legislator said. There was something in her voice—a note that sounded harsh, but that Tennal hadn't heard before, even when they'd argued viciously enough that he'd left. "But this can't go on. Everything else aside, Zinyary is a bright girl and doesn't deserve being at the mercy of your constant crises. When you disappeared she was a wreck for days."

The small flicker inside Tennal that was still trying to make escape plans abruptly died. He stared at the fabric of his trousers over his knees and said, "All right."

"I shouldn't have to tell you—"

"I said 'all right,'" Tennal dropped his hands and lifted his head again. Everything was gray and dull, as if all his senses had been muffled. "Duty officer. Cavalry Division. Property of the military as of twenty-two hundred hours. I was listening."

The legislator eyed him mistrustfully, but she'd intended to back him into this corner. She'd corralled him through every step of this conversation, and Tennal hadn't even been in good enough condition to give her an interesting fight. She nodded.

Tennal levered himself out of the chair. "Think I'm going to drop in on Zin," he said. "Seeing as I'm going to be disappearing

on her again. Any objections?" He didn't have the energy to spin
defiance into his voice. It was pointless anyway; she'd already an-
ticipated a parting shot, and he didn't want to read off her script.

"I can give you an hour."

"That'll do." Tennal walked past her without further word. He
could feel her gaze on him as he stepped out the door.

His escort was already waiting in the cooling dusk outside: a
low-grade ranker obviously more curious than they were allowed
to let on. They wore some kind of ship insignia—Tennal had never
bothered to memorize the different shapes—so they must be
from a spacer division in dock. It proved easier than Tennal had
thought to get them on his side. Tennal struck an upbeat, last-
night-before-deployment note, leaving out any mention of his
reader abilities or conscription, and within a few minutes they'd
agreed to a quick present-shopping diversion on the way to Tennal's residential enclave.

The apartment was still keyed to accept Tennal's retina print.
He stood in the dark entranceway, balancing two chain-store gift
boxes, and saw light coming from under the door of Zin's room.

When he opened the door she had four screens going, all covered with schoolwork, and two tiny chat projections of friends
Tennal didn't recognize. She didn't immediately hear the door.
One of the tiny head-and-shoulder projections pointed behind her,
and she spun in her chair, flinched, and said, "Guidance Lights."

"Hey," Tennal said. "Yup. It's me. Large as life and twice as
great. You don't have to kill the chat," he added, as Zin frantically slapped the tiny projections into nonexistence. "I'm highly
respectable now."

"I'm *sorry*, Tenn," Zin said, whirling back to him once her
friends' heads had winked out. "I didn't know they had a flag
on my comm, or I would have warned you, I promise! She never
said—"

"Hey, it's okay." Tennal put the boxes on her desk carefully
and squashed the part of him that had expected this to be

uncomplicated. "It's okay, really. How's my favorite relative? How was commencement?"

"Oh *Lights*," Zin said, and hugged him.

Tennal swallowed. "Missed you too, pipsqueak."

Twenty-six minutes later, Zin had made them both some tea, opened her gifts, been polite about the expensive earrings that apparently weren't her style anymore and more genuinely enthusiastic about the sweets. Everything about her was as familiar as Tennal's own face in the mirror, but he kept coming across small differences: all her clothes were new and bright, maybe as a reaction against the gray Legal tunics. She was taller. The earrings she favored now were colorful chunks of plastic set around ostentatious beads of flint.

Although there were variations and local practices all over the place, the Orshan sector loosely adhered to galactic customs of showing gender. Wood was a clear request for a gender reference of *he,* flint for *she*. Everything else depended, but *they* was usually a polite choice for a stranger, though Orshan was less formal about it than other sectors. Zin had been experimenting for a few years and tentatively wearing flint when he'd left, but it looked like she'd landed firmly on *she* while Tennal had been gone.

Zin scavenged a mismatched collection of leftovers from the kitchen and pressed them on Tennal: fried vegetables, millet, tiny spiced crayfish. Tennal discovered he was ravenous and ate all of it, then he raided the open gift box for the coffee and cream–filled pastries he always pretended were only Zin's favorite. He kept up a patter of stories about gambling dodges and outrageous parties. Zin laughed in all the right places—but a split second too late, watching his eyes. He wasn't sweeping her along anymore.

Zin's room had also changed. Tennal didn't recognize any of the posters that papered the walls with bright division colors. The divisions were a military thing, officially, but they sponsored sports teams, businesses, industrial bodies, festivals—everything went more smoothly if you had division connections. If one member of a family joined the army, their relatives could draw on their division connections for life. The Halkana family had been Cavalry for generations. Zin's posters mainly *weren't* Cavalry red, though: she followed debate teams, where Pilot Division dominated, and her flavor of the month seemed to be an unusual one that wasn't affiliated with anything. That was new.

"Oh, Tenn," Zin said, "I got my apprenticeship placement! It's a reader rights group!"

"Nice one," Tennal said. He bit into another bitter coffee pastry, then replayed what she'd said. He swallowed too soon. "Wait, what? What rights group?" Zin was supposed to be learning law, not getting into politics.

"It's all signed off," Zin said, which didn't answer his question. "Look, though, I took a commencement capture! This is where I come in." She pulled up a screen and jabbed him with her elbow until he paid attention.

Tennal spent the next ten minutes watching the capture of the commencement ceremony, with additional irreverent commentary from Zin, while he finished his pastry. They didn't have them in Sanura, and he'd forgotten the way the crisp buttery flakes broke on your tongue; it seemed unfair of the universe to remind him just as he was about to lose all those small luxuries. His time ticked down. He was putting it off.

"So," Tennal said eventually, from his perch on her desk. "'Fraid this isn't a long visit."

Zin lowered her mug. "I thought maybe it wasn't." She turned the mug around in her hands. "You've seen her, haven't you?"

Her usually meant the legislator. "We've sorted things out," Tennal said. "I'm taking a tour with the army. We're just going to see how it goes."

"The army," Zin repeated. She turned away from him and started to tidy the things on the other end of her desk, usually a giveaway for a conversation she didn't want to have. "You hate the army."

"It's the best option I've got," Tennal said. "Honestly, it's not that bad. Research fleet, she said. Sounds like they're going into disturbed space to study it." Tennal knew absolutely nothing about how space screwed itself up near the galactic link or why anyone would want to study it. It wasn't as if his aunt would care either. She just wanted him somewhere else. "Might find an alien."

Zin shut her book, extinguishing the light inside it, and moved it onto a stack of other specialist legal texts. "Really."

"Well, maybe not the alien," Tennal said. He was confident in his ability to out-brazen a sixteen-year-old. "I'll be running my unit in a year, no sweat."

"Which unit?"

Tennal realized he hadn't asked. It hadn't seemed important. "We're still sorting that out," he said. "I'll be out of touch for a bit, but she'll know where I am if you want updates. And I'll be back on leave in a few months."

Zin turned back to face him. She had that grave, unfamiliar expression again. "Did she conscript you?"

"No," Tennal said. "Lights, Zin, it's not like that. Don't get in knots about it."

There was a long silence. Zin had a vintage-style clock above her bed; Tennal could hear it ticking. "All right," Zin said, and Tennal recognized his own inflection with a mild jolt of surprise. "When are you leaving?"

"Tonight."

"Of course you are," Zin said. She took a slow breath. "You know she can't legally conscript you, don't you?"

"She's not," Tennal said. He could imagine what would happen if he challenged the legislator on those grounds. She didn't *need* to conscript him legally—she only had to have a word with the people who could. "I already said it wasn't like that. We just agreed I needed a change of scene."

Zin ignored the interruption. "The army needs a documented violation to conscript anyone, did you know that? One that relates to one of three relevant acts. And she never let them document anything on you," she added. "I checked."

Tennal paused. "You've been working hard on this pre-Legal course stuff, huh?" he said. He flicked the pile of books. "You know the world's not going to end if you take a break."

Zin shrugged, an air of embarrassment clinging to her. "You should know," she said. "It's important."

"I'm not saying it's not important," Tennal said slowly. He could feel the wheels in his mind start to spin again. "I'm just saying it's not relevant to the situation right now." His wristband buzzed. Shit, that was his escort. He was out of time. "Okay, I've got to run. Hey, though, can I get a reading recommendation from the Honorable Counsel Zinyary? For boring stretches on the ship?"

Zin silently pulled one of the books from the pile. The glowing letters on the side said *The Law and Codes of Manual Neuromodification.*

Tennal wasn't sure if it was a good thing that she'd had it right on hand. "Thanks," he said, folding the book into block form. Her half-hopeful, half-defensive expression was so familiar from many years needling each other, but there was so much seriousness to it now that Tennal had to look away. It wasn't really Tennal's fault that he was abandoning her this time, except it was—it had all been his own doing.

The folded book was now a slim block the size of his palm. He tossed it in the air and caught it before sliding it into his pocket. "Don't worry about me. I think I can make this trip interesting."

CHAPTER 4

"Thirty *thousand* liters of goats' milk," the district captain said despairingly. "Chicken eggs! Livestock! Fifty tons of feed pellets! And that's not to mention all the damage to the hardware!"

"Sir," Surit said neutrally. He stood in the district captain's small, bare-bones office with his hands linked behind his back and stared at the Cavalry emblem on the wall behind the desk.

The district captain gave him an outraged look. More seemed to be called for. Surit cleared his throat. "I believe it was thirty-one thousand, nine hundred and fifty liters of goats' milk."

"The quantity of milk is *immaterial,* Lieutenant!"

"Yes, sir."

"And you crashed into this freighter because . . . ?"

"It wasn't us, sir. The freighter had to swerve, and then it hit the gunship."

"And why did the freighter have to swerve, Lieutenant?"

Surit continued to stare at the wall, wearing his best poker face. "That would be because we were in its way, sir." That didn't seem enough, so he added, "We were attending the scene of an accident. There was a pod in trouble."

Surit's unit—his first command, straight out of officer academy—crewed a tiny retrieval ship that patrolled up and down the edges of chaotic space, mapping the constant changes in the space-time disturbance and retrieving any salvage that the churning clouds spat out. This would be fine, except chaotic space tended to *drift.* A pod had run across some tendrils that had pulled it in like a riptide, and Surit's retrieval unit had gone to help. It was unfortunate that it had caused the biggest traffic pileup this side of Orshan Three, but in Surit's view, not really his problem. He had followed the regulations. Everything else was merely a side effect.

As his direct commanding officer, the district captain knew all this. It was in Surit's written report. This was more in the nature of a dressing-down than a real debrief.

"The module with all the chickens was retrieved in an orderly manner," Surit added. "No chicken casualties were sustained. We do have some egg damage to our sensors."

The district captain looked down at her desk, apparently fighting strong emotion, and put her hand over her mouth.

Eventually she removed it and said, "And the bodywork damage sustained by the gunship . . . ?"

"That was when we were attempting to rescue the goat crates from the freighter, sir."

"You did *extortionate* damage to the navigation systems of a mind-bogglingly expensive gunship in order to rescue some goats?"

"It's not fair for goats to be in space, sir," Surit said. "They don't know which way is up."

There was a short silence. Surit maintained his poker face. The goats hadn't seemed to appreciate being rescued much, but in Surit's experience, livestock seldom did.

The district captain, a short, voluble type who probably didn't deserve to be responsible for all the traffic snarls in one of Orshan's most crowded space zones, sank further in her chair and put her head in her hands. "Produce all *over* space," she said. "*Thousands* of chicken eggs—"

"They were in containers," Surit said factually. "Five hundred to a crate, and only a few of them opened. It just gets a bit chaotic when they depressurize—"

"Yes! Thank you, Lieutenant!" She tapped a screen on the desk. "Needless to say, I have Command on my back about the gunship, and it turns out the freight company had links to Infantry Division, so I'm getting calls about *that* as well."

Surit stared straight ahead. "I take full responsibility for the incident, sir."

"So you've said!" She pulled up a file. "In fact, you've said it several times in your sixty-page report. Do you know what it *means* to take full responsibility in writing, Lieutenant Yeni? It means I've had three separate requests for your removal, personally, by name."

This was a blow, though not unexpected. "Sir."

The district captain drummed her fingers on the arm of her chair. "It was also the fault of the soldier piloting your ship," she said. "We might be able to do something with that. I don't particularly want to lose you, Lieutenant Yeni. It seems unfair to let a wayward herd of goats take out the career of one of my better officers."

"All the pilots in my unit are competent, sir," Surit said flatly. "Any fault was in my orders." This was not strictly true. Retrieval ships were the most despised assignment in the army, and the soldiers who got shuffled into them were the unambitious, the unskilled, and the very new. But they were Surit's unit, and Surit had a duty to them. He had been the officer in charge.

"Guidance *Lights*," the district captain said. "Are you just determined to kill your career? Is this what it was like talking to your mother?"

Surit stiffened. Most people knew about his mother—the traitor general Marit Yeni was a household name, even twenty years after her death—but most people didn't mention her to Surit's face. Surit very carefully counted to five, bringing his vocal cords under control enough that he could say lightly, "I don't know, sir. Do you have a way I can travel back in time and check?" That was rude. He added, "Sorry, sir. Sore point."

The district captain raised her hand, abashed. Surit had always found her a solid commanding officer, cautious with her architect abilities, responsible with her orders. But she had no way to resist pressure from higher up the food chain.

She shuffled the glowing files around her desk. "We have to transfer you," she said. "I'm sorry, Lieutenant, but I haven't been given a choice. If you picked the right post, though, you could recover in a year or so. I've asked around for open assignments. Look at this."

She opened a diagram of the sector on her desk, the same one that hung above every bridge. This one centered on the whirling galactic link and on the silver clouds of chaotic space that surrounded it.

There were advantages for Orshan to have a galactic link so close to their habitable planets. It meant they were tied closely to the interplanetary trade networks, active members of the galaxy-spanning Resolution treaty. But the downside of having an active link so close was the disturbance it caused in the fabric of space. Regularly—on a deep-space scale, over decades—clouds broke off the maelstrom around the link and drifted out into the rest of the sector, where they caused trouble for ships.

Surit's mother had died in the outskirts of chaotic space in a vicious civil war. Now Surit patrolled the edges to stop inexperienced pilots from wrecking their ships. Things were better now.

The district captain tapped several highlighted dots on the map. "Most of the posts I managed to scrape up are retrieval units, but, you know, at least you'd keep your current rank. Think of it as a temporary setback."

As Surit looked at the dead-end postings with some dismay, one of the dots caught his eye. The rest of the assignments were near major traffic routes, like his current post, but this one was different. It sat near the link itself, on the outskirts of the whirlpool of chaotic space. "Can I ask what that one is, sir?"

She hesitated. "That request was for you, specifically. It came in this morning."

After the accident, then. The district captain tapped the map.

New text spilled onto it: very short, only a set of coordinates, a chain of command, and a ship name. Surit didn't recognize the division, and then he realized it wasn't a division at all.

"Regulators," the district captain said.

Surit blinked. As it sank in, he felt a spike of wariness. The regulators dealt with military discipline and investigations, and oversaw the army's architects and its handful of readers. Surit had never encountered them.

"No details, of course," the district captain said. "I don't know why they want you. That looks like a Cavalry ship, but the request definitely came through the regulators. You're an architect, aren't you? But you're not strong enough for them to recruit you in the normal course of things. They've said it's promotion-track." She killed the screen and turned her face up to him again. "I intended to turn it down," she said, "because it smells bad. Why do they need a random junior officer? I don't like the regulators, and I don't like setting my soldiers up to fail."

"I'll take it," Surit said.

The district captain put her hand over her face. Surit waited patiently. Eventually she dragged her hand down and said, "Consider why the request was for you."

"You think they want someone disposable for . . . whatever they have in mind," Surit said. Even if Surit hadn't just accepted responsibility for this latest screwup, Marit Yeni's legacy limited his options. "I know." He'd rather risk it and try to succeed, however small the chance, than spend years out here. "I still want to take the assignment, sir." He needed the captain rank; once he was a permanent captain, they'd restore a military pension to his alt-parent. Another quiet backwater post wouldn't get him there for years.

The district captain threw up her hands. "Well, then!" She entered something on her wristband. "I'll forward you the briefing. Say your goodbyes and pack fast. It's on the other side of the sector, and they want you in three weeks."

"I'll find a shuttle," Surit said. He paused. "Sir—"

"Yes?"

"My unit," Surit said doggedly. "I don't want any disciplinary marks on their records. They—"

"Will be *fine*, Lieutenant," his superior officer said irritably. "I'll make sure their records remain unblemished. Though the next time they make my traffic routes into a giant omelet, I make no promises."

Surit saluted. "Thank you, sir. My regards to the goats."

"I'll pass them on," the district captain said. She regarded him with friendly exasperation. "And I suppose I should say—good luck, Lieutenant."

It took Surit two weeks of traveling to get to the refueling stop.

He spent some of it reading the briefing pack, which was unhelpfully minimal. A Cavalry Division fleet was going on a salvage retrieval mission. What they were trying to retrieve was unspecified. The *location* of it was unspecified, until Surit looked more closely at the fleet rendezvous coordinates and realized they were inside the maelstrom of chaotic space around the galactic link itself. There must be some mistake. The mass of disturbed space-time around the link was active and dangerous.

When he'd been a teenager, Surit had spent years obsessed with chaotic space. The army had fought battles at the edges of it, back in the Reader War. His mother's ship—or the fragments of it—must still be in there somewhere, drifting eternally. For a few years, Surit had even tracked the currents to work out where the wreckage might have ended up. He didn't do that anymore.

Surit dealt with uncertainty by making lists in his head. He started another one.

List: Queries He Probably Wasn't Going to Get Answered.

Item: Why him? If this mystery post was a salvage mission, he could be useful, but retrieval units of the kind Surit ran were as common as waste-disposal workers. You didn't headhunt a junior retrieval officer from halfway across the sector.

Item: Did they know about Marit? Surit considered the question for a few seconds then discarded it as useless. Even if someone did have some sort of grudge, they wouldn't tell him.

Item: Why was this coming from the *regulators*? Regulators had nothing to do with salvage. Regulators didn't even belong to a division. They were there to oversee breaches of military law.

Thinking wasn't going to help. Surit wrote his list of questions down instead and resolved to ask.

When he came within range of the refueling post, his mail caught up with him. The only comm was from Elvi Tamori, his alt-parent, who sounded enormously proud that he'd rustled up two dozen neighbors from their village to congratulate Surit on his new job. Elvi knew about the accident with the goats, of course. But Elvi didn't believe in dwelling on things that went wrong. This was why he never talked about Marit.

Surit smiled at Elvi's voice anyway as he recorded replies and used part of his allowance to put them back on the priority channel because he hadn't had any leave in six months and didn't see why he shouldn't splash out.

He reported to the station administration office the moment he docked. He'd expected to be assigned Study and Training, the usual code for soldiers on standby, but the duty officer scanned his ID and said, "Lieutenant Yeni? Confined to quarters."

"Excuse me?"

"Says here *confined to quarters pending interview*," the duty officer said. He held out a hand. "Wristband." He took Surit's wristband and scanned it, clearly distracted by the screen playing a drama capture in a corner of his desk. A light on the wristband started to glow orange, indicating Surit was out of his assigned area. "Habitat two-oh-six A. You've got twenty minutes to find it."

Surit counted to five in his head. "Does it say why?" he asked politely.

"Classified," the desk officer said.

Surit stowed his pack in his assigned quarters. They were standard issue for a base or station, almost identical to the ones he'd occupied at the academy. *Confined to quarters* included the officers' canteen and the gymnasium, so it wasn't as if he were under arrest, but he still felt uneasy.

The interview notification chimed onto his wristband late at night, two hours into his sleep cycle.

It pointed to a room deep in the secure station core. Surit stopped trying to suppress his uneasy feelings and dressed swiftly, readying himself as if he were going into battle. Regulators. This was starting to feel personal. As far as Surit knew, his mother hadn't had any enemies in the regulators specifically, but it wasn't as if he had a list.

The interview room was gray and featureless, designed to unnerve the interviewee. There was one metal chair. Surit looked at it, decided he didn't want to put himself at a psychological disadvantage before he really had to, and took up a comfortable at-ease stance instead.

It was a good half hour before the door opened. Surit had fallen into a half-meditative state, replaying the message from his parent in his mind, and had to cover a start when the official arrived. He had no rank tabs. Regulators didn't display them.

"Yeni," the official said, not offering him the courtesy of a title. "Don't like the chair?" He was unremarkable. His hair was mousy and his face forgettable. He had a wooden gender-mark button in his cuff—standard uniform positioning, for those who chose to wear a marker—and no other decoration. But when he looked at Surit, his next words had so much architect force that they hit Surit like a blow. "Sit down."

Surit found his teeth were clenched tightly. It was like a magnesium flare on his exposed brain, so bright it hurt. It didn't come close to making him obey, since he had natural defenses, but the official was very strong, and that had been the intent. If Surit's defenses had been weaker, the command might have hit. The use of architect powers on an unwilling subject was illegal. It didn't matter that it was common between soldiers. It didn't matter that it hadn't worked. It was the principle of the thing.

Surit breathed out slowly and didn't move. "Is that an order, sir?"

"I said, sit down." This time the write command was stronger. Surit guessed the official was putting everything he had into it.

Surit stared straight ahead, not moving a muscle. "Unfortunately I have no way of identifying you as a superior officer and therefore cannot comply. Are you able to provide proof of rank?"

The corners of the official's mouth lifted in something like a smile. He waved the door shut behind him. "Very nice." He pulled his tags from under his jacket and displayed a colonel's etching. "Sit down, Lieutenant Yeni." There was no write command under the words.

Surit sat. He tried to gather fragments of the equanimity he'd had a few minutes ago, but his jaw kept clenching when he wasn't focusing on it. "Sir."

"It's come to light," the official said, "that you've been lying to us for quite a while."

"I absolutely refute that allegation," Surit said. "I have been nothing but honest. Sir."

"The test you took at the academy placed you as an architect of middling ability," the official said. Surit realized with a shock that this wasn't about his mother at all. "You're much stronger than that. You lied to the testers."

Surit took a moment to switch gears. So this whole conversation was about architects.

Some people were more susceptible to architect commands than others. It didn't necessarily relate to your own abilities. You could be born with natural defenses—even neutrals or readers could. You could discipline your mind and learn techniques to make yourself harder to affect. But very strong architects—the level the army called *Rank One*—were, to a person, almost impossible to write.

Surit had learned that fact once and compared it in his memory to the occasions people had tried to write him, and to the few times he had used his own architect abilities—and to the shocked and dismayed expression on Elvi's face, quickly hidden, when he had seen what Surit could do. Then Surit had very deliberately never thought about it again.

Surit supposed, when he thought about it, that you *could* class that as a lie. He'd always known he was a stronger architect than was listed in his file. The test they'd all taken in the first year of officer academy had seemed perfunctory, just a physical fitness test where the whole class took turns shouting orders. Most families who suspected their child was a strong architect would have had them professionally tested when they were a teenager. "I didn't lie," he said. "I didn't know what it was supposed to feel like."

"I can almost believe that," the official said easily. "I doubt anyone's succeeded in writing you in your life, have they?"

"I don't know," Surit said. Honesty compelled him to add, "Probably not."

"Then why didn't you get your file corrected?" The official seemed entirely comfortable standing while Surit sat: Surit guessed this was an interrogation technique. "Odd behavior. You'd be much better off in your career."

"That's not a fair way to select for promotion," Surit said. It was true that stronger architects ended up with better postings and tended to float to the top, but Elvi had always been stubbornly against that. He'd always said Marit had never liked it either—not that it mattered what Marit would have thought about anything, but Surit cared about Elvi's opinion. "Someone's architect abilities shouldn't matter. Writing without consent is illegal."

"Except for reasons of military necessity," the official said. "Know what else is illegal? Lying to your superior officers. But good news, kid. We don't care about that because you're strong enough for a regulator-approved assignment." Just as Surit was opening his mouth to request a professional retest, the official asked, "Ever met a reader?"

Surit hesitated. The army had stopped making readers decades ago. The first readers and architects had worked together, but the readers had started a coup—Orshan's history was littered with coups—and the military had hastily stopped making them and started churning out architects to quell it. Now the only new readers were genetic throwbacks in architects' children.

He might have passed one in the street, but that was private information, so he wouldn't have known. "No."

The official gave that non-smile again. "We're giving you one to sync."

Surit gripped the arms of the chair involuntarily. "What?"

"Congratulations," the official said. "Not even all our Rank Ones get that. You'll have to make some sacrifices, but in the regulators, it's a golden ticket for your whole career. You could make general in ten years."

Even the ability to count himself into calming down had deserted Surit. "You can't be talking about a permanent sync." Surit didn't know much about advanced use of architect powers, but even he knew you couldn't sever a sync. Both the architect and the reader were so bound into it that their brains would shut down if they tried. That must be bad enough for the architect, who controlled the whole thing, but for the reader—Surit had barely ever *thought* about readers. He pried his fingers from the arms of the chair. "My briefing—"

"You still have a mission," the official said. "Standard salvage operation. They're jetting into chaotic space to take apart an old space station. You'll have a retrieval unit to command as usual. Think of the reader as an . . . add-on. A bonus. You can use this assignment to get to know them, and they can start their pilot training. And after that—much more interesting assignments and guaranteed promotion. You'll make captain permanently by next year. I understand you have some benefits for your parent hinging on it."

Surit sat still in his chair, reason and dismay warring inside him. Surit had never shirked an order, never failed a challenge. The regulators were the most powerful body outside the division commands. They could make difficulties for him wherever he went. "What happens if I refuse?"

"I really hope you don't," the official said. "It would be a shame to have to court-martial the only person from your province on the command track."

Surit had half suspected it. The time to turn it down would have been in the district captain's office. And even that might not have worked.

This reader had joined the army and agreed to sync, willing to serve their planet. The knowledge sent a stab of shame through him. Surit had signed up for this too.

"Who is the reader?" he said.

"We prefer to call our agents by number," the official said. "He'll identify himself when you board your ship. He's under orders to assist in your mission as a learning exercise. Is this acknowledgment of your movement orders?"

Surit tried to realign his attitude. He'd been asked to do this; this was how he could be most useful to the army. It sounded like the reader had military experience. Hopefully he would know more about successful syncing than Surit did.

"Yes, sir," Surit said. "I accept."

CHAPTER 5

"What is going *on* here?"

Tennal didn't turn around. "Six inches to the left," he said, waving at the ranker carrying an armchair. "Yes, in the corner, thank you. Secure it there."

The ship's warrant officer, towering and irascible, stood in the door of the small cabin and glared at the clutter of furniture. Tennal had been briefly introduced to them earlier that day and the two of them had not gotten on, but if that was going to be anyone's problem, it wasn't going to be Tennal's.

The warrant officer snapped, "Explain yourself, Fifty-Six."

"My name," Tennal said, finally turning to face the door, "is Tennalhin. Tennal, if you want to be friendly. I don't think I'll go by my code name, thanks. It makes me feel like a box of groceries. Can I help you?"

The warrant officer gave the armchair, the three trunks, the decorations, and the cushions a further incredulous look. Tennal had covered an entire wall with old sports banners: most top racing teams had designs in Vanguard blue, and most of the best wrestling teams were Cavalry red. There had been some gaps, so he'd filled them with banners from Zin's debate team. "You can get this crap out of my ship, is what you can do!"

Tennal opened his eyes wide. "But I'm within my allowance, Officer."

"You have a fifty-pound clothing and effects allowance, same as any ranker," the warrant officer said, their patience visibly fraying. The two rankers Tennal had co-opted to help him move furniture were barely hiding smirks. "It may be that I'm somehow walking around with my *eyes* fucking *shut,* but none of this shit is in your allowance so far as I can see."

Tennal opened his mind, focused on the warrant officer, and unrepentantly read their surface feelings. He got impatience, worry at this new responsibility, and a crack of uncertainty at how they were supposed to handle a conscripted soldier who was also the legislator's nephew. Good. All of that was useful.

"That's very strange, Officer," Tennal said, overflowing with baffled innocence. "Let me just—oh, look, here we are, knew I'd marked it somewhere—" Shipboard regulations spilled over the wall, projected from his wristband. One section of text was marked by a soft blue glow. Tennal made a show of rereading it. "It *looks* like—and correct me if I'm wrong—a civilian is entitled to reasonable adjustments in living quarters, pending approval of the commander or other delegated authority *and*—this one is interesting—if a dispute arises, the civilian can be removed to appropriate commercial transport. Do we have a dispute?"

"Do we have a fucking *dispute*—"

"Here are some commercial transports," Tennal said, waving up a link search he'd done half an hour ago. "I'd be very happy to take any of them to our destination." The destination the fleet had registered was a patch of uninhabitable chaotic space, which Tennal assumed had something to do with *research mission.* No commercial transports would go near it. Tennal had highlighted a few pleasure-cruise tours to Archer Link Station instead. "What do you think, Officer?"

The warrant officer stared at him for a good three seconds and turned to the rankers. "You two, get the fuck out. We're launching in thirty-two minutes. Stations." The two rankers saluted, one of them doing a better job at a poker face than the other one, and left. Tennal heard their footsteps slowing as they walked away, clearly angling to hear the rest of the argument.

The warrant officer took a heavy step into the room, right on the deep-pile rug Tennal had borrowed from the legislator's storage without her permission. "For a start, you'll stop calling me *Officer* like a fucking civilian. You call me *sir* or *Captain*. And second, you aren't a fucking civilian, and you aren't covered by this—this regulation-grubbing. Third—"

"Oh, but I am," Tennal said.

He opened the channel again just in time to feel that derail the warrant officer from their train of thought. "What?"

"A civilian," Tennal said helpfully. "Up until I either sign a recruitment form or sync with a serving architect, I'm not actually classified as military personnel. I've had to dig into the regulations a bit, but it looks like the best description for me on this trip is *civilian adviser,* as I'm voluntarily contributing my knowledge and expertise. Not a big deal, by the way," he added. "Always happy to help our brave protectors."

The warrant officer glared at him, a tic jumping in their forehead. "Show me these regulations."

"Of course. Let me just—here we are—" This time, the text that filled the wall was ant-sized. Page after page of laws and codes crammed in, highlighted here and there in blue. Tennal hadn't read half of them—he only ever learned enough about any one field to be dangerous—but he was fairly sure they backed him up. "So that seems clear," Tennal said blandly. He turned away to rearrange the gaudy decorations he'd picked up for his wall-mounted Guidance shrine. He'd unearthed a string of red novelty lights in place of the oil lamps, and when he clicked them on, they started flashing in an immensely satisfying way.

"Turn those bloody things off," the warrant officer said irritably. "My orders say differently. You're a normal ranker being transported to meet up with an architect. The only special instructions I have are not to spread your name around, and to arrest you if I find out you've read anyone."

"I'm not going to read anyone," Tennal said. This was true in spirit; he didn't plan to deep-read anyone, which was what non-readers were afraid of. He couldn't turn off every hint from his reader senses any more than he could turn off his ears. "I also don't intend to murder anyone or siphon off credits from the ship's funds—is it *that* hard to believe I don't plan to commit a crime on a tiny ship full of soldiers?" A buzzer blared to indicate thirty minutes until departure. "Don't you want to be on the bridge or something?" Tennal added. "I thought you'd have important buttons to press."

The warrant officer yanked the flashing lights away from the Guidance shrine and turned them off. "You won't be laughing when I send back a report about this."

"Please do," Tennal said, "I don't want to stand in the way of our fine military traditions." He was fairly sure no report would go back—it was only nine days before Tennal was due to become a Rank One architect's problem. Tennal had picked up a fine sense of how far people would go to get their own back.

The warrant officer looked in increasing frustration at the other bed, which Tennal had used to lay out his clothes. It was meant for the architect who was supposed to sync him. "This is a double cabin," the warrant officer said. "You may not report to me, but *your* commanding officer is going to have something to say about it when he joins us."

"Again," Tennal said, "I really don't like to correct you, Officer, it does pain me, but: *not military personnel*. That bit's very important. I can't actually have a commanding officer at this moment. Could I have my important devotional material back, please."

The warrant officer stood there, their fist clenching around the string of novelty lights, then abruptly shoved them back at Tennal. "Listen to me, you fucking weasel," they said. "You have nine days before your architect joins us. Once you've synced, then you're a ranker. And if you cause trouble for me before that, I will come down on you like a shipload of girders in double gravity."

"Of course, Officer," Tennal said. He gave them a smile. "I don't mean to cause any trouble."

Once the warrant officer had gone, Tennal stowed the rug for takeoff because it wasn't actually fastened to the floor. He strapped himself into a launch chair and spent the burn time reviewing the assignments that had been sent to the new queue on his wristband. There were still no notes on his assigned architect, but he'd apparently been assigned enough learning modules—*Study and Training* modules—to fill the next six months, let alone the next nine days. He rejected all of them and meticulously noted his civilian status on every rejection.

None of the officers had told Tennal anything, but he'd picked up from the rankers that this was the *Fractal Note,* the deep-space flagship of the research fleet. It only had a skeleton crew now, but it was heading to a string of staging posts to pick up its commander and the rest of its crew. After that it would rendezvous with the rest of the research fleet in whatever part of chaotic space they planned to study.

Tennal couldn't care less about the crew's research mission. He'd found a schedule, and the only important thing on it was the refueling stop in nine days: the one where they were due to pick up his architect. That meant he only had nine days left of being alone in his own head. He'd vainly hoped the mental itch of the priming might wear off before he met his architect, but no such luck so far. Tennal knew what enhancers felt like, and the itch in his brain wasn't totally different, but it hadn't worn off after a few hours like enhancers did. It felt much, much deeper. He was stuck on a ship with his defenses down and there was nothing he could do about it.

They all expected Tennal to be cooperative. It wasn't as if he had a choice. A shame that he'd never been cooperative in his life.

He spent the first day meandering around the poky corridors— half-familiar from occasional deep-space trips with his aunt before she'd left the army—and familiarizing himself with the people on it. His wristband kept pinging at him to report to the gymnasium for an assigned exercise program. He ignored it.

The second day, Tennal discovered the senior officers on the crew held an operational meeting every morning. He turned up early to the next one and put his feet on the table, casually acknowledging everyone who trickled in after him. Most of them were architects, none very strong; Tennal's reader senses picked up faint flares as they came in. "Civilian adviser," he said, when the commander's chief of staff walked in, surrounded by a stronger glow. "The legislator arranged it. Don't mind me."

He was counting on the fact that his aunt worked at the highest levels and so had probably only briefed the ship's commander, who wasn't here yet. When he focused his reader senses on the chief of staff, he found that had been a safe guess: she was suspicious but confused, and the mention of the legislator had thrown her off. "Take your feet off the table," she said as she took the top chair. Tennal widened his senses to sample everyone else's reactions. Mainly they were mildly irritated or distracted, thinking about the meeting. The warrant officer near the foot of the table was spiking with fury but not going to overrule the chief of staff. Tennal smiled and removed his feet.

The meeting got very quickly into dull details of ship maneuvers and mapping chaotic space. It took Tennal all of ten minutes to figure out ways to relieve the boredom. He waited until two members of the meeting had a dispute, then he dropped in an obscure fact or metric—true or made-up—that supported the weaker side, then sat back and let them forget he hadn't sourced the data at all.

Finally, one time Tennal spoke, a mid-ranking officer looked at him with deep suspicion and said, "Why is he here unsupervised? Isn't he a *reader*?"

"I'm the legislator's nephew," Tennal said blandly. He'd always been careful not to name-drop before, mindful of her position, and it gave him a sharp satisfaction to do it now. "Is there a problem? You don't have something against readers, do you?"

"He's under regulator orders and his architect's on the way," the chief of staff said, in the irritated voice of someone who wasn't entirely pleased with the situation but didn't know what to do about it right now. "Can we get on? We're overrunning our time."

It was two hours before the meeting finished, largely due to Tennal's helpful contributions. He thanked the frazzled officers sitting next to him and bowed to the warrant officer on the way out, touching his throat in an aggressively civilian gesture.

Half the rules on a ship were custom, not military law. Tennal had talked about that with Zin once, back when they'd regularly eaten dinner at the legislator's table. Now that fact got him onto the bridge, where he helped steer any discussion he heard into an unproductive spiral. A couple of times someone tried and failed to write him quiet. The first time it happened it gave Tennal a nasty shock, suddenly aware of the priming in his head, but it turned out the priming *didn't* have exactly the same effect as enhancers. Tennal was still hard to write. Just not, presumably, hard to sync.

He knew he'd pushed it too far when an exasperated captain tried to put a compulsion on him. Compulsions were lingering commands that could be reactivated by a trigger phrase until they wore off, which would have been a good way of stopping Tennal's meddling. It was a shame you needed to be very strong to have any hope of laying one and that Tennal had never encountered anyone who could get one to stick.

All the officers had him pinned as a troublemaker by day three. The warrant officer started to assign rankers to cleaning chores wherever Tennal was, but Tennal had been working on the rankers, and had blown most of his allowance before he boarded on brandy that he'd shared on the first evening. It didn't make him one of them, but it produced a derisory atmosphere on the subject of Tennal between the rankers and the officers, with the rankers ready to mock both sides. Tennal was satisfied with that.

A couple of them were more disposed to be friendly. Tennal

hadn't realized he'd been flirting with one of them—a male ranker with curly hair just outside the bounds of a regulation cut—until the ranker made a bad excuse to lean in and fix the lie of Tennal's collar. Tennal almost accepted; it wasn't as if Zin was going to call him the next morning *this* time. But something stopped him.

If the ranker had offered a couple of days later, he would have gotten a different answer. Tennal was aware he was getting worse as the days wore on. He'd never been very good at suspense. He'd poked at the new data they'd put on his wristband and there was a space for the details of his architect, a file he was *supposed* to have access to, but all it said was *pending details*. He didn't know who the architect was. He couldn't even remember if the legislator had said anything about them. He wouldn't put it past her to withhold the details until Tennal could do nothing about it— she'd always preferred a fait accompli—but he should have those details. He was owed them.

On the ninth day, four hours out from the staging-post rendezvous, a notification pinged into his queue. Tennal stopped in the middle of a corridor and opened it.

The file was three lines long. *Surit Yeni. Junior lieutenant, first rank. Graduation average: 96/100.*

That was it. Not even a picture. That was *it*. Tennal leaned against the wall, a surge of rage sticking in his throat. They wanted him to sync to this architect for life, and they didn't even have the common courtesy to give him a full file.

He made his way back to his room and lay flat on his bed. He wished he'd kept a bottle of the brandy back, though he wasn't sure whether he wanted to drink it or smash it against a wall. "Ninety-six percent," he said to the ceiling. "What a model fucking soldier we have here. Found that one yourself, did you, Auntie dearest?" The room panel lit up, recognizing he was alone and speaking. Tennal flung out his arm to wave it off.

Yeni. That probably wasn't the same as General Marit Yeni, the architect who had blown herself up in the Reader War around the time Tennal was born. There must be thousands of unrelated people called Yeni.

It sounded provincial. Provincials didn't make officer very often. Maybe the legislator had picked Surit Yeni because there was no possibility he and Tennal had any friends in common. Or maybe the legislator just couldn't be bothered to vet the architect at all. She wanted Tennal rewritten inside out, and it might as well be done by a martinet who knew the rule book, whatever their name was.

Tennal already hated them. It was an energizing kind of hatred, like warming his hands at a fire. It was one of the only distractions he had left.

He lay there with his eyes shut and considered the limited supply of soothers hidden inside the armchair. He'd been saving those since he wasn't sure where he could replenish them. He shouldn't take them now. He should be planning how he was going to play the first meeting with this architect—*Surit Yeni*. The perfect soldier.

He rolled over and flipped up the armchair cushion with his foot.

When the *Fractal Note* docked, Tennal was already feeling better. He slipped out with the shore-leave rankers. He'd thrown his military-issue identity pins in the back of the storage cupboard five minutes after he'd been handed them, but he got a commercial pass easily enough by just presenting his biometric details to immigration. It was a minor space station, with only a small population there to serve the passing ships, but there were three bars. Tennal picked one by instinct and was gratified when it got loud and anonymous at barely the beginning of the night cycle.

After his first drink, he started speculating about escape. After his third, he admitted it wasn't going to work. He had no idea how you got hold of a fake identity, and his legal one would be flagged before he'd even made it on a ship. He had no allies and no plan.

The remainder of his allowance lasted him well into the night shift. He was still there, trying to persuade someone he'd never met that he was a famous regulator detective, when a handful of rankers from the *Fractal Note* rolled in. The curly-haired one met his eyes and grinned.

Tennal drained his shot and bought a round.

The two of them ended up in Tennal's cabin. As a partner, the ranker was enthusiastic and good-natured, but when Tennal opened an experimental channel to read his surface feelings he got something not quite complimentary about Tennal himself, so he shut it again. Casual encounters were a bad time to read people. His partner wasn't as good as an architect—getting wasted on cheap drinks wasn't as effective as someone writing you—but between fooling around and the lurching blurriness, Tennal unwound enough to sleep.

The day cycle started with a soft glow in the cabin walls. Tennal shoved himself up on his elbows, dislodging his partner, as the door buzzed.

He didn't have to open it. The person outside had entrance access.

"I know I'm late," a voice said as the door slid aside. "I didn't get the docking notification until just a few—" The newcomer broke off.

He was young. All the Rank Ones Tennal had met were senior officers with graying hair and cutlery trays of decorations on their chests. Tennal wasn't ready for this fresh-faced lieutenant straight out of a recruitment promo, hesitantly blocking the door with the width of his shoulders. He *should* have been ready, Tennal realized: he should have expected every bit of him, from the fastidious hang of his belt to his clean shoes to the pleasantly blank look on his face. An oak-wood button on his cuff gave his gender reference in a neat, military-approved style. His hair was thick and sandy, cropped close to his head.

But the one thing Tennal had been ready for wasn't there. There was no light coming from the soldier in front of him. As he stood there in the door, Tennal was sure—absolutely *certain*—he was an architect. It didn't make any difference what his rank tabs said; this instinct could have picked him out in the blackness of space. Tennal had always assumed architects couldn't help the light they shed, as if their intentions spilled it into the universe undirected, like a lamp with no shade. But he could see nothing from this newcomer at all. Tennal had never experienced this certainty combined with this total lack of presence. This soldier had defenses so strong that nothing showed through.

The perfect soldier was frowning now, a frozen expression with a gaze that didn't quite land on the curly-haired ranker in Tennal's bed. He said, "Fifty-Six?"

Tennal gave him a cool, artificial smile. "Surit Yeni. I don't recall inviting you to my cabin. Did you come to watch?"

Surit rarely forgot things, even under pressure. Even—like now— under the pressure of being faced with an unexpectedly attractive, unexpectedly naked stranger at what Surit had thought was a routine introduction. Surit remembered faces and images particularly easily, so easily that it had almost felt like he was cheating in exams when he read the answers off a mental picture of the textbook. And so he was sure he hadn't met this smoothly confident civilian, one with an intensity that belied the sallowness under his eyes, but he'd seen that face before.

The defined features, the strong nose, the green eyes, and the sweep of brown hair over his forehead. Not on a capture; it had been a still image. On a trip to Exana, on the *news*—

"You're one of the legislator's family," he said, more in shock than anything else. He could see the caption under the billboard image. "Sen . . . Tennalhin?"

"No, I'm the commander's hired courtesan," Tennalhin said, swinging his legs over the other person in the bed. The other *naked* person in the bed, as Surit was trying not to officially notice. "Thanks for visiting—now get out. Not you," he added to his partner, who was stirring at the noise. "Go back to sleep. I don't know who this lump of muscle is. He just walked in."

"Lieutenant Yeni," Surit said. He could have commented that Tennalhin had known his name seconds before, but Surit didn't like to give in to someone baiting him. "I'm sorry to—" He swallowed, deeply uncomfortable with the whole situation. He knew soldiers slept with each other, even though it was officially disapproved of, but he had taken care to avoid anything he wasn't supposed to see. Tennalhin was supposed to be a ranker, as was the curly-haired person half-buried in the blanket, so at least there weren't any chain-of-command relations going on, but Surit still didn't want to see it. "I didn't mean to interrupt," Surit temporized. He looked at the other ranker and said, "I think maybe you lost your way to your room."

"Well, you fucking are interrupting." Tennalhin unfolded himself to his feet. He shrugged a civilian wrap-jacket onto his shoulders, obviously from last night, which just drew deliberate attention to the fact he was wearing nothing else at all. "In fact," he said, with the precise, razor-sharp diction that Surit had mainly heard from the very rich Exana set, "you are interrupting my fucking."

Surit felt the heat of embarrassment rise to his face. "Do you think," he said, carefully measuring his tone, "that you could get dressed?"

"Can't see where I put my trousers," Tennalhin said, without bothering to take his eyes off Surit's face. Behind him, his partner gave a bleary groan and put a pillow over his head. "Are you offering yours?"

It galled Surit to realize Tennalhin was enjoying his discomfort. He let out a slow breath to control his embarrassment and let his expression go entirely neutral. "I'm not really here to discuss uniform," he said. "I was told I was sharing this cabin with a ranker code-named Fifty-Six."

"Were you?" Tennalhin said.

Surit's new-assignment nerves twinged as the ground of his own certainty cracked beneath his feet. This wasn't a ranker. No ranker would be allowed to cram their cabin full of non-regulation furniture. And everything Surit knew of Orshan high society didn't let him believe a relative of the legislator would join as a ranker. "I was told to expect a reader."

Tennalhin gave him a smile with edges in it. "Oh, I'm the only reader on this ship."

The spike of embarrassment hadn't faded. Surit felt a deeper mortification stirring in him. His briefing had been wrong, and he had a suspicion as to why. He continued doggedly, "Were you ever code-named Fifty-Six?"

"You know," Tennalhin said, "I don't really remember." The smile melted off his face as he took another step toward Surit in the cluttered cabin. Surit tensed and didn't back up, even when Tennalhin rested a fingertip on his chest. "You're supposed to be a regulator-approved architect, aren't you? Write it out of me."

"Please take your hand off me," Surit said.

"Can't do it?" Tennalhin said, an undertone of mockery to his voice. "Not strong enough?"

He'd had a warning. Surit took his wrist firmly and moved it aside. Tennalhin put up surprisingly little resistance. "Writing without consent is illegal."

"So you know that," Tennalhin said. Something in his eyes made Surit feel as if he'd avoided a trap by a razor-thin margin.

Surit said, very carefully, "Are you the agent I'm supposed to sync with?"

Tennalhin removed his wrist from Surit's hand and stepped back. The smile he gave Surit this time was pure malice. "You've been misinformed," he said. "I'm very sorry, Lieutenant Yeni. I'm a civilian, a nephew of the legislator, and I haven't consented. If you make any move to sync with me, I'm afraid I have lawyers waiting to take you and your promising military career apart."

Surit's nagging suspicions coalesced into full, mortifying certainty. He'd been set up. Either the regulators had another goal here, one they hadn't told him, or someone with connections wanted to take down the family of the traitor general. He might have avoided the obvious trap of writing a civilian, but he'd still landed in this mess. He'd been sent here to embarrass himself.

Tennalhin was watching him, that sharpness still gleaming in his eyes like the arming catch on an incendiary. "I see," Surit said stiffly. He switched to a non-military form of address. "My apologies, Sen Tennalhin. I'm sorry for disturbing you." He didn't look any further at Tennal's bed partner, who still had his head under a pillow, or at the rest of the cluttered cabin. He went to salute, realized Tennalhin wasn't a uniformed soldier, and touched his own throat in a civilian gesture instead. "Excuse me."

He saw a flash of surprise in Tennalhin's face, then the return of that sharp defensiveness. The door closed between them.

Surit picked up his bag, turned around, and went straight to the ranker cabins. The logistics officer was surprised at his request for accommodation, but they were still running with a skeleton crew, and she found him a bunk in a dormitory. Surit stowed his things swiftly and went to seek out the highest-ranking officer currently on board the ship.

"What do you mean, you can't carry out orders?" the chief of staff said. "He's right bloody there."

Surit maintained his salute until she belatedly answered it. She'd activated the privacy field around her desk when Surit mentioned this was regulator business, but Surit checked the blue line on the floor was glowing before he spoke. "There's been a mistake in my briefing," Surit said, though he was almost certain whatever cock-up had happened was intentional. "Fifty-Six—I mean, Sen Tennalhin has not agreed to sync."

"We're not supposed to be throwing his legal name around," the chief of staff said irritably. "Orders. Why's he not syncing? He was dumped on us from your people in the regulators. I was told he'd sync as soon as you turned up,"

"I'm not privy to all the details," Surit said carefully. "My briefing pack from the regulators was minimal."

The chief of staff muttered something that sounded like *fucking regulators*. "Report back to your seniors, then, and await orders. Who do you even report to?"

Surit pulled up a mental image of his briefing. "My acting CO is the commander of this ship," he said. "Until I'm notified further, the regulators say."

The chief of staff cast a harried look at the calendar glowing on her desk, as if she could hurry up the commander's rendezvous date. "Then bring it up with Commander Vinys," she said. "The moment he steps on the ship. Please fucking Lights he's had a better briefing than they've seen fit to give me, because if he doesn't have a solution, I'm going to throw that bloody reader into a nova."

Surit almost opened his mouth to ask why, but then had a sudden flashback of Tennalhin's blazing presence inches away, his finger pressing into Surit's chest. Maybe he didn't need to ask.

A buzzer sounded, indicating their departure from the space station. The chief of staff took down the privacy field and spoke into her wristband. "Countdown to launch," she said. "Lieutenant, find a seat."

Surit saluted. He wasn't going to argue further if she wasn't. But as he buckled into a launch seat, he felt an uneasy prickling down his back: that didn't feel like the end of it. Surely it must be. This was illegal. They couldn't make a *civilian* sync if he didn't want to.

This whole thing was a mess from start to finish. Surit shut his eyes and tried to put Tennalhin out of his mind.

CHAPTER 6

It had worked. Tennal saw his bed partner out, dressed and showered and ate in the rankers' canteen, and then allowed himself thirty seconds to sit on his bed and stop hiding the shivers that chased over his body from the ball of tension in his chest.

He didn't trust the relief, and when he made himself look at things objectively, he was right—it had only worked for now. Lights knew what Surit Yeni was planning, or who he'd complained to after he'd left. Tennal had been trying to read him every moment he'd been in the room but it was like getting blood from a stone. Surit's surface emotions were muted in the same way his architect presence was muted: all Tennal had gotten were small spikes of confusion and horrified embarrassment.

But Tennal wasn't synced. The exposed itch of the priming was still there in his head, so Surit would have been able to force a sync if he'd tried. He hadn't tried.

Bile roiled in Tennal's stomach, strong enough that he had to go and breathe deeply in the bathroom. He made himself think. He had to keep Surit Yeni at bay for three more days now, before the fleet's commander boarded and Surit was no longer the biggest threat. Surit—nice, rule-abiding graduate that he was—had seemed revolted at both Tennal's habits and personality, which was a good start. Tennal wouldn't have much trouble keeping that up.

His headache was bad enough that he had to stop thinking there. He wasn't used to looking beyond the next few hours. The morning strategy meeting was about to start. Tennal shoved himself to his feet; that was an important part of his weird outsider status, and if he stopped going, someone might get ideas about treating him as a ranker again.

Over the next couple of days, he kept an eye out for Surit around the ship. The lieutenant was easy to catch sight of because his walk was distinctive: careful and oddly silent for his build. Tennal saw him coming in and out of the gymnasium, or the showers, or the tiny study terminal closets provided to stop soldiers from going mad in their rooms. He seemed to be on facilities duty a lot, a dull chore usually given to a ranker. Tennal checked his schedule and realized Surit had signed up for extra chores—in the time slots, it looked like, that were assigned for him to test Tennal's abilities.

It was Surit's presence, in the end, that made Tennal overstep in the next strategy meeting.

He had taken his last two soothers beforehand, but that was just to calm himself. He had the pressure-chamber feeling that was usually the harbinger of his biggest mistakes. Soothers aside, it still gave him a caustic pleasure to have his feet on the table while the chief of staff dealt with the logistics officer, to sip his coffee noisily enough to annoy his neighbors, to ask nitpicky questions about the topic at hand.

It was the day their new officer, Commander Vinys, was due to board, so everyone was on edge and trying to pretend everything was under control. The morning meeting was frantically worried about the new scanning ships that were supposed to be joining the fleet. The ships, Tennal gathered, were Resolution-loan technology, imported through the link from the wider galaxy, and they were apparently stuck at Archer Link Station because Archer Division wouldn't clear them for import.

There was no love lost between Archer and Cavalry. Tennal could recognize and admire obstructive fuckery when he saw it.

He couldn't give a shit one way or the other, personally, but it was fertile ground for argument. It was cheating to read the table just to figure out the best way to keep the members of the meeting at one another's throats. He did it anyway.

"Do you have a *better* idea, Sen Tennalhin?" the chief of staff finally said, rounding on him in exasperation. "We've been through five proposals now, and you've undermined all of them. Give me yours."

Tennal sat up straighter, taken aback. The way she was looking at him suggested he hadn't been nearly careful enough to hide what he was doing this time. "I—" he said, then looked more closely at the import regulations on the screen. "Okay. Reclassify all the scanners as livestock. They're Resolution tech, so they're weird as shit. I bet nobody on Archer Station can prove they're *not* alive. Send in the vets to check them for foot mites or whatever, clear them, and bang, you've got your scanners."

The chief of staff suddenly looked thoughtful, but her reaction was lost in the infuriated backlash from around the table as three people at once told Tennal why that was a ludicrous idea. Tennal smiled viciously, bile still sitting in his stomach, and made up two obscure past cases where they'd done just that. Because he was doing badly at being convincing today, someone tried to look it up on the ship's databases, and the meeting divided over whether they believed him or not.

"Will you all *shut* the hell *up!*" the chief of staff snapped. "This is a meeting, not a zoo." Into the moment of silence that fell—they were soldiers, after all—she said, "Does anyone else have something of value to add? If not, I'm declaring this the shit show it is and putting it on Commander Vinys's desk when he boards."

"If I may?" someone said from the back of the room. Tennal didn't immediately recognize the voice, but he recognized the blank space in his reader senses: Surit Yeni.

Surit was sitting with a couple of other very junior officers in observers' chairs at the back. They'd been asked to fetch coffee a couple of times and were occasionally allowed to participate. The chief of staff waved permission for him to speak.

"It would work," Surit said quietly. "Given sufficient authority for reclassification. But the problem is that you would then have to provide your 'livestock' with a suitable environment, which in absence of prior documentation means human-survivable conditions. So you couldn't operate them as spaceships. You'd lose the import license, and Archer would have grounds to seize them back."

For some reason his artificially calm voice annoyed Tennal more than all the people who hadn't really thought about it. "Do you *memorize regulations for fun*?" he said, over whatever the chief of staff was attempting to say. "What's your alternative? Launch a fucking missile strike on Archer Link Station?"

It was the wrong tone of voice, he'd sworn in front of senior officers, and he'd talked over the chief of staff. All rookie mistakes. He was braced before she even rested her hands on the table, said, "I've had enough," and wrote him quiet.

Or tried to. The chief of staff wasn't a weak architect, but her write command slid off Tennal's defenses like most of them did. For a brief, destructive moment, Tennal considered pretending he hadn't heard, but he couldn't afford to get thrown out. Instead, he said, "My apologies, sir," in the flattest voice he could summon, and looked away. He felt her flash of annoyance that it hadn't worked. Still, she wanted to finish up more than she wanted to waste time on him. Tennal kept quiet for the rest of the meeting.

He'd pushed it too far. He could tell after the meeting that more of the officers were wondering what he was doing there, why he wasn't synced. A couple had brief, inquiring words with Surit as the group broke up. Tennal avoided them. Not well enough, though, because he ended up in the lift alone with Surit, who had also made a surprisingly fast exit.

Tennal stuck to the corner, keeping his breathing even, aware of the priming itch in his head like a siren blaring in the distance.

Surit didn't seem any more comfortable. He folded himself into the opposite corner without much success. The lift wasn't big.

"Do you think I'm going to bite?" Tennal said.

"Excuse me," Surit said, shifting his hip against the wall. He looked steadily past Tennal at the floor.

Tennal was prickling with the effort of navigating his way through the meeting, synapses still firing in random and unhelpful directions. It would be a terrible idea to pick a fight with the man he needed to keep at a distance. "So," he said, "is this your new strategy? Maybe *engaging* with me will convince me to sync with you?"

Surit lifted his head. His flat, brown-eyed gaze met Tennal's with an impact that made Tennal feel like he'd just run into a wall.

"No," Surit said.

Tennal tapped his fingers against the wall behind him. "You were lying, weren't you?" he said. "About the import regulations. You couldn't remember something like that."

He saw Surit stiffen—not so impervious after all. Tennal still couldn't feel anything from him. There was a long pause, during which Tennal wondered if Surit was even strong enough to write him. Maybe he *wasn't* a Rank One. "I remember things," Surit said at last. "Details. I would prefer it if you didn't accuse me of lying."

"Oh, well, in that case," Tennal said. "You should try it. It makes meetings go so much faster."

"I'm sure it does," Surit said. "You didn't seem keen on shortening that session."

Tennal gave him a broad smile. "You should have written me quiet instead. Maybe you could have succeeded where our honorable leader failed."

Surit looked back at the door and said, "She shouldn't have done that."

"Guidance lead us," Tennal said, his voice overly shocked. "Casual writing? In the Orshan army? What are we coming to?"

"*You* shouldn't have sworn in front of a senior officer," Surit snapped. "Nor should you have gone to an officers' meeting high on mood alterers! You were lucky she didn't notice."

The remnants of the soothers were still in Tennal's system, softening the worst of the edges, but they had nearly worn off, and he was frankly surprised Surit had noticed anything. "I do my best thinking when I'm high."

"No you *don't*," Surit said. "You were forgetting details. You couldn't process more than one person speaking at once. If you can think on that level when you're chemically altered, you'll think twice as effectively when you're not. I know you don't answer to me, but I strongly advise you to ask the medics for a withdrawal shot and break that habit."

The doors started to open on the cabin level. "To hell with that," Tennal said, nettled. "Last time I got one of those, they slipped in a priming shot. Fuck if I let someone near me with a needle again."

"A priming—" Surit said, looking bemused, as if he'd never heard the word. To be fair, whatever the medics had used for priming might have been in the scanners instead of the shots. "To do what?"

Tennal didn't have to hand Surit that information if he hadn't worked it out. He pushed past Surit to the door.

Surit put out a hand and grabbed Tennal's arm as he passed. A glimmer of light brushed Tennal's mind, something like a write command but much more distant, faint, and unfamiliar, like the light from a new star. It touched the itch in the back of his head—*the priming*—like the sun lighting up a vein of crystal. The refractions sent a shudder straight through Tennal's brain. He jerked his arm violently out of Surit's grip.

"They've taken down your defenses." The mental touch withdrew. Surit sounded blank, so blank that Tennal wasn't expecting it when he said, "That's barbarous."

Tennal swallowed in shock. The elevator doors beeped a

protest, unable to shut. "Welcome to the *military*," he said. "Is this your first day?" He pushed himself away from the wall and started down the corridor to put distance between them. Both their wristbands pinged at the same time: a troop muster. Tennal didn't plan to attend, but he knew why it was there. He had been counting down the days to the new threat. "Isn't your fleet commander due to board today?" he said over his shoulder. "Don't you have some shoes to shine?"

CHAPTER 7

Surit couldn't get the sound out of his head as he reported to the bridge: Tennalhin's bitter, casual voice saying, *They slipped in a priming shot.* As if what they'd done to him were a minor indignity and not viscerally shocking, not a crime. But was it a crime if the army had done it? Had they planned this? Surit couldn't believe they'd genuinely meant him to sync with an unwilling civilian—an unwilling civilian who was also the nephew of the Orshan legislator. But it disturbed him more than he could articulate that he felt he *could* have made them sync, could have fallen into Tennalhin's orbit and Tennalhin into his, like they were mirrored binary planets—

He flinched. The thought of someone falling into a sync because their brain chemistry had been forcibly rearranged was vile.

Surit had expected his career to be difficult. He'd known the Orshan army didn't live up to its ideals. He'd thought he was clear-eyed: it was often inefficient, occasionally corrupt, frequently prejudiced. But it wasn't as if non-military organizations were all that much better, and it was the only way to restore Marit's pension—and besides, divisions like Cavalry had their tendrils in so many parts of society that it was difficult to get anywhere without one of them.

He hadn't considered he was signing up to the same body that ordered readers to sync. He hadn't considered he might be asked to do anything like this.

He wanted to sit down and methodically think it through, but he didn't have time. All officers were under orders to assemble on the bridge and welcome the fleet's commander. Surit had to put a lid on his inner agitation and follow orders.

Surit had caught a glimpse of the fast courier that had brought Commander Vinys to the ship—a service expensive enough that it was only extended to senior officers—but he hadn't seen him disembark. So the first glimpse he got was when a solid figure with gray hair and a short beard came into the bridge. Like other effective senior officers Surit had seen, Commander Vinys had a personal presence like a dense mass in a star field, and everyone else in the room angled themselves around him as they came to attention.

"At ease," the commander said, with a crack of a smile. "We'll run the briefing once the rest of the fleet is here. I'm expecting this to be a nice, clean trip into chaotic space and back. Almost a holiday, if we do it right. I expect you all have your sunscreen and beach loungers packed." He snapped his fingers to break the silence. "Carry on."

He picked out the senior officers. At his elbow was the chief of staff, who seemed relieved he'd arrived. Surit took a step forward to ask if he could have an audience later.

But as he did, Commander Vinys was already turning to him. "Our regulator-assigned rookie," he said, clapping him on the shoulder. He let go and measured Surit with a glance. "Where's your reader?"

Surit came to attention and said, "I don't know at this moment, sir. He might be in his cabin."

"Why don't you know?" Commander Vinys said.

"I wanted to raise the matter with you, sir," Surit said, staring straight ahead. "There have been some issues with my briefing."

"What issues?"

"Sir, the classification—"

Commander Vinys raised an impatient hand and stepped into the privacy zone around the command desk, which had been vacated for him. Beyond the privacy shield, the air took on a gray tint, and the bustle of the bridge was suddenly muted. "Explain," he said, his voice cooler, "because from what I can see, you've left your reader running around the ship unsupervised."

"I—sir?"

"Have I misunderstood? You don't know where he is. Military readers should make their architect aware of their whereabouts at all times." The commander killed the privacy screen just long enough to say curtly to the chief of staff, "Ping Agent Fifty-Six for me. Flag chamber. Fifteen minutes."

Surit needed a moment to process his shock. Of course, strong readers could theoretically make other people uneasy, he knew that, but he didn't realize that extended to keeping tabs on their movements. "We're not synced, sir. I was misinformed about the situation. Tennalhin hasn't volunteered to sync. He—" Surit didn't even know how to say it. It was a wild accusation.

"Why?" the commander said. "I understood he was primed. Has it worn off?"

Surit stared at him. It wasn't appropriate behavior in front of a senior officer, but he didn't feel in full control of his reactions. The commander had been briefed that Tennal would be primed. That meant this wasn't some accident, but a legitimate order from high command.

Surit picked up the pieces of his voice and assembled them enough to say, "I don't see how that can be legal, sir."

The commander let the pause stretch out this time, regarding him for so long that Surit's neck prickled. "I'll say two things, Lieutenant. The first is that when you put on this uniform, when you accepted the role of wielding force in service of the state, you agreed to be commanded by the state. That's the justification for all military action, right across the whole Resolution. Are you on board so far?" He waited for Surit's stiff nod. "The second is that you are not privy to what regulator-assigned readers have done prior to recruitment. I doubt you've seen what an unscrupulous person can do with deep reading. Take my word for it: it isn't pretty."

Surit instinctively opened his mouth to reject that. But it was true that he didn't know anything about Tennalhin except who he was related to. And if everything had been aboveboard, surely Tennalhin wouldn't have joined like this, synced to a junior officer who'd only been requested at the last minute. Surit had known there was more to this than he'd been told. He was just starting to realize how much more.

"Sir," he said neutrally. "I still don't—"

The commander glanced at the time on the desk. "Report to the flag chamber in fourteen minutes. Bring your reader."

Surit cut himself off. He could hear when an order was an order. "Sir."

The commander beckoned the chief of staff again as he strode off the bridge. She fell in beside him, speaking in the level tone of someone giving a briefing. Surit heard *refuses to acknowledge orders even from the bloody regulators* and guessed what the commander wanted to be briefed about.

The short break gave Surit time to write down a brief outline of his concerns, including the conversation with Commander Vinys. He encrypted the report but then realized the regulators hadn't given him a contact to send anything to. He couldn't just raise it to anyone: Tennalhin could be in danger if the information got out. By this point he was pushing his fourteen minutes. He saved the report for later.

He had to push his time even further, as Tennalhin's wristband wasn't immediately accessible from the ship's network. It took Surit a further two minutes to figure out Tennalhin had somehow registered himself as the only civilian on the ship. Surit had to come out of the military network entirely and approach it from a less-secure commercial interface just to open a line.

"I'm so glad you called," Tennalhin said. His head and shoulders appeared in a tiny projection above Surit's wristband. "You never call. It's like I'm a stranger you met three days ago."

Surit ignored that. "The commander requests you come to the flag chamber."

"Does he?" Tennalhin said. "That's not what the last message I got said."

Surit paused. "What did the last one say?"

"That one wasn't a request," Tennalhin said. "But I suppose, if you're asking nicely." He stretched in a way that was obviously meant to indicate relaxation, but even through the projection Surit could tell he was faking. "Tell our new commander I'll be there in a minute."

Tennalhin was late. By that time, Surit had already arrived at the flag chamber: a large, shielded space that was a fleet commander's office, war room, and meeting hall rolled into one. The commander sat, flanked by the chief of staff, at the table they used for the morning strategy meetings. "Let's see your regulator stamps," he said, as soon as Surit walked in.

Surit opened the sync authorization he'd received in his briefing. It floated onto the table in silver layers, each of them a filigree visualization of an encryption algorithm. The layers coalesced into the most formal style of document, identifying Surit—and presumably Tennalhin—by a long identification number that must correspond with the regulators' databases.

Commander Vinys took his time examining it. "Those are in order."

"You're late," the chief of staff said as Tennalhin came through the door.

Tennalhin took a seat, uninvited. He wore a deep green wrap-jacket and an ostentatiously civilian earring. "Yes, usually," he said. "You asked for me?"

The chief of staff was too professional to glance at Commander Vinys as if to say, *Look what I've had to deal with,* but Surit felt she wanted to. Surit wanted to mentally shout at Tennal to stand up, to warn him the commander didn't like readers out of control.

"Agent Fifty-Six," Commander Vinys said, putting his elbows on the table, "it has been brought to my attention that you're the nephew of the legislator."

Tennalhin wasn't dense, at least. He could feel the trap in the words as much as Surit could. Surit could see the tension radiating from him, but based on Surit's limited experience, that didn't necessarily mean Tennalhin was going to say anything polite. "I am."

"My staff tells me you're claiming that you're a civilian adviser," the commander said. "That right as well?"

"It is."

Commander Vinys leaned back. "Then that'll be news to your aunt," he said, "because it sure wasn't what she told me when she put you on my ship." There was a moment's silence before he continued. "But I hear you've got documents to back you up. Some nice regulations lawyering. That's just fine. You'll understand, though, that I can't have a reader running around unsynced. A reader who's read and blackmailed two people on my own ship."

Tennalhin flinched with his whole body. "I haven't done anything like that. I wouldn't—obviously I—" Then, as Surit's mind spun wildly, Tennalhin said, "Which two people?"

"Private Ashahil," the Commander said, "whom you took to your cabin four nights ago to sleep with."

"A *normal* bloody thing to do—do you think I needed to blackmail him to—"

"And Lieutenant Yeni," the commander continued, "who had a perfect record right up until he boarded this ship."

"No," Surit said, in some shock. "Sir, that's not it at all." He wondered belatedly if his own actions could have been somehow manipulated. But he had had *reasons,* and those reasons were the same way he always thought.

"I have *not fucking blackmailed Lieutenant Yeni,*" Tennalhin said through his teeth.

"Both of you quiet down," the commander said. He nodded to the chief of staff. "Let's get some answers."

The chief of staff looked slightly embarrassed. "I can't, sir," she said. "Lieutenant Yeni will need to do it."

The commander pointed at Surit and indicated Tennalhin. "Go ahead, Lieutenant." Surit realized the commander must be a neutral, with no architect abilities himself. He wanted Surit to write the information out of Tennalhin.

"Wait a minute," Surit said. "Sir, please." Tennalhin had put his head in his hands.

That coolness came back into the commander's voice. His eyes were flat. "Lieutenant Yeni, this reader is a danger to your fellow soldiers. I didn't have you marked as unreliable, but I swear on the Light of Guidance, if you refuse orders, I'll give you to the regulators along with him."

"I—" Surit said.

Tennalhin put a hand up, the palm facing Surit. "Do it!" he said. "Just do it! You're a fucking *architect*. This is what your brain was built for! Do you think I want to take this to the regulators?"

Surit was trapped. He hadn't written anyone in years: a few times as a child, then once when someone dared him at officer academy, and he'd regretted it afterward. Both the subject and his commanding officer were telling him to do it. Logically there was no reason for him to feel this wave of stubbornness. "You have the right to refuse, Sen Tennalhin."

"I'm not refusing," Tennalhin said flatly. "I told you to get on with it."

Surit tried to clear the unpleasant taste from the back of his mouth and said, "Please ready yourself." He reached out and directed a command at Tennalhin's mind.

Every architect saw minds differently. Surit hadn't written many people—Elvi had valued strict mental discipline and raised him that way—but when he had, it had always been like shining a light into water. Sometimes it was a sparkling pool of icelike fractals; sometimes it was dark and mossy like a stone well. When he reached out to Tennalhin's mind, casting light on the currents within it, he was expecting something deep and difficult to influence. But he wasn't prepared for what he plunged into.

Tennalhin's mind was like the sea.

Surit nearly lost himself. Tennalhin's subconscious intentions were all around him like swirling currents. Surit had to will himself to keep his own mind together. As he sank further, illuminating the ocean around him, his mind threw up images to try to make sense of it: there were dark shapes in the depths, unfathomable shadows, leviathans that floated in the distance or turned away with the flick of a tail. He sensed that if he sank deeper, there would be swaying tendrils and reefs and rocks. The sea of Tennal's mind stretched beyond anything he had ever experienced—one mistake, and Surit knew it could swallow the faint, steady light he brought with him.

The currents grew more violent as he sank, trying to toss him out. Surit struggled to stay focused. He usually picked out intentions by leaning over the surface and looking for them, but he would have no chance of that here: Tennalhin's intentions were wide currents that rose and fell from miles deep. With every movement, the water made new efforts to tear Surit's consciousness apart.

The intention he needed was the urge to *expose information*. He could see the texture of the different currents, although he couldn't have said what they were—he could only recognize one when he was looking for it. *Expose information* wasn't too far in the depths, and when he found it, he took it and shaped it to what he needed.

A force stirred the waves as the sea churned around the stray current. But Surit had it, he felt it. He shaped the command like a hurricane.

Tell me if you've read anyone on this ship.

Back in the command room, Tennalhin sat up and said emotionlessly, "I've been reading surface thoughts a lot. Not deep reading, though, and I've never blackmailed anyone in my life."

"You read serving personnel?" Surit heard the commander say.

Surit came back to himself slowly from that endless sea, his skin pricking with wonder. It had never—*never*—felt like that to write someone: exhilarating and terrifying and like you were wrestling with nature itself. He wondered if all readers had minds like that.

Tennalhin blinked and shook his head as if he were the one emerging from water. He gave Surit a startled glance. His uncertainty only lasted a moment, though; a split second later, Tennalhin had pulled the sardonic expression back onto his face. "Was that fun, Lieutenant?" he said. "Apparently I'm horrific to write when I haven't taken enhancers. Yes, serving personnel. Who else have we got on this ship?"

Surit didn't know what enhancers were, but he could make a guess, and that was another repellent concept. He forced himself to concentrate on the conversation.

"Okay, then," the commander said. "You're a civilian, and you're conducting espionage on my soldiers. Here's what I'm going to do."

"Who would you say I'm spying for? My bingo group?" Tennalhin rested his elbows on his knees, sounding blasé, but the defensive hunch of his shoulders gave him away.

"I'm putting a civilian emergency order on you," the commander said. Surit frowned. The commander was well within his rights to put an emergency order on a civilian on his ship, but there was no way that extended to syncing. But what the commander said next didn't cover that. "Confined to cabin. All extraneous equipment confiscated. You don't leave the room unless you're told. If you agree to follow Lieutenant Yeni's instructions and speak to no one else, you may accompany him around the ship, but further interference with the crew or with my staff will lead to indefinite confinement. Unless," he said, slowing to a drawl, "you're going to let Lieutenant Yeni sync you?"

"No," Tennalhin said, his mouth barely moving. He was staring at the floor now.

"And you, Lieutenant Yeni"—here the commander pointed a crooked finger at Surit—"are wasting space. Move into your assigned quarters. You're on babysitting duty until you have a sync."

"What?" Surit said blankly. "We can't—" Then he realized the commander *hadn't* ordered either of them to sync. He'd just put Tennalhin under what amounted to brig confinement. Brig confinement with Surit. But he had grounds for that, as Tennalhin had just admitted to using his reader powers, in however minor a way. He'd dealt neatly with the obstruction and would clearly drive Tennalhin mad if that was what it took to get a sync. It was all legal. And all Surit had to do was wait until Tennalhin couldn't take the four walls of the cabin anymore and then bribe him with time outside.

Surit was not an angry person. But that was purposeful: when he felt anger rise in him, he stopped it or redirected it. So it was a surprise to take a step back from his conscious thoughts and realize he'd been letting his anger build around him, breathing it— *swimming* in it.

"Any questions?" the commander said.

Tennalhin moved his shoulders in a silent shrug. It was all legal.

Surit saluted stiffly. "No, sir," he said. "I'll get my things."

They were thorough, Tennal gave them credit for that. The commander assigned two of the crew's security personnel overseen by the warrant officer, who seemed to find it immensely satisfying to strip Tennal's cabin of the unauthorized decorations. At least this was making someone happy.

Tennal's civilian clothes were on the list of unauthorized items. Tennal took the outfit of ranker casuals one of them handed him and changed in the middle of the furniture moving, because he wasn't too concerned about anyone's comfort levels.

"Where are your division marks?" the warrant officer said when he was done, looking over Tennal's ranker outfit critically.

Every soldier wore a set of metal marks pinned to their collar to show their current ship or station. The *Fractal Note*'s showed a pair of crossed lances. "Lights know. Lost them."

"You're a fucking idiot, then, aren't you?" the warrant officer said. They were looking slightly to the side, as if it made them uncomfortable to see a soldier without any kind of affiliation. Tennal watched their discomfiture. "I'll have another set found."

Tennal shrugged and flopped back on his bed, now stripped of the garish fabrics he'd covered it with. "List."

"What?"

"List of what you're confiscating," Tennal repeated. "You're legally obliged to provide me with an inventory." He didn't know if that was true. Right now he found it hard to give a shit about what they were taking—he couldn't even remember half of what he'd brought with him to decorate—but it made the warrant officer turn back to their immediate task in annoyance.

Tennal lay unmoving on the bed for some time after they'd all left. His mind ticked over like a malfunctioning drive, spitting out heat and movement without purpose. He watched it from inside his own head. He didn't even wish he still had his last soothers. Two soothers wouldn't do anything for this. He'd need a pack.

It was another short while before the door opened again. Surit had been held back by the commander, Tennal assumed for orders on how to sync him. Tennal had his eyes shut as the door opened. He could feel Surit's presence by the faint traces around him, like a cloaked module moving deep underwater.

As a rule, Tennal didn't deep-read people. Reading wasn't quite as unobtrusive as people thought, and the deeper you went, the more likely they would notice something was wrong and get you in trouble. But it wasn't as if Tennal could sink much lower now. He pushed his reading senses at Surit Yeni with everything he had.

It was no fucking use. It wasn't that Tennal was missing something. Surit's thoughts emitted no light at all, no clues, no crack in the shell he surrounded himself with. Strong architects had natural defenses against being written, but reading was more delicate and could often slide around them. Not here. This was someone who had practiced keeping himself under control, probably because some fucking self-help guide had told him to.

Tennal raised his head. Surit's face was completely blank, like someone had programmed a perfect military AI, and he held himself as stiffly as a marionette. Surit hadn't even noticed.

Tennal couldn't help it. He laughed.

Surit turned from placing his small military-issue holdall and weapon case by the spare bed. "Do you," he said, sounding closer to anger than Tennal had heard from him so far, "have something to say?"

Tennal took a dark, amused moment to appreciate that even the perfect soldier didn't like being ordered around when he wasn't expecting it. Then a lurch in his stomach reminded him Surit was about to sync him, and he didn't need Surit to hold a grudge. Tennal threw a forearm over his face to block out the light. "Not really."

Tennal could still feel the itch of the priming in his head like burned skin, too sensitive to touch. He braced grimly for the brush of Surit's mind against it.

"I'm about to use the desk," Surit said. "Do you need it?"

"What?" Tennal said, opening his eyes. "No."

Surit sat at the desk and tapped his wristband for a screen. As Tennal watched incredulously, Surit pulled up some sort of tactics study module.

"Putting it off?" Tennal said.

"Until you ask me to," Surit said, "I have no intention of syncing you." He tapped a command in too hard, realized it was wrong, and had to redo it. "Excuse me. I have to get this done."

It looked like the kind of routine study you picked up when you had nothing better to do. Tennal watched him for a few minutes, gradually recognizing the leaden ache that sank through his muscles and prickled in his feet. Usually he made his own horrors, but thanks to the generous resources of the army, he didn't have to do that here. He was aware of every movement Surit made, every twitch of his hand at the console. *Until you ask me to.*

Tennal found another reserve of spite under the dread. Surit might want to feel better about syncing him, but Tennal had no reason to play along.

When he turned to his wristband, Tennal wasn't surprised to find they'd already cut off most of his network access. He could still get to basic systems, army regs, and his schedule—which was blank. He didn't have access to the room panel, so he couldn't open the door. No surprise there either. Nothing to do.

So Tennal lay on the bed, his thoughts spiraling into an abyss, and did nothing.

There had always been times when he'd wanted to shut his brain off. And there'd always been times when he'd been unable to do anything about it, lying there with a blank ceiling and a head full of live wires, no pills, no one else awake, nowhere to take his particular brand of rich-kid bullshit. Each time he'd catch himself thinking, *This is the worst point of my life*, then he'd realize he'd tipped into melodrama and make fun of himself for playing the same self-pitying tune again. He could do that in an army cabin just as easily as in a cheap Sanura hotel.

Surit pushed his chair back after about an hour. Tennal's eyes flicked open, which was futile; Surit didn't have to move to sync him. Listening wouldn't give Tennal any warning.

Surit cleared his throat. "I'm going to the canteen," he said. "You can accompany me if you abide by the rules the commander set."

"No," Tennal said. He was aware of his diminishing supply of refusals, dwindling to the uncertain point when Surit decided Tennal wasn't going to consent to sync and went ahead anyway. He might as well use them all.

Surit nodded as if unsurprised. "You're on the basic rations list. I'll bring you a pack."

"So kind," Tennal said to the ceiling. "I'll have the lobster."

Surit brought back an unappetizing box and a report that they were settling into their final three-day trajectory to chaotic space, whatever that meant. Tennal wasn't hungry and didn't care. The blue tint had faded out of the cabin walls as the day cycle ended, leaving a warmer light, but Tennal didn't feel the slightest bit tired. He waited the evening out with his eyes shut.

He couldn't stop his brain from circling what it would feel like to be synced to an architect. Tennal tried floating the thought: *maybe it wouldn't be so bad.* After all, Tennal had let people write him before. He'd asked for it; he'd even taken enhancers to let them—anything to turn his brain off for a few hours. Would a sync feel any different from enhancers? They both brought your defenses down and let someone else in. The only distinction was that enhancers were temporary: Tennal had come back to his own head, every time, prickly with aftereffects and his emotions ringing like a bell struck by someone else.

Because it had never been good enough, had it? Even letting someone else take control had never given Tennal the relief from his own thoughts that he wanted. It worked for a few hours, and then the dissonance got too much, and the jagged edges of Tennal's thoughts reasserted themselves, and all Tennal could think of was *escape.*

There would be no escape from a sync. Tennal didn't habitually acknowledge fear, but it was hard to ignore the crawling feeling on his skin, like terror was a slowly tightening net.

"Excuse me," Surit said.

Surit was standing in front of the Guidance niche. Tennal

couldn't shake an absolute awareness of where Surit was from the tiny sounds he made, even with his eyes closed. Nor could he stop the surge of adrenaline as he opened his eyes. "What?"

"Do you mind if I take half of this?"

They'd stripped most of the elaborate decorations Tennal had put up, leaving only his personal Guidance icon, a glassed-over picture he now noticed was getting faded. He and Zin had picked that out years ago. It looked shabby without any lights around it.

It was such a reasonable request, Tennal couldn't find the barb in it. "It's a double niche," Tennal said at last. "It's supposed to be halved. Move mine to the side of the shelf."

Surit hesitated. "Really? I don't want to touch it, but I just need space for an incense burner . . ."

The noise in Tennal's brain paused long enough for him to experience a minor shock. "You *are* rural."

"I never said I wasn't," Surit said stiffly. He had put an incense heater at the very edge of the niche, precariously balanced. Some sort of rural cult.

I don't give a shit if you touch my icon, Tennal nearly said, but he found he did. He got up and shifted the picture to the side of the niche, leaving Surit room for the heater and the miniature books he seemed to want to stack.

"Thank you," Surit said. "Do you mind incense for a moment?"

Tennal shrugged. Surit hesitated, then sat cross-legged in front of the niche and shut his eyes.

Tennal sat on the edge of his bed and watched him meditate. Tennal's skin was still prickling. His clothes felt too rough. The thin mist that came out of Surit's incense heater smelled of wood smoke and greenery. Surit's back was ramrod straight, but as an hour ticked on, and then another, eventually the line of his muscles relaxed.

Tennal fought down a spike of white-hot envy and lay back on the bed, rolling over to face the wall.

He didn't sleep that night. Surit slept like the dead, a motion-less lump on the other bed.

The next day Surit left for breakfast and brought back another pointless ration pack. "We're nearing the fleet rendezvous," he said, apparently under the misguided impression that Tennal might want to know. "The rest of the expedition ships are already collecting at the edge of chaotic space. We'll catch up with them in forty-eight hours."

Tennal didn't answer. Surit didn't make another attempt. In-stead he left again for his exercise routine, then later for his chores. He returned just as Tennal was coming out of the bath-room after dealing with his soother hangover.

Surit didn't comment then, but the next time Tennal had to get up, he found Surit filling the bathroom door behind him. Tennal drew a unit of water and washed his mouth before deliberately turning around.

"Are you all right?" Surit said. "Is this substance withdrawal?"

"It's a hangover," Tennal said, then realized it probably was soother withdrawal. He hadn't noticed because he was too hung up on the sync. No wonder he felt so spectacularly bad.

Surit was eyeing him with that small frown which was the only expression he ever seemed to wear around Tennal. "I could ask Medical for a withdrawal shot."

The priming itch in the back of Tennal's brain tingled, and he flinched. "No more shots."

Surit apparently remembered their conversation in the lift, be-cause he gave a slow nod. "Painkillers?"

Painkillers wouldn't do anything. "Sure you don't just want to sync me?" Tennal said. "I hear if you go deep enough, you might be able to share what I'm physically feeling. There's a treat for you."

"No," Surit said, brutally short. He took a breath, then said, much more evenly, "I'm sorry. I'm snappish."

Surit didn't mention syncing that day. So there was one last-ditch tactic: feel physically bad enough that Surit didn't want to try it. On the other hand, Tennal was kidding himself if he thought that was a real solution.

Besides, Tennal didn't have any control over how he felt. It wasn't intentional that he didn't sleep the next night; he couldn't shut his brain down. The only thing between him and a sync was Surit's decision. When Tennal thought about it, random muscles hurt in the space between his ribs.

It became obvious what was happening around dawn on the third day, when Tennal finally acknowledged his heartbeat had probably been elevated for thirty-six hours straight. The uncertainty was as good as an interrogation technique. Making him wait wasn't just something Surit was doing so he could feel better. It also worked to break him.

Tennal held out throughout the day. The army regs they'd left him access to gave him something else to try to focus on, though he had almost no focus left; he read the same sentence over and over as he tried to lose the hyperawareness that was keeping him jittery and exhausted. Surit came and went. Tennal thought he was doing well, all things considered.

So it was a mystery to him why Surit sat up in the middle of the night, threw the room lights on, and said, "That's it. I'm getting a medic."

A layer of unreality had settled over everything from the lack of sleep, distorting Tennal's reactions. "Why?" he said. The word echoed oddly in his head.

"You're hyperventilating," Surit said.

Tennal wrestled just enough distance away from his body to realize Surit was half-right. Tennal's blood had been hammering in his ears anyway, from the soother withdrawal and insomnia, so he hadn't linked it to the way he couldn't quite get enough air. It wasn't something he remembered doing before. He was having a *wealth* of new experiences on this trip. He made himself slow his breathing. "I'm all right."

Surit had gotten up by this point, all six-feet-something of him in pajama trousers and a white top that had been washed repeatedly within an inch of its life. "You're not," he said tightly. "You haven't eaten in three days. I don't think you've *slept*. I keep waking up to check if you're still breathing. If you're on a hunger strike—"

"I'm not on a hunger strike," Tennal said. It was noticeably easier to speak now that he'd forced his lungs into doing their fucking job. The idea was ridiculous. "What good would that do?"

"Then you're ill, and you need medical attention."

"No," Tennal said. He wasn't really ill, and by now everyone on the ship would know the commander had slapped him down. They'd think Tennal was sulking if he suddenly claimed he was ill. A medic would either laugh at him or sedate him.

Surit took an obvious moment to keep his voice calm. "Then what do you suggest? I know you don't like me, and I know the situation is difficult, but if you're going to play games with your own health—"

Tennal started laughing, which was a mistake. It came out ugly, each breath more violent than the last, and once he started, it was difficult to stop. He covered his face with his hands. "Fuck this," he said. The inside of his head was an awful void. "I know what you're doing. And you win, understand? You *win*."

"I—what?" Surit said.

"I can't take any more of this." Tennal had lost control of his mouth; the words spilled out before they'd even formed in his head. "Put me out of my fucking misery. Sync."

The way Surit stood still was something more than an absence of motion. Tennal's hands clenched in the sickening silence before Surit finally said, "We have a misunderstanding. When I said I wouldn't sync you until you asked, this wasn't what I meant."

Tennal's mouth tasted like bile. Surit wanted more than a brief crack. There was nothing to stop him from stringing this out for weeks until he realized he was never going to get an easier version of the reader on the other end of it. Tennal curled his nails into the edge of the bed he was sitting on and said savagely, "*Please.*"

Surit blinked. The tiny movement broke his blank expression, and he raised a defensive hand, looking almost disturbed. "I don't—" He looked at his hand as if he hadn't seen it before, then pulled out the desk chair and sat down hard. "I think I haven't been clear."

"For fuck's sake," Tennal said bitterly. "This is as much as you're going to get. Just take it."

Surit spoke over Tennal as if he hadn't heard. "I thought I was taking an assignment to sync with a volunteer," he said. "I assumed you were a citizen who'd applied for a career in the army because you wanted to use your reader skills for piloting. I thought you were trained and briefed and had joined to protect the social contract."

Even in the dark groove Tennal's mind was running in, he took a moment to be incredulous at this. "Is that what *you* joined up to do?"

"My briefing had a lot of holes," Surit said, apparently ignoring him, "but even I can figure out you're not here voluntarily. I know who you are, and the law should apply to everyone, but none of this feels right." Tennal couldn't even laugh. The law didn't have anything to do with it, but it wasn't as if he were an innocent victim. "I'm not law enforcement," Surit continued, "and I haven't been made aware I have any rehabilitative responsibilities. Have you been sentenced under the laws and codes of the Orshan Fedstate?"

Tennal's throat was so dry he couldn't swallow. "No."

He expected *then what did you do?*—but it didn't come. Surit seemed to weigh each slow word as he put them together. "Then I should have been clearer," he said. "There is literally nothing you could say to make me sync you."

Tennal sat bolt upright on the edge of the bed. "How about, *you have orders?*" he demanded. "How about, *you signed up for this?*"

"Not all orders are legal," Surit said.

"You're going to risk a court-martial? Over this?"

"Forcing a sync like this is wrong." Surit's voice was rough and tightly controlled. He turned away, hunching over his light-screen. "I didn't realize I was causing you stress, and I apologize. I thought you knew I wouldn't carry it out."

Those weren't reasons; those were excuses. Tennal's hands were shaking, which was a useless distraction. "You don't have any family obligations to me," he said. "You're not my friend. You're not even sleeping with me. Although," he added, suddenly seeing a way this might make sense, "if that's what you're angling for—"

Surit tensed further. "Please take this seriously, Tennalhin." He magnified the screen and angled it so Tennal could see. "I wrote up a formal assignment rejection. I haven't submitted it yet because it doesn't fix things. You'll still be chemically altered, and they'll probably find another architect to sync you the moment I tell them I won't do it."

Tennal gripped the edge of the bed convulsively and stared at Surit. He was a solid, unwavering presence in the chair three feet from Tennal, silhouetted in the dim glow that was all the lights would give out during the night cycle. The screens shed more warm light onto his face. The frown was back, that slight crease between his eyebrows. Tennal had thought he had a handle on understanding Surit, but he'd been wrong. He didn't know him at all.

"You really won't do it?"

"Of course not," Surit snapped.

"Why?" Tennal's voice was a needle looking for weak points. "Are you feeling sorry for me? You shouldn't."

It gave Surit the perfect opening to interrogate Tennal about what he'd done. It was bubbling at the top of Tennal's head: *drugs, organized crime rings, a fucking liability.*

Then Surit said, "Because you have that covered?" and Tennal choked on the first real laugh he'd had since Orshan.

"Was that a joke, Lieutenant?" Tennal said, when he'd finished coughing. The pain in his chest eased a fraction. "Shame on you."

"Absolutely not," Surit said. "Let's focus, please. I thought I'd have a few days to come up with something, since I doubt there are any other Rank Ones on this ship to sync you, but I didn't realize the confinement effect would get this bad, this fast." He looked as if he'd come to some resolution. "You have to leave the army."

"Leave the army?" Tennal said incredulously. "What a thought. This must be the kind of bright idea that gets you into officer academy. I'll just find a spacesuit and stroll out the nearest airlock, shall I?"

"Can't readers breathe in space?" Surit said, so earnestly that Tennal nearly fell for it.

"*Lieutenant,*" Tennal said severely.

Surit raised his eyes to glance at Tennal's face. For the first time, there was something hesitant in it, as if he hadn't been sure if Tennal could take jokes about this. Tennal loathed being pitied, but this wasn't pity. Tennal didn't have time to work out what it was before Surit carried on, as if nothing had passed between them. "This fleet is on a salvage mission. That means three weeks in chaotic space. When we've completed the mission, we'll have to return to a station, where there'll be other ships and chances to travel. Then we'll get you temporary movement papers and—"

Surit came to a halt. Tennal got the impression he had just come up against the same problem that had occurred to Tennal: Tennal would need a fake identity to travel, and he didn't know how to get one. Maybe this was the first illegal thought Surit Yeni had ever had in his life. Tennal watched in dark fascination as Surit squared his shoulders and said, "We'll find you another identity."

"You have no idea how to do that."

Surit's tone brooked no opposition. "I'll find out when we get there. First we figure out how to get out of this room."

Tennal's heart was still a vicious beat in his rib cage. "Surit.

Lieutenant Yeni. Our finest and best. Spend two minutes listening to me, since you apparently haven't considered listening to your own common sense. You're a perfect junior officer. Your shoes are shiny, you've memorized all the regulations, you're practically vibrating with eagerness. I bet your academy teachers marked you as the cadet most likely to go out in a blaze of glory saving a ship full of kittens and senior officers' children." That was probably uncalled for. Tennal didn't care. "You want a promotion, and you want it really badly. Why?"

He thought Surit wasn't going to answer. But then the crease between his eyebrows deepened, and he looked away, as if he couldn't meet Tennal's eyes. "It's the money," Surit said. He sounded ashamed. Tennal should feel bad about that, but he didn't have any energy left over from feeling shitty about everything else. "My alt-parent should be getting a bereavement pension. The army stopped it. If I make captain, I can get it reinstated."

Surit's alt-parent. Everyone had a gen-parent who formed their main ancestral line, whether genetically related or polite fiction. But it helped to have more adults around to raise a child, and so most children had an alt-parent, or more than one: a romantic partner, someone who had contributed genes, or just someone reliable who could help. Tennal's alt-parent was his aunt. He was willing to believe most people loved their alt-parents; at least, Surit's voice cracked a little when he talked about his.

"There you are, then." Tennal couldn't be kind, not when it felt like there were flakes of rusty metal circulating through his veins, but he could tell Surit the truth. "That's what you'll lose."

"No," Surit said. "I'll earn it another way. There'll be another chance."

It was a nice story. It had the advantage of Surit already believing it. If Tennal was less stupid and less self-destructive, he could have agreed. All he needed to do was nod.

He should've agreed.

Instead, Tennal said, "You're lying to yourself and, relatedly, you're the most gullible person in the sector. I can't believe I even have to explain this to you."

Surit stiffened, offended. That was better. "There won't be another chance," Tennal said. "The army's not *fair*. Nothing's fair. If you let me walk out of this room without syncing, your career is over, you're heading to detention, and then they'll discharge you back to your village to dig ditches for the rest of your life. *I* don't fucking care. I don't have any good options. You only have one." Surit was going to abandon him anyway. Tennal had always wanted to get the worst over with quickly—it was easier when he courted the worst-case scenario, flirted with it, threw himself into it. He felt like the wick of a candle on the wild edge of flickering out. "Do it. *Sync us,* you conscientious, rule-spouting fucker. Because I'm walking out of this room one day either way, and your time is running out."

Surit flinched at every sentence. Tennal was used to working people into a rage. It was a shitty way of doing things, to press every button until someone was so furious they couldn't hide anything from him, but it was what Tennal was good at.

But Surit wasn't in a rage. Something behind his eyes hardened with every shot Tennal fired, like carbon compacting under pressure. Tennal couldn't break it, and he didn't understand it. He didn't understand, either, when Surit pressed his lips together and said, "We're both walking out of here." And before Tennal could take a breath for another salvo, Surit said, like a carefully placed missile, "Fake it."

Tennal lost all his tactical high ground. His mind went blank. "What?"

"Fake that you've been synced so we can leave," Surit said. "What does a sync look like to other people?"

What *did* it look like? Syncs were reserved for hushed stories from old veterans, most of whom Tennal would bet had never met a synced reader, or for wildly inaccurate war films. Somehow Tennal doubted you started radiating ominous background music when you synced. On the other hand, a sync had to be something like enhancers, and nobody had been able to tell Tennal was on enhancers when they'd passed him in the street.

Tennal felt light-headed. Everything took on the clarity of total exhaustion. Surit might not be an ally, but even the prospect of *someone* who didn't want him brainwashed was firing some neurons that the last few days had paralyzed. "I don't have the faintest idea what it looks like. Do you?"

Surit shook his head, looking taken aback, as if he'd been sure that Tennal would know. But why should *Tennal* know? The army hadn't sat him down with an instructional video.

"I bet nobody on this ship knows either," Tennal said. The thoughts running through his brain felt so electric that he could almost taste them. "There aren't many readers. What if we kept faking it? What if we faked it for the whole mission?"

Surit placed a hand flat on the desk in front of him. Tennal could have reached out and traced the line of solid tension across his arm muscles and all the way back to his shoulders. "That will be weeks," Surit said. "We'll need to keep it consistent. We don't have a lot of data."

Tennal dismissed their collective lack of knowledge with a wave of his hand. "We know you should be able to write me without any effort. You can fake the writing—we'll work out some signals. Or if you're strong enough to really write me and pretend it's easy, you can do that." He pushed to his feet. "I know what being written feels like. I can put on a show. And after that, it's only convincing them you have me under control, isn't it? We can act that out, no problem. I'll shine my emblems and stop insulting the commander. I'll be a fucking model recruit. It's only until I can escape. This will work," he said, tasting the words in pure shock. "This will work. We can do this."

There was a yawning silence. Tennal stopped.

He recognized that silence. The problem was always this: there was too much of Tennal. There was too much of him for his own head, too much for other people, too much to let him settle into any respectable niche in society. Certainly too much of him for Surit.

It was a bad enough feeling that he almost avoided looking at Surit. But when he did, he got something he wasn't expecting. Through Surit's inscrutable expression, Tennal thought he could feel a crack—just a tiny crack—in Surit's defenses. Surit was totally focused on him. Behind that focus, Tennal didn't sense caution, or bafflement, or anything Tennal usually engendered. Instead there was a single glimpse of clockwork arranging itself around Tennal's quick-fire ideas, of a vast, immovable will bending itself to a purpose. Something that never let itself be stopped. Something that could meet Tennal and not be knocked off course.

Tennal would not admit he had stopped breathing for an instant.

"Yes," Surit said at last. That was it. *Yes.* No bargaining, no equivocation, no price.

Tennal still had the self-destructive urge to push him harder. *There must be a catch somewhere*—or, no, he was lying to himself. Tennal pushed because there was too much of him in his own skin, and the energy had to go somewhere. He felt himself open his mouth to ruin it.

In the instant before he could, a light pulsed between them. Surit's wristband glowed blue in the dark room.

"What's that?"

Surit looked down. "Oh," he said. "That's the ping I set up for the fleet rendezvous. We must have arrived."

Tennal said impulsively, "Let me see."

"Ah," Surit said softly. Tennal got the impression he had asked for something Surit had been waiting to see himself. Almost reverentially, Surit touched his wristband, and the light grew into a projection that filled the room.

Stars rose over the walls. Silver ships wheeled in a tiny cluster in the distance. Clouds of dust glinted in the light from the faraway sun, and above it all, covering the ceiling and walls at a scale incalculably vast, was a churning cloud that made something in the lowest, most unconscious layers of Tennal's mind leap up like the spray from a breaking wave.

"Chaotic space," Surit said, his eyes following Tennal's as Tennal threw himself back on the bed, with stars and the tides of unknown space circling over his head. "We're here."

PART TWO

CHAPTER 8

Chaotic space, that vast, churning sea of pressure and distortion, lapped at the edges of normal space like a hungry tide. At the fringe of its massive clouds, dozens of silver specks converged slowly as the new Cavalry fleet formed and gathered its ships. It took days. When the ships reached the rendezvous, they flocked and wheeled around one another like seabirds in slow motion before settling into formation, a stately dance that kept them just out of reach of the disturbance.

This whirlpool was the source of all the disturbed space-time that littered the Orshan sector. At the center of it sat the galactic link: the eye-watering fold that was their gateway to the universe. Only Resolution scouts took ships through the stormy center of it, through the link to distant planets. Even here, far from the link itself, you needed scanning ships to probe the turbulence and avoid being torn apart by its currents.

Chaotic space was never still. The boundaries of it ebbed and flowed, and no map of its interior would stay accurate for more than a few weeks. This had been clear space once. The army had built covert military stations here: it was always useful to have a place where most ships didn't dare go. But, in the past few decades since this section of chaotic space had started expanding, they'd all been moved or abandoned to the currents.

The only remaining space station was the gracefully rounded shape of Archer Link Station, far off in the distance. It had to be there: Orshan needed a staging post near the galactic link for both spaceships and passengers, so it sat out of reach of the currents, some way from where the fleet gathered. It was too small to see from here, but most Orshans knew its distinctive stacked discs, like a spinning top gently rotating in the void.

The wheeling ships took care to stay far out of range. They had their sights set on a particular abandoned facility, and nobody wanted the complication of alerting Archer Division.

In the middle of all this, the *Fractal Note* eased into the waiting fleet. It stood out, with its seven troop decks and bristling shuttle berths—the largest ship present, though *large* meant nothing this near chaotic space, where every ship was a speck of grain against the unimaginable scale of the universe. It took its place amid a hail of polite comms salutes to its commander. The flagship was here. The mission could commence.

None of these polite exchanges made it down to the level of its dormitories, or to the ship's insubordinate reader and its single, conflicted Rank One architect.

Surit woke up angry. He had been angry through the rest of the night, long after Tennalhin had finally fallen asleep with the rag-doll stillness of the truly exhausted, and meditating hadn't helped. Surit wasn't owed explanations from anyone, he knew that. He wasn't owed the army's reasoning, or a statement about what they'd planned for Tennalhin, or any information about his own mission, but part of him still wanted to shake all of those out of anyone up to and including his division command. It was unthinkable to push for an explanation from Tennalhin himself, who was a mess of cracks apparently patched together with bent tacks and recalcitrance. He shouldn't be in the *army,* let alone conscripted into a sync.

Surit had known, when he joined the army, that he wouldn't have a lot of choice about what he did. He'd just thought it would get easier after academy and its hothouse of status connections and public exam results, not more complicated. He'd been prepared to work hard to make captain, harder than people with a high birth class might have to, but he hadn't been prepared for this sort of morass.

He realized, at that moment, that he'd been thinking of those elite, well-connected cadets as coming from families like Tennalhin Halkana's.

Tennalhin looked peaceful when he was asleep, if you ignored the shadows under his eyes. It was so much better than the glassy-eyed stares he'd been giving the ceiling the past two days that when Surit woke, after an hour of sleep, he left Tennalhin to rest.

Surit's first duty was to send an update to the commander on the successful sync, which he did. Then he reported to his assigned morning exercise session. Now more than ever, there was no room for negligence.

The movement of the *Fractal Note* felt different as they neared chaotic space. It was traveling more slowly, taking the cautious approach any vessel relied on near disturbed space-time. Hit the wrong patch of disturbed space and the navigation would go haywire; hit a really bad cloud and it would rip the hull apart, aging parts of it to dust in seconds. Surit had flown near disturbed space, of course; that was what retrieval units did. But the maelstrom around the galactic link was another order of magnitude.

One of those retrieval shuttles in the new fleet was Surit's. He had been promised a unit to command. He'd been looking forward to it before all this.

Lights knew what the average unit would make of an officer who was synced to a reader. Surit worried, as well, how his new unit would treat an acknowledged reader. Among civilians, readers were vanishingly rare and under no obligation to disclose their abilities. Once people knew about them, they reacted differently. Surit hadn't liked the sheen of suspicion and contempt from the commander when he'd dealt with Tennalhin.

On the other hand, this wasn't just any reader. This was Tennalhin. Lights knew what anyone would make of Tennalhin Halkana.

As Surit was on his way back from exercise, the ship sent out an all-hands ping. At least they would get a briefing. The commander had promised that. Maybe a description of the salvage they were here to find. Surit would give anything to wrestle with a nice, straightforward logistics problem again. Then he remembered he and Tennal would have to fake a sync whenever they were in public and resisted the urge to press his hands over his eyes.

When Surit reached their cabin again, he found Tennalhin fastening a wooden button through his cuffs on a clean uniform, the discarded wrapper of yesterday's ration pack on the table. He looked better—no, Surit realized, that wasn't true. Tennalhin still had the pale shadows of exhaustion under his eyes, but you could easily miss it behind the low crackle of energy. He had pinned the *Fractal Note*'s lance-shaped mark to his collar. The points glittered like needles. He gave Surit a smile that even Surit could see was mechanical. "Sir."

"No," Surit said abruptly.

Tennalhin narrowed his eyes at the non sequitur. Surit could see a comment surface before Tennalhin shoved it down again.

"You don't want to be here," Surit said. "You don't have respect for the uniform, and there's no point in you faking it." Tennalhin straightened and leaned back against the pair of lockers behind him. His lips twitched with the effort of holding back whatever he wanted to say. Surit met his gaze levelly. "Go on."

Tennalhin's mouth twisted to the side in something that wasn't a smile. "I thought we had a deal," he said. "Did I dream that? I thought we had a deal that we were going to pretend to sync until I found a way out, but it's possible I've just lost my tenuous grip on reality."

Surit abruptly revised his assessment of the whole conversation. He wasn't sure how it was possible there was any doubt, but apparently Tennalhin had found a way. "In *public*," Surit said. "You'll need to do some pretending in *front of other people*. Of course we had a deal. I wouldn't go back on something I agreed to!"

Tennalhin always held himself like someone relaxed, so it wasn't obvious how tense he'd been until the tiny shift of his body showed it dissipating. The realization gave fresh fuel to Surit's anger. Half of it was at himself.

"You're more duplicitous than you first come across, Lieutenant," Tennalhin said. His generous mouth curved. "I think I like it."

"I'm *not*," Surit said. He needed to meditate, but with the ping on his wristband summoning them to muster, he wouldn't have time. "This all flows logically from you being primed without formal grounds. I don't know what's going on, and none of this is right."

"My aunt wanted me off-planet where I couldn't cause trouble," Tennalhin said. "You were the right person at the right time." He sounded more cheerful the more Surit had to battle his cresting frustration. "Only it's starting to look like you're exactly the wrong person, if she only knew. Fantastic. There's a red light on your wristband."

Surit closed his eyes, forcing his thoughts into the bounds of his assigned mission. He was an officer with a briefing to attend, whether or not he had the legislator's illegally primed nephew fake-synced to him. "I have to report for a command muster. We've reached the fleet rendezvous. Tennalhin—"

"Tennal. *Tennalhin* is what my aunt calls me."

"You'll have to come with me," Surit said. "You'll have to act synced if we're to make this work." He had very little idea how that should even look. A sync meant he should have write access to Tennal: defensive techniques wouldn't work, and writing itself should take very little effort, since Surit's commands would go straight to Tennal's subconscious. Surit remembered the vast, mesmerizing sea of Tennal's mind and had to push the memory aside to think. There had to be a way.

Tennal didn't seem to share Surit's apprehensions. His eyes had gone harder, something vicious and crystalline about him. "Showtime," he said. "I have an idea."

A few minutes later, they emerged into the corridors, where the bright day-cycle light and the vivid Cavalry emblems on the walls made Tennal wince and put up a hand to protect his eyes. The *Fractal Note* was busier than it had ever been. Soldiers passed them, saluting Surit and glancing askance at Tennal. Surit's entire back felt tense as he returned the salutes. As they left the dormitory level, Tennal looked around, narrow-eyed, then dropped back until he was walking one pace behind Surit's shoulder. That didn't make Surit feel better at all. It was technically correct for Tennal's nominal rank, but having Tennal behind you felt like turning your back on a tiger.

As they crossed into the command module, transparent panels opened on a wall beside them, showing the black tapestry of space and the distant clouds of turbulence. Surit knew roughly where they were—he'd tracked the currents of chaotic space for years, since he'd tried to figure out the coordinates for the remains of Marit's ship. It had taken him until much later to realize there was no point. Her ship would be a heap of scrap.

The rest of the fleet maneuvered behind the viewing panes. Shuttles passed back and forth around the larger ships like silver birds. One of those shuttles would be Surit's new unit. Surit had memorized their docking time and set a counter in the back of his head.

Tennal's gaze tracked the new fleet outside. "Fantastic. I was just thinking we didn't have enough soldiers around. What's that?"

Surit followed Tennal's gaze to one of the larger ships. It must be one of the scanning ships that they'd bought from the Galactics. Tennal had immediately zeroed in on the most interesting part: one of the antennae produced a mild distortion field that Surit associated with Resolution tools.

"It finds paths through chaotic space," Surit said. "It can shape them as well. They must have worked out how to solve the import problems."

Tennal glanced sideways at Surit. "You're an officer, aren't you? Don't you get your own ship?"

"I've been assigned a retrieval unit," Surit said. "It's a shuttle, though, not a ship."

Tennal had to lower his voice as they passed a group of soldiers jogging past. "You mean syncing me wasn't your only very special project? I'm hurt. What's a retrieval unit?"

Surit explained, in snatches between passing soldiers. Tennal's face grew more and more incredulous.

"A *debris retrieval unit*?" Tennal said. "I thought you were an army lieutenant, not a low-tech trash collector."

"A retrieval shuttle is just as useful as that scanning ship," Surit said, gesturing to the research ship with its bristling array of antennae. "Chaotic space is unpredictable. Sometimes you need a sonic manipulator. Sometimes you need people with pliers."

"That has to be the worst assignment in the army," Tennal said as they stepped off the bridge. Surit couldn't immediately find a way to deny that, though he objected to the way Tennal said it. "Why did *you* end up with it, Officer Ninety-Six-Percent-in-My-Exams?"

"Someone has to do it," Surit said. He didn't mention his mother. If Tennal didn't know, he'd find out soon enough. "All jobs are worth doing."

Tennal frowned. "You're a Rank One architect with a synced reader," he said, as if to a particularly slow pupil. "If you couldn't parlay that into a better assignment than *trash collector,* you desperately need advice on how to play politics. Though obviously not from me."

Surit was prepared to take that as a gibe, but it didn't sound like one. Something about the way Tennal said it made Surit's hindbrain uneasy, as if he'd just unwittingly started a timer on an explosive. "It's fine. I do what I'm told."

The sound of their footsteps disappeared as they crossed into the command module, muffled by the wine-red carpet underfoot. "Do you?" Tennal said.

He'd timed it just as they turned a corner that led to the bridge, so Surit couldn't answer. They both stopped when they saw the officer coming up the corridor.

Commander Vinys. Tennal's breath came out in a low hiss.

The commander was flanked by the chief of staff, trailing some ghostly documents behind her while she explained something. He raised an eyebrow when he saw Tennal.

"Fifty-Six," Commander Vinys said. "Lieutenant Yeni reports that you've decided to join us."

Surit was prepared for almost anything from Tennal, but despite their deal, it was still a shock when Tennal drew up to a reasonable copy of attention beside him and colorlessly said, "Yes, sir." His posture wouldn't have passed muster at academy classes, but it might have fooled a civilian watching a media drama. His eyes were hooded, as if he didn't usually have a gaze that could set light to charcoal.

The commander raked his sardonic gaze over him. One of Tennal's feet started to twitch.

"Go on," the commander said. "Salute."

Surit must have imagined the way Tennal's expression flattened, because he could have sworn none of his facial muscles moved. Tennal's arm came up. The salute was so bad that it would have been funny, if Surit's nerves hadn't been jangling like storm warnings.

The commander snorted. "So we'll all get some amusement value out of this. Three days, Yeni. Did the priming not work?"

At the key moment, the enormity of the lie stuck in Surit's throat. He couldn't find an answer.

Tennal's gaze flickered to him with irritation, but it was all gone again the next second. "Lieutenant Yeni has completed the sync, sir."

Surit wasn't an actor. On the other hand, he knew he wasn't expressive either. He concentrated on maintaining military poise and fixed his eyes on the corridor behind the commander. "Agent Fifty-Six was recovering from mood-altering drugs. I don't think his withdrawal symptoms will be a problem now that the sync is active."

Tennal picked it up seamlessly. "I'm cooperating. It was just the soothers. There's no need to write me. I'd be more cooperative if I had my possessions back, though, and while I'm making requests, an encrypted comms channel to talk to my family would also be nice. If you're *asking*."

That was a cue. *Don't try and ham it up,* Tennal had warned, a sentence that had never been said to Surit before in his life. Surit glanced at Tennal and said flatly, "Agent Fifty-Six."

He wasn't sure what Tennal had planned—walking it back, maybe, to prove to the commander that something had changed. Instead Tennal shifted on his feet, his back straightening as if someone had lifted him at the shoulders. His head tilted back, as if unconsciously, and his eyes flickered shut. He frowned for an instant before his forehead smoothed out. When he opened his eyes again, his shoulders relaxed, and his gaze went straight to Surit's face as if drawn there. His expression was calm and empty.

That was what Tennal looked like when he was written, Surit realized. He'd been so lost in Tennal's mind the only time he'd actually written him that he hadn't looked at Tennal at all. It was fake: Surit knew he hadn't written him, and the commander was neutral, but Tennal acted it out so naturally that he must know the feeling as well as he knew his own breathing. Surit found a knot forming in his stomach.

"My apologies, sir," Tennal said calmly. He turned his gaze to the wall in front of him.

Surit tried to look as if he'd expected that.

The sudden silence made his nerves worse. He knew he'd given no sign that he was trying to write Tennal, so at best the commander would assume Surit's commands were effortless now that Tennal was synced, and at worst he would see straight through the whole thing. Surit swallowed.

The commander grunted. "Good. I won't be able to carry a rogue reader once we get into chaotic space, Yeni. Other senior commanders are not as fluffy and sensitive as I am. Fifty-Six will be faultless, or I'll hand him to the regulators for them to fix. I trust I won't have to explain that again?"

He believed them, Surit thought in disbelief. They'd gotten away with it—the first part of it, at least. Even when Surit had hatched the desperate idea last night, part of him thought the commander would just send them both to the regulators and cut the whole thing off at the knees. "We understand, sir. You won't need to remind us."

The chief of staff, behind the commander, was not quite buying it. "To remind *either* of you?"

"Oh, I hope not," Tennal said. He was still at some form of attention, but the strain was showing: his foot tapped arrhythmically, and he had to wet his lips before he spoke. "Sir."

"Good," the commander said, and dropped Tennal from his attention completely. He tilted his head at Surit. "Get into the briefing, Yeni. We're wasting time. I'll speak to you afterward."

He no longer paid attention to Tennal, as if Tennal had just winked out of existence now that someone had leverage over him. Surit, not for the first time, felt a deep unease about the observational skills of his senior officers. A lit fuse didn't stop being a lit fuse just because it had decided to burn politely. Tennal gave Surit an inscrutable glance and fell in behind him.

The flag chamber usually held a table for the morning strategy meeting. Today that had been cleared away in favor of close-packed rows of chairs. The chamber was full.

Dozens of ships had just joined the fleet, from sleek scanning vessels to enormous grappling frames to the retrieval shuttles that clamped onto the *Fractal Note* like barnacles. Thirty new emblems hung on the walls of the room between the *Note*'s crossed-lance flags. The officers of all the new ships were all here, groups of them talking quietly with crimson Cavalry panels on the shoulders of their immaculate uniforms.

As he entered the grand room, Surit felt the nerves of his first day at the academy all over again: he was too rural, too big, too clumsy. His accent didn't fit, his parentage was a liability, and being half a head taller than average just seemed to add insult to injury for everyone else. He felt himself duck his head, trying to make himself inconspicuous.

He heard someone say, "That's him," and he tensed.

The murmur had come from a group of young officers with pilot stripes. Tennal, who had been inspecting the faces around the room with sharp interest, glanced over at them and smirked in return. Surit realized the comment hadn't been about Marit Yeni at all, but directed at Tennal—the only reader in the fleet.

Smirking as a response had never even occurred to Surit. The blank, baffled reaction it got from the elite young officers was strangely gratifying. Surit filed that away to consider.

The chief of staff snapped a command, and the chattering assembly quieted. Surit slipped into a chair at the side next to some other junior officers. He saw Tennal glance around at the handful of other rankers who'd been allowed in to assist officers and then, without turning a hair, take up a standing position behind Surit's left shoulder. He linked his hands behind his back in a reasonable approximation of an at-ease stance.

Commander Vinys took the front of the hall. He turned the wall behind him into a display screen, tuned to a view of the nearest opening in chaotic space. Clouds of color broke like slow-motion waves across the blackness of the void.

"Soldiers," he began, "wherever you've just arrived from, welcome to the next stage of the mission. Welcome to the gateway to chaotic space."

Surit gratefully focused all his attention on the briefing. He had worked with disturbed space before, even if not this kind—the mother lode, the chaotic space around the link itself—and retrieval missions into it held no moral ambiguity at all. You went in, you picked up any useful hardware or debris, and you came out. He and Tennal could fake their sync all the way through that.

"Some of you've got experience in salvage retrieval," Commander Vinys said. "Some of you've been yanked from other jobs and are probably wondering why you're here. Let me answer your question."

Behind him, the display changed. A smooth, quartz-like object rotated in midair. It was impossible to tell its scale from the projection, and even in the recording, it glowed with a light that was slightly *off* in some way.

The commander waved a hand at it. "Remnants," he said. There was a murmur of interest around the room. "The lost technology of something that was alive before we were even plankton in the sea. Those of you with neuromodifications, this is what made you who you are—or, for the kiddies here, your parents. This is what we're looking for."

Surit frowned, taken aback. That might explain the secrecy around the mission.

Orshan hadn't owned any remnants in a couple of decades, not since the ones they'd excavated and used in the first architect experiments. The Resolution didn't like individual planets to have them; Orshan had surrendered them as part of the deal that had kept the whole sector in the galactic protection treaty. That also explained the size of the fleet and the expensive scanning ships. Remnants were dangerous in the wrong hands.

"Why do we think they're in there?" Commander Vinys continued. "Well, the currents have shifted over the past few years, and we might find a few things we've lost. We're hoping to get at this."

The screen changed again. This time it was a schematic of a space station: a small installation, with a handful of modules circling eternally around a central hub. It was an old type, ordinary and unremarkable.

Surit's throat went dry.

He recognized that station. The silhouette was burned in his memory from the time he'd spent obsessing over old newslogs. It was the research laboratory where they'd made the original architects. They hadn't stopped there: just a couple of years later, during the reader rebellion, that laboratory had made the war machines that mass-produced architects, modifying the brains of tens of thousands of soldiers.

That was the laboratory his mother—his *architect mother*—had tried to seize. She'd wanted a power base. Lights knew what she'd have done to Orshan if she'd succeeded.

Instead she'd blown up her own ship, destroyed half the station, and taken hundreds of lives with her.

Surit didn't hear the rest of the briefing. He sat motionless as the commander droned on about trajectories and drifting paths into chaotic space.

That explained why he was here. Someone had known about Surit's parentage and wanted to give him a chance to repair some of the damage. Or someone with a sense of irony had thought it was funny.

Or maybe not. Maybe this was the Guidances making a very intricate joke.

The commander had reverted to a flat screen with a schematic of spatial paths. "There are no recent maps," he said. "The far side of the zone is Archer territory. The governor there doubts our ability to retrieve the remnants safely"—he sounded contemptuous—"and so we'll be keeping well away from her station and the space around it. This fleet brings together some of the best pilots in the sector. I know you'll manage."

"Question, sir." A wristband chimed, and one of the pilots leaned forward, a glossy and well-groomed lieutenant with an accent from the rich merchant cities of Orshan Two. "Aren't we carrying some unacknowledged risks? Isn't one of our officers Marit Yeni's child?"

Surit stiffened. Eyes were watching him from all around the room.

They *had* known.

This was always something Surit was afraid of when he boarded a new ship. This time he'd been sickeningly right about it. In the sudden susurrus of murmurs, Commander Vinys paused, expressionless.

More officers indicated they had questions with chimes from their wristbands. Surit's hands clenched so hard that his knuckles stood proud against the stretched skin. If the commander wasn't going to squash this, Surit would have to find something to say himself. He felt sick as he raised his head.

"Excuse me," Tennal drawled from behind him, just before Surit could ask for permission to speak. His voice was pitched to cut effortlessly through the muttering. "Who is Marit Yeni?"

The entire room stopped whispering to turn and stare at him.

There wasn't a single person in the military who didn't know who Marit Yeni was. She was infamous: the only architect to join the reader rebellion. Children in tiny villages used her name in playground games. It was almost inconceivable that Tennal, the *legislator's nephew,* wouldn't be familiar with the history.

Tennal looked around, meeting people's eyes with an air of genuine confusion. "Sorry, did I say something wrong?"

Surit wondered wildly if Tennal was somehow using reader powers to draw everyone's attention to himself. He had never seen someone hijack a room so completely.

"Enough," Commander Vinys said impatiently. "Personnel matters are not up for discussion in this briefing."

Surit's mouth snapped shut. If the commander had really wanted to stifle the topic, he should have said that thirty seconds ago.

That was it for mentions of Marit, at least. The commander wrapped up the meeting by running through assignments; Surit mechanically noted his new command: *Retrieval Unit Two-Eight-Seven.* His nerves were jangling so much that he had to force himself to remember his part in the syncing act. He didn't have to look around for Tennal, though; Tennal glued himself to Surit's elbow the moment the meeting finished.

As they turned to leave, Tennal murmured, "So when were you planning to tell me your mother was a celebrity?"

Surit had been expecting the accusation, though not the edge of prurient curiosity in Tennal's voice. "Celebrity isn't the word," he said. *Infamous* was more like it. "Tennal, do you really not—didn't you learn about her in school?"

"Boarding school was a busy time for me," Tennal said. "I had my hands full committing mind crimes against my classmates."

"There was a *civil war!*" Surit said, his ferocious whisper a bit louder than it should have been.

Tennal checked that the dispersing officers were out of earshot. "Oh, for Lights' sake, of course I know who she is," he said. "Don't ask me to take a test on her—I meant it about boarding school—but you wouldn't have liked any of my other ideas for a distraction."

Surit stopped. Tennal had done it on purpose. He had meant to draw the other officers' attention. For a moment he saw the exchange as Tennal had clearly seen it: as a game where all the words were weapons. Part of Surit wanted to say he hadn't needed help, but that wasn't true. Instead, he said, "Oh. I see. Thank you."

Surprise crossed Tennal's face, quickly covered by something else. "Well," Tennal said. "Keep up your end of the deal, then. *Sir.*" The *sir* was tacked hastily onto the end as the commander gestured them both over.

The commander stood with someone Surit recognized as one of the fleet's new pilots: this one had the rank tabs of a full wing leader and a grave, square-jawed face. There was something about him that suggested a funeral director. The commander was already speaking, with a short gesture toward Tennal; Surit caught the tail end. "... the fleet's reader and the architect who's synced him."

Surit saluted. "You wanted to see us, sir?"

The wing leader ignored Surit and looked down at Tennal somberly. "Is he a pilot?" he asked. "The readers I worked with before had pilot training."

"I can fold a paper dart," Tennal said.

"*Agent Fifty-Six,*" Surit said desperately.

He had a sudden fear that Tennal was going to act as if Surit had written him again, but Tennal only put on a moderately contrite look and saluted. This salute was better, as if he'd been watching Surit to copy him. "I don't have pilot training, sir."

"Yes, I can see," the wing leader said, frowning further as he looked Tennal over. Surit followed his line of thought easily: Tennal didn't have the build of a soldier who had gone through even a week of boot camp. It was obvious he wasn't meant to be in the army—because he *shouldn't* be in the army; Surit found he still had room to be angry about that—and that meant he would be of limited help to the pilots. He wouldn't know the vocabulary to tell them what he saw with his reader senses. The wing leader seemed to come to the same conclusion. "I can't make use of him until he has some of the basics."

The commander gave a short nod. "Lieutenant Yeni, you have a retrieval unit, don't you? When are they docking?"

"Around now, sir," Surit said. "They should be on the final approach." He was counting down in his head, *Three and a half minutes until scheduled docking,* but he'd learned that level of detail worried people.

"Get one of your rankers to give Fifty-Six the basics," the commander said. "We have a few days until we're in the real danger areas. Even someone with school-grade science should be able to pick up the bare minimum by then." Tennal opened his mouth, appeared to think better of it, and shut it again. "Do you have something to say, Fifty-Six?"

"No, sir."

"No. Too busy making a spectacle of your ignorance in briefings," the commander said coolly. "I understand. Yeni, make sure he's caught up with his basic training to third-class ranker standard. I will check." Surit's interfaces pinged quietly in his ear as Tennal's schedule updated itself. From the number and pitch of the pings, Tennal wouldn't have any free time to come up with an escape plan.

Surit gritted his teeth. There was no way you could pick someone off the street and get them up to ranker-level education and physical condition in a handful of days, especially if Tennal was also expected to get through basic piloting modules. "Understood, sir. If you'll give us permission to leave, my unit is docking soon. And Agent Fifty-Six—"

"I'd better get started on my remedial training, hadn't I?" Tennal said, with a quick, insincere smile. "Proud to join the fleet, Commander."

CHAPTER 9

Tennal felt ten times more alive as they left the flag chamber—the lights were brighter, the Cavalry-red emblems more vivid. He was walking a tightrope over his own destruction, but now Surit had handed him a balance pole. Tennal could have talked the top brass of every division into believing he was synced. He could have fooled the world.

The only nagging question was how long he could keep this up. Adrenaline cracked under his skin as he followed Surit to the shuttle where they were due to meet their new unit, one pace behind as he'd seen other soldiers accompany their COs. They'd have to fool Surit's new unit as well. Tennal had avoided the rankers—the *other* rankers—so far, but he needed to maintain the pretense until this mission was over, and that could be weeks away.

Tennal had once managed to pretend to be a nice, amenable person for one of his exes. He'd kept up the act for two whole weeks before he'd cracked under the strain and reverted to his normal personality, and that had been the end of that relationship. The ex was married to two bankers now, and the three of them together still added up to less of an asshole than Tennal. It was hard to turn yourself into somebody else.

Tennal's whole future and mental freedom hadn't been on the line then, though. Maybe that would be enough motivation not to screw up everything this time.

Surit had been characteristically quiet, but he looked up as they stepped into the bustling rotunda of the ship dock. The space was an enormous spiral of walkways with offshoots to individual bays where large ships touched gantries or sent shuttles, and small ships nestled like birds coming home to roost.

It might just have been because Tennal had eaten and slept now, but he could feel the disturbance of chaotic space acutely, waiting behind the layers of metal hull like a stirring beast.

"It's a tiny shuttle," Surit said, sounding happier now that they were done with the lying and he could get on with being a shining beacon of an upright staff officer. "Twenty people. They'll be staying on the *Note*—the shuttle doesn't have permanent quarters—but I sent an order for a muster before everyone disembarked. This is my second command," he added, apropos of nothing. Tennal realized that Surit was nervous for reasons that had nothing to do with the sync. The mindset of a career military officer was like an alien artifact to Tennal.

"Get in there, O Glorious Leader," Tennal said. "Bowl them over with your encyclopedic knowledge of the regulations."

It *was* a small ship, for something that carried twenty people for days on end. When Tennal ducked in through the hatch of the shuttle, he found himself in an operations room barely large enough to contain the three rows of workstations squeezed into it. It was walled on either side with the bare metal of the shuttle's hull. Through a door there was a cramped mess room with pull-down beds lining the walls; this ship was clearly only made to house people during hops from one mothership to another.

It should have been crowded with nearly two dozen of Orshan's finest in there. But there weren't twenty soldiers. Instead a single first-class ranker—tall and solid enough that the chair was a fraction too small for her—huddled in a chair and stared at a screen. Tennal got her gender reference from the flint button in her cuff. She'd collected styli from the empty desks and made a pyramid out of them on the desk in front of her.

Surit looked around the room, examining the empty chairs with the same blank expression he'd worn the whole morning.

When Tennal had first seen it he'd assumed that Surit was putting on a look of noble aloofness to impress his commanders, but now that he'd had some time to study him, Tennal was starting to realize that was just what Surit's face defaulted to.

The ranker hadn't seen them. "What a shame, Lieutenant Yeni," Tennal said. "My first unit muster and nobody's here. Or is this a unit of one?"

The ranker looked around belatedly and twitched like someone had electrocuted her. She scrambled to her feet—Surit was generally the tallest in any room, but she was nearly the same height—and saluted. "Sorry! Sorry. I didn't see you come in"—a moment's hesitation as her eyes went to Tennal then to Surit's lieutenant rank tabs—"um, sir."

Surit wasn't thrown. "At ease, Private . . ."

"Basavi, sir," the ranker said.

"Thank you. I'm Lieutenant Yeni. I've been assigned to Cavalry Retrieval Unit Two-Eight-Seven. I take it you didn't get my message about the muster." Surit looked around again at the notable lack of soldiers mustering. "However, we're thirty-four minutes into the start of shift two, by standard schedules. This class of retrieval shuttle requires a minimum of four people on shift. There should be at least three other people here."

Basavi shifted from foot to foot. "Yes, sir."

Tennal leaned back against the doorframe to enjoy the show. Surit said patiently, "And where are those people, Private Basavi?"

"Some of the unit went to get breakfast, sir. Everyone was excited to land."

"Did they offer to get you breakfast, or did you get the short straw?" Tennal said, and slightly regretted it when she flushed. He wasn't here to pick on people who weren't picking on him. "Ignore that. They all left together?"

"Some of them went to their rooms, s—" She cut herself off as she took a closer look and realized he wasn't an officer.

"This is Agent Fifty-Six," Surit said. "He's seconded to our unit."

Tennal could see the gears turning. "Call me Halkana," he said. "Ranker, third-class. The lieutenant is my architect."

It took a moment, but then it clicked. She visibly swallowed and took a sharp step backward. Tennal narrowed his eyes. Of course, soldiers only came across the most powerful readers: the ones the army had decided were useful, and so they'd dug up a crime or another reason to sync them. Of course Private Basavi was afraid of him. As far as she could see, the only thing stopping him from reading her mind was Surit's sync.

Tennal had been trying not to think of how close he'd come to being synced, but her reaction made it roar up in the back of his mind. All Surit had to do was give in to the pressure and do it. Tennal wrestled the thought back down. *Lights* but he could use some soothers.

"All right," Surit said mildly, as if he hadn't noticed the sudden tension between them. He tapped his wristband, pulled a list of names off the network, and projected them above Basavi's desk. "We'll take these one by one."

Basavi turned helpful once she realized Surit wasn't going to demote her on the spot. Surit took notes on each name—*notes!*—as Tennal grew bored and started poking into the nearest workstation.

"Thank you, I think that will do it," Surit said, and Tennal jumped, but Surit was only turning toward him with the sort of cast-iron optimism he'd shown last night. "Shall we go and find our unit?"

"I wasn't planning to do anything else with my morning," Tennal said, then when the ranker looked confused, added, "sir."

They left Basavi focusing on her workstation with renewed determination and made their way back through the docks to the living habitats. "They did see your order to muster," Tennal said, in case Surit really was too good for this world. "I saw it on someone's workstation. They're skiving because you're new, and they think they can get away with it."

"I guessed," Surit said neutrally. They stepped onto the lift platform to the residential level. "I had the same problem before. The small ships aren't exciting, particularly when they're not attached to a mothership, and everyone wants a break the moment they dock. But keeping order is important." He looked up something on his wristband and set off purposefully down the corridor. Tennal had to hasten to keep up.

"You went pretty easy on that ranker," Tennal said. Surit had been much more patient than Tennal would have been.

Surit sighed. "I checked her work," he said. "She'd been running all the assigned maintenance scans. That usually takes three people. I don't see any point in dressing down the one member of the unit who seems to be genuinely working. But she *shouldn't* have been left to cover that shift by herself; that's against the safety clauses."

"Is it?" Tennal said. "You know, when I said 'wow them with the regulations,' I didn't mean for you to take that literally."

"The regulations are there for a reason." Surit looked at his list, then at the door in front of them. "Let's start with this one." He put out his hand to give his bios then glanced at Tennal and hesitated. "Maybe I should do the talking on this one. It will make it easier for you to integrate."

It would, but that just made Tennal want to do the opposite. That was a bad instinct, though, so he bit his tongue and leaned against the wall of the corridor. "Oh, I won't interfere, Lieutenant," he said. "I am *agog* to see how you handle this."

Surit flashed him a quick, undeserved smile, which threw Tennal, and buzzed at the door.

The ranker inside had clearly taken the opportunity for a quick nap. "Good morning!" Surit said in stentorian tones. He waited just long enough for them to wake up in confusion, then clapped them on the shoulder. "I'm very sorry you're unwell. *Health of Soldiery* paragraph forty-two says if you are too physically exhausted to carry out your duties, you need to be seen by medical personnel. Shall I get someone?"

The ranker almost levitated out of bed, stuttering excuses. Tennal had never seen someone move that fast. "That's your new officer, by the way," Tennal said sweetly, as Surit politely ushered him out the door. "Muster in ten. See you on the ship."

"That went well," Surit said, and he proceeded to repeat it three more times while Tennal trailed behind him in growing fascination. The fifth ranker was in the sixth's assigned quarters. "Two of you at once!" Surit said cheerfully. Neither of them had Tennal's lack of shame: they blushed all the way through getting dressed, while Surit stood in the doorway with his arms folded and his expression amiably neutral, and Tennal struggled to keep a straight face.

"You're making me laugh on purpose," Tennal murmured, when they'd sent the latest two down to the shuttle to keep Basavi company.

"Absolutely not." Surit might even have been telling the truth; not a muscle had moved in his expression.

"Really?" Tennal said. He'd taken a copy of Surit's list and was following along. "Next five are in the rec room."

Surit produced all five plus a tagalong from a table in the rec room. It turned out none of them could recite the subclauses that dealt with drinking on shift, so Surit quoted them in full, in the hearing of two dozen people, until the rankers in front of him had gone through all the stages from incredulity to awkward fidgeting to full mortified silence. There were no protests as he suggested they relocate back to the shuttle.

Part of Tennal was enjoying himself immensely. He hadn't considered it might be possible to cause more low-level chaos with a rule book than without. "That's nearly all of them. I'll get the last one from the canteen, shall I? You said muster would start now."

Surit frowned at his wristband. Tennal was starting to understand he didn't like missing a deadline, even one he'd set himself.
"Yes. Would you mind?"

"Let me be useful *somewhere*." Tennal waved a finger in a mock
salute and left him.

The corridors of the *Fractal Note* were much busier now that
there were all these other ships around. Tennal was used to his
civilian clothes attracting stares. What threw him was these new-
comers *weren't* staring at him. Now that he was in a ranker's uniform, nobody watched him suspiciously or gave him space. It was
like the uniform had made him invisible.

It was when an officer glared at him until he saluted her that it
really sank in: he wasn't playacting as a ranker. Until he escaped,
he was one.

The canteen was a large, low-ceilinged space divided by rows
of tables. Tennal had avoided eating here up until now, instead just
stalking into the officer side, daring anyone to comment, and taking a meal tray to eat in his room. Now his stomach grumbled
at the smell of food—a really inconvenient time for his body to
remind him he'd only had one meal in the past three days—but
he was still coasting on adrenaline, so he ignored it.

The large screens set at intervals around the wall were all showing newslog broadcasts. In this area of space, local news was all
about Archer Link Station: Tennal recognized Governor-General
Oma, surrounded by a sea of golden Archer banners and talking
into the camera. Oh yes, she ran Archer Link Station, didn't she?
Tennal had last spoken to her when he'd answered her call in
the Legislator's Residence. He hadn't passed on her message. He
hoped she was making life difficult for his aunt.

A bunch of rankers around Tennal's age crowded around the
meal dispensers, where a small, wiry ranker and a wrestler type
were having a shoving match. A small crowd watched.

Tennal glanced over the onlookers, checking their rank tabs
for the number that would indicate his unit, but he didn't see it.

He gave the onlookers his most unpleasant smile and didn't stop walking. They parted to let him through.

His stomach growled again. He had to do something about that. He scanned the less crowded dispensers at the edge to see what was easiest to carry and grabbed some sort of wrapped cake, hard and square, and thought regretfully of the real, oven-baked pastries he'd left with Zin. It would have to do.

He remembered Private Basavi, abandoned to hold down the fort while everyone left to get breakfast, and the thought irritated him so much that he took another one. The dispenser beeped in protest when he used his military identity, so he gave it his civilian keys—it was hard to think of them as his *old* civilian keys—to make it disgorge the second cake.

The dispenser flashed up empty once he'd taken it. Someone tapped him on the elbow, not gently. "Hey, bozo, *one* each."

Tennal turned to see the short, wiry ranker who had been in the fight when he'd entered. He put one of the cakes in his pocket. "I'm bad at counting."

"Hand it over." They didn't recognize him. Tennal still hadn't gotten used to his new invisibility.

"Think I won't, actually," Tennal said agreeably. He scanned for exit routes—it would look bad if *he* didn't turn up at the muster on time—but the other rankers had started to notice.

Because soldiers were Tennal's least favorite people, this one of course took that as a challenge. They squared up to him, shorter than Tennal but with the impression of a pine marten in a corner, and said, "I'll write it out of you."

A switch in Tennal's head flipped. He raised the cake in his hand, took hold of the wrapper tag with his teeth, his eyes not leaving theirs, and ripped it open. "Oh, *try* it." He took a bite.

To be fair, part of him regretted it immediately. That part had listened when Zin had exasperatedly told him that making bad choices wasn't a personality trait. Unfortunately, that part was being carried along as a passenger by the majority of Tennal, who chewed and swallowed without breaking eye contact. It wasn't even good. It tasted like dust and sweetener.

The ranker—who was skinny, with a long ponytail and a pugnacious look—squared their shoulders and clenched their fists. A couple of the others laughed. Tennal hadn't been in many fights, but he could read the room. "Hand it over, smug ass."

"Did you call dibs?" Tennal said insincerely. "Is that some kind of army rule?" He was concentrating on them, but the write command actually came from one of the bystanders. Tennal's head snapped around as he felt it splash off him like water on a rock.

That was when the skinny ranker swung at him. Tennal dodged backward, nearly knocking over a table. He should have planned an escape route before picking a fight, but he'd never been good at plans. He backed against a chair, kicked it over, and jumped over it, buying some space. The wiry ranker came after him. They lunged.

At that moment, Tennal read the number under their rank tabs.

Tennal dodged behind another chair. "Wait," he said, faking urgency. "*Wait.*"

They hesitated, just for a second. Tennal raised his arm and tapped his wristband. A ping sounded on theirs.

"We're unit-mates," Tennal said, with one of his best fake smiles. "And you're late for muster."

Tennal learned on the way back that the wiry ranker's name was Istara, they were first-class grade, and they wouldn't talk to him without glaring, which Tennal admittedly had asked for. They had an array of tiny glass, flint, and silver studs decorating their cuff, which was nonstandard—flint was common, and glass was a galactic way of indicating nonbinary, but silver didn't have a meaning Tennal knew. Either they'd explain when they wanted to, or they wouldn't. Tennal vaguely settled on *gender irrelevant, maybe fem-aligning.*

When Istara and Tennal reached the retrieval shuttle where Surit was waiting, Tennal gestured Istara through the airlock first then ate the rest of his cake behind their back. His limbs felt like they were at least one tenth putty. The days after withdrawal were only marginally less rubbish than the peak of it; he never remembered that when he took a soother.

The tiny operations room was bustling with the errant rankers Surit had rounded up. Retrieval Unit 287—they seemed to call themselves *Retrieval Two*—was all here. Surit himself leaned over a workstation with a ranker; Tennal shouldered his way toward him through the cramped space between the chairs. When Tennal passed Basavi, still hunched earnestly over her workstation, he waited until she wasn't looking and dropped the extra cake on her desk as he went. He noticed someone else had put a meal tray there, so maybe the rest of her unit wasn't entirely shitheads after all. Istara had taken the workstation next to Basavi, and Tennal heard *Halkana,* not in a complimentary tone, as the two bent their heads together.

That wasn't his problem. Everyone in this unit was just a minor obstacle in Tennal's eventual escape. Except for Surit, admittedly, who could scotch the whole thing with a single word.

Tennal owed Surit. The knowledge loomed over him like the ever-present rumbling of chaotic space. Tennal still didn't fully understand why Surit hadn't gotten cold feet yet—principles, sure, but nobody was principled enough to risk a court-martial for someone like Tennal—which meant he had to find a way to pay him back. There was no way Tennal could escape until after this mission, so he needed Surit's finer feelings to last for a few weeks, until they were at a more populated spaceport.

Getting someone to like Tennal for a few weeks was a tall order.

For now, he stopped in front of Surit and saluted. "Last ranker accounted for, sir."

"Thank you," Surit said, as the rankers next to him gave Tennal curious glances. "I think that's all of us." It was still enormously frustrating that Surit's mind was too locked up for Tennal to read him, but Tennal caught the glance he gave the room before he pressed the buzzer for attention. Surit was still nervous.

That made sense. Despite his bulk and his supernatural grasp of the rule book, Surit was the type of *nice* that wouldn't have survived in high-society circles, let alone among a bunch of soldiers. Tennal leaned against the wall and folded his arms as Surit cleared his throat.

"Good morning," Surit said to the two dozen people crammed into the operations room. Tennal was expecting a jolly all-in-this-together speech, but what Surit said was, "Is Comms Technician Thet present, please?"

There was a moment of murmured confusion among the rankers. Eventually a burly ranker tentatively raised her hand.

"I think there's a problem with your comms rig," Surit said. "When was the last time you ran a daily test routine?"

"Yesterday?" the ranker said.

"It was last week," Surit said. "I checked. There's no need for concern, though," he added. "I found the problem."

Tennal wondered if Surit was going to give them an excuse for ignoring the muster order. The ranker said, "It might've dropped a couple of messages—" though she was clearly on shaky ground, and she knew it.

"The stage at which the messages are getting dropped," Surit said mildly, "is between the message arriving on the ship and the message going into the recipients' eyeballs. What do you think the best fix is?" He dropped the suggestion into an awkward silence among the rankers. "Possibly some mass eye surgery?"

Surit wasn't so bad at this. Tennal's mouth curled up in appreciation. It took some artistry to make an atmosphere this excruciating.

"I hope that will be the only time this happens," Surit said calmly. The shuttle was dead silent. He had them, for now. "Please

listen carefully. I have made some changes to your task alloca-
tions."

The detail of tasks and shift patterns that followed made Tennal's brain shut down from immediate paralyzing boredom. Tennal
occupied himself with scanning faces and very carefully sampling
currents around the occupants of the room—not really *reading,* just
taking the temperature of the unit. Stress, anxiety, boredom: normal reactions for a group that had just been yelled at, even if it was
by Surit, which was a bit like a recruitment poster had come to life
in order to be gently disappointed in you.

"I'll take hull-inspection duty. And finally, Private Halkana
needs basic pilot training," Surit said, pulling Tennal's attention
back. There was a new bustle in the room as the rankers settled
down to new tasks or clambered out of the airlock to the mothership. Surit didn't falter for an instant on faces or names: he zeroed
in on Istara at the desk next to Basavi. "Private Istara, you have
the highest piloting scores. I want you to train Private Halkana
on—" He hesitated as he saw the obviously horrified looks Tennal
and Istara gave each other.

At least half the room was listening to this exchange. Tennal could see them trying to place where Tennal fell in the unit
dynamic—most of them would know he was a reader by now, if
gossip spread the way Tennal thought, but a tiny unit like this
would never have encountered a fleet reader before. If it looked
like Surit was trying to be *nice* to Tennal, Surit would look weak.

"Private Istara and I have already met, sir," Tennal said, with
an elaborate bow in Istara's direction. "It would be an honor to
work with them."

CHAPTER 10

Tennal did regret saying that, but of all the consequences he'd experienced during his life, eight hours of grindingly dull mathematics and charts, cramped at a desk with a grumpy ranker, wasn't the worst of them.

Istara turned out to be a loud, prickly personality who was quick to take insult but equally quick to forgive, and they didn't seem to hold a grudge about that morning. They obviously weren't thrilled to be landed with Tennal, but they knew their stuff. They threw a pile of basic instruction work at him, gave him a few hours to plow through it, then quizzed him mercilessly. Once they were satisfied about his fundamental physics—Tennal hadn't had to engage his brain for a long time, but he still had one—they took him through some mocked-up interfaces on their workstation.

By hour six, Tennal's brain was leaking out of his ears. A couple more weeks of this study program and he might be able to pilot a bathtub around a very small artificial vacuum.

Istara was apparently best friends with Basavi, the tall, quiet ranker with the impressive biceps. They spent the time in between blithely chatting—Istara was brighter and more cheerful with Basavi than anyone else, though Basavi's answers were too low and soft for Tennal to hear. Istara broke off when they saw Tennal had finished the latest exercise.

"Done?" They slapped down a light-screen on Tennal's desk. It lit up to show a grid of lines and colored symbols. "This is the chart of our current position."

Tennal stared. There were hundreds of symbols, only a dozen of which he'd memorized. But it didn't matter. As soon as he saw the chart, it made sense. Like someone had just opened a window, he felt the looming presence of chaotic space settle into those spirals and lines. He knew where every twist and distortion was on the map like each was a ridge or a dip on the back of his teeth. If he shut his eyes, he could feel a new space in his head like his vision was expanding, like his mind was leaving his body. He could see the ship as a speck of dust approaching a vast maelstrom, as if he floated in the darkness of space next to it.

So this was why a reader was useful to the pilots.

Istara was watching him. "You can feel it, huh?"

Tennal tore his attention from the map, still reeling. At the desk next to them, Basavi watched him sideways, nervously. Tennal could still feel the ghostly shape of chaotic space in his head. "Why doesn't the army just employ readers as pilots without syncing them?"

Istara snorted. "They burn out," they said, as if this were obvious. "And nobody trusts a strong reader. But you don't need a reader, really, not if you're maneuverable enough. A bunch of us in Retrieval Two have got the knack."

"A bunch of you are *readers*?" Tennal said without thinking.

The look Istara gave him was withering. "A bunch of us are architects, dickhead. Readers aren't the only people who can sense those currents, even if you're supposed to be better at it. Get on with the mapping module." Tennal was expecting them to back it up with a write command, but Istara didn't even try.

"Shift's nearly over," Basavi said, quietly and unexpectedly.

Tennal's wristband was pinging urgently for him to report to the gymnasium. Istara gave him a half-mocking, half-sympathetic look. "Remedial fitness, huh?"

"Guidance Lights," Tennal said, looking at the drills that had landed on his schedule like a particularly unwelcome vulture. "When do you *eat*?"

"Not all of us are entitled little rich kids," Istara said, getting up. "Hey, Savi, we're on cleaning duty."

Tennal gritted his teeth, made his way to the gymnasium bay that he'd ignored with prejudice up until now, and for once in his life, he made a good-faith attempt to exercise. He hadn't done that since boarding school.

Afterward, he felt as awful as he had felt in weeks—in a novel way—sitting sprawled against the treadmill with the back of his head pressed to the cool metal. And he'd only done half his fucking program. He had to find a way to catch up by the rest of the week, or the commander would realize Surit wasn't in control of him.

Maybe Surit *would* write him. Tennal briefly entertained the thought of relying on something other than his own wet-paper willpower but reluctantly concluded that if Surit wouldn't break his principles to save himself from court-martial, he was unlikely to do it to motivate Tennal into push-ups.

Instead, brooding over thoughts of weeks of this schedule, Tennal dragged himself to Medical. It was a clean and impersonal bay with military-standard equipment, which wasn't reassuring, but at least these medics didn't know his aunt. There was only one senior medic there, covering the night shift: a tall, grave person with a gloomy air, a wooden pin on his sleeve, and lieutenant tabs. Tennal draped himself over the medic's desk and said, "I need soothers." When the medic looked skeptical, he added, "It's a reader thing."

"Symptoms?" the medic said. "We don't give out soothers for anything less than limb amputation."

"I've just got a headache," Tennal said, smiling over the sudden spike of desperation. "What else do you have?"

Eventually Tennal got shop-bought analgesics—which were as much use for this kind of thing as an umbrella in a tornado, but the alternative was a shot—and a sedative strip. He didn't want a sedative. He needed something to lift his mood and distract him from the muscle aches and the headache, not smother him until he fell asleep. If he could get his hands on some enhancers, he could get someone to write him into distraction. He remembered with a jolt that there was an architect on the station who didn't *need* enhancers for him. Surit could have written this whole shitty feeling out of him, if he didn't have all the adventurous nature of a tax accountant.

He had to work out what to do about Surit.

Tennal tried the canteen for dinner. It turned out, at the end of a shift, one of the dispensers disgorged a brightly colored cup of alcohol that tasted like you could pour it into a fuel tank. Tennal took the cup, used his civilian codes to get another one, and downed half of the first as he thought. He could swear he had seen hints of Surit being attracted to him, if at an odd, different angle to the way people were usually attracted to Tennal. That might explain why Surit had volunteered to help him escape.

Tennal could work with physical attraction, though he wished he knew why Surit hadn't acted on it already. Surit was so fucking hard to read.

He picked up the unopened cup and left the canteen for the room he and Surit shared.

As he gave the door his handprint, it occurred to Tennal that Surit might not even be in—didn't officers socialize after their shifts or something?—but he relaxed a moment later when the door folded itself aside to reveal Surit and his neutral expression filling all the available space behind it. Surit's mind was locked down tight as usual.

Tennal held up the drinks in their bright cups. "Lights guide your path, my brother," he said. "Blessings on this holy meal."

Surit accepted the proffered cup with careful, controlled hands. He stepped back and broke the seal without jolting the liquid inside. "Are you all right?" he said. "Sorry I couldn't check in with you. I had to go over the hull."

"I don't need a babysitter, and I'm just peachy," Tennal said.

"Did six hours of mathematics and half my exercise program, and it nearly killed me. Don't let my ambulatory corpse distract you from your work."

Surit had projected a spiderweb of notes over the wall, stretching from one corner of the small room to another. Tennal glanced over them as Surit awkwardly stepped aside to give him space. Surit had noted down the name of everyone in Retrieval Two, plus a bunch of other people, and seemed to be linking them. "Is this what they teach you at officer school?"

"They're just notes," Surit said, as if someone had asked him to defend himself. Not an army-approved technique, then. "I know I'll remember things if I write them down."

"Hm." When Tennal examined the notes closer, he saw the linked fragments were things like *wiring specialist, wants promotion,* and mysterious notes like *Ext. Hull Qual Lvl 2.* He looked thoughtfully at the blank spaces between them, thought back to the low chatter around him while he'd worked in the shuttle, and said, "Do you take input?"

Surit stopped where he had just jotted down *claustrophobic* next to a ranker's name. He said, with some wariness, "Go on."

With the hand that wasn't holding his drink, Tennal tapped the projection on the wall and added a line between two points. "I'm almost sure these two just broke up and hate each other's guts," he said. "I heard one of them talk to Istara. Also, not our unit, but I've heard *these* two names: they're rankers, and they're both fucking the Retrieval One lieutenant. Which means Retrieval One is currently a toxic shit show. And no, I didn't read that from anyone, I was too busy being flattened with gravitational equations. Does any of that help?"

He'd meant the last part sarcastically, but Surit gave him a startled look. "You've been around them less than a day."

Tennal couldn't see how eavesdropping on a couple of rumors was impressive, when Surit had apparently done a full exterior-hull shift *and* memorized everyone's qualifications, but he wasn't sure how to phrase it in a way that didn't sound snide—sincerity was not one of his talents—so instead he dropped back to sit on his bed. "I'm good at picking up the worst side of human nature," he said. "Or gossip. One of those."

Surit snorted, which was close enough to a laugh for Tennal to count it as a success. Under the pretense of reading the notes, Tennal shifted himself over to sit on the storage chest jammed by Surit's bed, half an arm's length away. He kept one eye on Surit's reaction. Surit didn't tense, just sipped the eyebrow-scorching spirits and stared contemplatively at his notes. Tennal leaned back against the wall, letting his uniform crumple, and stretched his legs out. He'd meant to say something likeable and non-assholish, but his mind was blank. It was oddly not awkward. A placid silence emanated from Surit like a field of static. Tennal watched his hands as he made more notes.

It felt like a bubble of safety: a tiny, private room in a station packed full of soldiers they had fooled, floating in the vastness of space. When Surit finished his drink, he gave a long, heavy sigh, sat on his bed, and laid out a light-screen like a table, floating horizontally between them. "I found the refueling schedule."

"Fascinating," Tennal said lazily. "Why did you think I'd be interested in this?"

Surit gave the ghost of a smile. "I thought you'd want to know the first place the fleet will stop after we leave chaotic space. It's the first chance you'll have to leave."

Tennal sat up and gave the light-screen a closer look. It named a station, one of the midspace posts that meant refueling ships didn't have to enter planetary orbit. There might be commercial transports docking there. "Where is this?"

"About three days from when we come back out," Surit said, "providing chaotic space lets us leave in roughly the same place we came in." Tennal took from his tone that this wasn't a given. "It's right on the border with Archer territory. There'll be a constant flow of traffic to Archer Link Station."

The words *Archer Link Station* were jarring. Tennal had vaguely assumed he'd hop from station to station before he eventually managed to disappear somewhere in the megacities of Orshan Two or the sprawling farmland of Orshan Three. But Surit had clearly thought about it more than him: that was a risk. As long as Tennal was in Orshan space, the army could eventually track him down. If he made it to the wider universe, though, they stood no chance of finding him. "You think I should try and get out-system," he said flatly. "Through the link."

"Yes," Surit said. Tennal saw that even getting this far was costing him. Surit had probably never thought about how to outwit the army in his life. "It might be easier to fake some temporary documents to take you through the link. Something permanent for our own sector would be harder. And you can't stay here."

"I'm *illegal* outside Orshan space," Tennal pointed out. "So are you. When the Resolution let us back in, they made us sign that treaty that promised no neuromodified citizens would leave. They teach this every year at school. Remember? If I read a galactic citizen, I'm pretty sure that's both a treaty violation and an act of war."

"Yes, but if you don't, would they notice you're a reader?" Surit said, still frowning earnestly. He wore exactly the same expression discussing intergalactic warfare as he had when he'd found out a ranker hadn't turned in the last weekly report. Tennal was starting to suspect that in Surit's world, it was not possible to give less than 100 percent of your attention to an issue. "Other Resolution planets have neuromodifications. The High Chain has had them for centuries, for a start, though I don't think they're the same as ours. Orshan just wasn't authorized when the army started experimenting."

"Oh, so I'll just pass myself off as High Chain royalty?" Tennal said, but his brain had started to whir. He hadn't paid much attention to wider galactic politics, but he knew what Surit was talking about. The Resolution was huge. Orshan hadn't managed to secure acceptance of architects or readers—possibly because the reader powers creeped everyone out—but other planets *had* managed to get acceptance for their own people with weird quirks. There were trillions upon trillions of people in Resolution space. Tennal could disappear much more effectively out there than leading a paranoid half-life in a suburb of Orshan Two.

"You'll need documents for the link," Surit said. "Real or fake. Is there anyone . . . ?"

"No," Tennal said reflexively. Nobody was close enough to him that they would risk helping him commit a crime, except maybe Zin, and he'd cut his own leg off before he got her involved. And any attempt to reach out to his aunt's allies would get back to her before the data packets had even finished transmitting.

Then he realized: it didn't have to be an *ally* of his aunt.

Archer Link Station was in the hands of that terrifying general with the nuclear-reactor smile: Governor-General Oma. Archer and Cavalry didn't get along. Governor Oma didn't have any reason to be fond of his aunt. Of course, she didn't have any reason to be fond of Tennal either, but that was a problem for later. "Hm," Tennal said, the corners of his mouth turning up. "I've got some thoughts."

"Then don't tell me," Surit said, a crack of worry showing through.

Tennal understood. What Surit didn't know, he couldn't tell anyone else, even in a court-martial. Orshan's justice system didn't allow the use of reader or architect powers in court, but there were other ways of putting pressure on a junior officer. It brought into sharp focus just how much of a risk Surit was taking. Tennal's thanks dried up in his throat: what would he say, *Hey, thanks for putting your whole career on the line. Shame it wasn't for a better cause?*

Instead he watched as Surit reached out and shut down the light-screen. The evening-cycle lights were turning steadily dimmer and more orange in spectrum, nudging them to sleep.

Tennal shifted so his leg was casually pressed against Surit's. Surit froze.

A ping broke the atmosphere. "Sleep cycle," Surit said. He leaned down to check his wristband, breaking the warmth where Tennal's shin had rested against his calf. "We should have gone into it a while ago."

Tennal smiled lazily. "Hard to tell, on ship." His internal clock was off after the past three days, but then, he'd never slept regularly. "Your alert might be misfiring. Let me check." He reached over and rested his hand on Surit's bare wrist, angling the hovering screen so he could see.

He saw Surit swallow, confirming Tennal's suspicions. Tennal took his time, leaning forward in the sudden silence. He could hear both of them breathing. He kept his hand a second too long on Surit's wrist then let one of his fingertips brush the skin as he drew his hand away. Surit's forearm lifted infinitesimally, following the touch.

That was enough confirmation. "Looks like it's right," Tennal said. "We're supposed to be relaxing." He stood, turning a stretch into an invitation, and saw the way Surit's eyes tracked him. Surit stayed frozen on the bed like he couldn't remember how to move. Tennal leaned over and rested a finger lightly on Surit's chest, at the hollow of his neck. "I can think of a couple of ways."

Surit's intentions barely sent out a flicker of light around him, so little that Tennal had stopped even trying to read him. But he felt something this time, something as faint and deep as the shifting of earth beneath a continent. Surit wasn't even breathing.

"No," Surit said.

Tennal stiffened. "I'm sorry?"

Surit didn't move under Tennal's touch. When he breathed in, his rib cage moved with a noticeable effort. "No."

Tennal had never mistaken someone this badly, not even if he couldn't read them. He took his hand away, which did nothing for the heat in the room and his hyperawareness of Surit's every movement, the way Surit's eyes were focused on him. "How sure are you?"

"I'm sure we shouldn't do this," Surit said, a rough edge to his voice. "Are you reading me?"

"I fucking can't," Tennal said. "You're closed up like an airlock. Maybe it's all that meditation—no, I just have *eyes,* Lieutenant. I can see when someone's interested."

The stain hadn't left Surit's cheeks. "As a rule, I try and make my decisions with my brain."

"And what objection is your brain putting up?" Tennal said. His lips were dry for some reason. The fucking *obstinacy.* "You want this. I want this. We're two adults in a private room. Have you ever slept with a reader?"

"Does that have anything to do with it?" Surit said, which was a *no.*

Tennal recognized the bite that had crept into his own voice and made an effort to tone it down. He knew the steps that worked in this dance—Surit's case was harder because they were both too sober and Surit was obviously not used to getting what he wanted—but Tennal was usually good at this. "If you put your walls down and let me read you, we don't even need to talk."

If Surit had been wavering, his expression hardened when Tennal took that tack. "You've been conscripted," he said, "and that's not right."

"Guidance *Lights,*" Tennal said. "That doesn't have anything to do with it. If I walked into a party and saw you, I'd be trying to get you into a hotel room by midnight. You own a mirror—I mean, I assume you own a mirror, you might consider that an unmilitary luxury—but take it from me, that's not the issue here."

"You're in my chain of command," Surit said.

Tennal recognized the stony look in his eyes that meant Surit was about to dig in his heels until they took root. Tennal had to cut that off fast. "Not relevant. We're not in work hours."

"Tennal," Surit said, with a sudden gentleness that made Tennal's breath hitch. "That doesn't make a difference."

"*Explain*," Tennal said, shoving the storage chest out of his way with one foot. His control of the exchange had already broken, and he wasn't going to get it back, but it spilled out of his mouth anyway.

Surit just sat there, looking down, his presence as dense as a gravity field. He folded one of his hands into a fist and wrapped the other hand around it. "The fraternization rules are there for a reason," he said. "What if it gets messy?" He didn't pause long enough for Tennal to dismiss that. "What if you end up wanting to get away from me? They won't let you apply for a transfer. And you need me to lie about the sync."

Tennal's skin felt like something was burning under it. "I *know*," he said. The room was too small, and Surit was agonizingly close. But Surit wouldn't look up. "I'm one hundred percent aware of how much I need you," Tennal said, low and focused. "So will you just suspend your scruples for *once* and let me give you something to lie for."

Surit's head finally jerked up. If there had been any hint of indecision, it was gone, replaced by—something. Tennal tried to read him, but Surit was as devoid of intention currents as usual. Whatever the expression was, it wasn't flattering.

"I understand," Surit said. He sounded strangely empty.

Tennal mentally replayed what he'd just said. Surit had preferred him honest before. Tennal was starting to get the hollow feeling that dogged him whenever he was too sober. His head hurt again. "Listen. Surit. Lieutenant. I can be reasonable," he said. "I know you didn't want to end up with a reader. I know helping me out is bad for your career. All I'm saying is—" What was he saying? On the rare occasions when he'd started being honest, he'd never been able to find the right line between that and *too* honest. "It doesn't have to be all bad."

Surit was watching him steadily. Tennal felt like a gust of air battering away at a building. It wasn't fucking *working*.

"Do you get off on sitting there like a stone block when someone's talking?" Tennal said.

He was so on edge that he twitched when Surit moved. Surit didn't touch him, though, but got slowly to his feet, putting his hand on the wall behind him to balance so he wasn't in any danger of brushing against Tennal. Tennal didn't step back, which made it difficult, but Tennal wasn't in the mood to be considerate.

"Have you considered," Surit said, "that maybe I'm not lying for you?"

"If you try and tell me you're doing this for your meteoric career—"

"Don't go off topic, please," Surit said. "I've already told you I'm doing this because forcing either of us into a sync isn't right. It has nothing to do with who you are, or how you conduct yourself, or whether you're willing to sleep with me. Right now you're honestly the last person I could sleep with. I'll keep up our lie without being . . . bribed or whatever this is."

Something savage had risen in Tennal like a wave. "Oh, *thank* you," he said. He took a couple of steps back, putting half the tiny room between them. "How noble and gracious the officers of the Orshan fleet. Is this fun for you?"

Surit's eyes were like slabs of granite. "No," he said. "It's not."

In that moment Tennal hated the whole universe. "So you do talk back," he said. He raised his empty cup in a toast. "To the gallant impulses of the officer class! Long may those last." He tossed his cup into the recycler with unnecessary force and fished in his pocket. The sedative strip was still there: medical yellow and stiff to the touch. He slapped it onto his wrist, where the microteeth bit and the ends closed around the bones of his wrist like a bracelet.

"Tennal," Surit said.

"I'm going to bed," Tennal said. He kicked his shoes off and fell onto the stupid hard bed, fully clothed, and rolled to face the wall. "You can court-martial me tomorrow." He should have known he couldn't keep this up. He could barely be likeable for an hour at a time. If Surit gave up on him, and Tennal ended up stuck in the army with a sync like the good little marionette his aunt wanted, it was going to be his own Lights-forsaken fault.

CHAPTER 11

Tennal had crashed and burned worse before, though not for stakes this high. He went into the next morning knowing he'd fucked up—it had only been a matter of time—and grimly put together an apology in preparation. He could at least limit the damage.

When he tried out his apology over breakfast, Surit gave him a blank stare.

Tennal's insides curdled. He'd known he was going to ruin things, but even so, he'd thought he might have more time. He didn't know what he was going to do now. Steal a shuttle and dive into chaotic space, maybe. He was out of options.

"No, I think I should apologize," Surit said.

"What?"

Surit seemed entirely sincere. "I could have handled that better. I'm sorry. We're under a lot of strain, and I wasn't thinking straight."

It took Tennal a few moments to shut his mouth. "You weren't, were you?"

"The regulations—"

"*Don't*," Tennal said. "I cannot take you reciting the military sexual conduct regulations to me over breakfast. I will mutiny." Surit almost cracked a smile. Tennal forced himself to look away and return to his food. It made sense to drop the subject before Surit wrote himself up for breaking fraternization rules, which seemed like something he would do.

Maybe Tennal had been wrong. Maybe Surit would help him

out for two weeks without anything in return, though Tennal didn't understand *why*. But Tennal could handle another two weeks. He had to.

After breakfast, and another fleet-wide morning meeting where Tennal virtuously accompanied Surit and said nothing at all, Tennal's wristband pinged for the start of his shift. That heralded the start of something Tennal would not have believed he would ever end up trying: a serious attempt to fit into army life.

"Oh great, posh boy's back," Private Istara said, when Tennal slipped through the airlock into the shuttle's operations room. Tennal threw them a rude gesture, unthinkingly, and was surprised when they laughed.

Istara returned the gesture. "Not running home to auntie, then?"

So word had gotten around the unit about exactly who he was. Tennal met their smile with one of his own. "No, I'm going to have a long and storied military career and retire loaded with medals at forty. Then they'll make me legislator."

He saw Basavi twitch, as if not quite sure they *wouldn't* do that. Istara's eyes narrowed as their friend edged away. "You're not serious."

"That's step two of the plan, after I disband the army and replace all the supreme commanders with frogs." Tennal threw himself into his seat. "What are we doing today? I was told army life was glamorous."

"*You're* still in baby pilot school," Istara said, swiping another pile of exercises onto Tennal's desk. Tennal groaned. "Have fun," they added callously.

Tennal grumbled but bent his head to the screen and started working.

It wasn't so bad. He started to pick up more about the unit as he worked and listened. It turned out that nervous, conscientious Basavi was the child of a teacher who lived on rural Orshan Three; Istara, loud and brash, was from a huge family of construction workers the next village over. They'd met at basic training and apparently managed to stay together through all their transfers since. Tennal didn't understand people who made friends like that.

Tennal had thought Basavi didn't like readers, but he tentatively concluded he might be wrong. When he read her, he got no hostility: only a slow, strong curiosity. She just seemed to take her time to work through things.

Eventually she asked, "Do you read people?"

It was the first remark she'd addressed directly to him. Tennal was willing to take any excuse to stop working. "Are you worried I'm looking at your deep, dark secrets? I'm not, I promise," he said. "I can't even tell what you had for breakfast, not without a deep reading. And you'd feel that."

Basavi seemed to think about this. "So you do read people, just not deeply," she said, displaying a concerning ability to see straight through Tennal's wording. "How often?"

Tennal considered lying, but Basavi had been reasonably friendly so far. "I don't know. It's like looking at someone, you know? You can look at someone and see they're in a good mood, or they're sulking, or they're going to punch the next person who gets in their space. Or you can choose not to look at them. For example, I can tell hotshot pilot Istara over here doesn't like me and didn't want to be responsible for me," he said, waving a hand. "But I don't know *why*. I'd have to guess. Obviously I'm a delightful person, and everyone else loves me, so that will be hard."

"It's your sweet and humble nature," Istara said caustically. "We can't measure up." Tennal was starting to like them.

"So it's just on *all the time*?" Basavi said, startled. "You must be strong."

That wasn't what Tennal had meant, exactly. It was just the sea he swam in—sight, sound, occasional waves of emotion. He got one of them at that precise moment from Istara: a strong spike of discomfort. Interestingly, it was too delayed to be a reaction to

Tennal's admission that he read people. It must've been Basavi saying he was strong.

"Lights, of course he is! He's the fleet reader!" Istara slid a file to Tennal's desk with a gesture and slapped it for emphasis. It unfurled on the glowing screen. "Here, stop slacking off and memorize this." Tennal poked it. It was a simplified version of the map he'd seen yesterday. "We're moving into chaotic space tomorrow."

"Can't wait," Tennal said. "What does that mean? We're not actually doing any piloting." The shuttle was still nestled in the *Fractal Note,* unmoving, like a cannonball waiting to be fired.

"We'll be traveling separate," Istara said. "The scanners found a clear route inside, but we have to get past a patch of disturbed space at the entrance."

Tennal had picked up enough to know *traveling separate* meant the bulky *Fractal Note* was unsure it would be maneuverable enough, so it would eject all its shuttles—including them—before the difficult part. He'd learned yesterday that it was good to be lighter and faster when you were in the shifting cloud banks of chaotic space. Less chance of hitting something unexpected.

"Out on our own in the cold, hard universe," Istara added. "With you, Halkana, unless you get yourself moved to a cushy post on the bridge, or whatever fleet readers do."

"I'm working on it," Tennal said lazily.

He'd better hurry up and get a message to Governor Oma on Archer Link, since Lights knew how long a message would take to get out of chaotic space. They wouldn't let him contact Archer Link's networks directly, but if he could use his civilian identity and get to a relay point, he might be able to get something through. "Hey, who's on comms duty? My aunt said she'd message me, and I want to pick it up."

"Oh," Basavi said. From her great height, her expression softened in a way that made Tennal feel like he'd just accidentally played the pity card. "I am. Stara, you could put him on shift with me later."

Istara threw up their hands. "He's the *fleet reader,* not a stray puppy," they said. "You're going soft again."

"It's not soft to want to hear from your family," Basavi said defensively. Damn it, now Tennal owed her as well. He had enough on his hands with *one* do-gooder.

"Ugh, all right, all right," Istara said. Tennal was still getting a feel for how the unit worked, but *ranker, first-class* seemed to mean Istara and Basavi acted as deputies for Surit, and Istara certainly seemed to have access to the duty roster. "Fine, you're on comms for the afternoon shift, Halkana. Lights. Fuck off and get me a coffee. Get everyone else one while you're at it."

By no means unsatisfied with this outcome, Tennal got up and stretched, just as Surit stepped through the airlock and saluted the room. Istara and Basavi scrambled to their feet with the rest of the rankers, and Tennal had another opportunity to practice his salute. He reflected that anyone who had known him up until one month ago would be laughing themself sick right now.

"You knew the lieutenant before, right?" Istara said under their breath, as they all settled down again. Surit took the lieutenant's workstation overseeing the room, earnestly greeting a technician who opened three light-screens in front of him. "What's he like?"

Tennal glanced over at Istara. There was still suspicion there: the soldiers of Retrieval Two had been temporarily brought into line yesterday but still hadn't decided what to make of the new lieutenant. Tennal rolled several answers around in his head. He didn't feel *guilty,* as such, that Surit was going to deal with the fallout from Tennal's escape, but it did infuriate him that the army seemed not to realize they had Surit working for them. It was just such a waste. Surit could at least be properly in charge of his own unit. "Oh, didn't I mention?" Tennal said. "He's my aunt's handpicked choice. Top scores in everything. He fixed an air leak in her shuttle when she visited the academy. Got a commendation."

Istara paused, apparently reevaluating their first impression. Pleased with the effect, Tennal left to get cups of coffee and did a round of the room, dropping more Surit-related stories at every opportunity. Surit himself was discussing something with two mechanics at his workstation, and occasionally glanced suspiciously at Tennal whenever a pair of rankers turned to look at him.

Tennal considered that a good morning's work. He plowed through more pilot-training modules, leveling up from a bathtub in a small vacuum to maybe a dinghy in very generous gravity. Istara was witheringly scornful of his efforts to memorize the right terms, but the point wasn't to make him a pilot, Tennal reminded himself. The point was to give him more than a kindergartener's understanding of ship navigation so he could tell the real pilots what his senses were telling him.

And besides, his scraping of knowledge just needed to carry him through this mission. Then he'd be gone.

He absently read the temperature of the room as he worked. Istara and Basavi had definitely been friends for years; they talked and thought like people who had lived in each other's pockets. The rest of the unit wasn't quite as tight-knit, but they all had a working familiarity with each other. Tennal and Surit were the unknown quantities.

Basavi and Istara disappeared at lunchtime. For once Tennal didn't get to play the outsider, because Surit scooped him up on the way to the canteen like this was natural, sat them both over trays in the officer section, and gave him a long stare with a crease between his eyebrows.

"What did you do," Surit said.

"Absolutely nothing," Tennal said virtuously. "What are we talking about?"

"Half the unit started being polite to me this morning for no reason," Surit said. "I saw you talking to the rankers."

"I was fetching coffee," Tennal said, neglecting to mention that Surit was now responsible, in the eyes of the more credulous half of Retrieval Two, for three heroic rescues and a shoot-out with freight smugglers. "I'm very dedicated to the comfort and well-being of my unit."

Tennal was rewarded for his public spirit by his comms shift with Basavi.

A comms shift was much less headache-inducing than pilot training, and Basavi didn't really need the help. When she wasn't paying attention, Tennal surreptitiously went looking for the public Archer Link channels.

A surprising number of the station's public channels were restricted or throttled. Tennal thought back to when Governor Oma had called his aunt. He vaguely remembered her referencing an attempted coup. He wondered if that was related.

But that was none of his business. The governor had her own public channel, and Tennal still had codes for some basic anonymization services from his misspent year with the gambling rings, so he could do just enough obfuscation to let his message blend into the flow of outbound traffic.

The message he wrote was a reference to his name and a vague offer to pass her information in exchange for help. That would have to do.

He hesitated, hovering over the other public channels. Zin would have started her apprenticeship by now. But there was every possibility this escape was going to blow up spectacularly in a couple of weeks, and he shouldn't—*wouldn't*—bring his sister into that.

He left it. He'd done enough to screw up Zin's life as it was.

On day three of Tennal's shining military career, he woke up and knew the fleet was entering chaotic space.

The sense of distorted space hummed around him, no longer the sound of churning waves in the middle distance, but the tide lapping at his doorstep. It was almost like an extra pair of eyes had opened in his mind.

If Tennal tried, he could see the disturbed space around them as clearly as if he were floating outside the *Fractal Note*'s hull. He didn't even have to look at a chart. He could *feel* there was a stable opening into the chaos nearby, hidden behind a veil of clouds, like a tunnel into a cave system. That was where the small constellation of ships was slowly heading.

He and Surit threw themselves out of bed and to their shuttle. Surit took the morning meeting over comms as the *Fractal Note* started to discharge all the small ships it was carrying. In the operations room of Retrieval Two's shuttle, the early shift hummed with a new urgency.

The countdown for entry was still nearly an hour away. "I thought spaceships were fast," Tennal muttered, the echoes of chaotic space tingling like a far-off earthquake in his bones

"Did you hear space was big?" Istara said.

Tennal couldn't even insult them back, because his wristband started pinging urgently. *Movement orders for Agent Fifty-Six,* the ping said. *Leave shuttle and join pilot specialists on* Fractal Note *bridge. Report immediately.*

So the commander wanted to get some use out of his fleet reader, did he? Tennal looked at the ping contemplatively. Istara and Basavi had spent three days running themselves ragged to give him basic pilot training. It would be a shame if they didn't even get any use out of him.

He deleted the ping.

Now free of distractions, Tennal shut his eyes to feel the shape of chaotic space and their entry into it. There were patches of disturbed space floating across the entrance. They'd have to weave around those. He could see it in much more detail than their scanning tools. In fact, given the right chart, he could probably draw it.

After nearly an hour, he had a full chart that felt close enough to the maelstrom outside. He handed the results to Istara.

"I think you might actually be able to help," Istara said. They sounded even more surprised than Tennal felt. "Grab a headset."

Tennal took a headset and tried to process the crowded interface of a real pilot's station. It was three times as complicated as the training interface. He couldn't shut out his mental awareness of the rest of the unit bustling around, like flickers of light behind him, and Surit's locked-down mind moving between them. Surit kept disappearing and reappearing, once with a mechanic in an ex-vehic suit. He looked more concerned every time.

As he approached, Tennal caught his eye and acknowledged him with a half wave of his fingers. *What are you looking like that about?*

Surit gave a tiny shake of his head, a twitch of his shoulders. As clear as saying: *I don't know.* "Status?" Surit said aloud. "Are we in shape for entry?"

Tennal glanced at Istara, who nodded back at him. It seemed a formal query, so Tennal got to his feet. And with the very odd feeling of being a lever fitting into a larger machine, he saluted. "Yes, sir, all correct."

Surit saluted back. Tennal resumed his seat, put on his headset, and sank into a private world with the pilots, the white lines of his chart, and the rapidly approaching vortex.

The roiling chaos outside tingled distractingly on his skin. "How's our course?" Istara said abruptly.

"What?" Tennal said. "You're the pilot."

"You're the reader, aren't you?"

Istara couldn't know about the hot-cold radiation Tennal felt from chaotic space, like spray from a distant sea, but Tennal suddenly realized he *could* do more. Chaotic space was a glow on the edge of his senses, like the faint light he felt around people when he wasn't actively trying to read them. He had been trying to block it out. He could let it in.

Tennal shut his eyes and tried to read the universe.

A vast space opened inside his brain. He had a hazy vision of their shuttle from the outside, as if seeing with something other than his eyes: he sensed the fleet approaching the gap in the mass of distorted space like a handful of birds gliding into the tunnel of a great cliff face.

One side of the tunnel was less stable, its side bubbling gently with distortion. They should probably correct their course. Tennal opened his mouth to explain, but all he heard were some garbled vowel sounds, faint and far off. He raised his hand instead, impatiently, and gestured how they should correct. Operating his body was like trying to move a puppet on a string that stretched across the room, but Lights knew he couldn't get to the delicate controls around his mouth.

Tennal felt as if he had flung open a window and leaned out into a freezing wind. It wasn't *comfortable*—the fabric of his mind was stretched, as if the churning cold of deep space itself were leaching it away—but there was an exhilaration to it, like he was stepping over a cliff. His heart must be thumping. Strangely, he couldn't feel his heartbeat at all.

His shriveled sense of caution sounded a warning bell. Tennal ignored it. He could go further. At a much greater distance, he could even feel the link: not Archer Link Station, but the *link* itself, like a whirlpool, like a maelstrom, its faint currents touching everything else in the sector.

The chill made him sluggish. His thoughts came slow and deep. He was vaguely aware of a blaring alarm sounding back on the ship, and another one, of people tapping and shoving his body, but that was all happening a long way away.

Then an immense and searing presence touched an exposed part of his mind from back in the shuttle. The touch sent lines of fire through his whole being. Tennal felt a momentary exultation: he could draw on this, use the bright strength to ground him and sustain him in the vastness of space, if he just reached out—

As he reached out, he remembered he was primed to sync at

the exact moment that he collided into Surit's controlled machine of a mind. The shock was so great that he opened his eyes.

"—Halkana!"

There was a warm pressure around his wrist. Istara stood in front of him, looking frazzled. Tennal's muscles, coming back online, reported an escalation of forceful attempts to get his attention. But the touch at his wrist wasn't Istara: it was Surit, who was leaning over his chair with a crease of earnest consternation between his eyebrows, rather like, Tennal thought irrelevantly, Tennal was a badly filled-out form that Surit had found himself responsible for.

The mental presence he had felt was Surit.

Surit didn't remove his grip on Tennal's wrist immediately. An alarm whined overhead. Tennal was vaguely aware that the instrument screens were showing an awful lot of red and that half of Retrieval Two had left their stations, but from the increased tingling on his skin, he assumed they'd made it into chaotic space. He looked at his wrist, and Surit looked down as well, as if he'd just remembered he was holding it.

"*Don't do that again,*" Surit said. He let go.

"That's so sweet, boss," Tennal said, mostly as a way of checking if his hoarse voice still worked. "Do you have any idea what I did? Let me know, because I don't." If that was what they expected a fleet reader to do on a regular basis, just to help the pilots with their route-finding, he was surprised he hadn't heard of more readers going mad.

Behind Istara, Basavi pulled off her headset. The short curls on her forehead were damp with sweat, though the room wasn't warm. "We're out of distortion range, sir," she said to Surit. Her gaze skittered around Tennal then landed squarely on his face. "Your trajectory was right, Halkana. Thank you."

"Yeah, if you could not do it in *interpretive dance* next time," Istara said. "I know you know how to quote a relative trajectory. I taught you bloody yesterday."

"I don't teach well," Tennal said automatically. He was distracted by the noise of the alarms, which hadn't stopped, and a ringing noise from whatever he had just done. He had *gotten* things from Surit's mind when it had touched his. Tennal ran his tongue across the back of his teeth as if it had left a taste he could investigate. Surit stored all his surface thoughts neatly, like each one was in a filing tray. Above a driving obsession about something unrelated, Surit was preoccupied with a series of neatly filed concerns about *safety failures.* "Suri—Lieutenant, what's going on?"

Surit's hands were smudged with antistatic oil, and there was a smear of oil on his forehead where he'd wiped it. Tennal belatedly connected *safety failures* to the blaring alarms. "You've been out for an hour," Surit said tiredly. "We're safe, but we nearly lost one of our drives. Yes, I'm coming," he added, to a mechanic who had just tumbled into the ops room and was urgently trying to get his attention. "Check that the code patch uploaded."

Tennal was thrown. "Are we in danger?" He reconsidered and changed it to "Are we *still* in danger?"

"We should pull through, if we can find the last coolant leaks," Surit said. "It's going to take hardware parts and a code push from the rest of the fleet to patch us up. The shuttle's diagnostic alerts were lying to the mechanics. There was something wrong with the safety system."

Tennal hadn't seen that particular tension around his eyes before. Surit, who had spent the past two days diligently checking every comma of the shuttle's documents, had been lied to by his own safety system. Tennal reached out instinctively to read him, and for his pains, he just got Surit's closed-off walls and a sudden stabbing headache that meant he'd massively overstretched his reading abilities. He gave a blasé smile to hide it. "And you've got that in hand?"

"Not yet," Surit said, with the calm focus of a laser beam. "But right now, you're going to rest. I'm going to find out why our ship was falling apart."

"Can I help?" Tennal didn't ever recall offering that before, but, he reasoned, he had a vested interest in surviving this mission. "If the software's wrong, someone didn't check it. I can still read people." Basavi shifted uncomfortably, but it was too late to take it back.

Surit looked at him as if he took the offer very seriously. His intent brown eyes bored through Tennal, apparently noting the signs of pain, the lingering chill, and the bewilderment Tennal couldn't shake after his recent out-of-body trip. Tennal was admittedly not at his best right now, and Surit could *see* it. Tennal gave half a sardonic smile to distract him, but Surit's gaze was like an auger, drilling through every defensive layer of bullshit. "You could sit down for ten minutes and not die of overexertion," Surit said. "That would help. Private Istara?"

"Basavi and I have got him, sir," Istara said callously, while Tennal was still reeling from the brief moment of Surit's full attention. "I'll knock him out if he moves."

CHAPTER 12

"I don't understand, sir," the Retrieval Two mechanic said. He and Surit had scrambled through to the engine niche in the nose of the shuttle. The operations room was noisy and exhausted behind them, the pilots keeping the shuttle on course, Tennal a hair away from collapse by their console. Surit wasn't ready to think about what he had just felt Tennal do. "We should have known if the alert system was going wrong. It has fail-safes."

Surit had seldom used his wristband to keep track of what he had to do. Instead he carried a list in his head, and right now a good half of it was bright red and flashing. "It's not your fault, Private." He didn't understand how the shuttle had been in such bad shape without *him* noticing. He'd spent the two days before this carrying out every standard check. But he'd been using data from the alerts themselves. "Let's get this stabilized and worry about the root cause later."

Even if they hadn't nearly died in chaotic space, and even if Tennal hadn't just tried to throw himself out of his body like a missile with its own self-destruct button, the past hour of frantic patching would still not live fondly in Surit's memory. If they couldn't rely on their shuttle, they were in trouble.

And not only that. Surit couldn't forget their coordinates, like a constant running set of sums he could not make his brain stop performing. They were close to where he'd once calculated the wreckage of his mother's ship must be. Surit was *not* going to die of an accident near the same place his mother had blown up her ship. It would be the worst kind of irony.

It wasn't fair to take out his building frustration on anyone else, so he took it out on his work. Another three coolant fixes and they were through the worst. Surit had done this kind of thing on his last ship, because retrieval units weren't big enough that they could afford for the officer not to pitch in, but he'd never seen an engine fault this bad.

"*Fractal Note* is calling in shuttles, sir."

Surit straightened. That meant conditions were stable enough that the *Fractal Note* no longer needed the extra maneuverability. They could limp back to get their repairs and code patch. He said into his wristband, "Approve return."

He emerged from the engine niche into the operations room just in time to catch the moment they landed. One of the screens showed the open maw of the mothership as the Retrieval Two shuttle coasted up and clicked into its berth. A shudder ran through the flooring.

They were safe for now. The fleet had come to a halt to regroup and reorganize. It sat in a pocket of stable space while around it, like honeycombs, the clouds of chaotic space drifted, combining and recombining to create an unmappable maze of tunnels. Surit glanced at the main screen as he made his way back through the ops room.

Had Marit Yeni navigated the same space? It hadn't been so dangerous back then: chaotic space had grown in the two decades since. The laboratory-station had been on the edge of the disturbance, like a fortress surrounded by a moat, until Marit had tried to seize it and it had been blown apart in the fight. Surit had always known it was part of her plan to seize power, some vague connection to the neuromodification research they'd done there, but now he knew the exact reason. Marit must have been after the remnants.

What were you thinking, Marit? Why did you do it?

"Rotate crew out to eat and rest," he said. "I'll need everyone with maintenance ratings back for a late shift."

"What about us?" a voice drawled from the ops room door. Tennal was between the two pilots and leaning on Private Istara's shoulder reluctantly, as if he'd previously lost an argument with both Istara and his own legs. He looked like a garbage dispenser had just spat him back out.

"Pilots, double break shift," Surit said. "Private Halkana, go to Medical."

Tennal gave him an incredulous look through what Surit guessed was a migraine. "You think a random medic can fix a *reader*?"

"You don't need fixing," Surit said. He had no idea if that was true, but he didn't like the way Tennal said it, as if it were a lost cause. For a moment Surit wished there were another architect and reader pair around so he and Tennal could know what to expect of Tennal's abilities. Then he thought about the sort of architect who would agree to sync a conscripted reader and took back the wish. "You need analgesics. Not shots," he added hastily. "Ask for tablets. It will help."

Tennal looked torn between the dreadful banality of treating his universe-traveling mind with tablets you could buy at a grocery store and his agreement not to contradict Surit in public. "*Ugh*," he said. He made a face at Istara, who bickered with him as they helped him out.

Surit rejoined the mothership and spent some time sourcing materials for the fixes, organizing the code patch, and finding the captain on duty to report to.

When he did find them, Surit was—justifiably—reamed out. He accepted the lengthy censure with a blank stare at the wall. The duty captain was right. Surit had failed at his due diligence, and if they hadn't had Tennal's reading abilities, the consequences could have been much worse than an hour of panicked patching. Something had gone very wrong before Surit and Tennal had even set foot on that shuttle, and Surit hadn't caught it.

"You were lucky," the duty captain said tersely. "If you hadn't had a reader and a pilot specialist on the ship—"

"We didn't," Surit said.

They stared at each other.

"What do you mean?"

Surit had been told he was too detail-oriented, but he couldn't help who he was. "We don't have a pilot specialist."

"Aren't *you* a pilot specialist?"

"No," Surit said, puzzled. Any soldier could be taught the basics of piloting, but the specialists—the ones with years of training— were the smooth, highly educated types who had joined the *Note* at the fleet rendezvous and now sat on the bridge of the mothership, ready to guide the whole fleet through chaotic space. Pilot specialists were for big ships and fighters. You wouldn't find them on a retrieval shuttle. Surit privately thought his new unit's pilots were good, but that wasn't the same thing.

The duty captain frowned. "You must be. Readers are only recruited for pilot specialists."

"No," Surit said.

"Then why did they pick you?" the duty captain asked, nonplussed. "What was the plan there?"

Surit opened his mouth then realized, for the first time in years, he didn't have a reply.

Surit returned to his cabin much later, after a restless few hours overseeing the code patch. The shuttle had no extra room, so all personnel kept sleeping quarters on the *Note*. The lights in his cabin were down, but Tennal wasn't asleep; instead he was sprawled back on his bed, watching a training module on a light-screen over his head. He looked better than when Surit had last seen him. Surit realized he was watching the pale light flicker off the sharp planes of Tennal's face with a gaze that lingered too long. He made himself look away.

Tennal waved the screen aside lazily as he saw Surit come in. "Hey, boss."

"More pilot training?" Surit said. "It's halfway through night shift."

"One of the rankers you sicced on me has this way of looking like the world's going to end tragically if I don't finish this, and I think the other one might actually kill me if I slack off," Tennal said. "Also I can't sleep. Where have you been?"

"I was supervising the maintenance," Surit said, sitting heavily on his bed. He was almost too tired to start stripping his uniform off, but he did it mechanically. Tennal pulled the training module back up in front of his face. "We'll finish tomorrow morning."

"How's it looking?"

"I think we're safe to fly," Surit said. He didn't say, *I don't know what went wrong,* because there was no point unsettling everyone else, but it sat at the back of his throat like a lump. If he didn't know what had gone wrong, it could go wrong again. He pulled his sleep shirt toward him. "If you don't want to be aboard the shuttle tomorrow, you can stay here on the mothership. The commander said you should be spending more time in solo study."

"Fuck that," Tennal said cheerfully. "You don't get rid of me that easily. Want the ops room gossip from when you were at dinner?"

"I thought I asked you to go to Medical," Surit said, his voice muffled in the fabric over his head.

"I went to Medical," Tennal said. "Then I went back to the shuttle to help because I'm a model soldier and deserve a medal. Well, actually I hung around and watched. Half the unit blames the maintenance crew for screwing up, but the rest of them think their last mothership fucked up and gave them a dodgy patch."

It was still completely new to Surit, this experience of having an ally to feed him information, rather than having to run a unit on orders and guesswork. "I've been on that kind of ship," Surit said. It wasn't impossible.

"Mm," Tennal said. When Surit came out of the bathroom, he'd killed the screen entirely and was sitting straight up. The only light was the room's low red safety glow. "That's not the only thing, is it?"

Surit paused, one hand on his locker.

"Go on," Tennal said softly, with the air of someone poking a firework with a match. Tennal had said he couldn't read Surit, and Surit believed him, but Surit's face must be more transparent than he'd thought. "What's on your mind, Surit Yeni?"

"I looked up the other military readers," Surit said carefully.

He hadn't been looking for other readers when he'd started. He'd been looking for information on the sync. Military briefings were a byword for being full of holes and leaving out vital information, but it was incredibly frustrating how little they'd been told. The regulator who'd assigned Surit to the post had given the impression that this was a test period and, after this mission, they'd be given regulator training and guidance, but that seemed irresponsible. As far as the regulators knew, he and Tennal had already synced. What if they'd done it wrong? Didn't the regulators care?

Surit had scoured all the networks he had access to for more about readers, but the only mention in general military guidance was a note that synced readers must receive orders through their designated architect. Public networks had an array of lurid dramas about syncing, which didn't really help. There were rumors that had entered popular culture, some of which Surit recognized—synced architects could write readers with no effort, they couldn't spend too long apart, they died if the sync was broken. The way synced readers could teleport ships, had red eyes, and exploded people's heads from a distance was probably artistic license.

It had taken Surit some time and a lot of stubborn attempts, but eventually he'd found a file full of numbers. And for each number, a unit.

"So . . . ?" Tennal said.

"There are fifty-two synced readers on active duty. Ten of them are with the regulators."

"And the others?" Tennal said. "The fleet readers?"

"They're all synced to pilot specialists," Surit said. "All forty-one of them."

Tennal made the leap easily. "The forty-second is me." His eyes narrowed. "I'm the exception. I should be synced to a pilot specialist, if I'm supposed to be helping with navigation, and instead I'm synced to you. And you don't know why."

"I don't," Surit said. He carefully stowed his clothes and shut his locker. "I've been thinking about it. It would have been very easy to put me in pilot training; it's not as if the army desperately needs me to command Retrieval Two. They want to transfer *you* to help the pilot specialists, but they obviously don't want to transfer me. They just want me to control you from a distance. That doesn't seem efficient."

"Maybe they just don't trust you to drive," Tennal said flippantly.

Surit sat on the side of his bed and looked down at his clenched hands. "Maybe," he said. "They offered me a promotion. They never gave my family Marit's pension; they knew I needed the promotion. I don't know why they picked me. None of this seems normal."

Tennal drew his legs up and loosely wrapped his arms around them. "Did I ever tell you how much time it took?" he asked conversationally. "To get me on this ship?"

Surit shook his head.

"Twelve hours," Tennal said. "Twelve hours for my aunt to get my location alert, arrest me, call her Cavalry connections, find *you*, prime me to sync, hand-wave my enlistment paperwork, and get me bundled onto a ship. She works fast."

The back of Surit's neck prickled. "Your aunt . . . put you here."

"How else do you think I got here?" Tennal said. "Don't blame her too much. I was a nightmare. Am a nightmare. Anyway, the point is, I don't think that's the normal way you recruit a fleet reader. She wanted me off the planet that day and had to find someone to sync me. You were just convenient. Once we finish up this mission, they'll probably stick you in pilot training."

"Maybe," Surit said.

"Or the regulators," Tennal said. "Except I think you'd have to be a lot better connected for that than you obviously are. No offense."

Surit managed a half smile. Tennal had his measure. And he was probably right: Surit had inherited a bad reputation from his mother, but he'd been given Tennal, and a reader who could help with navigation was an *asset*. This couldn't be personal. "None taken," he said. "Good thing you're going to escape before it becomes a problem."

There was a long silence, and then Tennal blew out his breath in harsh amusement. "Yeah," he said. "Good thing."

The next day Tennal didn't mention the conversation. Surit spent the early shift checking on the code patch (successful), the crew (jumpy), and the newly mended drive (radiating innocence, to the extent that hardware could). He could almost forget he was in chaotic space, if not for the way every external viewport had been closed and every screen showed ominous bulges of static.

Tennal accompanied Surit to the morning command meeting. They had fallen into a pattern of not speaking to each other or to anyone else while they got through it. This time, at least, it was short. "We're in range of the last known location of the laboratory," the commander announced. "The far-range scanners will be picking our route for the day. Every piece of debris could be a clue to our target. Shuttles are to take a perimeter position and stand by for retrieval."

"I don't see the other teams volunteering to retrieve anything," Tennal muttered, after the meeting dispersed. "Don't their fancy Resolution scanners do anything useful?"

"Sometimes you need a pair of pliers," Surit said.

Back in the ops room, the shuttle launch was tense. Surit went over and over the checklists in his head: Had he forgotten anything? The drive should be able to handle the load. The alert system was working again. He'd had the maintenance team double-check every diagnostic test and had rerun half of them himself. There was no reason to believe they were in trouble.

Tennal settled back into his seat by the pilots, whom he seemed to have found an equilibrium with based on, as far as Surit could tell, gossip and mutual insults. Surit took the lieutenant's station. "Authorize launch for patrol." The floor shuddered as they slid gradually from the haven of the *Note*'s bay.

"We're out, sir," Private Istara reported. The screens started to blur. "Status clean."

"Want me to check out the landscape?" Tennal asked, leaning back in his chair until his eyes caught Surit's. "Your instruments are crap at showing chaotic space. Let me do the reader thing."

Surit looked down at him. Tennal had an insistent grin and a glint in his eye, as if he'd forgotten that whatever he'd done yesterday had wrung him out into a wet gray rag. A shiver went down Surit's shoulder blades. He'd tried to follow the current of Tennal's mind and guide it back toward his body, and instead he had found himself caught in a riptide. Tennal had welcomed him, pulled him in, as if he'd expected Surit would follow him out to the universe. As if Tennal had instinctively wanted something from *him*. And Surit's first instinct hadn't been to pull back and protect himself from danger—it had been to fling himself forward and sink into Tennal's mind. He'd only just stopped himself in time.

Yet he had to let Tennal practice; navigating was what readers did. This was exactly what the mothership's pilots would want from him. "Later. Wait until we have something to retrieve. And Private Halkana—when you do, be careful."

"*Care* is half my name," Tennal said. "Don't speculate on the other half."

"I mean it. Don't go far."

Tennal gave a ghost of a salute, with the impression that it could have been a rude gesture. Surit was about to return to his station when the shuttle gave a ping.

"They want to cut our patrol short, sir," Basavi reported, sounding as baffled as Surit felt at the news. "Return to dock?"

In the same data burst, Surit and Tennal's wristbands both buzzed. Surit looked down automatically at what could make it do that: a communication of high enough priority that it overrode everything else.

The Archer symbol pulsing on his wristband didn't even make sense at first. Then he realized it was a modified version of Archer Station's stamp. The Archer Station governor.

The instant it came, another order followed on its heels, from the commander:

NO COMMUNICATION IS PERMISSIBLE WITH NON-FLEET OFFICERS. REPORT IMMEDIATELY.

He looked to Tennal, who had his own fingers frozen in a gesture over his wristband as if he knew what this was. He met Surit's eyes unrepentantly.

"Whoops," Tennal said.

CHAPTER 13

It was hard to say who was more in trouble.

Governor Oma, projected at twice life-size on the screen of the flag chamber, was just as Tennal remembered: a serene presence with a close-shaved head and gilt Archer pins at her neck. She sat framed by golden drapes in what must be the station governor's office, a large space with high ceilings built for beauty, not utility. Like Tennal's aunt, she favored a civilian-style wrap-jacket; unlike his aunt, her broad face gave off a general air of benignity, as if the stars were permanently aligned in her favor. "A whole cavalcade!" she said. "Commander Vinys, thank you for joining us! I thought I only placed a call to one of your soldiers."

Tennal, by now a connoisseur of ways to enrage his senior officers, admired the sheer speed at which this made a vein in the commander's cheek twitch. Tennal raised a hand and waved from the spot where he had been told to stand. "I think you were trying to get to me, Governor. Pleasure to see you. How are you?"

Commander Vinys made a curt chopping motion with his hand, and Tennal fell quiet. The flag chamber should have felt larger when empty of its normal audience, only the commander seated at a desk and Surit and Tennal standing, but the commander's rage occupied the whole space like a bad-tempered cloud. "Governor-General Oma."

The face on the screen smiled. Every space station and planetary district had a governor. They should've been a civilian; it was unusual for a serving general to be in charge. But hadn't she mentioned a coup, earlier, when she'd called his aunt? The military took charge where there were problems; it was what they did. Found a power vacuum and filled it.

Tennal wasn't sure what he'd expected from his risky attempt to contact Governor Oma. His anonymizer service clearly hadn't been good enough. As Surit had said, Tennal needed some sort of help if he was going to get out through the link, and there was no love lost between Governor Oma and the legislator: it was possible she might help just to provoke Cavalry Division in general and his aunt in particular.

But mainly, Tennal had no idea what was going to happen. And although the past few days had been surprisingly bearable compared to the rest of his short military career, he'd missed this— the dizzying, toe-curling rush of gently kicking a stone off a mountaintop and seeing which rocks were ready to slide.

Governor-General Oma regarded the commander. Even on what must be the fleet's highest-priority channel, with the Resolution scanners boosting the transmission, it was clearly difficult to get a good signal in chaotic space: parts of her face kept fuzzing out, and her voice was on a slight delay. "In fact, I'm glad you intercepted this call, Commander," she said. Her voice was musical and pleasant; she didn't look like someone who had just put down a coup. "I've been trying to get hold of you for a while. I've been given very minimal information about why you felt the need to take a fleet into chaotic space right next to my station."

"You've been given what you need to know," Commander Vinys said. "That's not what this is about. I'd like to know why you placed a private call to my fleet reader."

Governor Oma ignored that with a tranquil air that, to Tennal's interest, aggravated the commander's twitching vein further. "I don't think I *have* been given everything I need to know," she said. "If all that Resolution equipment destabilizes chaotic space, not only will the disturbance chew you up like a dirt grinder, but the shock wave will endanger the civilians on Archer Link Station."

"My orders come from high command," the commander said, his deep voice measured. "My teams are experts. Your station is safe."

"You may have heard I am trying to deal with a coup on the station," Governor Oma said. "I still have restive elements. Safety concerns aside, it does not *help* to have a military fleet with mysterious objectives right next to my borders."

They stared at each other, the tension broken only by the fuzzing static that occasionally enveloped the projection screen.

"I am retrieving lost military hardware," the commander said. "It's none of your concern."

"Oh, don't try and equivocate, Commander," Governor Oma said. "You're looking for the old laboratory Marit Yeni tried to blow up. The remnants. Who told you to go after them? The legislator?"

Tennal felt Surit flinch, as he did whenever his mother's name was mentioned.

"I don't take my orders from the civilians," the commander said shortly—and, Tennal thought, inaccurately, since the legislator might not directly command the army, but he'd definitely done the legislator a personal favor by getting Tennal out of her way. "If you need to know the details of the mission, apply to high command."

"I will!" the governor said. "I'm so glad we had this chance to talk. Do you also want to tell me what in the infinite annals of Guidance is going on with your fleet reader situation?"

Tennal straightened.

"I have sign-off," Commander Vinys said.

"You received sign-off for two mid-ranking regulators," Governor Oma said. "What you brought on the *Fractal Note,* according to my sources, is a previously unknown Rank One architect and a synced reader. While I am the greatest supporter of our neuromodified soldiers, I agreed to two normal regulators traveling along my borders. Not a reader and a weapon of war."

Interesting. So they were last-minute substitutions. Tennal glanced sideways at Surit. The weapon of war gave a tiny, baffled shake of his head; he hadn't known that either.

"Your 'sources'?" the commander said, in a considering voice like the pressure of thunder on the horizon. "So this is why you were calling my reader."

"No, your reader is not one of my sources," Oma said impatiently. "This is the first time I've seen him. Let me lay out the problems. Your Rank One is a recent graduate. He's barely out of the academy, and he's at least three years away from the regulator's minimum service period for synced architects." She gave Surit the sort of look you got from disappointed relatives, which would have had zero effect on Tennal but made Surit wilt. Tennal would have taken a great deal of vindictive satisfaction in that, four days ago. Now he found he didn't like it.

"And then there's your reader," Oma said, "who doesn't seem to come from anywhere." Tennal raised his eyebrow at her as she transferred her gaze to him, expecting the same treatment. But all he got was a clear, level gaze with a steel core behind it and a question that stopped Tennal in his tracks: "Are you here of your own free will?"

Tennal opened his mouth, then shut it. Wheels in his mind started to spin frantically.

"He's authorized to be here," the commander said.

"He's not," Surit said abruptly, and all the wheels in Tennal's head jammed to a halt. "He's not here of his own free will."

Commander Vinys gave Surit an incredulous look that showed just how much Surit had damaged his reputation as a golden junior officer. "Agent Fifty-Six is on the conscription list. If you want to know why, you can ask the regulators."

Oma tapped her fingers on the desk in front of her. It was an aesthetic surface, covered with milky-white nebulas that swirled like clouds under the movement. "The regulators are notorious for telling people exactly what will benefit the regulators," she said.

Tennal couldn't believe he was hearing this—criticism of the regulators, from someone as senior as this—and had a wild urge to agree with this shorn-headed general with the pleasant stare and the hidden bite under half the things she said. *Take me out of here,* he almost said. *I can work for you instead.*

No, think about it logically, said the cold portion of his brain that always sounded disturbingly like his aunt. Oma didn't have any authority outside her station. The best he could hope for was her help *after* he escaped, and for that, he needed to get through this mission without the commander deciding to handcuff him to his workstation while they were in port.

"If this is why you called—" the commander said irritably.

"Then it's completely unnecessary," Tennal cut in. "I'm perfectly content on the *Fractal Note* at the moment, Governor."

"Does that end this circus?" the commander said. "This is my fleet, *Governor,* however much control you have on your station."

Oma had narrowed her eyes when Tennal said *at the moment.* Good. She might or might not want to help him, but he'd gotten his message across; you didn't rise to governor-general and put down a coup by being slow on the uptake. Tennal ignored Surit's repeated glances at him. Surit should know Tennal would lie when it was useful.

"I see," Oma said, sitting back in her chair. It was dark wood, inlaid with a fan of gold behind her head, and she looked uncomfortable in it. "In that case, I seem to have wasted your precious time, Commander. I do apologize." She smiled, pleasant but unconvinced. "I look forward to the results of your mission."

She didn't spare Tennal or Surit another glance before killing the connection. The wall shimmered back to dull gray.

Suddenly the flag chamber *did* feel empty. Commander Vinys leaned back in his chair and contemplated Tennal and Surit standing in front of him. "So. I don't suppose I have to tell you this threatens the operational security of the mission."

"No, sir," Surit said, before Tennal had time to reply. "No communications will go out from my unit. I'll make sure."

"She mentioned her sources."

Tennal felt the chill of exposure. The last time the commander had accused him of spying, they'd both known it was just a tactic to keep Tennal in line. This time he had more grounds for real suspicion, even if Tennal's initial message to Oma had been as bland as he could make it. But all Tennal had given away was that there was a Cavalry fleet in chaotic space. The rest she must have guessed.

Surit stiffened, apparently not having Tennal's rosy optimism.

But Commander Vinys didn't have time to do any worse, because an urgent alert came from his wristband. "*Sir, bridge reporting,*" a pilot said, as soon as the light-screen came up. "*Course update. The currents have shifted. We think our scanners have found a structure.*"

The pilot officer was trying to sound professionally neutral, but their excitement leaked through. "What size?" the commander asked sharply. Surit had also leaned forward. Tennal couldn't care less about the remnants, but he could see Surit did.

The pilot looked away from the screen as if for information. "*Several modules,*" they said. "*Sir, I think this is it. I think this is the lab you were looking for.*"

Commander Vinys rose to his feet. Tennal and Surit were forgotten as he brought up an all-comms channel. "Summon all personnel to retrieval stations."

Surit saluted, but Commander Vinys ignored him. He narrowed his gaze at Tennal instead. "Not you, Fifty-Six," he said. "*You* report to the pilots on the main bridge. Let's see if you can be any use yet."

CHAPTER 14

Surit was still buzzing with uneasy adrenaline as he pinged his unit to get ready for launch. He wished he could clear his head. It was unbearably distracting, to know how close they were to the laboratory Marit had attacked, but he had to remember Marit wasn't his business: his shuttle and Tennal and Retrieval Two were his business. It was just hard to keep that in mind.

Tennal split off in the corridor, but not before grabbing Surit's wrist and setting up private voice and location channels between their wristbands. "Keep those open."

"Why do I need to track you?" Surit said. "You're staying on the *Fractal Note*. You'll only be on the bridge."

"Lieutenant Yeni," Tennal said, deceptively smooth, "I'll be on the bridge, but *you* are going into deep space in a tiny shuttle. And besides, if you think I'm going to sit with those fuckers on the bridge without an open comms channel to the *one person I trust in this whole Lights-lost fleet,* then please have your cognitive functions checked."

Surit saw his point. He opened the channels.

Tennal threw him a casual salute. "See you on the other side, boss. Give my love to Istara. Bet they'll be disappointed they wasted all that training."

When Surit arrived at the shuttle without Tennal, Istara just said, "Typical! Sorry, sir, didn't mean any insubordination. But it's all right. It looks like conditions are clear at the moment. Basavi's handling the navigation. I'm on tugs."

Istara stood at one of the airlocks to the single-person tugs nestled in the shuttle like eggs under a bird's wing, just as the shuttle itself nestled in the mothership. Basavi had another assistant at the pilot's console. Istara and half a dozen other rankers were suited up; the life support in the tugs was flimsy, and the propulsion would only last a few hours.

"On your mark for launch," Surit said to the comms desk. "Please listen for bridge order." He glanced at their coordinates and regretted it. He wished he'd never traced the wreckage of Marit's ship. He wished he were better at letting things go. He was a regular soldier with a regular job to do, and his mother's history was a distraction.

"I'll take a tug," he added, standing down the ranker at the last airlock.

"Sir, are you sure?" Istara said.

Surit had been trained how to operate the little tug-pods, and he could command as well from one of them as from the main shuttle. It would be better than sitting inactive beside the pilots. *You're distracted,* part of his brain said, but he ignored it. "I'm sure."

"Shuttle launch!" the comms desk sang out.

There was a rumbling from the floor. Basavi pulled up a visualization of the ship and surrounding space: on it, Surit saw the *Fractal Note* disgorge all its ancillary shuttles. The tiny vessels flocked around the mothership like a school of fish, their own shuttle among them.

The screen also sketched a crude version of chaotic space's currents. It looked like the *Fractal Note* was cruising through the eye of a hurricane. On the screen, Surit could see it turn ponderously, its flock of shuttles around it, and ease into a narrow passage that had opened between the currents.

Surit and the others scrambled to get into their single-person tugs. It was familiar in here: cramped and smelling of heavily recycled air. Once he was in his seat and had checked his suit,

Surit opened comms to Basavi. "Tell me if you see any objects on the scan."

Basavi confirmed there were none yet. No facilities, no ships. Surit sat in his docked pod as their shuttle dutifully kept position in the slow-moving flotilla. The pod's rudimentary scanners showed tendrils of disturbed space creeping nearby. They didn't have Tennal to give them the bigger picture of the landscape, and the bridge wasn't sharing any information from the more powerful scanners.

As soldiers on the ground, Surit and his unit didn't need to know, did they? They were just there to obey orders. Surit tapped both his feet impatiently.

"*Does that question apply to me?*" Tennal's dry voice asked. Of course—the open comms channel.

"Yes, please," Surit said. "How is the bridge?"

Tennal paused. "*I'm in the fourth junior pilot's chair. The officers are models of open communication.*" Quieter, into his wristband, he said, "*Everyone here's an asshole. If they wanted me working on the bridge, why didn't they train me here? They haven't even told me to do the reader thing yet.*"

That was odd. But then, the whole setup around Tennal had been odd from the start, and Surit would have to give more thought to figuring it out—but it would have to be later, when he wasn't in the middle of an operation.

"*They've found a solid mass on the scanners ahead,*" Tennal said. "*Could be an old space facility, I guess. They haven't found any energy signatures that look like remnants. Ten minutes away.*"

Surit swallowed. He'd never known his mother. He'd only seen vids. So he'd never know what was going through her head when she decided to take her fleet to that old space facility to seize its remnants or die in the attempt. And she'd managed one of those.

Basavi pinged from the shuttle to tell him the same thing: a dark, modular station was on their long-distance sensors. The flotilla headed toward it, the *Note* at its head.

Marit had never set foot in the damaged facility; she'd blown up in the attack. Her ship would have been sent on a different trajectory. Wreckage in chaotic space often stayed together even after destruction, like detritus endlessly bobbing in a whirlpool. The ship might even be recognizable.

"*Look out,*" Tennal commented. "*Disturbance up ahead.*"

Basavi sent a course-change report. There was a knot of chaos in front of the fleet, drifting across the clear path. The flotilla of shuttles split to avoid it.

Surit sank his hand into the cool filaments of the pod's steering mesh beside him. He made the mistake of checking their position.

The flip side of Surit's good memory was that it was hard to forget things even if he wanted to. He'd worked out an exact set of coordinates, back when he'd been a naive teenager and had thought finding Marit's ship would solve everything. The numbers still blazed in his mind.

They were so close.

Surit kept his eyes on the screens and sensors as patches of chaos flashed past. He had lain awake at night dreaming of what finding her ship might look like. He'd simulated how a ship of Marit's type might fracture, what the pieces would look like from every angle, how the refracted light of chaotic space would hit the metal. The glimpse he might get.

For a single moment, a gap opened in the chaos patterns at the side of the tunnel. The screen showed something beyond. A lump that could be metal.

Surit's free hand hit the launch command for his tug.

"*Sir?*" Basavi said urgently. "*Sir, are tugs launching?*"

The gap was tiny and already closing. If a tug became trapped in the currents of chaotic space it would be torn apart. Surit wouldn't order anyone else to risk themselves. "No," he said. "Just me."

The tug dropped off from the shuttle with just Surit inside. Had that detection really been Marit's ship? Or just a piece of junk from the salvage that the rest of the fleet was flying toward? A deeper part of Surit didn't care. If he didn't try, he would never forgive himself. He flung his pod toward the gap in the currents.

"*Surit!*" Tennal said over comms. "*Guidance fucking Lights!*"

"I won't be long."

"*You're going to get yourself killed!*"

Basavi pinged Surit's tug urgently. "*Sir, you're out of range, and the bridge won't scan your path—*"

"It's all right," Surit said, as he drew on reflexes he hadn't used since training to avoid a strand of disturbance across his path. "Retrieval Two, keep your previous course."

"*You're heading toward a dead end,*" Tennal said sharply. Surit didn't understand how Tennal could see the patterns of chaotic space, but readers were clearly sensitive to them. Or maybe Tennal could see the scanners on the bridge. "*Lights, there's a lot of lag. Can you see a path?*" Tennal hesitated, apparently trying to read off unfamiliar equipment. The pilot jargon was clumsy in his mouth. "*Sternward, about two-ten.*"

Sternward meant in relation to the back of the flagship, the *Fractal Note,* behind him and traveling in a different direction. "I see it." Surit veered to the left, into a tiny gap that had just opened. He shot through it.

His tug ended up in a sudden ocean of silence.

He floated in a clear pocket within chaotic space, a smaller version of the ones the *Fractal Note,* now out of view, was relying on to travel. But this one was nearly entirely cut off from the safe paths. It was a pool of quiet.

And in it, tumbling quietly in an infinitesimally slow rotation, was a huge mass of jagged metal. A module of a ship, broken violently from its place. Still visible on the side—burnt, divided, but still recognizable—was Marit Yeni's twin-star mark.

Surit hadn't really believed he'd get here. He couldn't quite remember how to breathe.

His comms to Tennal were still working. *"Someone's behind you."*

Surit jerked his head around, absurdly, then looked down at his display. Another tug-pod had fallen through the gap. Its identity was Istara's.

"Picks sensible routes, doesn't he? Guidance Lights" came over the comms in Istara's sharpest tones. Then, unconvincingly: *"Sorry, sir, didn't mean for you to hear that. Is this our retrieval? Some kind of ship?"*

Surit's skin was tingling. It was hard to form normal words. "Yes."

The officer part of his brain, the part he'd carefully trained over the years, noted Istara was due a commendation for taking a risky action in support of an officer, that his unit would be wondering where he was, and logical concerns like that. The rest of Surit was entirely disconnected from it. He drew his tug toward the broken ship, anchored it to the side with the tug's spindly crane arms, and attached his tether like someone in a dream.

He vaguely registered Istara following procedure and anchoring next to him, floating out of their pod in their suit. It didn't seem important.

He didn't know what he'd expected to find. This was not a whole ship: it was an unsettling piece of carcass, like a detached limb. Only a quarter circle of the hull remained. Wires and insulation and fragments of flooring trailed out where it had snapped off.

The airlock was broken. It hung half-open.

When Surit let himself down through it, heaving it aside like a manhole cover, the gravity inside had given out as well. Surit floated down a dark corridor at the wrong angle. The only light was the built-in flashlight of his suit.

As he pushed himself down into the bowels of the ship, catching handholds on doorframes and ceiling fixtures, his beam of light illuminated a bare military corridor. Disappointment bit into Surit's stomach. This wasn't the living quarters, or a bridge, or anywhere that looked like it might have something for him. He recognized doors to energy and recycling systems. This was the functional heart of a ship. It could have been any aging Orshan vessel. No trace of Marit's unit remained.

But the last door, on the fractured upper level, was familiar.

That was a flag chamber.

Surit's heart beat painfully as he clambered into it and shone his flashlight around. He was at 90 degrees to the floor. Chairs, anchored to the ground, stuck out on the vertical floor like strange growths. There were no personal effects, no traces of people— everything ephemeral had been sucked out by the depressurization.

"*Surit?*" Tennal said in his ear. Surit ignored him.

Caught in the ruins of the wall below his feet, only a few strides away, was a strongbox slapped with an emergency seal. It was covered with Marit Yeni's twin-star mark. This one was her personal design.

A manual seal. Whoever had shut the box—*his mother*—had touched this with her own hand.

It was cracked. When Surit touched the strongbox, almost mesmerized, it beeped in protest. It didn't accept an emergency salvage key. Or—no, that wasn't it. Marit had set it to accept no key at all. She had never wanted this opened.

Shouldn't have blown yourself up, then, Surit thought. He couldn't parse the emotion attached to the thought. His chest hurt.

The silver strongbox had clearly been caught in a blast from somewhere else, embedding itself in this wall like shrapnel, which was the only reason it hadn't been sucked out into the cloud of debris outside. Surit stared at it, then knelt, clamped one hand to the surface beside it, and used the tool in the suit's wrist to break it open.

A dazzling light cracked from the box, spilling into the darkness of the ruined flag chamber.

It died away almost as quickly, leaving Surit wondering if he had hallucinated it. As it drained away, it was immediately replaced by a buzzing sensation, like a swarm of insects across Surit's skin. Surit barely stopped for a second thought. He levered open the side of the box.

Inside, heaped up like hundreds of shining pebbles, were more galactic remnants than Surit had ever thought existed.

Surit's breath caught. Marit had stolen these.

"The bridge knows you're there now," Tennal reported. *"Someone noticed. They're sending a scanning ship, looks like?"*

Surit did not really care. He picked out one of the remnants. It was a shard like a pearlescent piece of shell. It buzzed through the glove of his suit. He almost certainly shouldn't have been touching it.

Surit didn't know why the back of his throat tasted bitter with disappointment. He'd known his mother had started a coup for power. The remnants could have made more architects for her power base, so it made sense she wanted them. How had she planned to do it? Had she meant to bargain with the Resolution?

Did it even matter, now that she was dead? Her body might've been floating among the debris outside. Surit should have looked for that, not come inside the ship as if it would tell him something about what she'd meant to do.

There was nothing here for him. Only another crime his mother had committed.

"Sir," Istara said urgently over comms. *"Sir, there's a scanning ship from the fleet coming toward us. I don't know what it's fucking doing."* There was a pause. *"It's not slowing down. Lieutenant! Answer!"*

The world gave a shattering crash and turned over.

Surit's back slammed into the ceiling. He clutched the remnant shard in his hand. In the split seconds afterward, his head ringing, he tried to understand what had happened. A new ship must have collided with the wreckage he was in. Why—

"*Brace for recovery!*" Istara said in his ear. Surit choked, the air nearly knocked out of him, as Istara pulled fiercely on his tether. The remnant shard slipped out of his hand and floated into the darkness. Without gravity, the force of the tether yanked him backward, through the doorframe he'd entered, and down the corridor.

Surit fought to right himself. He kicked off the wall as he was pulled backward and grabbed at fixtures to control his momentum. Lights, Istara was right. You didn't stay in an enclosed wreck during a ship crash.

He grasped the edge of the airlock and pulled himself out.

The world spun around him. Surit stumbled and knelt on the hull, clamping himself to the metal below with magnets in his gloves and boots. They *were* spinning. He and Istara clung to the external hull of Marit's old ship, their tugs anchored beside them, while the whole ship tumbled nose over tail from the collision.

"*Snapped out of it?*" Istara craned their neck, scanning the space above them. Their expression through their faceplate was desperate. "*Because this is a really bad time for you to go silent!*"

"I'm okay," Surit said over comms. "Thank you for pulling me back." It had been wildly irresponsible to pick up a remnant with his own hands, even in a suit. It was hard to think straight. He followed Istara's gaze. "What hit us?"

"*That scanning ship,*" Istara said tersely. They detached the end of Surit's tether from the hull. "*What in the Lights' gaze does it think it's doing? It fucking rammed us!*"

The hull under their feet completed another revolution. Surit could see the other ship now, rising into view like the sun, bristling with lights and sensors and long antennae. There were gaps in the lights on its reinforced hull where it had just collided with them. Now it curved toward the edge of their oasis of clear space.

It was one of their fleet's own ships. Surit had watched it arrive at the rendezvous. He had seen the officer who captained it in the canteen.

"*It's coming back!*"

"Withdraw!" Surit said. He pulled himself hand over hand into his tug. Istara was already vaulting into theirs.

The looming bulk of the scanning ship glittered against the dim, churning wall of chaos behind it. As it looped back around, its antennae churned up disturbance behind it, like a plow crossing a field. That wasn't odd. The scanning ships were Resolution tech and had that capability. What *was* unusual were the reckless sweeps it was making, roiling the clear space into something dangerous.

"Ship," Surit said, trying to open comms with it as he and Istara floated their pods off the hull. It wasn't answering pings. "Ship, please respond. Please respond, you are making conditions untenable for—"

"*It doesn't care,*" Tennal said abruptly in his ear. "*Get the fuck out of there, Surit. I don't know why one of our own ships is trying to kill you, but if you stay there, you're both going to die.*"

Istara chimed in with the same thing. Surit watched in sheer confusion as the scanning ship turned and made another run at them.

"*Move!*" Istara said. They swerved their tug out of its path.

The tugs were not fast. Surit tried to follow Istara, but he didn't make it out cleanly. The scanning ship hurtled through the space where they had been, smashing the hull of the ship they had just left.

Surit was nearly caught in the backlash like a riptide. But he'd spent a year doing retrievals. There were some sounds hardwired in his brain: one of them was the quiet creak of his hull as it started to buckle under distortion, which no living retrieval unit had ever ignored. He rocketed away like someone had held an open flame to his skin.

The scanning ship disappeared back to where it had come, trailing a lethal wave of disturbed space-time behind it. Surit had used too much speed to get away. His tug tumbled precipitously toward the wall of true chaotic space, the currents that would tear his ship apart. He fought desperately for control.

Every retrieval unit knew they were always one mistake away from disaster. Get too close to disturbed space and the distortion would bend or crack metal. Soldiers who had been around it said it felt like a sickening change in gravity. A dense cloud of chaos might buckle a ship into pieces. It might age it to brittle fragments or preserve it for centuries. The organic matter of a pilot might also be preserved from aging—but that didn't make much of a difference when that same organic matter was smeared molecule-thick across a cloud of dust. The human body didn't survive.

Surit couldn't avoid the wall of chaos in front of him. He saw his death coming.

"*There's a—there's a—*" Tennal sounded frantic over the comms. "*Surit, I can see— I can— Let me in!*"

A flash of light. A searing pain in his head. And suddenly Surit didn't have control of his eyes anymore.

Tennal's presence was in Surit's head, filling it like a second passenger crammed into a single seat. Surit found himself shoved aside as Tennal grasped at his vision and his hearing.

Surit's first reaction was *terror*.

Tennal was a crashing wave breaking over Surit's thoughts. Outside, in front of Surit's tug, the oncoming wall of chaotic space seemed to slow—time slowed, death slowed—and the incandescent force of Tennal jolted Surit's thoughts into new paths. Surit's second, truer reaction was *euphoria*. He had never felt this alive.

Surit's third reaction was: *Is this a sync?*

The seething force of energy in Surit's mind paused, as if Tennal had heard that thought and hesitated.

But—no. Surit felt it. This wasn't quite a sync. Surit still had defenses, even if Tennal had reached out to flood his mind and Surit had let him in. Surit could visualize it: two hands touching but not clasping.

Even as he had the thought, Tennal was moving again. He had control of Surit's eyes and overlaid them with something else: his reader senses. Surit—Tennal—no, *both of them*—could see the flow of space around them with a startling clarity, as if they'd opened another eye with different vision. Where there had just been clouds, there was now a maze: a set of currents like they were a fish navigating water.

And they could see a way through.

The oasis of clear space was rapidly disappearing behind them, destroyed by the rogue scanning ship. Had it gone haywire? Was anyone piloting it? It didn't make any difference: the only way to survive was to get back to the fleet. "Istara, stick behind me," Surit managed. It felt like he was talking with someone else's mouth.

Better hope Istara's as good as they told me they were, a whisper came inside his head. Was that Tennal?

Surit-Tennal's tug dived into the currents. Surit couldn't tell how he was navigating, only that his knowledge of the controls and Tennal's reader senses gave them a path where there shouldn't be one. He could see Istara tracking him so close, the nose of their pod was nearly in his stabilizers. Surit-Tennal dodged and weaved and rode currents that threatened to smash them apart, until finally—

—finally, they shot back out into the clear paths.

There was no sign of the scanning ship. The *Note*'s fleet was scattered across the tunnel of clear space, much as it had been when Surit left. That was odd. The fleet should have moved on at a constant pace while they were out of sight. Instead they seemed to have halted, the smaller ships anxiously flocking together.

Surit blinked, reaching for Tennal's senses to understand—

"*Get out of my head!*" Tennal said desperately over his wristband.

Surit's mind reared back, horrified. He'd just tried to tighten his mental grip and complete their half-performed sync. He fe

another flash of searing pain, and then he and Tennal were two separate people once more. "Sorry! Sorry."

"No offense taken," Tennal said, though his voice was cracked. Amid a surge of guilt at his mistaken sync attempt, Surit remembered the last couple of times Tennal had used his reader senses. Tennal was probably head down with exhaustion on his console. At least he was awake this time. But after a moment, Tennal said in a different tone, *"Oh, wait. Wait! Lights, I think it's my birthday!"*

Surit noticed the same thing. Istara silently pulled into formation beside him.

The tunnel the fleet crept through snaked deep into chaotic space. Banks of turbulence towered around them, moving so slowly that they looked still. But the flicker of movement Tennal had noticed hadn't come from within the clouds around them: it came from behind, from the clear gap where the Cavalry fleet had first entered chaotic space. A rogue ship.

No—it was more than one ship. The first silver glint arriving at the mouth of the tunnel was followed by another. Then more.

The trickle of ships turned into a flood. Rank upon rank of gleaming warships poured into the entrance of the tunnel. They weren't cloaked in any way. Surit's tug sensors struggled to cope with the onslaught of identity pings; every single ship announced itself as *Archer Division, Archer Division,* one after another in an avalanche on his screen.

They came armed. Surit recognized some of the models and their attachments: holding fields, subduers, even burn cannons. This was a fleet on war footing, come to blockade an unarmed research expedition. And they outnumbered the Cavalry ships ten to one.

"They're from Archer Link Station," Tennal said gleefully. *"It's Governor Oma."*

Surit watched, his breath caught in his throat, as the ships

streamed in. He'd never seen an Orshan fleet in real force. They filled the hollow in the clouds like the stars in the sky outside.

"*Our dear commander crossed the wrong person,*" Tennal said in his ear. "*She must have already had ships on the way.*" He paused, savoring it. "*And Lights, I bet she's pissed.*"

PART THREE

CHAPTER 15

Somewhere, a bird sang. Dappled sunlight filtered into the room through gently waving leaves; the air temperature was perfect. There was coffee, freshly dispensed, by Tennal's bed.

Tennal had not felt *easy* or *comfortable* for quite a long time, so—instead of enjoying the unexpected peace—his brain pulsed with a constant drumbeat of suspicion.

He had nothing to complain about. Everything had come up like roses for him. From the first warning shot Governor Oma's forces had fired, it had been abruptly, starkly obvious that she took the Cavalry fleet's territorial violation more personally than Commander Vinys had expected. Tennal was going to treasure the moment of realization on the commander's face for maybe the rest of his life. The whole research fleet had withdrawn—under protest and under forced escort—to the stately spinning discs of Archer Link Station, where they were now.

Protesting had done the fleet no good, since Governor Oma had sent what amounted to a pacification force. Tennal himself hadn't been the point of it, but once the Archer troops poured on board and the mess turned hostile, all he'd had to do was say, *Tennalhin Halkana—I spoke to your boss,* to the nearest officer, and he'd been waved to a shuttle and treated like a guest. He'd passed out from exhaustion soon after. He didn't know where Surit was.

He should've been *happy*. The whole expedition to chaotic space had been a clusterfuck. Tennal had survived his first mission;

now he was, presumably, a free agent on Archer Link Station, under a governor who was sympathetic, and all his previous commanding officers were in detention. Maybe he could get in touch with Zin, make sure she was safe, then slip onto a link-bound ship and escape to the wider galaxy. Maybe *today.*

"This whole thing," Tennal said out loud, "is a Lights-lost mess."

His wristband flickered at the sound of his voice. After the poky sleeping quarters on the *Fractal Note,* this airy, high-ceilinged apartment was a luxury. Thin windows set high in the wall obviously led to the station's hydroponics facilities, doubling as scenery for high-status residents. The early morning sunlight effects were subtle. Guidances only knew why they'd given this place to Tennal.

Tennal sat on the bed, which had enough room around it that he could have driven a crawler from one side to the other, and drank a fresh cup of coffee that someone else had programmed last night. The one-way glass wall opposite looked out over the interior of the station.

The lower discs of Archer Link Station held docking rings and life-support systems, but the top level was occupied by a permanent residential city. It was covered by a series of soaring environmental domes that provided a blue and hazy artificial sky, kilometers across and hundreds of meters high. Into the domes rose silver towers connected by a web of clear walkways. The city below them was low and compact.

What gave Tennal a jolt were the golden Archer banners hung from every official-looking building: not Archer-sponsored teams or businesses, but the unadorned emblem of the division itself. This was a civilian city. Even Exana, which was a hotbed of division influence, kept the military symbols out of most public streets.

Tennal stared blankly at the banners flapping in a gentle breeze that came from the domes' hazy sky. His first priority was to somehow get a message to Zin. His second priority was to find out where Surit had gone. He opened his wristband to connect to the station network.

A light-screen flashed in front of his face, hovering at eye level. It said: OUTBOUND COMMUNICATIONS BLOCKED. EMERGENCY ONLY.

The universe of possibility narrowed very quickly. Tennal's mouth curled into a slow, unlovely smile.

First things first. He flipped his wristband to the standard room controls and tried the door. It was disabled, as he had half expected.

Whoever had locked him in here had done it with the permission of the governor's forces, which meant the emergency services on Archer Link Station were probably not his friends. On the other hand, he might as well start as he meant to go on.

He pressed the emergency button.

The screen flashed red. For an instant it showed a harassed-looking emergency operative, then the picture flickered out. It was replaced with a smooth man in a captain's uniform.

"Good morning," the captain said. "Is there an emergency?"

"I'm out of coffee," Tennal said.

The captain gave him a polite smile. "Apologies, sir," he said, which Tennal certainly wasn't expecting. "I'll send someone to refill the machine. Breakfast is on the way. Anything else I can get you?"

"Well, since you asked, I'll have two fried eggs, some fresh sliced fruit—nectarine, maybe, but make sure it's not preserved—some way to get a message to my sister, and, oh yes, a pack of soothers," Tennal said, and watched with incredulity as the captain nodded and made a list. Since Tennal had never let a stroke of luck go by without pushing it further, he said, "Oh, and unlock the door, will you?"

"Is the door locked?" the captain said. "I'm so sorry." Tennal couldn't read him over the screen, but he didn't look sorry. "Your appointment with the governor is coming up anyway. I'll be with you in a minute."

"*Is* it," Tennal said. "An appointment just for me? What an honor."

To Tennal's surprise, the eggs did arrive, sizzling hot, with orange juice that might have been fresh, and a neat pack of soothers on the side of the tray. Tennal stared at the soothers for several seconds before he crumpled up the cardboard and dropped them into the recycling unit in the corner, trying not to even look at his hand. He couldn't. He didn't have *time* to take the edge off. Then he ate the rest of his breakfast quietly, sitting at the room's wide table.

Part of his brain was trying to be grateful. Grateful for luxury and clean clothes, hot food, and for not being treated as a subordinate. For fuck's sake. He stopped eating and pressed his fingers over his closed eyelids until he saw stars.

He'd shaken off most of it by the time the door opened.

At the door was the same captain he'd spoken to on the screen. He was only a few years older than Tennal, with a pleasant face, a fashionable haircut, and an expensive tailored inlay on his wristband. After all this time stuck in the military, the tabs and badges on his uniform now meant something to Tennal. That service mark of crossed wheat stalks was exactly the same as Oma had worn. The border on the rank tab meant he was probably an aide to Governor Oma.

The captain saluted Tennal, which almost certainly wasn't correct. "I'm Captain Enahin Fari. Delighted to meet you." His accent was one Tennal recognized: the private schools in Exana took the children of the elite from the biggest cities across Orshan's three planets and gave their home accents that kind of Exana gloss. Tennal and Captain Fari might have met in class. If Tennal had made friends, and passed exams, and not gone off the rails, he could have *been* this smooth, successful officer in a few years. It was like looking at himself in a parallel universe.

The captain said, "This way, please."

Tennal automatically jogged to catch up. "You realize I'm a—"
He realized with a horrible lurch he'd been about to say *ranker.*
He changed it. "Civilian."

Captain Fari gave a polite nod without breaking his stride. "Yes,
sir." The corridor was hushed and carpeted. This was an expensive accommodation block. The only thing marring it was a burn
gun mark on the wall. Tennal's eyes caught on it, and he thought
about the coup that Governor Oma had mentioned.

"So I'm free to leave, then?" Tennal said.

"Absolutely, sir."

That was a lie. Tennal read the surface impressions coming
from the captain without any guilt at all, because Tennal might
not be conscripted, but he was still technically a prisoner. He got
nothing about himself; Captain Fari didn't know anything about
him. He was just impatient to do his job and deliver Tennal to his
boss. Bafflingly, despite the *sirs,* there was no mockery in him.

There was something bothering Tennal. It took him a moment
to put his finger on it. Captain Fari, like most officers, was obviously an architect. He gave off a corona of light to Tennal's reader
senses—nothing exceptional, only a presence that lay slightly
heavier on the fabric of the universe than a neutral. But there was
something *off* about the light around him. A haze, as if it were
reflected through water. Tennal didn't know what to make of it.

At the end of the corridor, a glass wall showed another vertig-
inous drop over the city. The huge, clear pipe behind it must be
the tube car system: Tennal had seen them before, though nothing on this scale. A panel slid open as a small four-person capsule
arrived outside their floor. Tennal settled into it gingerly.

The tube car accelerated fast. Tennal's breath caught as they
rocketed up the walls of the complex and joined a circle of transport tubes that ran around the dome. While their capsule coasted
along, the city nestled in the station's uppermost disc flashed by
underneath.

Silver towers and streets flickered by one after the other. Despite everything, planet-born Tennal felt an unexpected relief. Archer Link Station wasn't what he was used to, but it was still a *city*: there were neat blocks below them, scores of people walking to work, and tiny glass-enclosed gardens. After almost two weeks on a ship, it was such a relief to be able to see beyond the next corridor. Tennal missed the sprawling messiness of Exana so much that he ached, which was absurd, because he'd run away from Exana the first chance he'd had.

Tennal couldn't see any docks from here. They must be somewhere close, because Archer Station was a staging post for journeys through the galactic link. Orshan's link churned up an unusually large patch of chaotic space around itself, so the station had to be some distance away from the link—if it had been too close, it would have been torn apart. But every ship that went through to the wider galaxy docked here. Tennal just had to find his way onto one.

The tube car coasted down toward a shining set of buildings with official-looking domes and wings. That must be the governor's office. Tennal tapped his fingers on his leg. "You don't happen to know the whereabouts of Suri—Lieutenant Yeni? He's my synced architect, in case no one told you."

Captain Fari gave him a quick, tight smile. "Don't worry, don't worry," he said. "Lieutenant Yeni is under detention with the rest of the Cavalry intruders. He won't be allowed within writing distance of you, or even out of detention. Are you satisfied with that?"

"Am I?" Tennal said blankly. That sounded like Surit hadn't been waking up to a fresh-cooked breakfast. And, of course, they weren't really synced. But Tennal had spent so much effort lying about it that it had become habit. "What are you planning to—"

"The governor will sort that out."

"Oh," Tennal said. "Of course."

Tennal entered Governor Oma's office alone. The first thing he saw was the floor-to-ceiling window looking out onto the sea of space.

He nearly stopped breathing.

The viewing pane stretched across the entire office. Behind it, its vast tendrils uncontained by the field of view, was the pale, eye-watering maelstrom of the link. Tennal stumbled toward the glass. He pressed his hands against it.

The link, in all its star-spanning bulk, moved like spiraling water. Tennal couldn't tell how he knew, since it was so enormous and so far away that its pale clouds looked static. But if you looked long enough, the eye fell into it like a painting of windows within windows, spiraling into an unseen center where all sense of distance and time disappeared. Tennal felt *pain,* a sharp throb into his temple, and, at the same time, a stab of terrified awe like an animal emerging from its burrow and seeing, for the first time, the endless sky.

He wanted to get closer than the glass would let him; he wanted to launch himself into the void. He wanted to drown in it.

"It does take some people like that," a dry, amused voice said from behind him. "Welcome to Archer Link Station, Sen Tennalhin."

Tennal came back to himself slowly, feeling the coolness of the glass under his palms and the softness of the carpet beneath his feet.

He turned.

Governor Oma stood in front of her desk. Her bright, blue-eyed gaze was a bit like being pinned by a sudden searchlight; Tennal fought the urge to step back. Her office suite was a wide, open-plan affair that could have held dozens of people. One curved corner of it was taken up by the golden drapes and formal broadcasting setup Tennal had seen over the comm.

She looked at something on her desk and sighed. Tennal might have imagined the searchlight gaze, because when she looked back up and smiled, she looked trustworthy, the sort of kindly authority you saw on the newslogs, the sort that annoyed Tennal instinctively. She came across to him and made a gesture of greeting, her hand touching her throat. "I should have covered the windows; it seems to be worse for readers," she said. "Welcome anyway. I'm so glad you're safe."

"Governor Oma." Tennal touched his own throat in return. He had to focus. "Thank you for the concern. I'm *also* glad I'm safe. Such a pleasure that neither side of my own military killed me in a horrible misunderstanding over territory. Why, did you think they would? Am I a prisoner, by the way?"

He idly reached out with his reader senses and nearly swallowed his tongue.

Oma blazed white in his vision. Her presence wasn't a soft light; it was a controlled, white-hot furnace. Tennal had never felt anything like it; his half-formed intention to try to read her died on the spot. His hindbrain urgently informed him, like a mouse in front of a mink, that there was a narrow series of choices he could make to survive the next handful of seconds, and attempting to read her wasn't one of them. He didn't think he *could*.

Governor Oma's smile turned sharp. Tennal preferred that. It felt more honest. "You're not a prisoner, Tennalhin," she said. "Sit, sit, you must be exhausted."

She left her formal desk and led him to one of the scattered groups of low chairs on the other side of the suite, near the glass walls that let out onto space. Tennal was still destabilized by the view—he wasn't used to it; he lived on a planet—and picked the chair with its back to the stars. There was a low table between them, decorated with filament-thin lines that rippled like water.

On it was a bowl of fresh nectarines. Tennal did not take one.

"Not a prisoner, really?" he said. "So all those locked doors and blocked networks . . . your engineers up here are just *extraordinarily* bad at their jobs, are they?"

"I could certainly use better staff," Governor Oma agreed gravely. Up close like this, there was a fine web of lines over her face, gathering at the corners of her eyes. "But no." She took a nectarine. She wore a softer, more civilian version of a general's dress uniform today: her tunic was so dark green it was almost black, and the trouser folds draped in the liquid way of very expensive fabric. "In fact, I spent the night debriefing with officers from the *Fractal Note*." Tennal watched her hands as she sliced the skin of the fruit and efficiently broke it into halves. "One thing that came up was you. From what I've been told about your recent history, it seemed unlikely you'd stay in one place for very long, and I wanted to talk to you."

"People often do," Tennal said. "I'm a hot property. In some circles."

Governor Oma continued as if he hadn't said anything. "I understand you've been conscripted."

"Yes," Tennal said. His stomach lurched. "Are you going to send me back?"

Oma had cut a slice of the nectarine but stopped with it halfway to her mouth, looking at him in baffled incomprehension. "Guidance, what do you think of me?" She ate the slice neatly and touched the tips of her fingers to a napkin. "I'm not Legislator Yasanin, and I don't believe in forcibly breaking my own nephew's mind to, apparently, get him out of the way of my political career."

In the moment of silence that followed, she put the sliced nectarine back in the bowl.

Tennal felt transparent. It wasn't a reassuring feeling; in fact, it was excruciating. The way she said it made it sound like the sort of political scandal the newslogs like to report. Tennal could imagine his own picture up on a screen as part of an attack broadcast. "It was more complicated than that."

"It often is," Oma said reflectively.

Tennal should've explained he wasn't synced. He felt prickly and uncomfortable. He had the wild urge to defend the legislator's decisions: he might loathe his aunt down to the nail on her little finger, but he understood and respected how she thought. *You don't know what I'm like.*

Instead he gave Oma a false, earnest smile and said, "I appreciate the sympathy."

"I can see you've come through an ordeal," the governor said, her voice becoming brisk. "I respect that. I have neuromod medics on the station. They can have a look at you and see if there's any way to ease your sync."

"Can they break a sync?" Tennal said, before he'd thought about what that would mean. He could have told her he wasn't synced, but he didn't trust her an inch. The thing he really needed fixed was the priming. He had no idea if that had an expiration date, or if he could find a defense that would stop them from doing it again.

"Not without one or both of you dying," Oma said. Tennal appreciated that she didn't even try to make it gentle. "I believe neuroscience is working on it. But at our current level, no. I am sorry."

Tennal realized what he was doing. He was bargaining. Some small, naive part of him thought there was a way out of this. That he could undo the priming, announce he wasn't synced, and—then what? Go *home*? Go back to Exana and see Zin, somehow overlooked by the legislator, the regulators, and the combined Orshan military?

"Well, this has been entertaining," Tennal said, dragging the remnants of his dignity back together. "Don't get me wrong, I *am* very grateful for your help." Embarrassingly grateful, in fact; Tennal was trying not to think about how much he wanted to latch on to a governor treating him like an equal, like life could be normal again. But Tennal really didn't need any more medics poking around in his head, even to be helpful, and he was aware Oma's goodwill would run out as soon as she got to know him.

"If you could put me in touch with my sister," Tennal said, with his best imitation of *sincere and polite*—Lights, Surit would have been useful here—"and give me passage through the galactic link, I'd be in your debt." That debt would be completely useless to her, since Tennal intended to be on the other side of the galaxy as soon as possible, but Oma knew that. Tennal was trading on the hope that she'd do it to spite his aunt. It wasn't completely far-fetched. His aunt was an appealing person to spite.

Oma rose to her feet. She laid a hand on the glass of the outer window, contemplating the stars beyond. "Let me make you a counteroffer."

Tennal had heard *no* enough times in his life to recognize it. He leaned forward in his chair and discarded his attempt at sincerity. "That sounds fun," he said. "Go on."

Oma ran a hand over her shaved head. "Thanks to the attempted coup," she said, "I have much more on my plate right now than I thought I would. To be blunt, I think you've been wasted."

"In so many senses," Tennal said brightly. "What can I do for you?"

Oma looked over at her desk. "I have had some . . . staffing problems recently." Tennal followed her gaze. He hadn't noticed it, since the room as a whole looked undisturbed, but the surface of the desk was newly marred. There was a long, ugly burn mark right in front of where the desk's occupant might sit, gouged deep into the wood. Somewhere you might fire a burn gun right in front of the governor's face, if you had a lethal weapon and you wanted to intimidate her.

Oma turned back, the stars a milky background to her steel-trap presence. The thrumming in Tennal's bones grew stronger as his gaze was unwillingly drawn past her, out to the distant link. He had to look away. It must be something to do with the reader mutation. He hated not knowing what was going on in his own head.

"I'd like you to take a position as one of my aides-de-camp,"

Oma said briskly. "As a trial. Just to see what you can do when you're given scope for your talents."

"For how long?"

"Yes," Oma said gently, "or no?"

Tennal could play along with a fake military role if he had to. The last one hadn't killed him. He pushed himself to his feet. "Give me a deadline," he said. "It can't be a trial if it goes on forever. And I want a promotion on paper. I'm not spending one more day as a ranker."

"Two weeks," Oma said, as if this were her trump card in the negotiation. She strode over to her desk. Tennal followed. "Rank of captain. Wide-ranging responsibilities for keeping the peace. You'd have your own staff. Let me be clear," she added. "I consider what was done to you illegal. You have sanctuary on Archer Station if you want it. But it will take me a while to arrange passage for you through the link, and I'd like to see what you do when you're not being used as a tool for piloting ships."

Giving Tennal any kind of authority seemed like a bad plan, but that was her problem. "Two weeks," Tennal said. Twenty galactic-standard days. "Very precise. I like it."

A faint alarm chimed on Oma's desk. She silenced it. "Good," she said. "I know you have a . . . chaotic way of operating. I look forward to seeing what you do with a peacekeeping brief." Before Tennal could ask what *that* meant, she held out a bios pad. "You'll need to register your change of division. The *Fractal Note* commander has agreed to your release from Cavalry. All that remains, if you agree, is to enter Archer."

"Oh, Commander Vinys released me, did he?" Tennal said, fascinated. He took the pad and gave it his fingerprint. "Voluntarily?"

"In a way," Oma said, and smiled.

To be fair, Cavalry had given Tennal even less of a choice. He lifted the pad for a retina scan and completed the bios process. An Archer captain. His aunt would spit nails. "You know I'm still synced to a Cavalry lieutenant. Will that be a problem? Cross-division fraternization and all that, not to mention Surit Yeni can write me whenever he wants."

"Ah, yes, that," Oma said. She touched an area of her desk, and the chiming bell sounded again. "Enter."

After a few moments, the door slid open. Two rankers, armed with cappers, stood on either side of a third person: unarmed, uniform disheveled, head down.

The prisoner was Surit.

A shock ran through Tennal. He hadn't ever seen Surit less than fully put together before. Now Surit was in a uniform two days old, a shadow of stubble across his jaw, stumbling to a halt just inside the door. He looked up in naked surprise at seeing Tennal lounging against Oma's desk, then looked from him to Oma warily. As if Tennal had switched sides in more than just name. Tennal bit his tongue before he could say, *No, that's not it—*

"Lieutenant Yeni." Governor Oma's voice was velvet smooth. "Please be seated."

Surit carefully saluted: first Oma, then Tennal, who fought the ridiculous urge to salute back. "Governor," Surit said. His voice was rusty, as if he hadn't used it since Tennal had last seen him.

He avoided Tennal's eyes as he trod heavily across the room and sat in front of Governor Oma's desk.

Tennal had been in Surit's *mind*. He stared at the top of Surit's bent head as if his gaze could burn a hole in it. *Look up.*

"I understand you were the one to locate the remnants," Oma said gently, sitting with her elbows propped on her desk. Surit studied the floor by his own feet. "In a prohibited and unstable area, of course, as a side effect of a dangerous and dubiously legal mission"—Surit flinched—"but where would we be without soldiers taking the initiative? My fleet reports that you wouldn't help retrieve them."

"Remnants are classification level four," Surit said, still staring at the floor. "None of the soldiers detaining me had the authority to take custody of them." Tennal had a fleeting vision of Surit quoting regulations at a boarding party and was absolutely certain that had taken place.

"And did you have the authority to keep them hidden?" Oma said. Surit shook his head without looking up. Oma tapped the desk lightly. "They have been retrieved and neutralized. You will be glad to hear chaotic space is still—just about—stable."

Surit wasn't even going to bloody ask what was going to happen to him, Tennal suddenly realized. He didn't know what they did to soldiers caught in interdivisional spats—probably sent home with a scolding and a demerit—but that could ruin Surit's career, and he wasn't even going to *ask*. This fucking military obedience. Tennal had assumed Surit could take care of himself, but that was only true if other people were playing by the same rules as he was.

Well, Tennal had never agreed to the rules. "What are you holding Yeni for?" he asked Oma, leaning against the desk. "None of his unit wanted to go into chaotic space. They were doing what they were ordered."

Oma didn't take her gaze off Surit. "Yes, doing what you were ordered," she said. "Let's explore that. Lieutenant Yeni?"

Surit finally raised his head. "Governor?"

"You aren't a normal *Fractal Note* soldier, are you?" Oma said. "You were under a double brief from the regulators. Care to tell us what that brief was?"

Surit straightened his back as if reporting, his gaze just behind Oma's head. "Sir. My brief was to sync Tennalhin Halkana, identified to me as Agent Fifty-Six, and hold him ready for orders. I assumed that referred to orders from the fleet pilots. Sir."

Now that Tennal thought about it, it seemed even weirder. Why *not* sync him to a pilot specialist from the get-go? Or make Surit a pilot if they couldn't find another architect?

"And you agreed," Governor Oma said mildly.

Surit's shoulders hunched. Tennal's eyes narrowed: there was no reason not to tell Oma they weren't synced, except for the fact Tennal didn't trust her.

Surit shut his mouth and appeared to rethink something. It didn't look like a pleasant thought. "I agreed."

"Were you aware Tennalhin had not agreed?"

"I became aware of it," Surit said, more quietly. "Later."

"Are you familiar," Governor Oma said, "with the concept of an *illegal order*?"

"Yes."

Oma propped her elbows on the table and leaned forward. "So you knew you could have raised the matter through the appropriate channels and had Tennalhin returned home. You were intimidated by his . . . illustrious relative."

Surit was longer sitting up straight; he had slumped in the chair by invisible degrees. His mouth barely moved. "I suppose so. Yes."

This didn't make any sense. Tennal knew Surit wasn't that good at acting. This sounded like he was feeling actual guilt for something he hadn't even done. "Can I clear something up?" Tennal said clinically. "Lieutenant Yeni has been sickeningly noble about this whole thing, actually. He barely writes me."

"And yet not scrupulous enough to fight your forced conscription," Oma pointed out.

Surit's eyes flickered to Tennal, agonized. Tennal made one last-ditch attempt to read him, but Surit was still a complete void.

Oma's head turned to Tennal, and she raised a quizzical eyebrow, as if she'd felt that attempt. "Is he writing you now?"

Tennal gave her a bland smile. "No. You can tell because I'm much less obnoxious when I'm under write command."

"I'm not writing him," Surit said in a low voice. He'd linked his hands in his lap and was staring at them. "My conduct didn't meet ethical standards. I understand this." Tennal fought the urge to shout at him that he hadn't done anything.

"I'm glad you do," Oma said. "I've added the charge to the list that I'll be taking to Cavalry high command. You are also charged with entering a prohibited area with potential to destabilize local space-time, along with the rest of your fleet."

"I—I did that," Surit said. "I take responsibility. But—Governor. I know I have no right to ask questions, but . . . my unit. Retrieval Unit Two-Eight-Seven." It was a question.

"I'd also like to know where they are," Tennal said.

"Your old unit?" Oma said to Tennal.

"I'm not attached," Tennal said blandly. "I'm just very nosy, and I might have some scores to settle."

"All rankers have been offered a temporary reassignment," Oma said. "I'm not interested in low-ranking soldiers. Archer's only dispute is over the officers."

"So you're sending Surit back to Cavalry?" Tennal said. "You probably should. He can write me if he's here."

"Cavalry will negotiate for their officers," Oma said calmly. "But I understand your concern." She turned her attention back to Surit. "You understand your presence is a danger to Captain Halkana?"

"No," Tennal said.

"Yes," Surit said at the same time.

Oma gave a brisk nod. "I'm going to lay a compulsion on you."

Tennal blinked. A compulsion was an advanced form of writing. Usually a write command disappeared as soon as the architect stopped paying attention, but if they were really strong, they could lay down a command that lingered. It was rare to find an architect who could manage that even on a person with no defenses. There was no way she could lay a compulsion on someone as strong as Surit.

"It's very simple," Oma said, "if I or any Archer officers say the trigger phrase, *stop and report back,* you will stop what you are doing and you will present yourself at this office. You will then wait without further movement until I have acknowledged you. Is that clear?"

Tennal opened his mouth to say he didn't really *need* Surit to have a kill switch, but Surit just said colorlessly, "Yes, I understand."

"He's a Rank One," Tennal said. It was almost impossible to even write a Rank One, let alone start laying compulsions. "You're going to find it bloody difficult to—"

Oma wrote Surit.

The architect command came from her like a sunburst. Tennal's vision flooded with white. He could generally sense architect commands even if they were directed at someone else: they felt like a tendril of light, a flashlight beam. This was a supernova. It wasn't even aimed at him, and yet the glare was so bright that Tennal couldn't *see*. This was why Oma had looked like a furnace to his reader senses. She was stronger than Surit.

How was that possible? Tennal had never met someone as strong as her in his life. The white inferno in his eyes grew brighter and brighter. It was painful to look at. Tennal could feel a buzzing sensation in the back of his neck like crawling insects.

Then, like a vent puncturing the pressure, the sensation collapsed. The dazzling light disappeared. As Tennal's vision cleared, he saw Surit with his head in his hands.

Tennal couldn't say, *Surit, are you all right?* His hands gripped the edge of the desk.

Surit slowly and painfully raised his head. "Command acknowledged."

There was a long silence. Then: "Good," Oma said. "Dismissed."

"Can I have a word with him?" Tennal said, hastily pushing himself away from the desk. He remembered at the last moment that he shouldn't look too concerned, so he reached into the simmering resentment that hadn't gone away since he first crossed the threshold of a military ship, and let a flash of malice show. "In private. Unfinished business."

Oma looked at him, but she seemed to buy it. Nobody had ever looked at Tennal and had a problem assigning his motives to low-level malevolence. She turned to Surit. "Captain Halkana is now under the protection of Archer Division. If you write him, even once, I will exile you to a mining ship for the rest of your life. Clear?"

"Clear," Surit said, almost inaudibly. His shoulders were still hunched.

Tennal followed him into the corridor outside, where the two rankers were waiting to escort Surit back to detention. He grabbed Surit by the shoulder, waved the rankers back, and pulled him down the corridor. He shouldn't have been able to move Surit, but Surit stumbled after him as if he wasn't even thinking.

When they were out of earshot, Tennal grabbed Surit by the front of his uniform jacket and shoved him against the wall. Surit didn't resist. Tennal hissed, "Did you forget it was *fake*?"

Surit took a quick, sharp breath and finally met his eyes. "No."

"We aren't synced!" Tennal said, punctuating the point with a shake of Surit's uniform jacket. He might as well have tried to move a rock. "Stop looking like you've murdered someone!"

"Governor Oma was right, though," Surit said quietly. "I should have blown the whistle. I was afraid. I should have refused the order in the first place." His lips twisted in a struggle Tennal wasn't privy to. "Nothing I've done has been right."

"Because we agreed you wouldn't refuse it!" Tennal said incredulously. "Remember that?"

"It doesn't matter now anyway, does it," Surit said reasonably. He wasn't looking at Tennal anymore. He was looking at the bloody floor. This was the first time Tennal had seen Surit *humble* and he found he hated it. It was absolutely unbearable. "The governor will set it right. You'll escape. I'm glad."

"Are you finished, sir?" one of the escorting rankers called, hovering just out of earshot of the hushed, furious exchange. Tennal automatically stopped, waiting for Surit to deal with the distraction. "Only, the governor says to go back in for a briefing when you're ready, and we're supposed to take him back—"

Tennal realized *sir* wasn't Surit this time. It was him.

He let go of Surit. "Yes," he said. "Take him back to wherever you're keeping him. I'm done."

CHAPTER 16

They kept Surit on the *Fractal Note*. The ship was an empty husk attached to the station docks, its corridors silent, its rankers all disembarked and reassigned. The bridge and all ship systems were under the control of a small handful of Archer soldiers. The living quarters were prisons for its ex-officers.

Surit barely noticed he was a prisoner. He had spent longer detained on ship under the previous commander. He was in his original quarters: the tiny room felt empty without Tennal sprawled across the other bed complaining. Surit had noticed that at first. Then he had been summoned to the governor's office and told exactly how unethical his own conduct had been, while a distant, elegant version of Tennal hovered by her shoulder in an officer's green uniform, his profile like a hawk, and disowned Surit. That was probably as it should be. Surit had stopped thinking about Tennal after that.

He hadn't slept since his meeting with Governor Oma yesterday. Instead he sat at the room's cramped desk, staring at the collection of old newslog articles that he had carried on his wristband for years. His articles about Marit.

All of them were two decades old. He'd spent so much time trying to read a story between their bleak, matter-of-fact lines: *Conflict spreads to military bases. Neuromodified "reader" soldiers split from commanders. General Yeni defects. Battle at research laboratory. "This is a reader coup," declares military high command.*

Surit finally let the thought trickle in: *There's nothing here.*

He'd found his mother's ship, and he'd risked both Tennal's escape plans and his own unit to do it, and there was nothing to discover.

What had he expected? A letter from his mother, written just for him? A *confession*?

Surit scrolled through his hoarded newslog records again—dozens of screens, covering every day of the three-month rebellion—and the words blurred.

This whole thing was a dead end. He slumped onto the desk, his forehead against his arm. What if the whole concept of *understanding* was meaningless? Twenty years ago was ancient history. Nobody cared about Marit Yeni anymore.

And here he was, thinking he would do good where his mother hadn't, while he'd failed his unit and failed to help Tennal. Above his head, an address system reminded him that Archer Station was under martial law. Everything repeated. He'd found Marit's ship and *nobody else cared*.

The feed gently chimed, and a newslog reader gave a calm reminder about the legal purposes for civilians to gather on station decks.

If Cavalry and Archer high command couldn't agree on what was right, then what *was* right? Surit had been given responsibility for other people, and he couldn't even do the right thing for them.

This was all it came down to. Surit, in a small room, with no role, no power, no purpose. If the past or the present could be changed even in a small way, it wouldn't be by him. He shut his eyes.

After some time, there was a knock on the door.

A pause. Surit heard it unlock.

Tennal stood in the doorway, looking surprised that it had opened for him. Surit, sluggish from lack of sleep, blinked slowly.

Tennal had acquired a tailored officer's uniform in the two days since Surit had last seen him. He wore it carelessly, the jacket unbuttoned, the collar uneven. All his Cavalry colors were gone. Instead he wore Archer gold on his shoulders, and both his service tab and his personal tab glinted with crossed wheat stalks. Governor Oma's mark.

Tennal swept a look up and down Surit. "Guidance Lights, Yeni, get *up*."

Surit took a moment to rouse. "Tennal?" His voice was dry. "What . . . ?"

"When did you last sleep?" Tennal asked incredulously, pacing across the room with a rangy, electric energy. "Get up! Shave! Wash!"

Something in Surit's head responded to orders. He stumbled to his feet. Tennal caught his arm to stop him from tripping.

Surit looked down at Tennal's smooth, elegant fingers around Surit's crumpled sleeve. His thoughts short-circuited. The jolt helped him shake the fog in his head. "Tennal," he said. "What are you doing here?"

Tennal let go of Surit's arm as if it had suddenly grown spikes. "You're on my staff now," he said. "I'm the world's phoniest captain. I have a transfer order for you and everything. Washstand's *that* way, Lieutenant."

Surit pulled down his sleeve and lurched to the washstand, where he put his entire head under the tap to wake himself up.

When he emerged, shaking the water from his ears, Tennal was pacing up and down the tiny space, talking. He sounded slightly wild, as if he hadn't had much sleep either. ". . . no idea the amount of arguing I had to do. I *said* I already had a lieutenant. They were going to land me with some martinet they'd picked themselves. I told them you were the logical choice. I told them I couldn't sleep—"

"What?" Surit paused midshave. "Why?"

Tennal waved a hand. "The sync, Lieutenant Perfect. Don't you remember all those dramas about synced readers and architects? We're supposed to get antsy if we're apart for too long, and nobody out there can prove otherwise. I'm still giving out that we're synced, by the way, because I don't trust the gossip won't get back to my aunt. I don't trust anyone. Don't let it go to your head, but I need you. You have no idea how far out of my depth I am."

Surit dried his face, struggling to get on top of this. "So . . . you're not escaping?" he said, trying to fit this into his head. "You're joining Archer Division instead?"

"I am still very *much* escaping." Tennal's pacing brought him up against a wall and he spun on his heel. "Our dearly beloved Governor Oma says she'll give me passage through the link if I try out this job. I imagine Oma thinks the power will go to my head and I'll decide to stay and work for her. I know why she's doing it: if the legislator's nephew joins her side, it'll give her something to throw in my aunt's face. Not that I'm averse to that, but I hate being *dependent* on people." As he turned again, his gaze fell on Surit's screen.

Surit's throat tightened as he saw Tennal read the old newslog headlines.

"Your mother's ship?" Tennal said, more quietly. "Did you . . . find anything? Apart from the remnants?"

"No." Surit had to force the word out. There was a miserable prickling in the back of his head. "There was nothing there to find." He had to admit it. "I think there never was."

"Oh," Tennal said, with sudden awkwardness. "I'm sorry."

"It's not important." Surit sat heavily on the bed. He desperately didn't want to talk about it. "Go on. What were you saying?"

"I'm recruiting you," Tennal said. He didn't sit. "Oma's given me a whole district of the station to run. Peacekeeping, comms network, civilian complaints—it all ends up on my desk. I have a whole gaggle of civilian staff and rankers that I don't know the first thing about ordering around. As it turns out, I urgently need someone competent. All I need to do is fake my way through being a captain for another eighteen days, and I need you to help. It will get you out of here," he added temptingly.

Surit took a long, deep breath. "I have a condition."

Tennal stopped in the middle of his pacing. "What is it?"

"I need to know where the rest of our unit is."

"I *knew* you'd ask that. I bloody knew it." Tennal spun again, in an explosion of energy, and threw up an array of vids and still pictures on the wall. Each of them showed a member of Retrieval Two on Archer Station. "I thought of that. Here."

Surit's eyes went from one vid to the other, checking each soldier against his mental list. Most of the rankers seemed to be on patrols; some of them were shown directing ship traffic at a dock; some of them had been assigned to plumbing or maintenance. Private Basavi was frowning at a list of prompts at a terminal. Istara was on a sanitation shift. "I'm trying to get some of them reassigned to me," Tennal said. "But I have this horrible feeling that unless I have you on board, Istara is just going to tell me they prefer unblocking sewers. But Retrieval Two are all *fine,* even if they have been co-opted into dear Governor Oma's power base. Hitch your wagon to the stars and all that. Happy?"

Surit turned over the phrase *hitch your wagon to the stars* in his head. Tennal, when he wasn't high, afraid, or otherwise distracted, had an instinct for political currents that Surit couldn't match. Tennal clearly thought it was important to keep on the right side of the Archer Station governor. "Yes. I think."

"So does that mean you agree?" Tennal said. "I know I'm not an *officer you respect,* but if you can stand to pretend I am for two weeks, I think I can hold things stable. You'll keep your lieutenant rank. All you'll need to do is switch your registration to Archer—"

"No," Surit said.

Tennal stopped. He said slowly, like someone on the edge of a cliff, "What do you mean, no?"

Surit looked at his hands, bunching them together. "My mother was in Cavalry. It's my division."

"*That's* your problem?" Tennal said incredulously. His voice sped up, an edge of panic underneath. "Listen, before she went into politics, my aunt was so high up in Cavalry, she nearly ran it. My gen-parent was a Cavalry dependent, *she's* dead, are we going to have a family tragedy face-off? Your mother wouldn't care! Let it go!"

There was a horrible silence as Tennal finished.

Surit didn't look up. His chest felt hollow.

Tennal dropped onto the bed opposite Surit and put his face on his knees. "I'm sorry," he said. "I'm sorry. That was inexcusable. In my—well, my complete lack of defense—I'm incredibly stressed. Can we forget I said that?"

Surit breathed out. "It's all right." Tennal was right, maybe, though it felt like he'd dug his nails into an unhealed wound.

"Forget the transfer," Tennal said. "You don't have to leave Cavalry. I'll—look, maybe I can find you an adviser role." He straightened and rubbed a hand over his face. "Look. I'm a fuckup, promoted for political reasons, in a deeply shady situation. I don't have the tools for this. I need your help. I need you."

Surit, on a night of no sleep and a career in tatters, felt something under his feet stabilize. "You can command cross-division."

"What?"

"I can stay in Cavalry and work for you," Surit said. "It's not done much, but it's possible. We're all one army."

"You'll do it," Tennal said, sounding almost blank. "You *will* do it, then."

"I'll do it," Surit said. "If Governor Oma goes back on her word, how will you get through the link?"

"I have no bloody idea," Tennal said. "I'm an officer on this station, though—shouldn't that count for something? Maybe I can find out who runs the docks and bribe them."

"Who runs the docks," Surit said thoughtfully. A germ of an idea stirred in his brain. A germ of a purpose. "The best way into any area is to have an officially issued pass. The best way to get a pass is to be authorized on the system that issues them. Didn't you say Oma made you responsible for the comms network?"

"Not the useful bits of it," Tennal said. "Oma has about twenty aides running this place since they took over from the civilians. I'm just the newest. I only have a city district. Nothing to do with the docks."

"Then you need to expand operations," Surit said, thinking it through as he spoke. "Take on more work. Offer to help with other districts. Once you prove you can do the work, believe me, people give you more. We'll just be . . . very good at what we do."

He saw something go through Tennal like a shock when Surit said *we*. "Lights," Tennal said. He suppressed a flash of a smile. "You once told me you just do what you're told, Lieutenant Yeni. I think that might be the biggest lie I've ever heard."

Surit got to his feet, feeling the fog clear in his brain. He saluted.

After a long moment of stunned hesitation, Tennal raised his hand and saluted back.

"Let's see," Surit said, "what can be done."

CHAPTER 17

It was hard to put his finger on it, but even Tennal, who had spent the past year dabbling in underground gambling rings, thought Archer Link Station seemed on edge.

He and Surit emerged into the bright artificial light of the bustling city on the station's uppermost disc. Tennal enjoyed cities, and there was enough novelty about this one to keep his brain ticking over. It was the little things: the lack of road and air traffic, the cool haze of the artificial sky, and the way the food stalls used controlled heat packs and coated their awnings with spongelike absorbers to maintain air quality. Glass boxes rose at crossroads with tall, leafy plants inside them, waving fronds and flowers from their open tops. But there was an edge to the city's bustle, and he could tell Surit felt it as well. Some people on the street withdrew from their uniforms. More than a few soldiers took a close look at Surit's Cavalry tabs.

Tennal added Surit's name to his own accommodation and took him on a quick orientation tour. Archer Link Station's pride and joy were the enormous city-domes where most people lived beneath simulated skies. Below the city, the station had more functional levels that sat underneath it in a series of rings. The docks, where a steady stream of ships left for the galactic link, were on the lowest ring. Tennal hadn't yet figured out a good excuse to get there. Instead he took Surit on a lightning tour of his part of the city: apartment blocks, governing halls, the local food district, and the ever-present tube car system that spiraled up from the floor into all major buildings and residences.

Surit was quiet and kept his head down, but Tennal could see him noting everything around him. There were a *lot* of soldiers. Archer Link Station had always been a military base with a civilian population—the military ran most of Orshan's transport, and the link had to be protected—but normally *governor* was a civilian role. Now it was Governor-General Oma.

That wasn't Tennal's problem. Tennal was here to escape, not to get involved in Archer politics.

As they passed a blaring newslog screen, Surit said abruptly, "What happened to the old governor?"

"Caught embezzling money," Tennal said. "Arrested. Deposed. From what I can gather, they had a bunch of people loyal to them on the station, so their supporters kicked off and started a riot. Tried to put the governor back in office. That was when the army came in to restore order."

"Ah," Surit said. He had that frown between his eyebrows again.

Tennal remembered belatedly that Surit's parent had led the most spectacular failed rebellion in recent history. Attempted coups were probably a sensitive topic. Tennal changed the subject. "Come and see the office they've given us."

Tennal had been set up in a wing of the station's District Hall. The hall was the seat of government found in any Orshan province, though it was small compared to the Codifier Halls that Tennal was used to. Shrines to Guidances and to other deities nestled along the side of the building. Some of them were dark and shuttered.

Inside the hall, the staff barely looked up when Tennal entered. The offices he'd been given were cramped but bright, with a strip of glass windows at head height and colorful banners and stickers littering the staff workstations. Most of the stickers were smaller clubs or obscure sports teams. In Exana, all of those would be affiliated with a division. Here, it looked like the staff had intentionally steered away from announcing any affiliation.

There were whole rooms of people here, dealing with all the steadily turning wheels that made a city of people run. None of them paid attention to Tennal, and Tennal didn't blame them. He wouldn't have liked an incompetent prat parachuted into management either.

"I'm a figurehead," Tennal explained to Surit. He led the way into the back room they'd given him, which had two dozen workstations in it and was completely empty. Decorative banners had been ripped off the wall as people moved out. "The staff members are all civilians. Their executives were too close to the coup and got fired. The supervisors they have left all talk to me in monosyllables, and I don't have a military staff. Well, now I suppose I have you."

Surit looked at the empty office space, with the sad remains of old decorations on the wall, and said, "Hm."

After that, Tennal's empire grew fast.

The first thing Surit did was co-opt two of the fastest civilian administrators from the office outside and immerse himself in the pile of work that had been accumulating since the attempted coup. It was a stack of things Tennal had ignored as unimportant: hauler permits, contract disputes, complaints about soldiers, inquiries about why the district shrines were still shut. Surit started *answering* this pile of nothing.

Tennal had planned to spend the day trying to find out who issued galactic travel permits for his eventual escape. Instead he kept getting pings from Surit with painstaking case summaries of trivial local problems.

"What do you expect me to do with all these?" Tennal demanded, once his wristband started filling up.

Surit gave him a mildly surprised look and said, "Deal with them."

Tennal scowled, skimmed them, and signed off on Surit's decisions. Some of them seemed to need higher authority: Tennal spent an irritated afternoon hunting down Oma's aides—Oma's *other* aides—to find out who could do things like change minor laws and sign off on budgets.

This rapidly endeared Surit to the civilian supervisors. Tennal knew from experience that it was hard to withstand an onslaught of earnestness from Surit Yeni. When Tennal came back, there were ten people in his office all taking instructions from Surit, and three of the previously silent supervisors had gathered at Surit's terminal for an animated discussion. Surit looked up and broke off all his conversations in order to rise to his feet and salute Tennal.

Tennal stopped at the door. He did *not* laugh. Instead he saluted back. "Carry on, Lieutenant."

That night, as he fell into bed across the room from Surit, he said, "You don't have to help me, you know. I feel like I should say."

Surit was quiet for a moment. "You keep telling me this."

Tennal stared at the ceiling, where the shadows of the hydroponic vines outside the window waved in the last of the faint evening light, and didn't know what to add. He clearly hadn't fixed whatever was wrong in Surit's mind. He went to sleep unsatisfied.

Within days, they'd fallen into a double act. Surit, despite his quietness, did all the real work of keeping the district administration on track. Meanwhile Tennal faced off against Oma's other aides, most of whom had the same accent as him and reminded him of the people he'd gone to school with. This wasn't a point in their favor. After the past few weeks, Tennal had no problem smiling, insulting, flirting, and ruthlessly bad-mouthing them to their commanding officers when the situation called for it. It wasn't as if any of this mattered. The military shouldn't be in charge of this kind of civilian outfit anyway, and it couldn't last forever. Tennal would be out soon.

That didn't mean he could avoid all the work. On day three, Surit approached Tennal's ridiculous executive desk and saluted.

Tennal didn't get up from where he was sprawled in his seat, but he waved a vague acknowledgment. Surit seemed more certain in his step. Until now Tennal hadn't realized how much he'd been watching Surit out of the corner of his eye. There was no reason for him to do that anymore, except that it irritated him how Surit wasn't taking up as much space in the room as Tennal knew he should. At least now he had an excuse to look him full in the face. "Yes, Lieutenant Yeni?"

"We don't have enough people to take on the peacekeeping cases," Surit said. "They're all going to the District Five courts, and I think civilians are getting harsher sentences than they should. I need people we can trust." He hesitated. "Our unit."

Tennal hadn't been keeping track of Surit's caseload, but he had an answer ready for *where's our unit, Tennalhin?* "What do you think I've been doing, Lieutenant?" He'd nearly said *boss*—that would have confused everyone. He fanned out a dozen pending applications across his desk. The faces of Retrieval Two stared up at him. "I'm trying to get them transferred to us."

Surit touched the files with a fingertip. "I didn't know—that's good. Thank you." There was something about the way he said it, as if Tennal had found a way to quietly startle Surit. Tennal wasn't sure how he felt about that. It didn't feel fair to surprise someone by meeting the lowest bar possible.

"Anyway," Tennal said, to cover up his reaction, "half of them will refuse once they see it's me in charge and not you. It's obvious that the 'Captain Halkana' setup is fake. Well, all this rank hierarchy is fake, but more so than usual."

"That's not true," Surit said. "You were appointed captain by Governor Oma, who is the highest authority on this station. You *are* a captain. Otherwise all of it is—" He stopped.

Tennal felt like a hunter whose prey had run into a trap right in front of him. Surit made it so *easy* to skewer him. Of course it was all fake.

But, Tennal thought, Surit's alt-parent wasn't fake, and nor was the pension Surit was trying to restore. And the trouble Surit was going to be in when he got back to Cavalry wasn't fake either.

Tennal leaned back in his chair, watched the dismay on Surit's face, and for once chose not to drive the knife in. "All right," he said. "But the whole unit will take a cue from the first-class rankers, and I bet you Istara's going to take one look at my shiny new captain tabs and decide they'd rather shovel algae."

"Istara's an Orshan soldier," Surit said. "They took the oath to the state."

"That doesn't mean the same to everyone else as it means to you," Tennal said. Surit gave him a baffled look. Tennal raised his eyes to the heavens for guidance. "Let me prove it."

"They made *you* a captain?" Istara said.

They were knee-deep in coppery, rust-smelling water when Tennal found them at a water-treatment plant. "It's political," Tennal said, trying to keep his shoes out of it.

"I knew there was something fishy about your whole deal," Istara said. "Legislator's nephew gets synced—*are* you still synced?" They pulled themself out of the channel they were working in and knelt on the tiles at the side. Rusty water ran off their waders. The look they darted at Tennal while they were getting to their feet was too sharp for comfort.

"Why, did you come up with a cure for syncing?" Tennal said. "Your friend Basavi is doing sums in the accounting department. I checked. For some reason Archer thought she came across as more reliable than you. Listen, Archer's given me command of a city district. Su—Lieutenant Yeni says he needs your help."

That gave Istara pause. Tennal did *understand* why people liked Surit more than him. That didn't mean he wasn't going to manipulate it for his own purposes. "So why are you here?" Istara asked.

"It's my transfer request," Tennal said. "I'm the officer. It goes through quicker if you volunteer."

Istara peeled the waders off their legs, giving Tennal an incredulous look as they did it. "So you're here to . . . what, convince me?"

Tennal had notably failed to convince Istara of almost anything in their working relationship so far. "On behalf of Lieutenant Yeni."

"You're a captain now," Istara said. "However you did that—no, don't tell me, it was something to do with your family, wasn't it? So glad you don't have to be a ranker anymore. It must have been killing you not to hang around with your posh friends. You can just give the order, *Captain*."

Tennal took a deep breath—something he regretted in a sanitation plant—and said, not without difficulty, "You and Basavi taught me the basics of piloting. I'm not ungrateful." Basavi and Istara had been casually, acerbically kind when they didn't have to be, and Tennal found that hard to forget. "I'd rather not move either of you around like sacks of rice. It's been happening to me a lot, and I know how it feels, and I don't love it." He didn't say, *Is that enough of an explanation?* It felt like begging. He told himself he didn't actually need Istara. Surit could handle things without more staff.

"I'm in," Istara said. "Can't wait to watch you fuck this up from close quarters."

Tennal took a moment to register this as Istara saying *yes*. The world shifted onto a fractionally better axis. It was on the tip of his tongue to tell them he was only here until he escaped, but—no. He'd brought Surit into his plans because he absolutely had to. He couldn't trust *more* people. "You're welcome. Enjoy the show."

"Take me with you to Basavi's office," Istara said. "I'll tell her to volunteer."

While Retrieval Two, under Surit, managed the administration work and did Tennal the totally undeserved favor of making him look competent, Tennal started to get social invitations.

"I see you're settling in," Captain Fari said cheerfully, dropping by one afternoon at the end of the week. Tennal had seen quite a lot of Fari since he'd escorted Tennal to the governor's office that first time. Fari had taken it on himself to show Tennal the ropes. They both had the same job, after all: a young military officer thrown into managing a civilian district they absolutely weren't qualified to run. Fari seemed to think this was a good thing.

The office was full. People's personal decorations had gone back up as they trickled back in under Surit's encouragement, and the office walls were a jaunty blaze of color. Surit had judiciously hung several Archer banners and then stubbornly put up a Cavalry one. Tennal had bought a striped banner from Zin's favorite nonaffiliated debate team and hung it up, because it felt good to have something around that had nothing to do with the army.

Tennal had met all of Oma's aides now. They were the same type: bright, well-educated young officers who clearly thought Archer Division was a great place for their careers. In another world, Tennal could have met them in Exana's nightclubs. "We're having a get-together in a couple of days," Captain Fari said. "Dinner. Just our crowd. You'll join us, won't you?"

"Your crowd?" Tennal said, leaning back in his chair. He and Surit ate all their meals from food stalls or dispensers, but he knew there were exclusive restaurants patronized by the officers and rich civilians. Captain Fari hadn't even looked at Surit. "If it's for officers, then what about Lieutenant Yeni?"

Captain Fari looked surprised, as if Surit had only just winked into existence. "Oh, well—you can bring who you like," he said. "But not the wrong sort, you know?" He grinned, glanced around Tennal's brightly colored hive of operations, and left.

After he was gone, Surit said, "I'm not much good at parties."

"You do surprise me," Tennal said. "Anyway, I'm not going, so you don't have to."

"If you want to make connections—"

"Not with that crowd," Tennal said irritably. "Can't stand them." That probably wasn't fair to Captain Fari: there was something about his knowing gaze that Tennal didn't like, and Tennal had just enough self-awareness to realize it was something he saw in his own mirror. "Besides, if I ask them for a fake travel permit, they'll report me straight to Oma. They talk about her like there's a Guidance sitting on her shoulder."

He finally looked down at the work screens Surit had floated between them. There was a pile of thirty-seven items for sign-off. "Surit, I think you've forgotten we don't actually work here."

"We do," Surit said. "Work here, I mean."

Tennal shoved the screens around. "Complaints, damage compensation, missing people—Surit, this is not your *job*. They're not going to promote you for doing this when you get back to Cavalry, and Governor Oma doesn't like you."

"These things need fixing," Surit said stubbornly. "We're the only ones here."

Tennal recognized the tone. It was exactly the same obstinate certainty as when Surit had told him, *There is literally nothing you could say to make me sync you.*

Tennal put his head on the desk. "Fine," he said. "Fine."

Surit looked up from one of his work screens, frowning, and said, "I do think Governor Oma should have stepped down by now. Regulations say—"

The door to the outer office was open. "Lieutenant Yeni," Tennal snapped, "shut up."

Surit fell quiet. His eyes narrowed.

Tennal should have seen this coming. Of course Surit would know the regulations about how long martial law should last. But the politics of Archer Link Station wasn't their *business*. They were just passing through. And Lights knew there was nothing two junior officers could do about division-level games. "All right," Tennal said, much more quietly. "I'll help with whatever you think needs it, but don't rock the boat."

Surit hesitated, then nodded. "I'll keep that in mind."

By the tenth day of working with Surit, Tennal felt like he'd been doing this for weeks. Running a small district turned out to be mainly arguing and paperwork, and Tennal was good at one of those. He had a lieutenant with an encyclopedic memory for the other one.

It felt like an acrobatics act. Tennal would pick a fight with another officer over Surit's latest case review, make an outrageous claim—*This is how they do it on Orshan Central*—and Surit would unearth a fact to back it up. Their messages worked in tandem, both increasingly sure the other would catch them if they took a leap. It was a new experience for Tennal. Was this what normal people felt while they were doing their jobs? Surely someone would have told him if politics were more fun than it looked.

He was still working on his escape on the side. His biggest problem was the galactic travel permit: the one time he tried to get one, the system asked for authorizations Tennal didn't dare apply for without knowing who would see the request. He needed to find whoever was responsible for permits and work out how to bribe them.

"It would be morally bad to deep-read my way through the whole station," he said to Surit, in the spirit of testing out the theorem, one morning while they were both cramming down breakfast and hastily dressing.

"It depends on why," Surit said. He was distracted by trying to read two screens and find a lost sock at the same time. Then he seemed to realize what they were talking about and broke off to look at Tennal. "If you knew you were going to be handed back to Cavalry and synced, or if you thought *every* bystander on the station was complicit . . ."

"All right, all right," Tennal said. It was theoretical, since he didn't have the strength to read people on that scale, but he'd known going for bystanders probably wasn't ethical even by his own low standards. He didn't have any leads on who could issue passes. He *had* gone a few layers deep on Oma's other aides, even if he didn't dare read Oma herself, and had gotten nothing but internal Archer politics. "You should hire out your moral consulting services. Get a logo."

"I'll consider it," Surit said gravely. The dignity of the moment was somewhat spoiled by his one bare foot.

Tennal had slipped back into the habit of always having Surit there—when he went to sleep, when they woke up, every day at work—as easily as diving into water. Whenever he thought about it, it gave him a mild jolt of surprise. Tennal had thought his miserable claustrophobia back on the *Note* had been partly because he'd been forced together with Surit. But apparently the problem had been everything else.

Tennal had never been easy to live with. His record with a partner was two weeks, and he'd been sleeping with that guy. But Surit didn't pressure him or bother him. Surit was just . . . there.

Occasionally Tennal caught himself speculating about whether he still had a chance with Surit. Not when Surit came out of the shower or stripped down to his underwear to sleep—Tennal knew what a set of good abs looked like; he could find those anywhere—but when Surit absently passed him the water jug at breakfast, hair askew on his forehead, listening to whatever Tennal was complaining about, or said, "Tired?" with casual concern when they came back in late—then, Tennal was in unexpected trouble.

Tennal had tried moving on Surit once already, back on the *Note*. Surit had said no. The chain of command between them had flipped, but it hadn't broken. Tennal watched the way Surit meticulously drew back from touching him, and avoided looking when Tennal showered or changed, and he knew as surely as reading him that Surit had not changed his mind.

His attempts to forget this at work were thwarted by his own deputies.

"So, you and the lieutenant . . . ?" Istara said, late one afternoon after a particularly long day.

Surit was always *the lieutenant*, whereas Tennal was still, faintly derisively, *Halkana*. Istara leaned back in their chair, under a checkered banner hung by one of the station staff that advertised LOW-GRAV WRESTLING SOCIETY. Surit had tapped Istara and Basavi as his deputies the instant they came back into the unit. Basavi now managed day-to-day operations for two hundred staff members in their office. Istara wrangled freight supplies for the entire district. That was the thing about Surit: he had high expectations, and you found yourself living up to them.

Istara helped Tennal in their spare time. Tennal found himself leaning on them more than he'd meant to. He'd never had people he could rely on before.

Tennal looked blankly at his workstation then realized what they meant. "Me and Surit? Doing what, low-grav wrestling?" That made Istara snort. "We're not. Chain-of-command relationships are against the regulations."

"Yeah, so are all unit relationships," Istara said. "Didn't think *you'd* worry about that."

"I'm an officer now," Tennal said piously, to see if they'd rise to the bait.

Istara made a low, dubious noise in the back of their throat. Tennal wondered if they were going to tell him his rank was fake. "Do you know why the Governor promoted you?"

"I think to spite my aunt," Tennal said honestly. "Politics. But listen, it shouldn't affect you. I know that whatever happens, Surit will make sure Retrieval Two gets traded back to Cavalry. He's stubborn."

"It's not the trading—it's the risk they'll demote us," Istara said darkly. "I've only got three years left, and I don't want to leave at second class."

"Three years?" Tennal had never thought about other people's service periods. "I thought you lot were all in for life. Retiring with gray hair decked out with medals."

Istara lifted their feet up and *thunk*ed them on the terminal. A ring of smaller light-screens circled their chair. "What, are we just one faceless mass to you? I'm out as soon as possible."

"To do what?" Tennal said, fascinated. He'd never actually asked why normal people volunteered to join the army. He'd vaguely assumed it was about power and glory, or about *honor* if you were like Surit and could also ignore what the army actually was.

"Construction," Istara said unexpectedly. They looked at his expression and laughed. "What? My whole family is in the business. I'm the sixth of ten. But you gotta be ex-military to get anywhere with the suppliers, and Cavalry's a decent division. The plan was to transfer to an engineering unit once I got my pilot license."

"But you're still here," Tennal said.

Istara suddenly seemed very interested in the light-screen that held Surit's to-do list. "Well, you know . . . Basavi."

Tennal looked at them, and his mind circled back to *all unit relationships are against regulations.* He probably shouldn't surface-read them, but he did anyway and got an impression of undirected defiance. Tennal could understand that.

"Does she know?" Tennal said.

There was a pause. "Does she know what?"

"That you"—for once in his life, Tennal stopped and picked his words. He could at least not be shitty to the people who'd helped him out—"want a chance. With her. Do you?"

"Oh, *that,*" Istara said, with a wave of relief. Then they seemed to reconsider the relief. "No, of course she doesn't fucking *know.* That would be awkward."

"Who cares about awkward?" Tennal said. "Awkward's temporary."

"Oh yeah?" Istara said. "That works for you, does it?"

"It doesn't *work,*" Tennal said. "Nothing really *works,* I mean—"

"Are you giving me relationship advice?" Istara asked incredulously.

"Fuck no," Tennal said. "Definitely not. You should listen very carefully to whatever I say and then do the exact opposite."

"I got that already," Istara said. "I think the lieutenant's got it too." Tennal made a rude gesture at them, which they returned with a grin.

Tennal thought he'd headed that off pretty well. He couldn't afford to think about Surit. So, instead of obsessing about someone who wouldn't sleep with him or mind-reading everyone on the station for an escape route and turning his brain into a smear of pulp in the process, Tennal threw himself into forging a travel pass.

It was an amateur effort. Even he could see that. He didn't have the key pairs to generate the right encryption stamps, and he wasn't sure how to fake them. But it was his only idea right now, so he worked on it long after Istara had left, late in the evening in his darkening office.

It was at that point that Surit walked in, looking tired. "Tennal, I need a case review."

Tennal looked up. A file appeared on his desk, but Tennal squinted at Surit's face instead. Usually case reviews were traffic fines or minor offenses Surit had decided hadn't been proved. But, going by his face, something was different about this one. "What is it?"

"A citizen in detention has been receiving illegal communications. They're from—" Surit hesitated. "Well. See for yourself."

The file on Tennal's desk glowed red as Surit highlighted an information bubble. Tennal said blankly, "A rights group that advocates for readers."

"Yes."

Something nagged at Tennal as he stared at the file. "Is your prisoner a reader?"

"They must be. I heard about the case secondhand," Surit

said, slightly uncomfortable. "It's not related to our district. But Tennal—it's not illegal to communicate with a legal advocacy group. This isn't right."

Tennal realized why the name of the organization was familiar. "This is *Zin's* reader rights group," he said. "Lights lose it. My sister," he added, by way of explanation. "She just started her apprenticeship. She won't be involved with this—they must have dozens of law shoals in that group, and my aunt would have told Zin to stay out of anything controversial. But it must be legitimate if my aunt let her apprentice there. Surely you can't stop a law shoal from writing to a random citizen."

"That's what I mean," Surit said earnestly. "I think this accusation is being used to coerce the prisoner. I've been through their case, and I think the original imprisonment is on very shaky grounds. It's not our jurisdiction, but you have a brief for comms infrastructure, so I think you could make an argument—"

"Surit," Tennal said, "who is it?"

Surit paused then said, with the same precision as he read traffic reports, "The ex-governor of the station."

Tennal groaned. "Of course it is."

CHAPTER 18

The cell door slid aside with the faint hiss of a reinforced mechanism.

"Careful, sir," the detention guard said. "Are you sure you don't want them brought to an interview room?"

"What can they do?" Tennal said. "You said you had visuals in the cell. And I thought they were a politician, not a street wrestler."

He wasn't expecting what the guard said next, which was "They're a reader, sir. They might see what you're thinking."

"How do you know that?"

The ranker looked surprised. "Everyone knows."

The governor of a whole station, for years, had been a *reader,* and everyone on the station knew? Tennal didn't care about Archer Station's internal politics, but he felt like someone could have told him. "You know what," Tennal said, "I think I'll survive."

Tennal stepped through the door to the cell, Surit at his back, and let it slide shut behind them.

He had gotten the facts from Surit on the way over. Governor Birimi had been ousted for corruption, the same charge they were still sitting in prison to answer for. Oma had taken over to replace them. Birimi's supporters had boiled over a couple of weeks afterward, which had added *treason* to the charge sheet, but Birimi themself didn't seem violent.

The opposite, in fact. Surit reported Birimi had started in community government after leading a hobbyist group of historical fabric enthusiasts, leading Tennal to instantly dub them *Governor Knitting Circle.*

And they were a reader. Tennal wasn't sure why this annoyed him, except he should probably have some kind of commonality with a known reader, and he didn't, and also he wouldn't be caught dead at a historical fabrics society.

The room was a decent size, bigger than the quarters back on the *Note,* but it was clearly a cell. There was a table with a chair, a food dispenser, and a bed. A bunch of flowers on the table gave the room an unexpected splash of color. On the bed, a large person in patterned fabrics had settled down, seated against the wall, their linked hands resting on their stomach, and was taking a nap.

As Tennal came in, their eyes opened.

"Oh, hello," the prisoner said. "They mentioned a visitor."

Tennal examined the ex-governor of Archer Station. Their face was soft and rounded, their expression wary and mildly curious. The clothes they wore were strikingly, pointedly civilian: bright, intricate fabrics layered across each other in an explosion of color, and they wore no gender-marks that Tennal could see.

"I would introduce myself," Birimi said, "but it would be quite strange if you didn't know who you came to visit. You are . . . ?"

"Tennalhin Halkana," Tennal said. "Captain, as a matter of fact. This is Lieutenant Yeni. We work for Governor Oma."

"Oh," Birimi said. "That's a pity."

"Isn't it," Tennal agreed. He hadn't been invited to sit on a chair, so he sat on the edge of the table instead. "It's not entirely voluntary. Sorry to intrude on you. I expect it's a never-ending social whirl here—"

"Not precisely, no," Birimi said, a little wistfully. They didn't even seem offended. Tennal hadn't intended to let himself be interrupted. "I do appreciate visits, though. How can I help you? The charges are false, you know. But I suppose that's a little futile at this point."

Tennal was taken aback at the gently flippant tone, as if this were an old joke. Surit cleared his throat and picked up the conversation.

"Governor." His voice was polite: this was full Surit-on-Official-Business mode. "We're here about your communications."

"Goodness," Birimi said. "Remind me what it was that I did."

While Surit opened a screen and Birimi fumbled with some reading spectacles—most people who didn't want their eyes fixed used floating lenses; Birimi had their lenses set in artistic wire frames, probably because they were the type of person who would organize a knitting circle—Tennal read the room. He didn't get a lot from Birimi. Mild interest, recent regret, a thread of worry. Surit was closed off as normal.

"Ah, yes," Birimi said, squinting at the screen. "That was me. Am I not allowed to talk to rights groups?"

"Not through an encrypted channel," Surit said gravely. "But if you could decrypt the message—"

"No, I don't think so." The refusal was polite but absolute.

Tennal said, "Why not?"

"While I have the deepest respect for General Oma," Birimi said, "I'm not that keen to give her anyone else's messages. I'm not sure what she'd use them for."

Surit paused. "We're not here to accuse any more people."

Birimi blinked up from their seat on the bed. "Aren't you?" they said. "Your colleagues seemed fairly keen on that, after the protests."

"Did you do it?" Tennal asked abruptly. "The theft? The embezzling that got you deposed?"

"Well," Birimi said. "I realize this doesn't sound very credible, but no."

"You don't seem very upset about it."

Birimi scratched their head, dislodging the short curls. "I find you have to take politics as it comes," they said. "I'm sure General Oma can't keep up martial law forever. We had some *very* vicious exchanges in the historical fabrics society, and that was all smoothed over eventually." They glanced over at the cell door. "Of course, craft societies don't have the same facilities."

Tennal finally pinned down why Birimi annoyed him. Everyone Tennal knew had an edge or a hard shell. Even Surit. Even Zin, who had spent as much time around the legislator as Tennal had. But this ex-governor seemed soft through and through. They didn't feel like someone who could *survive* division politics. And they had somehow managed to get themself elected governor as a known reader? It was infuriating.

Surit shot an agonized glance over at Tennal. He recognized Surit in the grip of an ethical quandary. Surit believed Birimi, the same way he'd believed Tennal.

Lights lose it. Tennal cleared his mind and focused his reading more closely on Birimi.

Tennal had only meant to push his way in a little to see if he could pick up any clues. Birimi's mind felt like any normal person's: no flares of architect light, just the baseline of a living being. As Tennal focused, he caught fragments of thought and memory, in unhelpful formless snatches, and then—

—it was like someone had opened Tennal's brain with a crowbar. Something had changed in Tennal's head when he'd used his brain for piloting; a muscle had been used until it strengthened. He'd only meant to push a little way in. Instead he blinked and fell into space.

The room blurred. Only the life-forms in it were visible: Surit, a dim shape; Birimi, like a clear glass vessel filled with light. Tennal reached into Birimi without any effort. It was as easy as breathing.

A mistake. A torrent hit him: incomprehensible images, colors, emotions. And beyond it, a deep well of quiet anger, the knowledge of injustice, and—

"Goodness," Birimi said, the outlines of their mouth moving in Tennal's vision. Their thoughts closed. "You're a reader."

The shock made Tennal lose his grip. His vision snapped back to normal. "You felt that."

"You went very deep. It was almost . . . loud," Birimi said. A frisson of discomfort went up Tennal's back. He understood instinctively what Birimi meant: *loud* in the way architects were loud. "It's quite intrusive, how you do it. And illegal, of course."

They were watching Tennal with mild disappointment. The way they said *illegal* made Tennal feel that what he was really being censured for was being *impolite*.

Reading was not admissible evidence in court. Orshan's judges—none of whom had been in the military more than twenty years ago, when neuromods were created—had collectively decided that tampering with suspects' minds was not a route they wanted their courts to go down. The answers could also be slippery: someone could be on edge because they were lying or because they thought they might be accused of lying. It was a bad way to get at the truth.

Tennal's head was spinning. On balance, he thought Birimi probably shouldn't be in here. As he slowed down the whirling in his head and managed to think in a straight line again, he realized how much he had just screwed up. "I—okay, look, that was—"

Birimi appeared bleakly resigned. "So General Oma is now using readers to interrogate people."

Tennal straightened indignantly. "Lights, it was an accident. I fucked up. I'm sorry."

"Ah, I've triggered the defense condition," Birimi said. "Of course, it was nothing to do with General Oma. She has done everything legally and morally."

"Chances of that are low," Tennal said, with some asperity. He still had his reader senses open: for some reason he caught a glimpse of *surprise* from Birimi. Surely they knew that. "Oma hasn't gotten me to read anyone, though. That was my idea, I meant it to be shallow, and I'm sorry. Though, don't get me wrong, I'm sure Oma would have read you if she could."

Genuine surprise. "Hm," Birimi said. They appeared to relax. "My apologies. It's just that I have encountered some . . . strangeness in Oma's officers. Some odd reactions, maybe not of their own doing. I see that's not the case here."

"Strangeness," Tennal repeated. "What, you think she's writing them? She did put a compulsion on Surit."

"That was different," Surit said unhappily. "That was necessary."

"*Don't* start," Tennal said. "Look, I talk to the other aides every day. I think they'd have noticed if she were writing them. I get that you think you've been screwed over, but this seems paranoid." Also, importantly, not Tennal's problem. He wasn't getting involved in Archer Link Station politics.

"Perhaps I am paranoid," Birimi said, after a pause. "I have a very limited view from here."

"I think you should explain what you meant," Surit said. "You think Governor Oma is writing people?" By this point in their working relationship, Tennal recognized it: the painstaking inevitability of a cat that had been presented with the end of a piece of string; only instead of string, it was a potential injustice. Tennal couldn't even half-heartedly think, *Damn Surit*. It was just how Surit was.

Birimi hesitated. "I recognize this may add to the charges against me," they said finally, "but while I was still in office, General Oma and I had a dispute over some remnants that went missing on their way to the Resolution. I somewhat inadvisably accused her of keeping them, Lights know for what purpose. I think that may have triggered my removal."

Remnants. "Oh no," Tennal said, as he saw Surit's suddenly stricken face. "No, no, no, that does not make us more involved."

"We brought—"

"No," Tennal said. "Listen, this has gone too far, and we're not politicians. You"—he gestured at Birimi—"might have been screwed over. My lieutenant here is a bit like a dog with a bone when it comes to that kind of thing. Or you might be lying to us, honestly, I'm still not sure. But you're trapped here, and if you don't think you should be, well, join the club. Let's not start worrying about *remnant disposal*. What are we, Resolution Auditors? This isn't our business!"

"Ah," Birimi said, giving Tennal an uncomfortably aware look. "You say you're trapped. You were conscripted?"

Tennal hadn't meant to let that slip. "That's irrelevant. *Lieutenant Yeni*." Tennal waved at Surit, who, reassuringly reliable, brought up a screen with the list of illegal communications. "Get the headers, and show me who messaged him."

A palm-sized red seal materialized in the air between them. It was the standard seal of a law shoal, inscribed with the five names of its members. And it was up to date: at the bottom, where the apprentice slot went, was the neat signature *Zinyary Halkana*.

Tennal hadn't seen that before. And Surit hadn't been looking.

"Are you sure you won't decrypt their message?" Surit asked Birimi, not noticing Tennal's expression. "It would be easier to exonerate you."

Birimi's face gave nothing away. "Exonerate me of what?" they said. "Do you think a handful of lawyers could physically break me out of detention?"

"Delete the charge," Tennal said abruptly to Surit. "Make it disappear. I don't care what you have to do." He spun around to face Birimi.

Tennal's sister, unlike Tennal himself, did not get pulled into causes she didn't believe in. Zin had put her own name on a message to a deposed reader governor. Zin thought this was the right thing to do.

"If we got you out of here," Tennal said, "where would you go?"

He caught Surit's sudden astonished stare. But Tennal could

sympathize with wanting to leave. *Tennal* couldn't disappear into the Orshan sector: he had no allies, no documents, no rights groups backing him up. Tennal had to get through the link. But Birimi didn't.

"To friends," Birimi said immediately. "I would just rather be away from General Oma's sphere of influence."

"No promises," Tennal said. "All I can definitely say is we'll squash the communications charge because I don't want my sister involved in this." Birimi was visibly surprised at *my sister*. Tennal didn't plan to give them time to ask questions. "As for you—we'll be in touch. Don't go anywhere."

Birimi blinked and looked around the detention cell. The flowers were the only pleasant thing about it. Tennal wondered what it took to just sit there, knowing your enemy was in power, and patiently send messages until the wind changed. "I wasn't planning to."

Once they were out of the cell, Tennal and Surit said nothing to each other until they signed out of the building. The gates of the detention block crashed together behind them.

It was only when they were walking down the street under the city-dome, fresh air drifting down from the leafy hydroponics floors, that Tennal said, "We don't even know if Birimi was telling the truth."

Surit was silent for a long moment. There was no one on the street but a lone soldier patrolling at the end. Surit's footsteps were loud on the walkway. "Where are the remnants?"

"What?"

"The remnants should have been logged and handed over to the Resolution. The Resolution has the storage to neutralize them— and anyway, it's in all the treaties. Did anyone log them? Where are they?"

Surit had found a loose end and was not going to drop it. And something was nagging at the back of Tennal's mind as well. He didn't care about Archer Link Station, he didn't care about their politics or their power struggles, and he didn't even care about the remnants. But Zin had cared. And Surit cared.

Surit was getting to him.

"All right," Tennal said. "All *right*. I'll ask."

"Thank y—"

"Don't thank me," Tennal said. "You haven't heard how I'm going to find out yet."

Surit shut his mouth and looked sideways at him.

They turned a corner into a busier street. Banners floated in the breeze, advertising shops. Bright signs for bars and restaurants started to flicker into life on the buildings overhead.

Tennal said thoughtfully, "You know how you told me you weren't good at parties?"

CHAPTER 19

The restaurant was as elite and exclusive as Archer Link Station got, and it made Surit uncomfortable.

It occupied the whole top floor of a city block, covered with a glass ceiling open to the artificial night sky. In the hushed and spacious room, lamps shed golden pools of light and groups of couches were scattered over the floor. Carved wooden trays hovered in the air by each diner's elbow. This close to the galactic link, the owners had collected luxuries from outside the sector: Ecivit tree-branch art covered the wall, and underneath it, Nhäine goldwork pots stood next to couches, holding spindly alien flora in individual air bubbles.

Surit didn't belong here at all. He had standard dinner manners from officer academy, but he'd grown up on a small farm, and he knew it showed at places like this. But he didn't even have the chance for an awkward exchange with the doorkeeper, because what he did have was Tennalhin Halkana at his elbow.

Tennal flashed the doorkeeper a lazy smile, said, "Reservation for the group tonight," without even giving his *name*, and the doorkeeper waved them past. That shouldn't have worked. But it was Tennal; of course it had.

Surit had been on this station with Tennal for twelve days. Every single one of them had been like this.

He'd thought he was in trouble when Tennal had been a ranker on the *Fractal Note*. Surit hadn't been able to look away from the controlled chaos then, and he hadn't realized just how much that was Tennal being *discreet*. Now Tennal had a hundred places to channel his energy and Surit couldn't look away. They were working together, they were rooming together, and every time he turned around, there was Tennal—unpredictable and razor-edged, crackling like the end of a live wire. Surit worked in a universe of fixed possibilities. Tennal was a chaos event. Surit was drawn to it like a gravity well.

"Relax," Tennal murmured. "It'll be fun."

"Why am I here?" Surit asked quietly.

Without turning, Tennal gave him a lopsided smile. "Because I need backup. Don't let me get too drunk."

"Halkana!" a figure called from a group of couches. The officers' gathering was scattered over half the room. Tennal's moment of candor was gone as he pulled Surit with him to the nearest group.

Surit started getting looks the moment they slipped in to find seats. Tennal glanced at him, saw his uncertainty, and gave a dark smile.

"This is Yeni," Tennal announced to the group, as he insinuated himself into a space on the couch that was technically too small. "He's my synced architect. Yes, *that* line of Yeni; no, he won't tell you about it, the regulators have to murder anyone he mentions his mother to. Try asking him about military strategy instead. He could probably take over this station with two ships and a textbook. Someone get us drinks—no, not silverberry, does nobody here have any taste, *Lights*, did all of you grow up in a swamp? Here, someone make room."

There was a stunned silence, of the sort that frequently followed Tennal at full bore, and then the woman next to him laughed and waved for someone to pass them a different drinks tray. People shifted aside to give Surit a seat.

And that was it. Surit was in the group now. Someone handed him a tiny glass of something that seemed expensive, while across from him, Tennal proceeded to smile, verbally unsheathe his edges, and suck up all the air in the room.

Surit knew what the plan was. This small, noisy gathering held most of the younger officers who were closest to Oma, though not, of course, the governor herself. Someone here should know where the remnants were. If Birimi had been wrong, or lying, then the remnants should have been logged and sent to the Resolution. *Let's wait until they're drunk and then ask,* Tennal had said clinically. *We need them distracted. That way it's less likely to get back to Oma.*

"So, Yeni," a smiling lieutenant said next to him. "How's the station? You've got the problem district, haven't you?" Surit tensed, wondering if this was about their visit to Birimi, but she immediately clarified, "The traffic, that is. I've got the patch next to yours."

"Oh, that," Surit said, instantly relaxing. He could have talked about traffic patterns all day. If he'd known you were allowed to talk about work at this kind of party, he would have seen the point of them sooner.

They fell easily into a conversation. Surit was getting prurient sideways glances from everyone who passed—Tennal had admitted they were synced; of course that would cause curiosity—but he ignored them. Trays drifted around with sizzling roasted vegetables, seasoned and spiced, and morsels of expensive meat. Surit stopped drinking because it interfered with his ability to sketch an action plan for their joint traffic issues. At one point he had his message inbox up on a screen in front of him and caught an incredulous look from Tennal across the table, but just then Tennal was swept up to visit another group across the room.

There was only one odd moment with the other lieutenant. When they'd beaten the traffic problem into the ground, to mutual satisfaction, and Surit was finally closing his wristband screens, the lieutenant blinked, and a blank look came over her face. Then she looked seriously at him and said, "Halkana must be getting impatient."

It was her voice—Surit should know, he'd been talking to her for twenty minutes—but something was off about it. Some intonation wasn't quite the same.

"Impatient for what?" Surit said carefully.

"I heard he wanted to leave?" the lieutenant said. She glanced over at the gaggle of officers who had moved onto a drinking game—Tennal, of course, in the middle of it. The odd note in her voice was still there, as if her mouth were an unfamiliar shape.

Surit was not an actor, but he could make his voice politely baffled. "I don't think so. He seems to like it here."

For a long few seconds, there was no answer. The lieutenant just blinked. Then her face relaxed. "We all like it here," she said, and smiled in a distracted way. "Excuse me." She stood and wandered away to another of the couch groupings. A tray drifted hopefully behind her.

Surit thought of Governor Birimi saying, *Some odd reactions, maybe not of their own doing.*

Architects could write people temporarily. That was just a risk of living in the Orshan sector. A strong architect could manage a write command that would linger in someone's brain, activating on a certain trigger. But nothing Surit knew of would produce an effect where it looked like someone else was in your head.

Even the suspicion was absurd. Architects and readers were real; brainwashing was a myth. This was just a lieutenant who was very loyal to her commander. That was how the army was supposed to work.

"Hi," Tennal said from behind him. Tennal draped himself over the back of the couch, leaning on Surit's shoulder. Surit was so familiar with the sound of his footsteps that he didn't even jump. It was only a second later that he realized Tennal's face was so close that Surit could feel his breath on his neck, and Surit should probably be feeling uncomfortable. It was alarming— *dangerous*—that he wasn't.

"I'm a little drunk," Tennal said, without moving. He was a

warm weight on Surit's shoulder. Surit couldn't make himself move. "Most of these people are assholes. I shouldn't have mentioned the sync; that's all they want to talk about. Are you having fun?"

"I've solved our traffic issues," Surit said, which was both safe and indisputable.

Surit felt Tennal's laugh on his skin. "Of course you did. Do you want a drink?"

"No," Surit said. He had one thing to focus on this evening. "Give me yours." Tennal passed him his half-finished glass, and Surit replaced it with something nonalcoholic and poisonously sweet. "Try this."

Tennal pushed himself up straight, took a sip of it, and choked. "Ugh. Perfect." He glanced across the room. "Stand by, I'll need you later."

After he'd disappeared, Surit stayed in his seat for a while. The group around him had disappeared, leaving only empty trays hovering above the plush cushions and crescent dishes of fruit, half-eaten. He watched the other officers from a distance.

Birimi had accused Oma of—well, not much, now that Surit thought of it. Birimi had carefully avoided accusing her of anything. They had mentioned that some remnants had disappeared while Oma was in charge of them and that her architects were acting strangely. That was it.

Orshan's scientists had dug a set of remnants out of deep space to make the original architects and readers. It had taken years of research and meticulously built technology. The effect of the remnants had made Marit, they had made thousands of other architects, and a generation later, through inheritance, they had made Tennal and Surit.

Surit had brought more remnants to Archer Link Station. It made him uncomfortable, now, that he didn't know where they were. He had nothing to go on, only nebulous suspicions, but he had brought them here, and he needed to find them.

"Get Yeni to do it," a loud voice said. "You're synced, aren't you?" Surit's head jerked up.

The central group of officers had grown louder and louder. By this point they'd shoved the couches aside to make room for an enormous game board that someone had generated, hovering three feet above the floor and glowing. The owner of the restaurant looked on with wary tolerance. Surit made a mental note to check if officers regularly covered damages here.

Tennal stood at the head of the board, one arm stretched out, looking insufferably smug.

Surit knew this space-battle game. It should have tiny clusters of holographic spaceships crawling across the board like grains of rice. Instead, under Tennal's hand, a whole swarm of game pieces boiled up like locusts. Their tiny guns went off in a miniature firework display. Tennal had apparently not only won, but annihilated everyone. He'd said they needed a distraction: he'd certainly managed to get everyone's attention.

There was no way he'd done that under the legal rules of the game. The board shouldn't even *generate* that many ships.

The rest of the party knew that as well as Surit did. There were yells of protest, and the player next to Tennal hammered on his arm. As Surit made his way over, though, he realized that wasn't all that was going on.

Tennal brought his other hand up in a beckoning motion, as if saying, *Come on, try me.* In between the raucous shouts of *cheater!* Surit saw a few members of the group concentrating, and the small twitching movements Tennal made as he shrugged something off.

Tennal was daring the others to write him. They were trying.

Surit didn't have time to react before Captain Fari—the aide who kept shadowing them—turned around and spotted him. "Here's your *sync*, Halkana," Fari said. "Let's see him try writing you."

"Oh, leave Yeni alone," Tennal said.

"No, no, let's have it out." It sounded pleasant, but there was a note of annoyance under it. There were shouts of support. Tennal was good at riling people up, less good at recovering the situation. "Your defenses are so good that no one can write you, are they? I can't *wait* to see what happens when someone tries it through your sync."

Tennal glanced over his shoulder.

Surit recognized the glint in Tennal's eye as the relentlessness of a rising tide. By now, Surit knew what it looked like when things were about to escalate, because that was what Tennal did every time.

Surit tried to divert it. "That won't be—"

"We're a marvelous curiosity, Surit," Tennal said. His tone was overly sweet. "Let's show these provincials what a sync looks like—everyone here can tell Oma I gave permission. Write me. Tell you what, I won't even look." And he gave Surit his sharpest smile and turned his back on him.

Surit's mouth snapped shut.

Surit breathed out. He wasn't going to write Tennal, however much Tennal pushed. But there was something he could do. He thought of how Tennal's presence had felt when he'd guided Surit out of chaotic space. The edge of a vast expanse. A hint of salty wind, flung spray, a distant ocean.

He opened his hand to tell the onlookers he was writing and touched the primed weak point in Tennal's mind.

"*Lights,*" Tennal said in front of him.

Surit withdrew as swiftly as he possibly could. He opened his eyes, dizzy from the contact, to see Tennal breathing out and dropping his arm, winding up his fake writing performance.

They'd timed it perfectly.

Tennal clenched his fist, and the purloined game pieces on the board turned on each other, destroying themselves in an orgy of gunfire. "Fine, whatever, there you are," Tennal said in a more normal voice. "My forces are all down. Happy now?"

"How did you get that many ships?" one of the other players asked suspiciously. "Was that a reader thing?"

"Hardly. I just tweaked the probability settings when we started the game," Tennal said. With anyone else it might be an attempt at an apology, but Tennal sounded completely unrepentant. "Old trick I learned from a gambling ring."

Tennal had managed to sustain his distraction—every eye in the room was on him. Surit was trying to figure out where Tennal planned to go from here when Fari clapped a hand on his shoulder. "You're impressive, Yeni," Fari said. "You must be a Rank One—why are you just a lieutenant? Let's see you write someone else."

Tennal saw Surit's face. He moved before Surit could: he abandoned his place by the game board and squeezed past a chair to get to them. "Let go, Fari," he said, barely loud enough for even Surit to hear. "Yeni's mine."

Surit let his breath out between his teeth. That was a lie, of course. Surit and Tennal had invented so many lies between them that Surit was losing track. But Fari at least backed away, raising his eyebrows, and didn't tell Surit to write anyone. "I'll leave you to the game," Surit said.

"No, wait." Tennal turned back to the table, pulling everyone's attention to him again. "Lieutenant Yeni will take over my pieces," he announced. "Carry on!"

Surit looked at the board where Tennal had just destroyed all his own ships. "You don't have any pieces."

"I had two leftover scouts in the corner," Tennal said. He added softly, in Surit's ear, "Take them down, Surit."

Surit looked up at the game board and half of Oma's trusted aides watching him. Behind him, Tennal smiled at Fari and took him aside, not quite flirting, but not quite not. Nobody's eyes followed Tennal. Everyone was waiting to see what Surit would do with Tennal's abandoned game. Tennal had created a vortex of attention and then neatly—so neatly—slipped out of it and replaced himself with Surit. And now Tennal was holding a quiet

conversation with the person he'd wanted to interrogate, in a bubble of privacy so complete, he might as well be on another station. Surit doubted he'd planned it. Tennal just took whatever step seemed most likely to work.

But Surit *was* good at games that had rules.

Surit located his scouts. He looked up at the faces watching him and said, "My apologies, officers. Is it my turn?"

It was a long time before the campaign wound up and Surit carefully withdrew Tennal's rebuilt forces to a modest victory. The other players were drunk, which had made it a neat set of predictable outcomes. Real war didn't go like this, of course. This was just a lot of computational rules you could memorize. Surit wondered, sometimes, if he'd been born in a period with real wars or rebellions, if he would have had any talent at that. Then he remembered Marit, who had been so good at it that hundreds of people had died, and his thoughts stopped.

The party was winding down. Tennal emerged from the shadows and pulled him out of the group, his hand loosely around Surit's wrist.

Outside the restaurant, in the mouth of a service corridor, Tennal let go of his wrist and leaned against the wall. "I thought they'd go for that. I'm a genius."

Surit didn't immediately answer. The line of Tennal's throat was outlined in crimson and blue light thrown from a sign opposite. Surit knew his own tendencies, which had nothing to do with gender and everything to do with people who were lightning strikes on dead land. He didn't say, *Are you?*

He said, "How did you guess I played battle sim well enough to keep the attention off you?"

"Ninety-six percent in your exams, and every officer learns it," Tennal said smugly. "You have the right kind of mind. Was I wrong?"

"All right," Surit said, giving in. "You got yourself a private conversation with Captain Fari. What did you learn?"

Tennal raised a finger. "The remnants you found in chaotic space are currently in—totally legal—archival storage. They've been temporarily neutralized. There's a paper trail and everything, Fari thinks. Of course, he didn't know why I was asking, but if they *are* in the station archives, then Oma isn't using them."

"If they are?" Surit said. "There's no way for us to check."

Tennal pushed himself away from the wall and turned toward the clean air of the station dome. "I'm a little drunk," he informed Surit, "and I have a great idea."

CHAPTER 20

The hatch cover came off with a muffled *clang*. Light flooded the tunnel. Surit prudently dropped back down the ladder a couple of rungs; Tennal wrestling with a manual lever was not a picture of carefulness, and his feet were in Surit's face.

"Sorry." Tennal peered down. "Did I get you?"

"I dodged," Surit said.

"You know, your poker face is uncannily good," Tennal said, "for someone breaking several regulations at once."

"Thank you," Surit said mildly. Tennal gave a quiet, surprised choke of laughter as he squeezed through the maintenance hatch. Surit was now used to the way Tennal went for weak points when he was nervous.

It was the middle of the night. The archives building was quiet, nearly deserted. Surit would be lying if he said he weren't also uneasy, but something had changed in his thinking over the past two weeks. There were no answers, the divisions were fighting— why *not* do what was needed? After hours, the archive lighting was dim and blue-tinged, washing out the walls of the corridor. Surit climbed through the maintenance hatch after Tennal and shut it behind them.

"It may be an oversight," Surit added quietly, "but there aren't technically any regulations that forbid us from checking whether some galactic remnants are where they should be. And we have a valid pass."

Tennal twirled the pass on his finger. It was an emergency

electrician's pass that they had discovered, as a captain, Tennal could authorize to himself. "I'll tell them you told me that."

"You're the commanding officer, Captain Halkana. It's your responsibility to know the regulations." Surit counted off doors in his head. Tennal had inveigled a reference number out of Captain Fari, and there were plans of the archive available on the station's government network. "Fifth door to your left, up ahead."

Tennal was halfway down the corridor before he froze and held up a hand. Surit stopped. He heard it too: loud footsteps ringing on a metal floor.

There must be a security guard on patrol. The floors up here weren't metal: the footsteps sounded like the guard was on a catwalk on the warehouse floor below, where they kept the supercooled data cores. Surit trained his hearing on it for long enough to ascertain they weren't on the same floor, then gestured for Tennal to start moving again.

"At least that means there's no one looking at the cameras," Tennal breathed. "Unless that guard has a friend."

Both of them knew they would show up on any cameras. That probably wouldn't matter: as Surit had written painstakingly in his officer exam essays, security cameras were a reliable *audit* control but a poor *real-time* control, because expecting a junior guard to concentrate fully on several dozen feeds for hours on end, night after night, was a losing battle. That meant they'd be caught in a few days if the archivists realized there was something out of place and reviewed the footage. Tennal had grandly declared that to be a future problem.

As Surit listened, the footsteps on the floor below paused, then started again. "We have to be fast," Surit said, ducking his head so he could murmur in Tennal's ear. "That patrol route will cover the whole building."

Tennal was so close that when he turned his head, Surit could feel the warmth of his breath. "Watch me go fast, then." He slipped in the door and beckoned Surit after him.

It took Surit a long moment to move. He couldn't think about how it felt when Tennal was close. They didn't have time.

This storage room was small compared to the warehouse below. It held a series of metal frames that supported crates of all sizes, accessible by rotating belts that brought each one to the front in turn. A tap of Tennal's emergency pass gave him a screen where he entered the crate code. A frame sprung into quiet, whirring life.

The crate it brought forward was as tall as Surit. It hissed to a halt, and the hatch slid open.

Surit couldn't concentrate on looking for remnants. Because inside the crate was a rack of debris and salvage: scraps of metal, bits of fabric. The final remains of the ship Surit had last seen in chaotic space. Marit's ship.

There was no biological matter, of course. That would have been stored separately or sent to the planet for anonymous rites. But amid the panels and chips and parts, there was a heaped pile of old, silvery wristbands.

A wristband was like part of someone's body. These had just been casually slipped into protective bubbles and left abandoned.

But what caught Surit's breath was that he recognized the twin-star mark on one of them.

"Well, shit," Tennal said reflectively.

Surit tore his attention away from the sad pile of dead soldiers' wristbands and followed his gaze.

The remnants box was there. The remnants were not.

"So someone has the remnants," Tennal said. "We weren't just being suspicious bastards. I admit, this is not doing wonders for my paranoia. I wonder if the army offers therapy. I'm great at therapy. What are you—Lights, Surit, really?" He gave Surit a revolted look.

Surit straightened, the twin-star wristband in his hand, extracted from its protective bubble. It should have felt like taking a finger bone from a corpse, but it just felt like what it was: a thin strip of soft metal.

"I think it's Marit's," he said.

"Oh," Tennal said, his tone different. He tentatively reached out and touched Surit's shoulder. Surit recoiled.

Tennal pulled back, chagrined. As he did, the ringing footsteps came back, and they both froze. The direction had changed. Surit pulled up his mental plan of the archives and realized the guard was heading to the elevator.

"Patrol," he said. "We'll have to come back later."

Tennal's mouth curved. "Let's go."

They shoved the crate back and scrambled for the hatch, trading silence for speed. Tennal presented the pass while Surit took over the lever.

"Maybe we should stop and explain," Tennal said in an undertone as the hatch opened. "We might find out firsthand what happened to those remnants—"

"*In*," Surit said, seizing Tennal's arm and bodily pushing him toward the hatch. There were no metal walkways on this level, but he could almost imagine soft footsteps.

And then it wasn't imagination at all. Surit heard a *clank* as a door slid open a few rooms over. Surit threw himself into the maintenance tunnel, clung to the ladder, and shut the hatch in desperate silence.

Neither of them dared move. Surit could hear Tennal breathing on the ladder below. He felt the accidental press of Tennal's hand on his foot.

The guard was doing their patrol in a perfunctory way: only a quick look into each room. Doors slid open one after the other. Surit counted them in his head and held his breath when the guard reached the one they'd just left.

He visualized the room, trying to remember if they'd left anything noticeably out of place, but for once the memory was out of focus. He'd been distracted by the wristbands, and by the way Tennal turned everything else into background.

The door shut again. The footsteps receded to the far side of the building. Surit breathed out.

"Gone?" Tennal whispered from below. He sounded as if he were about to laugh.

Surit *didn't* want to laugh, but Tennal was starting to make him think he did. "I think so, but be quiet."

Tennal was already climbing down, slow and awkward, his feet making muffled sounds on the metal rungs. Surit followed, down several floors of ladders, at one point wordlessly pausing as Tennal ran out of breath.

"Did you ever complete that basic physical training?" Surit murmured, hanging on to the ladder as Tennal got his breath back.

"I wouldn't do it if the Resolution itself told me to," Tennal said. "I wasn't made for exercise. Thank *Guidance*, I can see the ground."

There was a tiny patch of corridor, little more than a landing, behind the heavy maintenance door where they'd originally broken in. The door, Surit suddenly remembered, that had a clear line of sight from the windows that lined the upper floors.

"Don't open it!" Surit said, suddenly urgent, clinging to the ladder.

Tennal stopped in the act of drawing the pass from his pocket. "Why—oh." Tennal apparently remembered the sight lines as well, and came to the same conclusion. "I suppose we'd better give our friend time to get away from this level before we run for it." He slid down to sit on the floor behind the door, his back against the wall.

"I would like to get off this ladder," Surit informed him. "If you could not take up all the space."

Tennal lifted his face to Surit, pale in the wash of blue light, and grinned suddenly. He reached up, grabbed Surit's ankle, and tugged as Surit got off the last rung. He moved over just as Surit stumbled to the ground.

One of Surit's hands landed on Tennal's head to save himself, which Tennal frankly deserved. Surit steadied himself on his feet and crouched next to Tennal in the cramped space.

Tennal tilted his head up when Surit released it. "Poker face still going strong, I see. You weren't worried about being caught."

"I got one hundred and three percent on my covert-break-in module," Surit said. "The examiner wanted to give me a prize after the test but couldn't find me to do it."

He saw Tennal believe him for a split second then catch on, grinning. "Oh, fuck off." Tennal fidgeted until he was leaning more comfortably, pressing back against Surit. "How long can it take to do a patrol?"

Tennal was right there. The lean blade of his shoulders was a warm line against Surit's arm and chest. Surit couldn't think of anything else.

"Tennal," Surit said. That only made Tennal turn to look at him, awkward in their cramped quarters. His face was too close. There was a seditious gleam in his eyes, his cheeks flushed with success.

Surit's memory, unbidden, presented him with a flash from the *Note*: Tennal, his presence like a lightning bolt, pressing his hand to Surit's chest and making an invitation. Tennal had not grown safer. Surit had only come to know him: the one burning star in a system of inert planets, flaring so brightly it was dangerous to orbit. Every layer of him Surit had witnessed was annihilating. Every step he got closer to Tennal was in full acceptance of his own destruction.

Tennal leaned in. They shouldn't do this. Surit couldn't remember why.

Surit closed the gap and kissed him.

Tennal didn't give him any chance to regret it. His returning kiss was fierce, his mouth against Surit's hot and urgent. It crumbled the walls of Surit's ordered thoughts. He had been lying to himself. He had never been indifferent—he wanted this, he wanted Tennal, and there was no space for anything in his head but the hot crackle of energy in Tennal's every movement. Surit gripped Tennal's biceps, urging him closer. Tennal was kissing him, one hand on Surit's neck, and Surit's control was starting to fall apart—

They broke away from each other.

"This is the first time I've ever said this," Tennal said, while Surit tried to gather his reeling thoughts, "but we should, maybe, stop."

Surit couldn't answer. His tongue was clumsy in his mouth. He swallowed.

"Don't take that as me not being into this," Tennal added, apparently both in full possession of his faculties and anxious that Surit shouldn't get the wrong idea. Whatever the wrong idea was, Surit was at least three steps behind and still adrift. "Would I: absolutely. Even more than before. Would I, in a *maintenance corridor mid-break-in*—actually yes, that would be hilarious, but—"

Surit choked with something that wasn't laughter. The aftermath of the kiss still rang in his body. This was an absolute disaster. "No."

"—not my point." Tennal touched his mouth, precisely and deftly, then looked at his fingers as if they were some sort of aide-mémoire. He made an obvious effort to slow himself down. "Surit, I'm leaving." It fell into a silence that suddenly sounded hollower than before. "The great escape. If I manage it, then I'm never coming back to any planet you can legally travel to. And if I don't escape, they'll separate us anyway."

Surit took a slow breath. He could hear the drip of a pipe somewhere far up in the tunnel. He said nothing.

"I have had many bad ideas in my time," Tennal said lightly. "*Not* running would be cataclysmic. Oma will lose this fight to the other divisions eventually, and if the regulators get us back, they'll make us sync for real or worse. And even with a few days to go before I run for it . . . I don't think you'd *do* short-term, would you? I don't think you're the type."

Everything in Surit wanted to say yes, to take what was offered, cup his hands under a firework and try to catch the falling embers. But he knew that wasn't how he was. He knew once he latched on to someone, he would try to hold on to them to the end of time, and that would be messy. His chest hurt. Tennal deserved honesty. Surit shook his head. "I don't work like that."

"Thought so." It was gentle. Tennal was softening his edges for Surit. That only widened the rip in Surit's chest.

Surit should have been sensible. That was who he had been his entire life: he was the dependable one, the one you could rely on not to do something rash. He pulled himself together and buried the part that wanted to fling his whole self at the coruscating sun in his flight path. "No," he said. "You're right. We have to do the job in front of us." *And there's no future for us together.* Neither of them had to say it.

Surit pushed himself up into a crouch, then to his feet. He wasn't unsteady; that was only a lie his brain was telling him. "The exit must be clear by now. We should get back."

Tennal pushed himself to his feet as well—careless, his elbow in Surit's chest, but not getting as close as they'd been before. His back pressed against the wall. "Yes," he said. "Let's not get arrested on top of each other in a maintenance corridor. Think of the paperwork." He gave Surit a rueful smile. "Lead on, Lieutenant."

CHAPTER 21

Surit sat up in bed in the early morning light, dappled through the hydroponics window, and stared at the old wristband.

He hadn't let it go since last night. He hadn't even really taken in that it was *Marit's* wristband. Surit's picture of his gen-parent was a hazy composite of family pictures and vids: his alt-parent, Elvi, had kept them all, as if Marit had never been declared a traitor. Surit had never known Marit, not personally. Elvi had raised him. Surit was a war baby, an old slang term for babies born from soldiers freezing their genetic material just before a big campaign, for their partners or families to raise their child if something went wrong. And, for Marit, something had gone wrong.

Surit wondered if Tennal had been a war baby as well. He was the right age, and his gen-parent must have been a neuromodified soldier.

Surit was putting it off. He brought up his family key and tapped the wristband.

The owner of a wristband could segregate files into compartments for access by someone with the right key, tiny message capsules for if they were dead or incapacitated. The most common one was a public prompt for urgent medical records, but a family key was common as well. Surit tried it.

Two images popped up. One was picture of Marit and Elvi in some tourist spot by a river. Marit, short and squat, looked suspiciously at the camera drone. The second—Surit blinked and stared.

Surit had seen this type of picture before. It was a commemorative shot, the kind you took on a special project. A dozen young officers stared back at him with varying expressions of pride and uncertainty. His mother, barely twenty years old, was in the middle.

That wasn't what had stopped him. Next to Marit—so familiar that Surit had to rub his eyes—was a person who looked almost like Tennal. It took Surit a moment to realize that it must be a younger version of the Orshan legislator. She had Tennal's edged, unsettled air, and an impression that she was uncomfortable with her own sharp face.

Once he'd recognized her, Surit understood what this was. Marit had been one of the first volunteers to be made into an architect. So, famously, had the legislator. This must've been the unit that had gone through the very first neuromodification project.

What he hadn't expected was Governor Oma, around the same age, with her arm slung around the legislator's shoulders.

Surit checked for more files. But that was it. That was everything. If Surit had been expecting some sort of explanation, some sort of confession, he'd been a fool.

As he stared at the wristband, he realized he hadn't tried the public prompt.

There was almost certainly nothing there. People used the public prompt for allergies and emergency medical information, not for anything they might want to keep private. Surit put his finger on the wristband and tried it anyway.

A light-screen opened in front of him. Text spilled into midair—but it was fragmented, unformatted. The underlying files had been corrupted. As if something had been transmitted and shoved hastily in here before its owner did something inadvisable.

—SHOULD PUBLICLY RELEASE INFORMATION ON—WHY HAS NARRATIVE TILTED TOWARD ARCHITECTS V READERS—YOU KNOW THE HISTORY OF THE OPERATION—

—OVER TEN THOUSAND ARCHITECTS AND FOR WHAT—

—HAS FOUND OPERATION NEUROMOD IS NO LONGER VOLUN-
TARY—

—THEY CAN'T JUST TAKE THE LOSING SIDE FOR EXPERIMENTAL
NEUROMOD WORK—

—ABDUCTION OF SOLDIERS UNDER MY COMMAND—THREE OF
MY READERS DIED IN THAT LAB—

That was it. The wristband's reconstruction program, which had been trawling the corrupted data, *beep*ed in resignation. That was all it could recover.

Surit stared at it for a long time.

Three of my readers died in that lab.

Surit was used to seeing his mother's face in pictures and vids. It wasn't as if Surit was grieving any more. He hadn't been for years. It had taken him a long time to come to terms with the fact his gen-parent wasn't the great general she'd thought she was, but just another power-hungry climber.

And now it turned out she wasn't. If this was true. *If* this was true.

Why didn't you tell Elvi that you'd assigned yourself a suicide mission? Surit thought, staring up at her face. Marit had given her life to the army, but she'd lived with Elvi for years and frozen her genes for Surit to be born. *Why didn't you leave any explanation for me? Didn't we* matter?

He looked up as Tennal emerged from the shower, doing up the tabs on the shoulders of his uniform.

"Tennal," Surit said.

He didn't give Tennal a chance to open his mouth. He threw the text onto the wall screen in front of him.

Three of Marit's readers died in that lab.

It played through Surit's head on loop. Three of Marit's people had died—read: had been *killed*—in the neuromodification experiments in that lab. They hadn't stopped at making the first neuromods. They'd moved on to new experiments, and they'd taken readers to do it, and those readers had died. Marit might not have been trying to seize power. She might have been trying to close the experiments down.

Tennal's expression went through several journeys before he apparently remembered he was trying not to care.

"Look," he said, "that's shitty. I'm sorry. The army is the worst. But it was twenty years ago, Surit, I don't know what you want me to—"

"*What were they doing?*" Surit said.

Tennal stopped talking.

"Marit went into that laboratory," Surit said. "They invented the architects and the readers. The readers rebelled. Marit joined them—she joined the *readers,* so she must have thought they had a cause. And now this. Three of her fleet's readers died. What were they doing, that the whole project was shut down after the war? Oma was there from the start. What does she know?"

A moment of silence. Tennal started to pace up and down the room, watching Surit warily. "All right. Let's think about Oma. Here's what we know about the Archer Link Station clusterfuck." He held up a hand to tick off his fingers. "One: Oma deposed Governor Birimi on shaky grounds. Two: Oma impounded the *Fractal Note* and its whole fleet, maybe just because Archer likes fucking with Cavalry, but she coincidentally got her hands on a massive trove of remnants."

"We brought her those," Surit said automatically.

"Quiet, Lieutenant. *Three:* Oma came to power weirdly fast and has a bunch of architects under her who Birimi says are creepy. You say Oma was involved in the original neuromodification project—so was my aunt. I'm not surprised. Marit tried to shut that project down. Maybe she died to do it."

Surit breathed out, remembering the weird moments of blankness he'd seen at the officers' party. He turned the wristband over in his hands again.

Tennal stopped pacing. "Which brings us to four: What if Oma has been using a remnant to fuck around with people's minds on this station? Maybe that's what the project was doing before Marit shut it down. What if Oma took that research and waited until she could use it?"

The way Tennal just *said* things out loud. Surit would have spent months quietly turning over those thoughts in the dark recesses of his brain. Tennal talked like he had stumbled into an armory and decided to explode every bomb at once.

Surit shut his eyes. "Let's say that's true," he said. "Oma took the confiscated remnants to use on people's minds. How can she do that? The only thing the army ever used them for was to make people into readers and architects. How is Oma using them for her own purposes?"

"I don't know," Tennal said. "I know *brainwashing* is a dirty word, but that's the logical extension of architect abilities, right? It's just writing you can't feel. What if Oma found out how to use the remnants to amplify her own architect powers?"

Brainwashing. It had been a fear, back in the early days of modification, before everyone had known exactly what architects and readers could do and that architect commands were obvious and temporary. The idea of architect commands and compulsions with no limit was terrifying. But if you wanted power, you couldn't do it on a one-to-one basis. "If I were brainwashing people," Surit said, "I'd brainwash the strongest architects I could. Then they'd be able to write anyone I couldn't reach."

"*Would* you," Tennal said. "Good to know one of us could take over the world if we wanted to. That explains why all her officers are strong architects."

That was a wild accusation, now that Tennal said it out loud. Oma couldn't possibly be brainwashing all her officers. Surit had never heard of anyone able to do something like that. His brain spun, trying to backtrack. "*I'm* a strong architect," Surit pointed out. "She hasn't done it to me. I wouldn't be working for you if she had; I'd be working for her."

"Maybe she doesn't know you're strong," Tennal suggested. "No—that doesn't track. It must be in your paperwork, since you synced me. And she knows *I'm* strong; I should be on that list myself. Readers would be useful too, if what you want is power. And I'm bloody sure she hasn't brainwashed me." He brooded for a moment. "Maybe we're up the wrong tree entirely."

"I suppose she could just keep you as a prisoner," Surit said. "She may not need to brainwash you."

"If she wanted me as a prisoner, I'd already be one," Tennal said. "And she doesn't have any other way to control me. She can't blackmail me: my family is out of her reach, and you'll be gone soon."

"She couldn't blackmail you with me," Surit said absently.

There was a pause neither of them had intended.

"No," Tennal said. "Of course not."

Surit didn't have the extra space in his thoughts to deal with his complicated feelings about Tennal. He looked down at the wristband.

"Given all our outlandish theories, I'm inclined to get the ex-governor out of here," Tennal said abruptly. "And after that, you and the rest of Retrieval Two. I don't think it's going to be safe to be on this station for much longer."

"And you," Surit said.

"*I've* still got to find a way to get through the bloody link," Tennal said. "But you and the rest of them can just hop back to Cavalry territory, can't you? If you're quick and careful and don't care about a *small* chance of being arrested or shot."

Surit had absolutely no intention of leaving Archer Link Station before Tennal escaped. He also recognized this was going to cause an argument. "I can start looking into transfers for our unit."

"And Birimi?" Tennal said.

"I'll find a transport we can slip them onto," Surit said. "We'll get found out, but they should be well on their way to Orshan Central by then."

"Fantastic," Tennal said. He fixed his collar, checked his Archer tabs in the mirror, and opened the door. "Do you want a written order? Might cover you when the shit hits the fan."

Surit straightened. "I've never needed an order," he said stiffly, "to do the right thing."

When Tennal met his eyes, Surit saw a brief glint of that heat he'd seen before. "I know," Tennal said, "it's infuriating." And he left.

It took Surit two further days to painstakingly line up all the pieces.

The first domino to fall was the ex-governor's escape. Surit's hunch had been right: it was easy enough to quietly commandeer a single transport seat under Captain Halkana's authority, no questions asked. Tennal could have done it for himself, if he didn't mind being caught by the other divisions the moment he disembarked.

But something made Surit nervous. Not just around Birimi's escape, although that was part of it. The station felt tenser.

He told himself it was his guilty conscience. He still went to witness the shuttle transfer, as if he could make it go smoothly by watching.

There were restaurants that looked over the concourse to the station docks. Surit picked one that accepted loiterers and settled down with some almond bread and a flask of bitter tea from his home province. It was dull work, watching dozens of people stream from the elevators to the docks. Surit didn't mind dull work. He would relax when all of this had gone off without any surprises.

"Lieutenant Yeni. Hiding in a corner to slack off?"

Surit would know Tennal's voice in his sleep by now, but he looked up anyway. "I thought you were busy."

"Something changed," Tennal said. Surit raised his eyebrows, but Tennal didn't elaborate, only sprawled in the chair opposite with his feet stretched out in front of him. "Have they made the handover yet?"

"No."

Tennal watched through the enormous glass windowpane with hooded eyes. They sat in silence for five minutes. Tennal absently took a drink of Surit's tea and choked on it.

"Surit, this is a travesty."

"It's a refined taste," Surit said calmly.

Tennal stole his almond bread instead. He ate half of it, contemplating the view of the concourse with his feet on the opposite chair.

"Did you ever wonder," he said conversationally, "if we could have been normal?"

Surit tore his eyes away from the concourse for a quick, baffled glance at him.

This didn't deter Tennal. He waved a hand. "You know. If we'd met on Orshan, we could have been meeting up like this *without* all the conscription and war crimes and everything. What if it had turned out like that? We could have both met in Exana—"

"I've been to Exana once, when I was thirteen," Surit said. "I don't think we would have met."

"Stop being literal," Tennal said. He turned the tea around in his hands. "Sometimes I think about—it's nearly summer down there, isn't it? I used to like summer. Do you remember what planetside dawn is like?" His tone was wistful. Surit didn't look at him. "Exana has . . . oh, this amber kind of light in the gardens. I used to just wander all night. And then people would come out in ones and twos, and the street carts would start up, and you could get hot flatbread. Crisp. I'll take you to get some."

Surit said nothing.

"Or swimming," Tennal said. "That's what you do in summer. By the city walls, where the concrete heats up the sea like bathwater."

Surit hadn't meant to say anything, his eyes still fixed on the

concourse, but Tennal's quiet voice made a cascade of images flood
his head. Surit had left Elvi and his home village behind, but he'd
never lost the furnace heat of sunlight on the trees or the soft sinking of the loose earth underfoot. "Rivers."

"Rivers, really?" Tennal said. "It was always the ocean for us.
Sun heats up the harbor wall until you could fry an egg."

"Frogs in the water," Surit said. "Wriggling where you step."

"*No*," Tennal said.

"I'll take you," Surit said recklessly.

"You have to exterminate the frogs first," Tennal said, "but I'll
hold you to that." Surit drew a sharp breath. It felt like something
had just clamped itself around his rib cage. He couldn't say anything, though, because Tennal leaned forward with the intent
twitch of a bird spotting prey. "There they are."

Surit spotted the figures a second later. Three of them: Birimi,
heavyset and dressed less colorfully than last time he'd seen them,
and a pair of Retrieval Two rankers who had just escorted the
ex-governor out of prison and were now trying to fade into the
crowd and pretend they were here coincidentally. A dockworker
came out and checked the emergency pass Surit had issued
Birimi. She nodded and gestured them to follow her.

Birimi looked around, peered at the windows of the concourse
above, and raised their hand in a gesture of thanks.

They disappeared through the dock gates. Nobody shouted.
Nobody ran after them.

"That's that, then," Tennal said brightly. He finished Surit's tea.

Surit made one last visual sweep of the concourse, unable to
believe it had gone off this smoothly, and switched his attention
to Tennal. Tennal was doing a reasonably good job of pretending
at insouciance, but his foot was tapping compulsively. And he'd
sought Surit out here instead of waiting for Surit to come back to
his office.

"What did you want to tell me?" Surit said.

"How did you—" Tennal said, then broke off and laughed. It

wasn't a particularly happy laugh. "All right, yes. Half an hour ago, someone sent me this."

He threw a small screen from his wristband onto the table, shielded for privacy. Staring back from it, wreathed in encryption watermarks, was Tennal's face.

Surit leaned over. It was a Resolution-issued pass. He'd never seen one before. With something like this, Tennal wouldn't need Governor Oma's permission to get through the link. The border guards would just wave him through.

"Is it real?" Surit said.

"I have no bloody clue," Tennal said. "It came out of the blue from our very dear ex-politician." His eyes flicked up to the bustling concourse where Birimi had just disappeared. "They couldn't spring themself from an Archer cell, could they? But they're a politician. They *do* obviously have friends."

"If it doesn't work . . ."

"Yes, I know," Tennal said impatiently, "if it's fake and I get found out, they'll deliver me to Oma tied up on a platter. At that point I imagine Oma will stop being nice." He paused. "I have to try it, though."

Surit couldn't look away from the small, rotating image of Tennal's head. If this was real, then that was it.

"You need to move your own escape up," Tennal said. "Once I'm gone, they might be more suspicious. You said you had plans to get our unit out."

Surit nodded.

"I have to get through the link," Tennal said, as if in answer to something Surit hadn't said. "Forced sync on one side, shady remnants business on the other—I'm a conscripted reader, Surit. There is no *good place* for me in this whole Lights-lost sector."

Surit was aware of that feeling again, like a tongue of flame licking at a cold piece of coal. What kind of sector was Orshan, if it couldn't even hold someone like Tennal?

But Surit was a Cavalry officer, and he had a unit, and he had his orders. "I'll get the rest of Retrieval Two out of here tonight."

Tennal collapsed a little, as if his shoulders had been held up by tension and relief had cut the strings. Surit wondered if he'd expected an argument. "Great. Fine. Fantastic. I have to book a ship. I'll leave on the next one I can get."

"Tennal?" Surit said, as Tennal rose to his feet.

Tennal stopped. "Yes?"

"Come back to our room before you leave. Say goodbye."

Tennal hesitated, then a flicker of a smile crossed his face. "I'll try. But don't wait for me, Lieutenant."

Tennal was gone. Surit didn't let himself pause, only went back to work and set the other dominoes in motion.

He'd planned Retrieval Two's escape back to Cavalry like he planned any other operation. He listed it out in his head. *Item: travel forms.* A dozen of them submitted and approved, for individual soldiers, each at a different time and for a different purpose. Half the unit had already left on those flimsy excuses. *Item: escape for the remaining soldiers.* Surit couldn't send away his whole unit without attracting attention, but he and the first-class rankers had a plan. Surit was almost certain the hull of the *Fractal Note* was empty, now, the officers moved to station detention or traded back to Cavalry. He still had the override codes that every officer serving on it had been given. If it was no longer locked down to keep in prisoners, those should work again. He had a plausible distraction: a leak of harmful radiation. He had a flight path, for emergency quarantine and maintenance in station orbit. The *Fractal Note* was their key to getting out.

Item: movement orders. All Surit had to do was give the word. In a few days' time, they'd be back under Cavalry authority. Of course, there would be explaining to do. His senior officers might see Surit as a hero for breaking away from—he couldn't ignore the evidence—what was shaping up to be an Archer coup, albeit one that would never succeed. Or Cavalry might court-martial him. They probably would, in fact, for losing Tennal. But he would be back under the command of his home division, and he would know he'd done the right thing.

Back in his room, he pressed his forehead against the window. Coolness spread from the reinforced glass. He opened his eyes and stared blankly at the view of Archer Station that Tennal's wild maneuvering had gotten them: the bustling city, the soaring towers, the pure sky.

Like a constant rumble of thunder in the back of his brain that hadn't stopped since he'd read Marit's words, Surit thought, *They lied to me about my mother.*

Marit hadn't tried to take over the sector. She had died avenging her soldiers who had been taken for experiments.

Surit wasn't responsible for every injustice in the world. He'd signed up knowing he couldn't even be responsible for every injustice in the army itself—*Marit* had told him that. She'd written it in a letter to Elvi, early on in her career. *The army doesn't work,* she'd said. *It's not fair. It's not equal. You have to let things go, over and over and over again. But it's mine, and it's important, and I'm doing what I can.*

And if Marit had followed her own *Lights-lost advice,* she might not have died.

He raised his head away from the widow glass. He'd spent the past two weeks just getting on with things. But in the silence of the room, and in the sudden absence of his daily duties, he finally acknowledged that ever since he'd first seen Marit's shattered wreck of a ship, his guts felt like they'd been ripped out with a fishhook, and he'd been bleeding out slowly ever since.

He looked at his escape plans. What was he going to do?

His job, of course. He always did his job.

It took him half an hour to put the final tweaks to the last permission forms. The *Note* needed refueling. That could be done on the way out. It was time to go into the office and tell the others.

But as he turned, the door chimed.

Surit opened it. It was Tennal's officer friend, Captain Fari. There was a ranker behind him.

"Did you want Captain Halkana?" Surit said. "He's gone to—"

"No," Fari said. "Actually, Lieutenant, I came here for you. We'd like to ask about the travel permits you've issued."

They'd been quicker than Surit had thought. He didn't move. "Can this be done tomorrow? My duties—"

"Your commanding officer will be informed," the captain said. "And going by your reports, Lieutenant Yeni, there seems to be a serious risk that you won't be here tomorrow. Am I wrong?"

Surit looked at the captain's eyes, which were blank, and saw someone else behind them.

Captain Fari smiled, apparently unaware he wasn't in full command of his own mind. He said, "Would you come with me?"

CHAPTER 22

So Surit was finally leaving Archer Station. That was good. Surit would organize his unit's escape back to Cavalry with his normal sickening competence, and the unit would give him three cheers and a medal, and Tennal would fade from all their memories in about a month. Tennal had been working for that exact goal for weeks, so there was no reason that this should make him irritated.

The thought kept stealing in like unwelcome morning light: he would miss Surit.

It didn't matter. They'd only met weeks ago. Tennal hadn't even written Surit a goodbye message, not after the effort of a message to Zin had nearly killed him. Tennal couldn't afford to care about any more people.

He took a small bag, left his district, and headed to the docks under the city.

Tennal hadn't yet explored the lower rings of Archer Link Station. Underneath the great dome of the city, the stacked discs were occupied by environmental systems and automated factories. The largest ring, and the reason for the station's existence, was the enormous circular docks. Ships flocked to its hatches like fish to a feeder. A constant stream of traffic went between it and the city; it was easy for Tennal to slip quietly into the flow.

The gates to the transit hub—the same ones Birimi had taken that morning—were bustling. Some civilians were being questioned, but Tennal was an Archer captain, so he presented his bios and walked straight through.

There was almost certainly a flag on his account. An alert would be making its way up the chain. But Tennal going to the docks would not, in itself, tell Oma anything. He could have legitimate reasons to be there. And she would know there was nowhere in-sector that he could run to.

Better be quick.

When the tube car disgorged him into the transit hub, Tennal had to stop, momentarily overwhelmed. There were thousands of people. Floating screens glowed everywhere. It took him a while to orient himself: *that* was retail, that way was transient hostels, and that way was the huge flow of traffic to the in-system planets. And at the far end, lit with an amber glow, was the gate to the link.

Orshan's link jumped straight into a major galactic hub where roughly thirty territories, polities, and empires met, so the transports ranged from commercial to high-end luxury to budget shuttles. If Tennal could get through this first link, he could go anywhere.

His brain stalled when he tried to imagine what *anywhere* would feel like.

He kept walking automatically. The Resolution border was a glitter of pale golden light stretched across the far wall. As he approached, Tennal watched travelers enter it: each of them presented their wristbands to a scanning wand outside it and walked straight through. It wasn't a normal force screen that switched on and off; it hung there like a cloud. The doorway to the universe.

The Resolution controlled the galactic link. Orshan was a member of the Resolution treaty, of course—it had to be, because without the Resolution, not only could you not use the links, but you were also fair game for invasion by any of the other powers.

They had nearly been kicked out of the entire treaty twenty years ago, when the army's reader and architect experiments had come to light. The Resolution hated unsanctioned neuromodification, which was a bit rich, because Orshan certainly wasn't the only planet ever to mess around with remnants. Regardless,

Orshan had friends and allies among the powers that made up the Resolution's committees, and they'd struck a deal to get back in good standing.

That deal forbade architects and readers from traveling outside Orshan without permission. Tennal, however, was pretty sure there was no way the Galactics could *know*.

As Tennal lounged against the wall to watch, a Resolution scout entered with a telltale shimmer over one eye—the visual implant all Resolution workers seemed to get. He wore a wooden gender-mark and embroidery in galactic designs Tennal didn't recognize, and his face was hard and intent. Tennal, for a moment, wondered what the difference was, exactly, between what the scouts could do and the feeling Tennal had when he tried to navigate. Were the scouts just better readers? Surely not. The Resolution had cracked down on Orshan precisely *because* the architects and readers were something they didn't want spreading. The scouts had the ability to pilot. Orshan's readers and architects affected other human minds.

The scout stopped suddenly at the edge of the amber field, looking over his shoulder. His eyes searched the room.

Tennal, through some sudden instinct, reached for a defensive technique. He let his mind clear. *Readers can't sense other readers.* But a scout was not a reader, unless the Resolution was a lot more hypocritical than Tennal had previously thought.

The scout paused then shook his head slightly, as if clearing it, and moved on.

As Tennal started to relax, his wristband beeped. *Urgent.* Tennal twitched before he realized it was probably just another traffic crisis. He shut the whole thing off. There was nobody in the sector he wanted to talk to now.

All right. Showtime.

When the scout had gone, Tennal walked briskly up to the border. A scanning wand shed a bright pool of white light. Tennal keyed up his wristband and presented the pass.

No noise. Tennal could barely keep himself breathing steadily. He had no fucking clue if this was a real pass or not. He shouldn't have trusted it. Birimi could've been trying to get him in trouble, or playing a joke, or simply bad at this. If Oma found out Tennal was really trying to escape—

The light turned gold. An arrow pointed Tennal through the barrier.

Tennal breathed out and stepped through it.

Amber light filled his eyes and his mouth. It tasted like freezing fog, though it wasn't cold. There was a buzzing in the back of Tennal's head. He forced himself to keep walking.

When the fog cleared, he was in a clean white corridor with a small stream of people heading from the barrier.

The ship he was booked on was the only one boarding among the dozens of hatches. Tennal couldn't see its size from the corridor, but the tunnel that extended from the hatch was sleek and black. The people boarding were all important-looking officials. Tennal looked down at the pass, and it occurred to him to wonder what documents, exactly, Birimi had wrangled for him.

A hand landed on Tennal's shoulder.

Tennal jumped. He readied more defensive techniques as he turned, but he saw a round, smiling woman in rumpled civilian clothes, who said genially, "Captain Halkana?"

"Yes," Tennal said, because there didn't seem to be much point in denying it. "Excuse me, though, I can't talk. I have a shuttle to catch."

"Yes, of course," the woman said. She tugged him politely to the side. "I'm the station manager; I won't hold you up. The governor just asked me to pass on this."

She opened a communications screen. It cleared to show Governor Oma frowning over the desk in her office. Oma turned at the faint chime and instantly dropped her work. "Ah, you found him."

The station manager made an apologetic gesture. "I'm so sorry,

I'm very busy. I'll just leave you two . . ." She waved a hand to tether the signal to Tennal's wristband. He let her. She wasn't involved.

"*Governor*," Tennal said, when it was just him, Oma, and the stream of passengers casting him curious glances. "What a delight."

"I see I've caught you at an awkward moment," Oma said. But the next thing wasn't about Tennal's escape at all. "The legislator has announced a surprise visit."

Tennal's face changed color, though not expression. "*Really?* My aunt's coming out here?"

"You're aware there's some tension between Archer and Cavalry at the moment," Oma said, as if this were all a regrettable argument in a schoolyard. "Nothing we can't smooth out with some face-to-face conversations. However, it does have some implications for you."

It didn't. Oma couldn't stop a ship cleared to go through the link. In five minutes Tennal would be out of here. "Does my aunt know I'm here?"

"Almost certainly." Oma propped her chin on one fist. "I don't plan to hide it. We need to talk . . . tactics. Come and see me in person."

Tennal took a long breath. "Of course, sir. I'll just be a few minutes."

He moved to cut the connection. Oma raised a hand. "Wait."

Tennal stopped. Oma looked at him through the connection. Something about her gaze made Tennal's mouth dry.

"I can't control you, of course," Oma said softly, "but you might want to know that I've just had to arrest Surit Yeni."

The blood drained from Tennal's face. "You've *what*?"

"I'll see you in a few minutes, Captain Halkana," Oma said genially. "Or not. Your choice." She cut the connection.

Tennal stared at his own wristband in the light from the golden barrier behind him. She'd arrested Surit.

It was as clear as day: if Tennal escaped, Surit would answer for it. She must have noticed Surit's escape plans, because Lights knew she couldn't pin any other charges on him. *She had Surit.*

The ship's gate chimed. An out-system dignitary hurried past in a heavy formal wrap.

The universe was waiting. A universe where nobody knew how much Tennal had fucked up, and nobody cared, and nobody had any claim on him at all.

"Guidance fucking lose it," Tennal said savagely. He turned his back on the link and faced the docks again. The barrier swallowed him.

Tennal had never found reflecting on *how did I get here?* a particularly useful or interesting exercise. But as he stepped into the office of the Archer Station governor, neatly dressed in Archer colors and captain's tabs, he touched the wheat-stalk emblem at his collar and thought, *Maybe you should have just let me carry on gambling, Auntie.*

The link swirled through the windows, silhouetting Oma's bowed head as she worked.

As Tennal entered she raised her head, sighed, and pushed back her chair. "We had to take the office back, you know," she remarked, in an apparent non sequitur. "There was hand-to-hand fighting in the building. The rebels reinstalled the old governor, albeit for all of twenty minutes." She laid her hand flat on the surface of the desk. "Exciting times."

For some reason, Tennal's eyes fastened on the burn gun mark he'd noticed before: a scar on the desk right in front of where the occupant would sit. Fired to intimidate. He'd always assumed the rebels had fired at Oma. But if the rebels had taken back Birimi's office, it must have been Birimi sitting there and Oma's troops with the burn gun.

He raised his eyes to Oma's. "Exciting times, sir," he said blandly. "Where's my lieutenant?"

Oma tapped her fingers on the desk. Despite his previous attempt, Tennal wondered if there was any chance he could read her. But when he reached out a tentative feeler, she was as sealed up as Surit and gave the impression of a shielded fusion reactor.

"Do you know," Oma said, "I seem to have lost Birimi."

"The ex-governor?" Tennal didn't turn a hair. "That's a shame."

"Two days after you visited them, in fact."

"Guidance takes strange paths," Tennal said piously. "When you say you *lost* them—did they die? Does that go on my permanent record? My very first murder; that's exciting. What have you done with Surit?"

Oma, rather unexpectedly, laughed. "I won't press you for an answer about Birimi," she said. "They're not relevant at this point. Your Lieutenant Yeni is under arrest for trying to desert."

"Trying to desert?" Tennal made himself sound incredulous. "Is that what you call it when a soldier tries to go back to a different division? Aren't we all Orshans?" There might not be any inter-sector fights while the Resolution was watching them, but the divisions were so entrenched that society was unimaginable without them. Tennal sometimes suspected Orshan had to have a standing army to protect itself from its own standing army.

"I have nothing against Cavalry," Oma said, without even bothering to sound sincere. "But obviously Lieutenant Yeni wasn't going back to Cavalry. He was going to follow you through the galactic link."

"Through the *link*?" Tennal said blankly. "Why would he do that?"

Oma frowned. Tennal got the impression that was the first thing he'd said that she hadn't expected. "Because he's synced to you," she said. "You can't be too far apart. There must have been a plan for him to go with you."

Tennal couldn't exactly say, *I assumed the shit we made up wouldn't matter once I was several light-years away.* He managed a shrug. "I'd like him released, please."

Oma sat back in her chair. "Well, there's also the charge of trespassing in the station archives," she said, "which you were also involved in. In fact, between that, breaking my prisoners out of detention, and trying to get yourself onto a Resolution ship, I can only conclude I haven't given you enough to do and you're getting bored."

Tennal opened his mouth to say he had excuses for all of those. But he hesitated. There was something about Oma that he recognized, something his aunt had, something Tennal unwillingly recognized in himself. There was no point smiling and treading in velvet slippers when what was underneath Oma's voice, always, was the bared edge of a knife.

She knew Tennal and Surit had been in the archives. She might've known they'd been looking for the remnants. Tennal wasn't too concerned about being found out: he'd expected it once someone checked the entry logs. But Oma hadn't asked for an explanation, which meant she didn't care that he was poking around. She didn't care that a pile of alien artifacts had gone missing.

Tennal said, "What did you do with the remnants Surit found in chaotic space?"

"Oh." Oma gave a smile that showed her teeth. "So you *are* Yasanin's nephew. It's well past time." She reached under her desk and pulled out something Tennal had mistaken for part of the desk, but he now saw it was a secure lockbox shaped like a cabinet. It hovered just above the floor as she removed it. "I only had about a dozen before Lieutenant Yeni found this windfall. The best outcome possible, really."

The cabinet was something more than a lockbox. It was encased in stained mahogany, like the sides of the desk, but when she lifted the lid, it was six inches thick with metal shielding. She took out a metal box from inside it, also shielded, and laid it on her desk.

"When I was at the lab, this was our talisman," Oma said, placing a hand on it. "They discovered it when chaotic space spat out a pocket of debris. I was nineteen. This was Orshan's hope. This was our chance of modelling ourselves after the High Chain. We could be *more than human*—that was the sales pitch I volunteered for." She gave a self-deprecating smile. "Unfortunately, we're all still human. Just human with some mild neuro abilities."

"And . . . what was the goal after that?" Tennal asked, fascinated. "Did you really think the Resolution wouldn't care?"

"Well, they didn't notice for a good few years," Oma said. "Even their first Auditor missed it. As for the goal, we'd genuinely thought we'd be an unstoppable fighting force. The High Chain architects—well, whatever they are, *architects* is an Orshan word—can influence whole crowds of people at once. But the Chain is much more advanced than us. The neuromodifications we managed were smaller. In fact, what we got was something very bad for interplanetary expansion but very good for internal coups and civil wars."

"Lucky us," Tennal said. "So your new readers started a coup, and your new architects followed right along with a civil war."

Oma didn't answer him. She opened the lid of the box she'd taken from the cabinet.

As she opened it, Tennal immediately felt a buzzing in the back of his head. The first layer was a black cloth tray with a dozen pearly fragments embedded in it.

Then she lifted the tray, and what Tennal saw was a mass of opalescent fragments heaped on each other, filling the box in a glowing pile, dozens upon dozens. Hundreds.

Tennal's mouth was open. He knew Surit had seen this when he found them, but Tennal himself had never come across more than one remnant in the same place. As Tennal watched, they seemed to move, like every fragment was a droplet in a wave. Then he blinked, and they were still.

"We used to call it the Constellation," Oma said softly. "Rather beautiful, aren't they? They were all found together. The biggest remnant discovery in our history." Her hand hovered over them. "It's inadvisable to touch them. But you do always feel a . . . compulsion."

Pressure gripped Tennal's chest. He tried to understand it. What he felt wasn't a compulsion to touch them; what he felt was a deep and debilitating *grief*.

That was impossible to explain. Tennal didn't bother to try: he knew remnants messed with your head. He was lucky he wasn't smelling sounds and hearing colors. "Does the Resolution know we have these?"

"The Resolution doesn't know. And it won't as long as we keep the power usage low. The trick is to use one at a time."

"One at a time?" Tennal said. "Is that how it works? The brainwashing?"

Oma said sorrowfully, "*Brainwashing* is a very loaded word." She shut the box with careful hands. "Imagine this."

Her mind cracked open like a fissure in the side of a volcano, and an image flooded Tennal's brain.

Tennal saw a single point of light, with countless lines out to other points, like a hub and spokes. Each bright, glowing line felt alien. It felt, Tennal realized, like the remnants. Oma was the hub. Each other point was *someone else's mind*.

"Calling it *brainwashing* really undersells the delicacy of it," Oma said. She withdrew her mind; Tennal didn't even understand what she'd done. It was like writing, only she'd made his eyes visualize something instead. That level of control was ridiculous. "It's only an expansion of the neuroscience we already had. It's a modification of the sync bond."

"The sync," Tennal repeated, trying to sound brightly clueless, which wasn't hard.

"The sync is two halves," Oma said, placing her hands together to illustrate. "The remnants have a dual nature, and to make architects and readers in the first place, we—well, the history of the research is complicated, but essentially the original researchers split that nature into *controlling* and *observing*. Then the observing side, the reading, was considered too dangerous—it was political—so after the first batches, only architects were made. A sync reunites the two halves in a one-to-one relationship. With the influence of a remnant, you can force a sync into a one-to-many relationship instead. Like a broadcast connecting to many receivers."

Tennal looked her in the face. "Is this what you're planning to do to me?"

Oma suddenly looked *very* like his aunt. "No," she said, with testy patience. "Otherwise I wouldn't have explained it. I would like you as an ally, Tennalhin, and you have no need to worry about this. You're a reader, and besides, you're already in a sync."

So whatever brainwashing Oma was doing, it wouldn't work on readers, and it wouldn't work on people who were synced. Surit was safe as long as she didn't notice. Nobody else Tennal cared about was anywhere near Oma.

"Shall we talk about you?" Oma said.

Tennal hesitated. There were still a dozen questions queued in his throat, including *why did you suddenly need a thousand more remnants?* and *what are you planning?* But the way Oma said it—steely, pleasant—made it quite clear she had finished answering. That wasn't an invitation that came with a *no.* Tennal gave her a bright smile and sat in a chair in front of her desk. "My favorite topic. May I say something?"

"Go ahead."

"I don't really care what you're doing," Tennal said. "I'm a very selfish person. Sue me. I just want to escape the army." He tried to keep his voice sincere. It helped that it was true—Tennal was as selfish as they came—but she didn't need to know Tennal could pass what he knew on to Surit, who could decide what to do with all this. This kind of division warfare needed someone responsible to know about it, and Lights knew that wouldn't be Tennal. He was going to be out of here. "And my trial period is over the day after tomorrow. We had a deal."

"We did," Oma agreed. "And I thought your trial period was very successful. You're a highly competent officer. A shame your aunt never gave you a chance to be one."

Surit was a highly competent officer. Tennal was just good at taking credit. "You don't need more competent officers. You don't need me. I'll only complicate whatever argument you're having with my aunt. Let Surit go, and I'll be through the link and out of your hair."

Oma sat back, a faint smile on her face. "Can I bribe you? I can offer a promotion, of course. But I would have thought you might be more persuaded by the opportunity to show the legislator she was wrong about you."

"It's very tempting," Tennal said. "But honestly, I don't trust that she doesn't have a way to make me come back. You don't *know* my aunt."

"I used to," Oma said.

"Of course," Tennal said. "I forgot. I'm sure she was just as terrifying when she was eighteen and volunteering for unproven neuromodification experiments." Of course, Oma had done exactly the same thing. "The thing is. The thing is, she's family." He stopped. He hadn't even meant to say that. But his excuses always worked better when part of them was true. "You don't know how hard it is to say no to family."

Oma pushed herself away from the table and rose to her feet. "I do understand," she said quietly. "And I understand it can be very difficult to be close to great figures. If you don't have your own drive, you just get swept up in their wake." This was cutting too close to the bone. Tennal opened his mouth, but Oma turned around briskly. "And she may not be as big a threat as you think."

Tennal's brain spun freely and uselessly. He stared at her in horror. "You couldn't brainwash the *legislator*."

"I won't try to influence Yasanin," Oma agreed, and it only then occurred to Tennal to wonder why not. "Call it shared history. But, let's say, we can open *robust* negotiations. And you'll have a part."

Things started clicking into place in Tennal's head. For a moment, almost as if he *had* read Oma, he saw the image she'd conjured: the legislator arriving at Archer Station to deal with Oma's growing power base and being confronted with Tennal, right beside Oma, wearing Archer colors.

Tennal had been right. Oma wanted him as a symbol.

"That sounds above my pay grade," Tennal said. "How about you just let me and Surit go? If not . . . well, as you've said, my aunt *is* coming tomorrow." He didn't have to point out that there were some secrets Oma wouldn't want him to pass on.

"Ah. We're at an impasse, then. I don't think you should go."

Bizarrely, this felt more familiar. More comfortable. Tennal put his feet up against the front panel of the desk. "How are you going to keep me?" he countered. "Lock me up, like you did to the old *Fractal Note* officers? I'd hardly be an asset like that."

"Let's see," Oma said. She blanked the wraparound windows and changed them to a screen. It was one of those enormous ones intended for mass transmission. "You haven't held a publicity post before, have you?"

"All the jobs I've ever had have been in quick succession over the past few weeks," Tennal said. He added warily, "I'm not a natural fit for publicity. Even my aunt's election team said so. Something about how my face looks on-screen."

"Oh, you should reconsider that," Oma said. "This one's just about to go out, as a matter of fact."

She gestured for a vid to start.

Tennal was used to news bulletins and political comms blasts. When he and Zin had grown up with his aunt, they'd been everywhere: feeds in her office, playing in the background at the dinner table, hovering around her as she walked out the door. Tennal was used to his aunt's face appearing on billboards or on the newslogs at school. He knew what government comms looked like.

This one started off the same as all the propaganda he'd seen. The Archer emblem. Majestic external shots of the station, its discs rotating slowly. Then the main reel: the shots switched to troop ships, and the voice-over announced, reassuringly, *"Archer Station prepares for a robust defense against recent Cavalry escalations . . ."*

"What Cavalry escalations?" Tennal said. "You didn't mention those."

"Didn't I?" Oma said. "Well, they haven't happened quite yet. But it won't be long. Your aunt is arriving tomorrow."

"For a *meeting,* you said," Tennal said. "Surely not with a fleet."

"I would be surprised if a fleet weren't following."

Tennal's mouth opened to say, *That would be civil war.* But before he could, the vid took on a new tone.

It showed sound bites from Oma, talking seriously at the camera about the need for calm. There were stock shots of Cavalry ships around Orshan's orbital stations. Upbeat interviews with the district leads.

And then Tennal himself walked on-screen.

He recognized the residential streets in the background under the domed sky. *Yes, we're all ready,* Tennal said brightly, in response to an unheard question. *Keen to get started.*

That had been one of Surit's shrine-opening ceremonies. Tennal remembered being impatient with the local reporter, trying to brush them off. The Tennal on-screen looked amused and remote. The subtitle said *Captain Tennalhin Halkana, previously Cavalry Division.* There was an inset picture of the legislator, just in case you'd forgotten whom Tennal was related to.

"Not subtle," Tennal managed. His own face was still on-screen. The superior look on it was absolutely insufferable. He wanted to punch himself.

"Did it have to be?" Oma said.

"I was talking about reopening a shrine," Tennal said. "Not fighting Cavalry."

The vid merged into more quick shots: Tennal at a factory plant Oma had asked him to visit. Tennal seriously talking to a group of staff. Tennal behind Oma as she gave a news conference. And Tennal realized she had nearly two weeks of footage to work from.

This was Tennal's own fault. He knew with a cold certainty that he was caught between two pincers: Oma could stop him from escaping because she controlled the link, and she had made the rest of his home sector unlivable for him. If he ever tried to go home now, the legislator would arrest him for treason. No more second chances.

Tennal was used to making bad choices. Four weeks ago, he would have put his head in his hands and felt like a stain on the ground until he could escape and drink himself into oblivion. But now—he could hear Surit's calm voice telling him to look at it logically. He hadn't been *stupid*. He had been *desperate*.

But what was the better choice? What choices were left at all? Tennal watched Oma's hands as she gestured to shut off the vid, and he tried not to despair.

"So that's gone out on all major comms channels on all three planets," Oma said conversationally.

"So glad," Tennal said. "I've always wanted to be famous."

"I can make this worth it for you," Oma said. "We can at least make sure your architect isn't a threat. I can get my medics to work on severing your sync."

Tennal's mind spun blankly. "So you can sync me instead? No, thanks. Anyway, you said it might kill me."

"I promise, you're more useful as an ally," Oma said. "But I'll be honest, it will kill your architect. You . . . probably not."

For some reason that was worse. "I'd rather Surit weren't dead, in fact. I do tend to leave a trail of spectacular fuckups, but I don't want to leave a body count."

Oma looked at him in a contemplative way that made Tennal even more unsettled. "Tell me," she said, "did you really not have a plan to have Lieutenant Yeni follow you through the link?" Tennal was too off-balance to pull up a good response. "No, I don't think you did. That's interesting."

"What do you want, a travel itinerary signed in triplicate?" Tennal said. "I was working things out. I don't need him dead."

Oma gave a terrifying smile. "Attached?"

The question shouldn't have knocked Tennal backward the way it did. Attached to *Surit*? What could he say to that: they were friends? They were partners in crime? Tennal had offered to sleep with Surit, *would* have slept with him, if Surit had been less sensible? Surit was like nobody Tennal had met before, and Tennal was going to leave him, and it was rare that Tennal saw a regret coming before it hit, but he was going to regret that for the rest of his life.

He had hesitated for too long. He said, entirely inadequately, "No."

That was when Tennal realized the question was a trap.

"Ah," Oma said briskly. "So you're *not* synced. Excellent."

Tennal had made his real mistake much earlier, when he'd told Oma they had separate escape plans. Oma had said, *You can't be too far apart.* She must have met synced pairs before. Tennal had let slip that he and Surit weren't acting like they were synced.

Oma wanted strong architects, and Surit, unlike Tennal, wasn't politically useful. If Surit wasn't synced, then she could use the remnants to brainwash him.

Tennal had sold Surit out without even realizing he'd done it.

Tennal pushed himself to his feet, terror sleeting through his brain. He didn't know what he would have done—she was a Rank

One; he didn't know what he would have been *able* to do. He was stopped by an aide bursting through the door.

"Sir!" the aide said, out of breath. "The legislator is requesting permission to dock."

"What?" Oma said, killing the screen as she turned. "Already?"

Tennal couldn't process the news. *Where was Surit?*

Oma stood like a statue for a moment, then shrugged fluidly. "Well, we're ready. Commence preparations for the meeting. Oh, and add to that"—the aide had turned to go; he stopped, attentive—"I need to talk to Lieutenant Surit Yeni. Urgently. Get him from detention."

Tennal could barely breathe. He had no time for a useful plan of action. "I'll do that."

Oma turned her head. "So you're in, Captain Halkana?"

Tennal tried not to let his terror show. She thought he was on her side; he'd burned enough bridges that joining her was his only real option. He gave her his most reasonable smile. "To get back at my aunt? Why not."

Oma smiled back. Even if she didn't trust him as far as she could throw him, there was no way Tennal could stop her from eventually getting her hands on Surit. This was her station. "Escort Lieutenant Yeni to the docking bay, then," she said. "There's no point in waiting. We can use him."

CHAPTER 23

Tennal didn't make a habit of being afraid. He had always dealt with problems by making himself into a bigger problem. There was no point worrying in advance about what would happen, especially if it was going to happen to someone else.

Tennal had never been this afraid in his life.

Even at his fastest walking speed, nerves singing like a taut wire, he couldn't outpace the aide Oma had attached to him on the way to the detention block. Thoughts and wild plans chased each other around his head. Apparently he and Surit had dodged a bullet by letting Oma assume they were synced, and Tennal's unforgivable slipup had put Surit right back in the bullet's path. Surit had no idea what was coming. He didn't know he was five minutes away from being brainwashed.

Of course Oma wanted Surit. Tennal kept forgetting, because Surit was so bloody quiet about it, but by raw power Surit was probably the strongest architect on the station after Oma.

Of course she wanted that. And Tennal had left him defenseless.

"Go on to the docking bay," he said to the aide. "I'll catch up with the prisoner."

"Can't, sir," the aide said apologetically. "Governor's orders take precedence."

So that wouldn't work. Tennal's thoughts swung from one thing to another like a bird throwing itself frantically around a cage. He could probably get the drop on this aide, who wouldn't be expecting a senior officer to tackle him. If he timed it right, he could do it when they'd reached Surit's cell. But after that? There were guards, alarms, prisoner sign-out procedures. It had taken them days to break out Birimi, and Oma hadn't even been paying attention to them. He couldn't get Surit out of there with a distraction less than a full-scale war.

He'd have to let Oma brainwash Surit. Surit wouldn't be completely lost—like readers in a sync, the architects seemed to be their own person unless Oma wanted something. Maybe there would be a way to undo it, like Oma had promised him a way to undo his own sync. That would at least give him more than *five fucking minutes* to solve this.

He could see Surit's stupid poker expression in his head. Tennal knew Surit lived and died by his principles. He might've thought of himself as a good little soldier, but the first time he'd been given an order he really didn't like—syncing Tennal—he'd gone rogue without a second thought. Without even a *first* thought. Surit was a menace and a danger to the military, and Tennal would rather die than let Oma control him.

Surit had gotten Tennal out of his worst nightmare. Now it was Surit in trouble, and Tennal was as much fucking use as a fish in an airlock.

Tennal didn't have time to come up with a clever distraction. Time drained away with every step he took. He had minutes.

The next thought Tennal had made him miss a step.

He stared at the wall. There was *one* answer.

Surit sat on a hard bench in a detention cell with his head in his hands, and tried to tell himself he had been in worse situations.

He'd failed to get his unit away and he was under arrest, it was true. But there was no point in feeling sorry for himself, or in going over the list of his own mistakes yet again. He tried pulling together another list: Tasks Completed Successfully.

Item: Some of Retrieval Two had already been transferred. Surit had been quietly reassigning people for days. There were only a dozen soldiers left.

Item: The *Fractal Note* was prepared and ready to launch. Oma's soldiers might not have noticed that. If his first-class rankers hadn't been arrested themselves, they could still get everyone else out. A unit like Retrieval Two was too unimportant for Archer to bother with much, as long as they were quick and quiet. Most of them would be both of those.

Item: Tennal had escaped. By now he might be halfway across the galaxy.

Surit stopped making the list and stared blankly ahead.

And Surit was in detention indefinitely, charged with aiding the ex-governor. He was a pawn in the middle of a coup. Not an important pawn, even, just one who'd failed to escape back to the right side.

Right side rang oddly in his head.

Surit thought, for the first time: if he were Governor Oma, there was no way he would let Tennal leave through the link.

He looked up as the door opened.

"Wait outside," a familiar voice said. "I want to ask him something."

"Sir—"

"*Do it*," Tennal said. His voice cracked in a way Surit had never heard before.

Surit stood and said, "Tennal—"

The cell was cold, but sweat prickled at Tennal's hairline as he stepped in. The first thing he did was turn to slam the close-door button and lock it with his emergency key, leaving his poor, bereft aide outside.

An alarm started overhead. Tennal hadn't set off one of those for a while.

He turned back with a feverish energy. "Surit! Hope they've been treating you well. Oma wants to brainwash you. I'm going to guess now that the alarm's gone off, we have thirty seconds."

Surit was on his feet, facing the door like a wrestler squaring up for a match. "Explain."

"It's the sync," Tennal said. "Oma's brainwashing works like a sync. She can't do it if you're already synced, and *she didn't try and brainwash you because she thought you were.*"

Surit's expression changed. "She found out our sync was fake?"

"I screwed up. I let her find out. Twenty seconds. Surit—" Tennal frantically met Surit's eyes.

Even in a crisis, Surit stood planted in the middle of the cell like an oak tree; quiet, assured, clear brown eyes fixed on Tennal as if absorbing every wild thing Tennal said. When he'd first met Surit, Tennal had taken that as arrogance. Now he knew this was just Surit existing. Surit ready to roll himself like a boulder into the path of anything he thought was wrong. Surit trusting him implicitly.

Surit had always treated Tennal like he could be trusted as much as Surit himself. Surit didn't seem to have noticed that bar was so fucking high, Tennal could only reach it by setting it on fire. Tennal could hardly breathe.

"Last idea," Tennal said. "It's one sync or the other."

He saw Surit's shock as he grasped what Tennal meant. In the same instant, Tennal plunged headlong into his reader senses. The color and light faded out of the cell until it was only bare white outlines over the blackness of space, and the dim, closed-off presence of Surit in front of him like a ghost.

There was a part of Tennal's mind that was exposed, that had been exposed ever since his aunt had dragged him back to Exana and chemically primed him. He didn't know if there was any way Surit could perceive it. But Surit had nearly synced him twice by accident, so he must know it was there. Tennal ripped that part of his mind out of the depths of his head and brought it up to the light, letting go of any defenses he had left. "How much do you trust me?"

For the first time ever, he saw something crack in Surit.

Surit broke like the core of a planet fracturing. A bright fissure, a ray of white-hot light. Tennal had seen that light in others, but he was so used to Surit being quiet and unreadable that the light hit him like a furnace.

Tennal read him.

> *—failed and failed to end up here. Failed his unit. Failed Tennal. Surit couldn't even think about Elvi, at home with the newslogs, hearing his child had ended up on the wrong side of a coup just like Marit. The fear. The cold cell air on the back of his neck. The desperation on Tennal's face. Tennal had been so afraid of this, Surit knew, Tennal had been running on pure fear for weeks. He didn't deserve this.*
>
> > *Don't do this for me, Tennal.*

Tennal felt like he'd been stabbed. "Your choice, Surit." It was hard to keep his voice steady. "It's not like last time, though, I promise. This time I'm in—if you say yes. My choice too. But I'll be honest, your options are bad: it's Archer Division or me."

—or you, Surit's thoughts echoed, and what had sounded disparaging from Tennal sounded different from him.

A shrieking, blaring noise came from the door. It started to open, agonizingly slow under the emergency controls.

"Five seconds!" Tennal said, with no actual grasp of how long they had. He threw himself into the thoughts coming from Surit, deeper than he had ever gone, as if they were skin to skin, and got—

> *—an endless sea in front of him, the endless astonishment of Tennal's mind, a huge and terrifying freedom encroaching on the structured way Surit thought and*

*lived, like a glimpse of the ocean from a dry valley. And
over it all, the fear of knowing this was wrong. Tennal
was going to put himself at risk, and all—*

"For once in your bloody life, Surit Yeni," Tennal said aloud,
through gritted teeth, "focus on saving *yourself*."

Surit's body was a chalky-white outline to Tennal's reader
senses, his physical dimensions were just a shadow, his eyes were
milky white. They opened wide.

Surit's mind touched the exposed root in Tennal's brain. The
touch sent stars all through Tennal's head, all through his nerves,
all through every physical and invisible part of him. Tennal barely
heard, behind him, the aide say, "Captain Halkana!" Tennal was so
deep in Surit's mind, the voice sounded like it was echoing down
a well.

"Sir! On the governor's authority, this prisoner—"

Tennal threw his whole self at the sync and met Surit, whose
defenses crumbled, fissures opening all over his mind like the shell
breaking away from a magma core. The heat of him was overwhelming. Tennal fell into him like a root system grasping the
earth, like nerves knitting themselves back together.

Tennal had seen the sync as a threat, as a punishment, as all
but a death sentence. This didn't feel anything like that—*this*
was a surge of life, a heady plunge into orbit. Tennal had thought
he would sense Surit controlling their minds, but all he got from
Surit was the same electrified wonder as Tennal as their fragmented selves coalesced into a newer and terrifying and alien
whole.

They took a breath. Tennal had a moment of terror when he
realized he didn't know which set of lungs was his.

After a horrible moment of hanging in the void, the sheer
force of twenty years' habit fired up nerves and synapses through
familiar paths, and he felt his way back into control of his own
body. His physical form was uncomfortable, like a badly fitting

pair of shoes. He snapped back out of his reader senses. The room flooded with color.

The door opened enough for the aide to force his way through. "Sir, please report! Is the prisoner attacking? Are you safe?" His tone suggested the questions were for form only. He stopped when he saw Tennal turn.

Tennal resisted the urge to balance himself with an arm on the doorframe. With every breath he took, an afterimage of Surit's mind burned in his brain. And Surit was still *there*, no longer a dim presence, but a blazing star that only Tennal could feel.

It was hard to focus on something as mundane as the aide. Then Tennal remembered. Oma. His aunt. Brainwashing. The coup.

They had to escape.

Must get all of us out, said a thought that wasn't Tennal's. *The unit too. Do what we have to.* And behind it, Surit's rock-solid, unending determination. Tennal saw with sudden, unnatural clarity how the military kept knocking down everything Surit had built and how Surit was *used* to pulling himself back up and putting one foot in front of the other. A defensive flare from Surit's mind. Tennal shut his eyes and reached to the wall for balance. He felt Surit wince and put his hand over his face.

"Are you all right, sir?" the aide said, in a tone with more than a touch of suspicion. "The governor said to meet her at the docking bay."

Tennal breathed deep. Two bodies opened two sets of eyes. "*Let's go.*"

CHAPTER 24

They were in the elevator to the reception bay before Tennal got the faintest semblance of stability back.

They were alone: the aide hustled him and Surit through the closing door, then once he was certain they were heading down, hurried to the next task. Tennal had a sudden, horrible moment when he couldn't remember which appendage was his left leg. He had to catch the rail for balance. The doors closed him and Surit into sudden, deafening silence.

This can't be how it's supposed to work.

That thought hadn't been Tennal. He didn't even need to look at Surit to know the terror wasn't just his; it bounced and refracted between the two of them. If Tennal didn't concentrate, he had four hands, two throats, two sets of arteries pumping blood to an upsetting multitude of alveoli. He could feel Surit's *spleen*. He'd never consciously felt his own, but his mind knew now there were two. Both felt like Tennal's. That wasn't good.

Surit was right; surely a normal sync couldn't be like this. The conscripted readers might not have a choice, but the military's architects would never have agreed to being stretched across two bodies for the rest of their life. Of course, a normal sync wasn't supposed to have both sides throw themselves at each other with everything they had. Surit and Tennal must have done it wrong. It was supposed to be a measured process where the architect took control.

Whatever this was, it wasn't one of them taking control.

Tennal couldn't get rid of the feeling that this wasn't two minds in a bond but two fragments of one thing—severed, alien—coming back together. Tennal had always thought of his reader abilities as part of himself. Now, for the first time, he thought about them as a genetic echo of the experiments their parents had gone through. An inherited passenger that Tennal would never really understand. He shoved the thought aside as unhelpful.

Surit slumped in the other corner. As the first stab of fear faded, Tennal felt . . . something else.

Like a drumbeat in the back of Surit's head, like a distant tide on a shore, Tennal felt something Surit had been trying not to think about. He felt a dizzying reflection of *himself*. Surit had an image of Tennal in his head that he was trying to hide, something made of lightning and razor edges and fireworks. Surit had been thinking about him for weeks.

Tennal realized, at the same time, his own speculations about Surit—what Surit's shoulders would feel like to touch, the heat of his skin if he was close—were escaping into their joined mind.

Of all the times to find out, Tennal thought, choking on the hysteria. He felt his own panic rebounding from Surit. If he thought of touching Surit right now, it would be like touching his own skin and expecting it to be someone else's.

They had a handful of seconds as the elevator fell toward the reception bay. Surit braced against the other side of the car. Slitted windows passed, showing stars. This time, Tennal didn't have to watch Surit; if he reached out with his mind, he could feel Surit's quick breathing.

It was Tennal who voiced the first thing they'd said to each other since they'd synced. "What are we going to do?"

He felt the question go through Surit like a frisson, the shock of Tennal's audible voice. And then the panic paused, and through sheer force of will, Surit stabilized himself. Tennal could feel him drawing away, painstakingly re-forming into the person who was *Surit,* rather than Surit-synced-with-Tennal. Tennal was barely ready for the sudden distance. It was as if Surit's heartbeat had been right next to his ear and was now across the room.

"I think the first thing on the list," Surit said, in a voice that seemed to come from a deep, dry pit, "is to disappoint Governor Oma."

"Oh," Tennal said, "my favorite hobby." He wasn't really thinking about what came out of his mouth. Two cut-together images of the legislator and Governor Oma flashed on the news screen in the elevator. Something moved deep in Surit's thoughts. Tennal reached out and found that reading Surit was effortless; he could just peel back the layers.

A flood of images came to him. Under its protective shell, Surit's mind ticked like a machine: a neat, ordered thing of shelves and categories. His memory was like nothing Tennal had ever imagined. Tennal lived his life in a haze of thoughts and impressions, but Surit had taken in and filed away thousands, maybe *millions,* of crystal-sharp images. No wonder he needed to keep his mind in order.

Even now he was running through a list. Tennal got more flashes of himself, of Retrieval Two, of the *Note*—Surit was still thinking of his escape plan, though he had mentally written himself out of it.

This couldn't be all there was. Tennal dug a layer deeper, past Surit's conscious thoughts. It didn't take much to find the emotions lurking at the edge of Surit's lists like a fog.

"Surit," Tennal said, "why do you keep thinking about your mother?"

"Don't *do* that." Surit drew away from Tennal, trying to mentally to fold in on himself, but there was nowhere to go. Surit was pressed against the far wall of their sync.

"Sorry. Sorry," Tennal said. He tried to pull himself back as well, but they were inextricable.

"It's not going to come to a civil war," Surit said.

Tennal caught a last flash of Surit's mother. "Obviously not."

Tennal could say, *This is just division posturing*. He could say, *Neither of them are Marit Yeni*. Instead he reached out. He concentrated entirely on isolating his right arm, his own muscles stretching and contracting, his own bones moving in their joints. He kept his mind to himself. He touched Surit's wrist.

Something in Surit changed, like a dull background noise that suddenly stopped. He mustered up a faint smile, which was a miracle given the amount of strain Tennal could feel from him. He said, "Showtime."

The docking level was like an anthill overturned. The legislator's sudden early arrival had thrown everyone. Rankers scurried down the corridor with comms equipment and Archer banners. Civilian passengers stood around in groups muttering about the sudden freeze on arrivals and departures. Sergeants shouted and chivvied. The legislator's still image was on every screen Tennal saw. *That picture's from two years ago,* Tennal thought irrelevantly. He'd bet she was a lot more furious now.

A wide, low-ceilinged room opened in front of them. The reception bay was usually another hall full of passenger crowds, occasionally repurposed to welcome VIPs like Resolution staff. It had been cleared and hastily turned into a conference room, with a negotiating table and Archer banners around the walls.

Soldiers were drawn up in ceremonial ranks at the sides. The legislator hadn't yet arrived, and neither had Oma, so there was a certain amount of quiet talking. Tennal and Surit slipped in at the side; Tennal was recognized and waved forward. He tried not to seem a twitchy mess. He still didn't have complete control of his left knee.

"Control says the legislator's ship just docked," one of the lieutenants reported.

The main doors on the other side of the room opened to admit Oma.

She'd come in strength. Tennal had never seen all her senior officers there at once, fanning out behind her as she entered, every one of them an architect. This was a major negotiation. As the officers broke ranks to sit, exchanging short words and taking half the seats at the table, Tennal had the uneasy thought: *could* any of them write the legislator? Surely not. The legislator wasn't a Rank One, but she wasn't far off. None of these architects were that strong. And Oma couldn't brainwash the legislator in a public meeting, not with everyone watching.

His aunt must've already known about Oma and what she could do with the remnants. The legislator had *intelligence agencies* reporting to her, for Lights' sake. There was no way Tennal could know something his aunt didn't.

Tennal had the horrible realization that he was going to have to try to warn her.

He'd have to catch her afterward. How he was going to do that and not get detained as a traitor by either side, he didn't know. *Surit?* he said, then realized his mouth hadn't moved.

Surit was already turning to him as if he'd heard. But Tennal hadn't said his name—he'd just reached out wordlessly to the other presence in the churning mess of their joined mind.

Surit was stopped by someone gripping his arm. Captain Fari had broken from the pack of aides, and now he'd obviously come to fetch them. "The governor wanted to see you, Lieutenant Yeni."

"*Surely* there's no time for that," Tennal said breezily, but Surit gave him a hunted look as he was drawn over. Tennal bit down on a swear word and followed. It took him a second to realize the fear he felt wasn't all his own. Surit was also afraid of Oma.

Oma was in conversation with one of her senior officers, but she paused as they came up, dismissed the officer, and glanced at Surit. "Thank you, Captain Halkana. I don't know if there's time—"

Tennal broke in. "Okay, let's not pretend I don't know what you're talking about." It took everything he had not to look at Surit, but he couldn't afford the distraction. "You can't brainwash Surit. You said it doesn't work if the architect is synced."

Oma blinked and looked at him. It wasn't possible to pick out a synced pair by sight, but it must be obvious something was up: one of Surit's eyes was unfocused, and Tennal kept having to move his left leg or forget where it was.

"*Interesting,*" Oma said. Her eyes rested on Tennal. "We'll talk after. Don't go anywhere."

"Sir," Surit said.

"Mm," Tennal said brightly. He didn't know if the immediate intention to be elsewhere came from him or Surit.

They had no time to hide even if they wanted to. A soft alarm came from the doors of the docking bay. The other side had arrived.

Tennal hadn't thought much about the legislator since he'd first been bundled aboard the *Note,* apart from the occasional vague stab of animosity, in the same way he didn't generally think about bad weather. There was nothing to be done about his aunt. There never had been. She spent her time immersed in cutthroat politics and endless committees; she approved of Zin, despised Tennal; and that was all that was relevant.

He watched as Archer officers ushered her and her party in. He'd expected the sight of her to be familiar—her faint, hard, media-appropriate smile, a familiar outfit with a bright swirl of flowers on both the jacket and the skirt—but it was like the past few weeks had given Tennal a feed of new information he couldn't turn off. She looked small. She wasn't armed. This was hostile territory.

She had a crowd of followers and aides, all in civilian dress. Tennal could now pin half of them as ex-military just from their posture, and reaching out with his reader senses showed him some architect auras. Most of them sported division emblems or jewelry: Tennal couldn't catalog all the emblems but spotted several Infantry onyx stones and Navy silver as well as Cavalry rubies. There were even some Archer diamonds, clearly not allies of Oma. Cross-division. That meant something. The politicians were here to face Oma with a unified front.

And there were others as well. Quiet officials in sober dress, a more serious version of the bodyguards who'd sat outside the residence back home. They were armed. Tennal had always ignored security at home, but now he found himself cataloging the number of them against the number of Archer soldiers in the room. At least there were enough people around his aunt to discourage anyone from starting trouble.

The legislator—sharp, powerful, terribly familiar—looked over at the quiescent camera drones. And just as Tennal followed her gaze and wondered why they hadn't launched yet, she spotted him.

Relief. And then, as her eyes fixed on Tennal's golden Archer stripes, terrible shock.

Tennal opened his mouth. He didn't know what he was going to say. He didn't know what he was going to do—they were half a room away, separated by the crowds of soldiers and hangers-on and by Oma, who smiled and approached the table in welcome.

Surit wrapped a hand around his elbow. "Stay back," he said quietly. The vortex of Tennal's thoughts registered *my hand,* then *not mine,* then *Surit,* then tried to spin in three directions at once.

After that brief moment, the legislator gave no other sign that she even knew Tennal. She approached the other side of the long oval table and touched her throat in a civilian salute to Oma. Oma responded in kind; both were wary, peremptory.

"Governor Oma," the legislator said, in that political way she had of sounding like a pleasant person who just happened to be holding a chain saw. At least she wasn't swearing. "In light of our long work together, I'm glad you finally agreed to this meeting. I don't have to tell you this contravenes—"

Oma pulled the burn gun at her side and shot the legislator in the chest.

It was, Tennal thought later, such a small, unfussy movement.

The burn gun left a tingling path behind it across the silent room. The legislator crumpled over her stomach, to her knees, to the ground.

The room broke into chaos around her body. Oma's architects shoved back their chairs and drew their weapons. The legislator's bodyguards shouted and tackled the politicians to the ground, but the military ones had come armed themselves and pulled their cappers to retaliate. Oma aimed at another politician, but she didn't get a second free shot; one of the bodyguards tackled her as the table went over with a crash.

Tennal felt the first architect command slung with the weight of a bulldozer, making one of Oma's soldiers drop their gun. In less time than it took to breathe, the air was thick with physical gun rays and the mental shrapnel of write commands.

"Sir!" an aide shouted to Oma, crawling behind the upturned table toward her. "They had reinforcements! Forty ships out of chaotic space!"

"*Forty*," Oma said, and swore. "Divert the first and seventh wings."

Tennal stood as if his feet were rooted to the floor. Everyone apart from Tennal and Surit had known this was the plan.

The legislator's body was so small on the ground of the meeting room. Oma didn't have to avoid consequences for starting trouble. She just had to be willing to make sacrifices.

Tennal lifted his foot, muscle by muscle, and took a step toward Oma. He took another. The vortex in his mind slowed, calmed, changing into a strange clarity. A shot from a burn gun crackled past his face. He barely noticed.

At least he knew who his enemy was.

When a soldier backed into his path, aiming at someone else in the chaos, Tennal's mind saw them before his eyes. In that peculiarly calm state, he read every flash of intention that went down the soldier's nerves and synapses. Whatever part of his brain was in charge, it gave his movements a new surety: he shoved an elbow in the soldier's back and threw them to the side.

He carried on walking into the firefight. His enemy was close enough to see.

All wasn't well. Tennal's skin felt too small, like the whole atmosphere of a planet forced into a bottle. On top of that, there were two of him where there should be one. But at least the *other* in his mind had power he could use to take out his enemy. He drained energy from Surit as he went. As he did so, he had something that wasn't a memory, more an ancestral instinct: a flash of duels where one mind the size of a star would shatter another open. He didn't have enough power for that, but he could try. He could try that.

"Tennal!"

The voice was irrelevant. Tennal's eyes were fixed on Oma's back.

Tennalhin Halkana! Withdraw!

The command went straight to his brain. Tennal's body stopped, then flung itself abruptly backward.

In front of him, a stray burn shot that would have killed him seared into the opposite wall.

Now run.

Tennal ran.

He abandoned the legislator's body. He abandoned his attempt to get to Oma. He dodged fighting soldiers and overturned chairs to get out of the room as fast as his body would let him. Everything narrowed to that single command: *run.*

Surit had backed up to a side door, his own capper out. His face was ashen. He didn't have to speak; Tennal knew he would lay down covering fire as Tennal dived for the door, then he'd back out after Tennal, frantically closing the service door as he went.

Of course, Surit didn't have to speak. It was *his* write command making Tennal run.

The command didn't let up. Tennal grimly sprinted up two flights of stairs, his breath ripping from his lungs with every step. Surit ran silently, efficiently. They had to flatten themselves to the wall to avoid a line of rankers hurrying the other way, reinforcements for the chaotic fight in the docking bay. An alarm sounded over their head, and another farther up. More were shrilling all over the station. Archer Link Station was at war.

Tennal's mind played, again and again, the legislator's slow collapse to the floor. The awful loop wouldn't stop. He couldn't make himself turn around. He ran away because Surit was writing him through the sync, because Tennal couldn't even *start* to defend against that. There was nothing foreign to defend against; it was like a decision from Tennal's own brain. Tennal had been written many times before. Never like this.

They broke into a corridor, and the command emanating from Surit finally stopped.

Tennal collapsed against the wall, barely standing. "You absolute fucker."

"You nearly got shot."

"You *wrote* me." It could barely be called writing. Surit's intentions had tapped straight into Tennal's spinal cord.

Surit stopped barely six inches from Tennal. His own terror and fury seeped into Tennal's mind through the cracks in his self-control. "I know you don't care right now if you die." Tennal opened his mouth to deny it. But Surit knew it, because he was as close to Tennal's skin as his tendons and veins, because his breath was indistinguishable from Tennal's lungs. Surit could see that was a lie. His clear gaze was terrible. "But I do. I care about that."

For an instant his memories leaked over into Tennal's, and Tennal saw the legislator collapsing from another angle. Her fall was Tennal's whole world, but Surit saw it differently: in Surit's mind it was only one of layers and layers of horror. Surit was visualizing not just the fight in the room but the dogfight between ships that must be happening in the orbit of the station, the mobilization of Archer ships, the path to Orshan. Fighting on the newslogs. Soldiers dead on both sides, soldiers he knew.

The balance between the divisions was delicate at the best of times, and now Oma had a trump card with her brainwashing technique. Coup and chaos: the same thing that had happened with Marit, the same thing was happening *again,* and Surit couldn't protect anyone, didn't even know where his unit was, had nowhere to go and no way to put it right.

The vivid terror behind his write command said: *Not you as well.*

Something inside Tennal quietly broke.

His whole chest hurt. Surit had given his life to the army and Tennal had fought tooth and nail against it, and it didn't even matter, because both of them had been broken in the impersonal grind of its wheels. Tennal had been useful; he had been used. Surit, golden boy Surit, had been inconvenient, so he had been sidelined and thrown away. Tennal's aunt had thought she had control of it. She was dead.

Tennal let out an animal noise and swung his fist onto Surit's shoulder like a hammer blow. Surit didn't even flinch.

Tennal pressed his fist into the fabric of Surit's uniform, the rough weave the only thing grounding Tennal as grief washed over him. Their minds swirled around each other, nearly drowned by the silent, earsplitting howl coming from Tennal's brain.

"Your face," Surit said.

It had only been seconds. Both their wristbands were giving urgent pings, which Tennal ignored. He raised a hand to his face and recognized part of the awful feeling as physical pain; the skin of half his cheek was dry and hot and hurt to touch. One of the burn gun shots.

He *had* nearly died, then. It didn't seem to matter.

"Ignore it," Tennal said. "What now? What's on your list, Surit? You didn't want me dying, so what *next*?"

It wasn't a fair question. But Surit took it as one, almost gratefully. Tennal felt it kick the machine in Surit's mind into life, start the cogs ticking over. He felt Surit rebuild his walls and pull himself together. At least one of them could do that. "Let me think."

Surit checked his wristband, which finally made Tennal do the same. The urgent ping was an emergency muster order—not just for Tennal himself, but for the whole of Retrieval Two. Tennal and Surit were supposed to report to Oma. The rankers had been assigned immediate berths on troop carriers.

"According to this," Tennal said, distantly hearing his own voice, "a *lot* of ships are going to be leaving. Quite soon, actually." He didn't say the words *Oma's taking a fleet to Orshan Central*.

"Not my unit," Surit said. He had gone pale. "Not us. I won't."

Tennal thought it through dispassionately. He couldn't engage his emotions or he'd admit he still had them, and that was a nonstarter. Oma and her inner circle had known this was coming, which was how they'd assigned everyone places on ships. But the rank and file were only now getting their assignments. Which meant everyone would be away from their normal posts, and most people hadn't trained for this; for the first few hours, this was *chaos*. And chaos was their friend.

Tennal met Surit's eyes. Their minds rang exactly in sync.

"The *Fractal Note*," Tennal said. "Your escape plan isn't spoiled yet."

Surit had already started running. Tennal was only half a step behind.

As they ran, Tennal noticed with surprise that he *could* still run, albeit at a slower jog. A few weeks ago, that first sprint would have left him floored. Now he had enough spare attention to spin up Basavi on his wristband.

Basavi wasn't answering.

"I can't get hold of any of them either," Surit said, throwing the words over his shoulder. "They might have been detained as well. We'll see when we get to—" He stopped as Tennal's captain's key opened the door to the bay where the *Fractal Note* was moored.

The *Fractal Note* had ceased to be a prison ship some days ago. Now it was just a quiet hulk, moored in an awkward place under one of the station's struts. The loading bay swept around three airlocks in a crescent of gunmetal gray.

Tennal was willing to bet the unconscious guards and a sleeping dockworker weren't normal fixtures here.

Surit passed them with only a glance. He strode unerringly to the airlock of the *Note* and presented his own keys. For a moment Tennal didn't think they'd work; then the door beeped and slid open. Surit and Tennal entered.

"Stop there!"

The moment they set foot on the ship, there was a ranker facing them. Not in guard position—the *Note* shouldn't have any crew on it apart from their own unit. Tennal stopped. He did not, at this point, feel shocked by someone pointing a capper at him. That was probably a bad thing.

Tennal slowly raised his hands.

The ranker's face was unfamiliar, but she was deeply suspicious of them. She looked to the side, still pointing the capper, and said, "I think it's their lieutenant! Call the bridge!"

Tennal breathed out. He didn't even have to make eye contact with Surit. They *could* blast their way out of here with Surit's architect commands, but Surit was reluctant to do that.

Tennal wasn't reluctant at all. If Surit wouldn't cooperate, he could just try to tackle this ranker for her weapon. It wouldn't work. But nothing *else* was working. Tennal tensed, ready to dive.

"Wait," Surit said, as a screen opened on the wall of the corridor.

A square, blocky face. An earnest frown that melted into relief.

"*Lieutenant,*" Private Basavi said. "You made it."

The screen showed Basavi on the bridge. The room behind them wasn't the neatly crewed bridge Tennal had known from the *Note*: there seemed to be only a few of them there, and they all looked like they'd just been in a fight. Istara was hanging over Basavi's shoulder to see Tennal and Surit on the screen. Part of their ponytail had been singed off.

"We all thought she'd gotten you," Istara said.

Surit—of fucking course—saluted the screen. "Private Basavi," he said. "Permission to come aboard?"

"Permission granted, sir," Basavi said. "*Hurry,* please." There were strangers on the bridge behind her.

"She was only holding back for you," Istara said, "and I don't think we could have stayed around five minutes longer." The door to the hull proper opened.

"Wait, though," the unfamiliar ranker said. She put a heavy hand on Tennal's shoulder and turned him toward the larger cameras. "This one's an Archer officer."

Tennal stared at Istara. He didn't have the energy to ask.

Istara gave him a hard, deadpan look for a good three seconds before they said, "Yeah, that one too." Apparently Tennal's brief career of being acknowledged as a captain was over. Then, in a different tone, "Are you all right, Halkana?"

"I'm peachy," Tennal said. "Absolutely fantastic." The vortex in his head crashed against itself like waves dashing themselves to pieces.

Istara glanced over to someone off camera. "Let them both in," they said. "We're launching or we're in trouble. Get up here. You know the way."

Tennal did know the way. He no longer had to even look at Surit to know where he was as they hurried to the *Fractal Note*'s bridge; he knew where he was with his eyes closed. There was a quiet sigh of static in Tennal's ear as someone patched him into a closed group channel, and Basavi's voice came into his ear.

She was briefing Surit. "—ships fighting even up to the docking struts, sir. Station traffic control is basically defunct, and it's chaos out there. We won't be stopped, but we could be shot at if we identify as the wrong side. We might get past Archer ships with our current keys, but the route we need is held by that Cavalry fleet right now. And I don't know if they'll believe we're Cavalry, sir. All the keys we have are Archer."

Tennal stared blankly ahead as they traced the familiar route up the corridors of the *Fractal Note* where he'd used to pace behind Surit's shoulder.

"I might be able to help with that," Tennal said.

Surit gave him a sidelong glance, because apparently you couldn't turn off Surit's habit of concern even when he was in your brain. "You're in shock," Surit said. "You should sit down."

"Let me be useful," Tennal said. "Lights know that would be new."

Three minutes and forty seconds later, they got their first challenge. The call sign was Cavalry. The fight had arrived in their path.

"*Identify?*"

Tennal took the comm on visual. He had refrained from doing this out of duty, then done it out of spite, and now it just hurt. He said, "My name is Tennalhin Halkana. I am the nephew of the legislator. Let us pass."

PART FOUR

CHAPTER 25

The *Fractal Note* shot from the fighting around Archer Link Station into deep space like a bird escaping a hunter. In the past few weeks, Surit had served on the *Note,* pretended to sync on it, fought for it, and been imprisoned on it. He had never thought he would be in command of it.

It was a good thing Surit was trained not to panic because otherwise his consciousness would be a smear on the floor of the nearest hull.

If normal syncing was like this, then Surit would eat an entire stockroom of parade hats. The regulators gave the impression that architects guided their pilot readers only when necessary, in a controlled and disciplined way. This wasn't that. This was like Surit's mind had been a neat and orderly house and he had flung open the door and let in the ocean.

Surit was prepared to believe this kind of sync did not happen with readers who weren't Tennal.

Since the moment they'd synced, the sea had come in roaring, a glorious, terrible torrent. Where there had been ordinary rooms and cabinets and stairs in Surit's neat mental house, there was now a tumult of swirling water, deep-sea caverns instead of foundations, whirlpools instead of floors. Fish chased each other down the corridors and seaweed grew through the windows. Surit's own consciousness tumbled along with the tide, and part of him just wanted to embrace the elation of it, the intoxication, but he could not *think* like this. He could not think while Tennal was part of him; he could only experience. And that wouldn't work.

So he built walls, and he shored them up, and he forced their minds to separate as far as they could. The maelstrom battered at his doors, and Surit doggedly made himself a small, clear space to think and talk. It was easier if he didn't look at Tennal. If he glanced at him, all he wanted to do was take down the walls and let himself dissolve in the storm. And they had to navigate their way out of this mess.

The *Fractal Note* was meant for a crew of two hundred. The ragtag collection on board now wasn't even a fifth of that; they barely had enough soldiers to cover a bridge rotation and skeletal maintenance shifts. But even that was more than Surit had expected.

"It seemed like the right thing to do, sir," Basavi said, staring at the wall behind Surit's ear. "Can't really say why, sir."

She had collected not just all the remaining members of Retrieval Two but a disparate group of soldiers who had been on the *Note* when Archer division had impounded it. Not the officers: those had been traded back to their division. But Basavi must have secretly been in contact with a dozen Cavalry rankers outside her unit, while they all quietly worked for Oma.

Surit recognized his own poker face in hers. "Very good, Private," he said, just as neutrally. "Would you join us at the command desk?"

That threw her, but Surit didn't wait, just walked past her to do a circuit of the bridge. Everything had to look normal, even in this, the most irregular situation possible. Orshan's military was at war with itself—no, *temporarily disrupted*—and it wouldn't help the straggling of soldiers to know Surit was on the edge of falling apart.

Don't think. The storm was at Surit's door. His walls were paper-thin. If he started thinking, he might not stop.

The remainder of Retrieval Two saluted him swiftly; salutes came slower or not at all from Basavi's new recruits. Some of the faces were familiar.

And Surit opened his mouth. And he said, "Here's what we know."

In his head there was suddenly a crystal clear memory of Tennal's conversation with Oma in her office, as if Surit had been there himself. He described the remnants. He described what he and Tennal knew, or guessed, about Oma's coup. About their suspicion that Oma was using the remnants to brainwash any strong architect she could find. About how it would help her take Orshan and install herself as the new legislator. There was a vacancy, after all.

Surit stood outside his head, watching himself give the briefing like watching someone do a circus trick, pulling inputs from two minds at once. The trained order of Surit's thoughts put Tennal's lightning leaps in a structure and gave them context. It wasn't overwhelming, this time. The tension between them was like they were both leaning on opposite sides of the same door.

Once Surit shut his mouth, the picture was stark and clear. This was absolutely a coup. Long planned and enabled by the remnants the *Fractal Note* had unwittingly delivered to Oma. And there was no reason it wouldn't work.

Some of the soldiers had guessed it was a coup already. Istara's eyes were wide. The medic winced a couple of times at the brainwashing parts.

It was only Basavi, of the people at the desk, who noticed that when Surit spoke, his consonants had been sharper, his intonation slightly off. Surit saw her look, disturbed, between him and Tennal.

Tennal lurched to his feet and caught himself on the desk. He brought one hand up to his neck, took hold of Oma's wheat-stalk emblem, and—after two fumbled attempts to unpin it—ripped it off his collar with a jerk. The mark tumbled from his hand with a metallic clatter. "We need to get to Orshan Central."

Surit could feel the force of Tennal's intentions like a tractor beam, dragging him in the same direction. He resisted. Oma and

"Oh," one of them said, with a faintly surprised look, "you're still alive."

Surit didn't pause. He recognized him: the tall, grave head medic from the *Note*. "We got out quickly," Surit said. The image of Orshans firing on other Orshans was burned into his brain. Surit couldn't forget the low pulse of Tennal's despair at the legislator falling; he had to pull his mind away from it. "Any casualties in your escape?"

"None yet," the medic said. His hair was graying; he might have served during the Reader War. "We'll see if we get through this without any."

Surit completed his loop of the bridge and ended up at the command desk with the small group he'd collected. Basavi had assigned subunit heads and already had a list of them on the table. She'd brought Istara with her. Surit had to figure out how to get Basavi in front of a promotion board when they were no longer in an undeclared civil war. The medic, who was technically a lieutenant, hung around the other side of the desk. Tennal sat in a chair to the side, his head in his hands like someone with a migraine. The sync hummed between him and Surit like a stretched wire.

"All right," Surit said, looking at everyone's face in turn. "I won't pretend the situation is good."

He had to stop and take a breath, as if he were physically incapacitated. He wasn't. It was just that the magnitude of the situation hit him all at once—chaos from all angles—and Surit's mind stuttered to a halt. He hadn't stopped moving since Tennal had flung himself through the door of Surit's cell and they'd both turned their minds inside out then stepped into the middle of a battle. Surit couldn't keep the confidence of the soldiers on this ship. Everything was out of his control.

Surit closed his eyes. Then he felt, from Tennal: a curl of salt water through the crack under the door. A wisp of spray flung through the window.

And Surit opened his mouth. And he said, "Here's what we know."

In his head there was suddenly a crystal clear memory of Tennal's conversation with Oma in her office, as if Surit had been there himself. He described the remnants. He described what he and Tennal knew, or guessed, about Oma's coup. About their suspicion that Oma was using the remnants to brainwash any strong architect she could find. About how it would help her take Orshan and install herself as the new legislator. There was a vacancy, after all.

Surit stood outside his head, watching himself give the briefing like watching someone do a circus trick, pulling inputs from two minds at once. The trained order of Surit's thoughts put Tennal's lightning leaps in a structure and gave them context. It wasn't overwhelming, this time. The tension between them was like they were both leaning on opposite sides of the same door.

Once Surit shut his mouth, the picture was stark and clear. This was absolutely a coup. Long planned and enabled by the remnants the *Fractal Note* had unwittingly delivered to Oma. And there was no reason it wouldn't work.

Some of the soldiers had guessed it was a coup already. Istara's eyes were wide. The medic winced a couple of times at the brainwashing parts.

It was only Basavi, of the people at the desk, who noticed that when Surit spoke, his consonants had been sharper, his intonation slightly off. Surit saw her look, disturbed, between him and Tennal.

Tennal lurched to his feet and caught himself on the desk. He brought one hand up to his neck, took hold of Oma's wheat-stalk emblem, and—after two fumbled attempts to unpin it—ripped it off his collar with a jerk. The mark tumbled from his hand with a metallic clatter. "We need to get to Orshan Central."

Surit could feel the force of Tennal's intentions like a tractor beam, dragging him in the same direction. He resisted. Oma and the rest of the divisions clashing were like titans above them. Them following the fight to Orshan Central was like a child running in with a toy capper. "We're not a military force. We're half a unit with one ship."

"This is too far," the medic said suddenly, apparently after wrestling with himself. "We can't have a legislator—brainwashing people. Not an entire political class. There should be an outcry. This is a scandal."

This made everyone look at him in incredulity. "But everything else is just fine and dandy?" Tennal said. "We're okay with a coup every now and then?"

"Well," the medic said, "not when you put it like that."

Surit cut them both off. "We have to get the message out about the brainwashing."

"I can put it on emergency bursts," Basavi said. "Flood our outgoing channels. It *is* like an SOS."

Istara muttered, "It won't change anything. When have the people at the top not done shady shit?"

Surit had nothing to say to contradict that. He gave Basavi a nod. "Put out the emergency messages. I'll write out what we know."

"Sir," Basavi said hesitantly. "We had an incoming message as well, ten minutes ago. A public circular with Halkana's key on it." She opened a light-screen on the table.

Some people might take that away to decrypt in private, but Tennal just tapped his wristband to release his personal key. The message resolved into text. "Let me guess," Tennal said. "Archer Station misses me desperately and wants us to come back. All is forgiven."

Basavi frowned over the short line of numbers the message revealed. "No," she said. "This isn't from the station. I don't know what it is. Coordinates? The headers say it's been sent to Orshan as well."

"Well, this is a great time for a mystery!" Tennal said. He shoved it at Istara. "You're the best navigator we've got, Lights pity us. Figure out where those coordinates are, and what under Guidance they mean."

"Yeah, okay, once we're not being *shot at*," Istara said. They glanced at Surit. "Sir, what's our path?"

"We'll cut close to chaotic space," Surit said, "just until we're sure we're not being followed. Then we'll work out where to go from there."

Newsburst after newsburst hit the screens. The crew had stopped looking up from their jobs for most of them, but Surit couldn't look away. Archer Station's transmissions were cleverly patched-together publicity reels. Seeing Tennal's face in them was a punch to the stomach.

Surit was always aware of where Tennal was now. In the hours since launch, while Surit had frantically schemed with Basavi to assign jobs, check ship parts, pull fuel reserves and get everyone rations and beds, he had felt Tennal sitting motionlessly in the chair he'd first fallen into, staring blankly across the bridge.

Surit couldn't stand it. He didn't know what to do. In desperation he weakened his mental wall; he cracked opened the door in his mind.

The storm that was Tennal had not abated. It came roaring at the door, and Surit braced.

In the real, physical world, Tennal looked up at him sharply. "I'm all right," Tennal said. "I am. Really. I know you don't—"

It was too late. Surit felt Tennal's despair like his own, a fast-flowing current through the crack in his mind, swirling in agitated pools. Surit's heart hurt, and he couldn't separate it from what he knew was *himself*, because he hurt for Tennal just as much as it hurt, right now, to be Tennal.

"Tennal—" Surit said.

Tennal rubbed a hand over his eyes in something between

uneasiness and an awful relief that Surit had let down more of his walls. "I'll help," he said. "I'm being useful. I'll help." He took a deep breath, trying to pull himself together. "You're worried about how close we are to chaotic space. You could use me with the pilots."

Surit stopped. That thought had come straight out of his head. As if, on the way to verbalizing it, Tennal had diverted the impulse from the neurons of Surit's brain to his own tongue.

Surit could almost see how to do the same. But he shouldn't; that way lay madness. He forced himself to speak aloud. "That would help, if you feel well enough. But don't do any reader navigation if you can avoid it." He didn't have to explain: in their current state, neither of them knew what would happen.

"I won't." Tennal gave him a sharp-edged smile. Surit could *feel* the muscle movements of Tennal smiling, brittle and intricate like sea ice. "Keep the ship together, Lieutenant."

Surit kept the ship together. He and Basavi hastily worked out how to spread the skeleton crew to keep the *Note* running, and the resulting chaos kept Surit on his feet for a double shift and half a third one. When the night cycle bled into its fifth hour, and Surit was frowning over a fuel report with bleary eyes and a cup of coffee, Tennal leaned over his shoulder and said, "That's not how you take your coffee."

"What?"

"You've put in enough milk powder to clog a drain. That's how *I* take my coffee," Tennal said. He picked up the cup and examined it. "You take it black." The smell was sweeter than it should be, now that Surit came to think of it, but another whisper told him he'd always had coffee that way.

It was like seeing double on the inside of his own brain. Surit pressed his hands to the sides of his head.

"Get some sleep, for Lights' sake," Tennal said. "You're not a machine."

"Ah," Surit said blankly. His eyes felt sandy. "Yes."

"Did you even assign yourself a bed?" Tennal said.

Surit brought up the ship plan on his wristband and frowned at it, his thoughts moving slowly. It hadn't seemed necessary. Anyway, they had hundreds of empty crew quarters. Surit found a ranker's bunk in the nearest dormitory and assigned it to himself.

"Really?" Tennal said. "Suit yourself, I suppose." He leaned over and prodded his finger at the light-screen. "*I'm* a petty bastard, so I'll take the commander's old cabin. See you in six hours."

Surit was so tired that he should have fallen unconscious as soon as he hit the familiar regulation-thin mattress. But he couldn't. He rolled in the bed, tried the cover on and off, wondered if he was ill.

What he had thought was generalized stress coalesced into one specific ache: he was missing something. Something should be there and wasn't, like an amputated limb.

This was self-indulgent and ridiculous. Surit put the pillow over his head and pressed his forehead to the mattress. He could go a night without sleep if he had to.

And ignoring it nearly worked, until his door opened without warning and Tennal stumbled in, flooding the room with light. Tennal looked as wild-eyed as Surit felt. "It's like I've lost my *hand*," he said, holding the doorframe like it might anchor him. "No, worse than that, it's like my hand dropped off and wandered to the other side of the ship. Is this the sync? This is the pits!"

Surit made an incoherent noise and put the pillow back over his face. The awful feeling of separation had stopped. He felt—not *whole*, but closer to it. And he was so tired. "Go to sleep."

"Get lost in a fucking swamp," Tennal said, without heat, and fell into the bunk across from Surit.

They fell asleep feet apart from each other. As Surit drifted off, he was aware of two sets of lungs rising and falling in perfect unison. And he dreamed of drifting through stars and nebulae and spinning galaxies, though he had never had that dream before.

The next day, they didn't talk about any of that.

The *Note* arrowed toward Orshan Central, but not on the straightest route. Instead they curved around the edges of chaotic space, not near enough for the disturbed space to be dangerous but enough to confuse anyone else's scanning equipment. Tennal attached himself to the pilot console alongside Istara.

Surit was busy from the moment he woke up. Half the crew members were on jobs they'd never done before. Half of them weren't even sure going back to Orshan Central was the right thing to do. Surit explained, listened, ordered, cajoled. And always in the back of his head, a wash of salt water, Tennal's acerbic awareness. Surit found himself watching people's eyes more than usual, playing to what they wanted, what they feared. He hadn't even known that was an option. It felt like he was constantly coming out with things that weren't quite *him* and weren't quite *Tennal* but somewhere in between.

The news bulletins continued to play. Tennal's cheerful, unwitting clips popped up in propaganda rolls about every half hour.

"If I have to see that smug prat on screen one more time," Tennal said conversationally, "I'm going to set our comms receiver on fire."

You didn't know, Surit said. Too late, he realized he was still watching the screen, and his mouth hadn't moved. The words had gone straight to Tennal's brain. Surit winced and forced himself to say what he meant out loud. "You didn't know. That matters." That was better. He could hear himself say it, like they were still two separate people.

Tennal rubbed his eyes and looked back down at the pilot's console.

Surit dimmed the screen and went to check on the oxygen levels. He hated this. And worse, he knew that if he'd had to sync with anyone, he would have chosen Tennal in a heartbeat. That felt like—not *taking advantage,* because Tennal had thrown himself into this as much as Surit—but it felt like they could have had something, if not for this.

Only that was another comforting lie, wasn't it? He and Tennal couldn't have had anything. They'd never had a future.

He hadn't been paying attention to the news screen until Basavi took a sharp breath.

This broadcast was a press conference. A girl sat at a dais in the Codifier Halls, looking grave, framed by flower sprays and the emblem of Orshan behind her. Two deputy legislators sat behind her in full formal wear. Surit had only a moment to sort out where he'd seen her before the audio kicked in:

"*My name is Zinyary Halkana. I am the niece of the legislator.*"

Tennal gave a low cry and shoved his chair back so he could see the screen.

The Zinyary on the screen looked nothing like the bubbly apprentice Tennal sometimes talked about. This version of her was somber, poised, pale. It was obviously a scripted statement, but she read it with enough assurance that she might have written it herself.

"*Yesterday, my aunt was murdered by General Oma of Archer Division.*"

The whole bridge was watching now. Istara muttered, "Took them long enough to come out and say it."

"*I am told General Oma intends to land on Orshan Central and take control of the government by force. I fully support my aunt's deputies until a new legislator is lawfully elected, and I appeal to you all to do the same.*"

"How did she get on a broadcast?" Tennal asked, his voice choked. "How did they get hold of her? Who's using her?"

"She doesn't look like she's doing it under pressure," Surit said.

"*I know my brother has appeared in General Oma's propaganda,*" Zinyary said, her eyes uncompromising on the camera. "*I believe he is under duress. Tennalhin, if you're listening, please be careful.*"

That was all of it. Tennal pushed to his feet, lunging toward the screen, but the clip winked out.

"She's in Exana, then," Surit said.

"She must have found my aunt's allies," Tennal said, pacing back and forth in front of the bridge's main screen. "Of course they'd put a sixteen-year-old in front of the cameras—looks better than a washed-out politician. Of course she'd volunteer. She's going to be top of Oma's fucking hit list now. What are you *doing*, Zin?"

The crew had gone back to their duties, though they were all eavesdropping. The one exception was Istara, who said suddenly and loudly, "Got it."

Tennal spun around. "What?"

Istara didn't seem to care about Halkana family politics. They floated their screen up from their workstation and expanded it. "The coordinates in that message," they said. "It's moved, because chaotic space does that, but I think that's where the lab should be."

"The lab?" Tennal said blankly, his thoughts still clearly on his sister.

"You know," Istara said, as if Tennal were being particularly dense. "The one where the remnants came from. Why would someone send you that?"

CHAPTER 26

"All right," Tennal said, slapping his hand on the wall. A light-screen spread from his fingers to fill the space. They were in the flag chamber: the table that had held thirty Cavalry officers now had him, the two first-class rankers, and the medic, who might know about remnants. *And Surit.* Tennal had to remind himself Surit was there, a separate person and not just another node of the Tennal-and-Surit hybrid. "So we have a choice. Oma will be landing on Orshan Central soon. On the other hand, some anonymous person has decided to send us a message about the old laboratory in chaotic space. There must be something in there. Relevant to our choice: Oma is an unthinkably powerful architect who can brainwash people who get near her. Surit and I should be immune to brainwashing, but that doesn't mean we're immune to her writing us. And I don't know how Oma's picking her targets, but *you're* vulnerable," he added, jabbing a finger at Istara and Basavi. "As is any other architect on this ship."

"Um," Basavi said.

"It won't come to that," Surit said. "We're—I'm not bringing this unit into a situation where that might happen."

"*Um,*" Basavi said again.

Istara gave Basavi a hard stare, and whatever they saw there made them give a heartfelt groan and drop their head onto the table in front of them. "*Savi.*"

"I'm not vulnerable," Basavi said, with the slow inevitability of a dirt grinder breaking through the side of a mountain. "I'm a reader."

Tennal found himself stranded in a pure vacuum of shock. "What?"

"Just do us both," Istara said, their voice muffled. "Lights, you might as well."

Basavi stared at the wall on the other side of the room and said, "Private Istara is also a reader."

Tennal reached out for Surit and found Surit's mind just as blank.

"I *know* you two," Tennal said to Basavi accusingly. "I've known you for weeks! Istara said they were an architect! They said you both were!" The two of them hadn't come across as much more than neutrals, but Tennal had taken Istara at their word: some architects were barely visible.

Basavi gave an unforthcoming shrug without taking her eyes off the opposite wall. "It's personal."

"Why lie about it?" Surit asked, genuinely bewildered.

Tennal, Istara, and Basavi all turned to stare at him. "Why lie about being a *reader*?" Istara said. "In the army?"

"Did you have a very soft and fluffy experience at officer training, Lieutenant?" Tennal asked. "Have the past few weeks been some sort of aberration? Did I just join at a particularly bad time?"

Surit flushed. "All right," he said, "that was an unhelpful thing to say."

Tennal forced himself back on track. He knew there were hidden readers in society, probably more of them than anyone suspected. You weren't in danger of conscription unless you were a certain strength, and Lights knew there was no good reason to wave the information around in front of people you didn't trust. Zin was very careful whom she told. Basavi had clearly decided they were trustworthy. Well—she had decided Surit was trustworthy, and Tennal was irrevocably along for the ride.

"I think we should go to the lab," Basavi said, apparently still on the original problem. "There might be something there."

Back into chaotic space. Tennal fed the thought into his and Surit's combined mind. It was easier to think when he used Surit's mind to do it: he wasn't as distracted by stray thoughts of his aunt's absence or of Zin. *What do we think of that?*

Surit's thoughts wrapped around his like two strands of a helix. Oma had an insurmountable advantage with her remnants. Nobody on Orshan was expecting what was coming. If they could find anything about how she'd done it, they could pass that information on to someone who could fight her.

The lab was their only option. They both dwelled for a moment on their last frenzied visit to chaotic space, but this time had to be different.

"You have neuromod medical training, don't you?" Tennal demanded, turning to the medic. It felt like there were harmonics of Surit's voice under his own. "You were a medical officer on the *Fractal Note* before, when half the crew were architects. You have experience treating neuromods—if we went to the lab, you'd at least know if we found anything useful. Like a way to stop Oma's brainwashing techniques."

The medic looked startled. "I—well, yes, I suppose."

"We're not on a known route into this part of chaotic space," Surit said aloud. Tennal felt an unvoiced echo of the words in his own throat. "We'll have to navigate the edge until we find a way in. Luckily—"

"—we've piloted this sort of route before," Tennal said, the train of thought switching seamlessly between them. He had to pull out of Surit's double vision so he could glare at Istara. "Can't believe I bought your line about *architects are sensitive to space.* That's why you're a good pilot, isn't it? You might not be a strong reader, but you have *some* of the same senses as me."

"I'm a good pilot because I trained!" Istara said. "You might be able to pull your mind out by its seams, apparently, but you don't know the first thing about physics."

"I know a bit. Stop that, Lieutenant," Tennal said aloud to Surit, whom he could feel in Tennal's head uncovering his scant knowledge of physics and looking at it in some alarm. "Anyway, I don't need to know as much as you two. That's why I'm the—"

"—assistant pilot," Surit said, completing the thought. "Private Istara, please keep command of the navigation bench. Captain Halkana will be there to assist only."

"Sir?" Basavi said uneasily.

Tennal and Surit now realized they had been passing sentences between each other, as if whose tongue touched the words were only a convenience.

"New course, then," Tennal said, after a tense pause. It would be dangerous to explore the edge of chaotic space for a clear way in, but the rest of the group looked to Surit, who nodded, and there were no disagreements.

"We must be more careful," Surit said to Tennal in an undertone, after the meeting. "This can't be normal. I think we didn't do it quite right."

"You *think*?" Tennal said. "In a normal sync, you would have brought me gently under control like good little puppet. You're not supposed to hurl yourselves at each other like two bits of space debris, *bam,* nothing left but mingled dust."

"That's not what I'm worried about," Surit said. He didn't meet Tennal's eyes. "I'm worried it's getting worse."

"We'll be fine," Tennal said. "Pilots and architects hold these syncs for years." He ignored the deep, rumbling current of doubt in Surit's mind. They'd make it work for as long as they had to. Tennal couldn't think more than a few hours ahead.

The ship was noisier, full of muttered conversations that died down when Surit or Tennal walked by, as the tense hurtle toward

Orshan turned into a slow crawl into the outskirts of chaotic space.

By this point, Tennal was so used to dealing with the difficult people Surit aimed him at that he did it without even prompting. Between Surit's exhaustive mental lists of everyone on the ship and Tennal's own nose for problems, he spotted the few soldiers who were grumbling about the new course and cut them out for a talk. Tennal was charming. He was sincere. He dangled the threat of Oma like a grenade. And he ran it all on autopilot, because Tennal's higher consciousness had just decided to pack up shop and stop thinking.

That was fine. Tennal didn't need to think because Surit was still thinking for him in their joined mind: solid, intent thoughts about divisions and coups and what might be happening on Orshan. Thoughts about their ship and their tiny, self-assigned mission back into chaotic space. Tennal tagged along with the currents in Surit's mind. This was much easier, in fact. It didn't hurt at all.

Days ticked by, two into three. Tennal had gotten over his aunt's death. He no longer thought about it, even when Surit was distracted.

"You used to talk more," Basavi said abruptly.

They were both at the pilot's terminal. Basavi was basically Surit's deputy lieutenant now, but since Tennal didn't have the training to handle even basic piloting by himself, she sometimes covered for Istara. Tennal looked up.

His eyes had been physically staring at a radar navigation screen, but all his attention had been focused through Surit's eyes down at the power generators. "Fifty-one, and the last power rack at half capacity," Tennal said. Then, "What?"

Basavi wore a miniature Guidance script on a bracelet; now she touched a fingertip to it uneasily. "I know you were always synced," she said, "but you and the lieutenant . . . it didn't look like this."

Tennal wrenched his attention back into his own head. It took

some effort. It took even more effort to realize he'd been riding
along in Surit's head for most of his shift. He'd sat next to Basavi
for—Lights, five hours—with neither of them saying anything. His
mouth was dry, his muscles were stiff, and he needed a piss. What
he really *didn't* need was ship gossip about how weird he and Surit were becoming.

"We're fine," Tennal said. "Nothing's different." He cast around
for a distraction and realized he wasn't the only one who had been
sitting here in silence for hours. "*You're* quiet."

Basavi brought up two more light-screens, as if she could hide
in her work. "No, I'm just—I've been distracted."

That caught Tennal's interest. "Distracted how?" He could feel
Surit's attention sharpen as well; a sudden spike of worry that his
most reliable deputy wasn't focused. Tennal could make a guess at
the cause. "Worried we're going to tell everyone you're a reader?
I don't know if you've noticed, but I don't care, and Surit only
pretends to be law-abiding."

Basavi moved one of the screens and looked at him in careful bemusement, as if she'd hidden the reader thing for so long,
it barely registered. Tennal had never really thought about just
how many people must've been hiding low-level reader abilities,
ignored by the army because they weren't useful. It wasn't as if anyone would announce it. "No," she said. "No, it's not, um, it's not
that."

Lights, maybe she had family on Orshan Central and was worried about them. "Do you need help?" Tennal said. "Because
there's probably not a lot we can do, but we can try." He didn't
think too hard about how *we* had just slipped out. About how *I*
was growing harder to grasp every hour.

Basavi's voice was stifled. "I don't need help." Her shoulders
had hunched up around her ears, as if she would have very much
liked to exchange her reader powers for the ability to haul her head
into a shell like a turtle. "If you have to know, it's just me and
Istara. And we're fine. Thank you."

"You and Istara . . ." Tennal looked at her properly. To his reader senses, she radiated discomfort, but it wasn't a bad kind of discomfort. Something had changed. "Wait," Tennal said, feeling a stab of glee for the first time in days. "*Wait,* did Istara finally ask you—"

His throat closed. Surit had tried to stop talking at exactly the same time as Tennal had intended to finish the sentence. Tennal choked, sucked in a huge breath and dissolved into coughs.

Basavi whacked him between the shoulder blades until they'd both ascertained Tennal wasn't choking to death. He didn't tell her why he'd choked, though he kept forming sentences like, *Okay, so what exactly did Istara say*—sentences that Surit, in their joined mind, dissolved in horror before they could come out of Tennal's mouth. "It's private," Basavi said. "I told xam—" She looked discomposed.

Oh, this must've gone further than Tennal had guessed. That sounded like Istara had a personal gender reference beyond *they,* and they'd let Basavi use it. Sometimes people had more nuances to their gender than Tennal bothered with for his own, and sometimes they were public about it, but sometimes they weren't; sometimes it was a major stage of intimacy just to let someone know. Unsurprisingly not many people had ever trusted Tennal that much. Tennal wasn't going to ask about Istara's personal gender, because he had some sense of propriety despite his best efforts and Basavi clearly hadn't meant to say it, but he *did* have questions about Istara and Basavi hooking up.

But what came out of his mouth, in Surit's phrasing, was: "I see. You're entitled to your privacy under the regulations."

It hadn't just come out in Surit's phrasing. It had come out in Surit's exact tone of voice.

Tennal's hand went to his own throat.

Basavi had noticed. It was impossible not to notice; it was Surit's voice, only changed a little by Tennal's lungs and jaw. Tennal didn't have any way to explain that. He had a sudden wild wish for a pack of soothers. He didn't have any.

Basavi made a worried noise, but Tennal got there first. "Just a side effect," he said. "I'm all right." He almost meant it. He might not have had any soothers, but he did have a safety valve now: he had the reassuring clockwork of Surit's mind when his own head got too bad. That was just as good. "Everything's fine."

It was fine.

Over the next three days in space, Tennal could see them both changing. There was more confidence to Surit's step, less erraticism in Tennal's. Tennal found it easier and easier to slip into the well-maintained structure of Surit's mind, the clean lines and organized thoughts. Tennal was only half-present during his pilot shifts, their snatched meals, the time he spent wandering the ship to make sure the soldiers were on task. The rest of his mind was in Surit's body.

When one of them opened their mouth, the other could speak with their voice. When Tennal found a soldier with no sense of humor, he could pull the harmonics of Surit's rock-solid certainty into his voice and steal Surit's phrasing to give himself credibility. When Surit, on the other side of the ship, was lost for an answer, Tennal could give him a sharp deflection.

It was a relief in a lot of ways. Whenever Tennal thought about something like the look on his aunt's face as she fell to her knees or the incredible stupidity of his past few weeks, and in fact his whole life, he could pack it away. He could neatly slip sideways into their shared thoughts instead—the ship, the unit, Tennal himself, all set out cleanly—and feel his previous mental tangles, his previous way of being *Tennal*, start to wither away. Surit's mind was neat and shining and dependable. It was as far as you could get from the disaster zone that was Tennal's head. It was an upgrade in every way.

Tennal had the lurching sensation that they were both losing their grip on something.

A couple of times, Tennal opened his eyes at his own seat and blinked away tears. Inexplicable. He wasn't sad. He wasn't anything.

He was covering the pilot console alone, late at night, when Surit burst in the door.

"You have to stop this," Surit said, wild-eyed. "We're losing parts of you."

Tennal stared at him. "What?"

"I don't know what you're doing," Surit said. "But you're letting yourself disappear."

This was ridiculous. Surit didn't know anything more about syncs than Tennal. And Tennal felt fine. "You're imagining things. What do you want me to do, call up the regulators and ask for a consultation? We're fine."

"*Look*." Surit's hand closed around Tennal's wrist, and Tennal felt a jolt, like an electric current, then—

—he saw what Surit saw.

In Surit's head was the same storm as in Tennal's, but the way Surit parsed it was different. Tennal had a sudden, lurching glimpse of an endless, ceaseless ocean and a rocky coast and knew this was how Surit experienced their joined minds. The ocean in Surit's head was unnaturally quiet. It drained itself away onto the land, lay stagnant in pools, sank into the sand. It was drying up.

"I don't think we can last like this much longer," Surit said. And now that Tennal was deep in Surit's head, he recognized the strand of fear. He understood, now, how good Surit had always been at hiding fear.

Tennal breathed out and said, like prying his own bones from his chest, "All right. Let's find a way to stop it."

The medic wasn't asleep, but Tennal summoned him from his shower, ruffled and grumpy.

"You said you knew something about neuromodification,"

Tennal said. Medical was quiet: the bay was meant for a team of four, but now it was only this lieutenant part-time.

"Is this an emergency?" the medic asked. "I have very *basic* training in neurology. We spent more time on burn wounds and transmissible diseases. I don't know what you expect of me."

"But you must know something," Tennal said impatiently. "This ship used to have dozens, hundreds of architects on it. You had a Rank One on the ship! What if the sync went wrong?"

The medic gave Tennal a slight frown, looking between him and Surit. "Has it? Gone wrong?"

Tennal and Surit shared a glance. *Maybe,* one of them said. Tennal couldn't tell which one of them it had come from, and he felt a stir of fear.

It was Surit who looked back at the medic and said, "Is a sync supposed to get more intense as it goes?"

The medic looked startled. "No. It's not a disease. It's a protective mechanism for the pilot."

Protective mechanism, Tennal said—or heard—disgustedly in their combined thoughts.

"Ours is," Surit said. "Getting worse."

"Is there any way to reverse it?" Tennal demanded. "They told me it's supposed to be impossible, but you know what else was supposed to be impossible? *Brainwashing.* The army's been doing shit with people's minds for twenty years, and fuck knows it never told the civilians much until soldiers started having kids."

"There has to be something you can do," Surit said.

The medic hesitated. "There's an experimental procedure," he said. "It's been around for quite some time. I understand they had . . . deaths in service. I'll be blunt: we're all mortal. One of the pair has to die first just by the laws of nature."

"Encouraging!" Tennal said. "Can we split *without* both of us dying?"

"What I'm trying to say," the medic said, "is that we can save the reader."

"That's—" *not helpful,* Tennal tried to say. But in his head, Surit faltered, and the words never reached Tennal's throat.

The medic continued as if Tennal hadn't spoken, in full lecture mode. "Readers are more stable. If the architect dies, they've had some success with treating the reader to keep them alive. But there have been no surviving cases the other way around."

"You could save Tennalhin?" Surit said.

What does that have to do with it? Tennal demanded, in the privacy of their thoughts.

"It requires a temporary coma and some specialized scanning equipment with traces of remnant infusion—I won't go into the details. The reader comes out of it altered, but alive."

The storm in Tennal's head grew louder, as if trying to crack his skull apart. Again, Tennal couldn't tell who was thinking what: *What if this keeps getting worse?* and *Nobody's going to die, fucker* swirled around like thunderclouds. The last one was probably him.

"What do you mean, the reader comes out of it altered?" Surit said.

The medic seemed to consider how to describe it, as if this might be unwelcome news. "In practice, the survivors exhibit traits we associate with architects."

"You mean," Surit said, then swallowed. "Like something is left behind. Something of the architect."

In the moment of silence, the air purifiers in the walls were very loud. Tennal could almost see the two of them from the outside, standing in the middle of the pale green flooring, surrounded by medical equipment and the smell of antiseptic gel. Tennal-and-Surit. Two nodes of one body, pretending they were still fully human. It seemed horribly plausible that if Surit died, parts of Surit's mind would linger in Tennal's. Tennal even imagined he could learn Surit's architect abilities if he tried hard enough and Surit's consciousness weren't there to get in the way. It would be easier as the walls between them eroded.

He had to stop thinking like that. They had merged far enough.

"But this is all irrelevant, isn't it?" Tennal said impatiently. Neither he nor Surit was going to die, so they might as well knock this on the head and look for other options. *There must be other options.* "You don't have the equipment."

"I do." The medic gestured to one part of the medical bay. Tennal had no idea what most of the scanners were used for, but one of them had heavy-duty shielding like there was something in it that gave off radiation. "The ship has it."

Surit had opened his mouth but stopped. "I thought you said it was very specialized."

"It's standard," the medic said, with only a fractional pause. "This is a well-equipped bay."

"*Why* do you have this?" Tennal said.

"It comes with—"

"No, it doesn't," Tennal said. Surit was trying to remember if he'd ever seen a list of standard medical equipment for a troop ship. Tennal, on the other hand, watched the medic's eyes.

Surit realized something was wrong, and his attention fell in behind Tennal's, focused along with him.

Their doubled attention magnified Tennal's senses until he didn't even need to read. They could see the medic's eyes dilate, see the pulse in his neck. Tennal-Surit felt like something so far up the food chain that this human was a grub crawling on the ground. They felt like a *predator*.

"Lieutenant Yeni!" the medic said.

Tennal-Surit jumped at the crash from behind them. Their new awareness broke apart. Tennal spun around and saw Surit had tripped—like his knees had just given way—and his body had fallen onto a counter, sprawled across a tray of empty glassware. None of the toughened glass had broken, but Tennal could feel his shock mirrored between them like a feedback loop.

"Good job, Lieutenant," Tennal said flippantly, to cover up what that meant. They'd let themselves get too distracted. It was getting worse. When he grabbed Surit's wrist to haul him to his feet, it felt like holding one of his own limbs.

Surit wasn't thinking about that, though. Tennal could feel him thinking about something else entirely. His gaze came up and focused on the medic.

Tennal let go of his wrist and turned his head.

"I should do an examination," the medic said. "Even if not a brain scan, a full physical—"

"No," Surit said, with the calm certainty of a riptide. Tennal could feel Surit's suspicion, even though Surit hadn't quite reached a conclusion. He just knew something was wrong. "Don't try and distract us."

In the quiet, several things clicked in Tennal's head.

"Why sync me to a junior lieutenant who's not even a pilot?" Tennal said softly. "There must be senior Rank Ones waiting for readers. Why have we never even *heard* from the regulators?"

The medic frowned. "I don't understand."

Tennal started to pace. "Why didn't I go straight to basic training?" he said. "It makes no sense. The regulators must have a way of inducting conscripted readers. I'm not the first one. Why not give *Surit* training? Why just tell him to sync and turn him loose with no idea what to do?"

Surit's head came up, watching Tennal. His mind had gone completely still. Listening.

"Why pick an architect, even a Rank One, who's not a pilot himself?" Tennal said. "Why send us off, on our *first mission,* to somewhere so out of the way that news wouldn't get back to the planets, under the authority of Cavalry Division, where my aunt has the *most* contacts, where she can cover up what she likes? You were fresh out of training, Surit. You shouldn't have been let near a sync."

Surit said nothing. From the depths of his thoughts, he let Tennal see the doubts, curling like wisps of smoke. An old misgiving, that he had been set up to fail. And a more recent one: the army that had lied to him about his mother had also lied to him about his appointment. Because working for the regulators was a prestigious career track, and nobody would recommend Surit for that.

"That's it, isn't it?" Tennal said. Their gazes bore into each other. "You're probably the least-connected Rank One architect in the whole damn fleet."

And last, in Surit's head, a very recent memory—the medic himself, as Surit had entered the bridge of this very ship, six days ago: *Oh, you're still—*

Tennal spun to face the medic. "'Oh, you're still alive,' was it?"

The medic was pale and still. He had a hand on his wristband, but he'd obviously realized there was nobody he could call.

Surit opened his mouth. The words came out like someone winding up a rusty chain. "If I'd died—"

"—like you nearly died in chaotic space last time we were here," Tennal said. "Like you nearly died under the commander my aunt fucking *gave you to*—"

"—you would have lived." Surit's voice was steady. "You would have survived the sync."

"More than that!" Tennal said. Every word was another pace closer to a precipice looming in front of him. He didn't want to press forward, but he couldn't stop. "If we believe this fucker, I'd have *kept* some of you. I could have passed myself off as an architect."

"Your aunt wanted that," Surit said.

Before the sync, it would have been a question: *Did she want that?* That kind of separation no longer existed between them. Tennal had nowhere to run. The only hiding place was in the negative space of the thoughts he had so far refused to think.

Tennal had finished running anyway. He and Surit were on the edge of this cliff together.

"My aunt wanted to fix me," Tennal said. He heard the words

come out of his mouth, high and thin and flat. "She must have known what was possible, because she knew the scientists who ran the first neuromod project. She thought my problem was being a reader. And she knew there was a way to *change* a reader so they had architect powers, so people would think they were an architect. This is Orshan. It's easier to live as an architect than a reader. She knew that."

As he said it, it rang true. It would have been funny: his aunt, blindfolded, reaching for the elephant of Tennal's inadequacies, catching the trunk, and deciding how to kill the snake. But it wasn't funny.

"Could she have passed me off as an architect?" Tennal said. The bay was horribly silent. Tennal didn't care about the medic. He only cared about the still, listening presence of Surit in his brain, like a low bank of cloud. "I don't know. Dozens of people know I'm a reader. But if I suddenly started writing people, some people *would* start treating me as an architect. Of course, that wouldn't have fixed anything. Joke's on her for thinking it would. But she *thought it would*." He met Surit's eyes. "So she needed an architect to sync me and then to die. A recruit to sacrifice for the greater good. She'd be used to that idea. It's something the military does."

Surit said nothing.

"And who better," Tennal said, "than the son of a disgraced general? Lieutenant Surit Yeni, Rank One architect, barely out of officer academy. No connections. Provincial. Expendable." Every word tasted like bile. "Who better than you?"

"Ah," Surit said softly. "Yes."

It was the quietness that honed Tennal's incredulous rage into something else. He wasn't angry. He was past anger. He was *complicit*. The Halkanas, the family of the legislator, had chewed Surit up and spat him out to make Tennalhin Halkana a normal, functioning member of society. Just like his aunt.

His aunt, who was dead.

Tennal's fury had no target. It spun sickeningly, floating free in his head. None of her plans for Tennal had gone right, of course, because Tennal could have made the Guidances themselves fuck up. His aunt hadn't foreseen Surit's conscience. She hadn't foreseen Oma. She hadn't guessed Tennal would throw himself so hard into the sync that they'd end up in an alien merge that was slowly consuming them both.

"Why didn't she tell you?" Surit said, as if he were talking through his thoughts out loud. "Why wouldn't she—oh. Of course." That thought was so strong that Tennal could hear it. Surit had absolute, cast-iron confidence that Tennal would never have agreed to it.

It nearly broke Tennal. He wouldn't have agreed to it, but nobody else would have believed that. He had never fucking deserved Surit.

Surit went silent. It killed Tennal that Surit was somehow hiding most of his thoughts, that he couldn't read anything more than the low thrum of horror Surit was privately sinking into.

"You fucker," Tennal said conversationally, to the medic. "You're involved, aren't you? You would have killed him. You were briefed to murder someone in cold blood."

"No," the medic said. "Absolutely not."

"Oh, you just *happened* to have what you needed for a broken sync?" Tennal said. "You just happened to have what you needed to dismantle Surit's mind for parts?"

"I was briefed to save your life, if and when it was necessary," the medic said with precision. "I was told nothing else. I am a doctor, not a butcher."

"Don't need to be, do you?" Tennal said. The medic was almost incidental to the wave of loathing rising in him. Surit had nearly died twice in chaotic space: once on the shuttle, and once in his tug. Tennal had been ordered away from him both times. "You don't need to be a killer if other people do it for you."

"Captain Halkana—"

"Well, none of that happened," Surit interrupted.

It stopped Tennal in his tracks.

"I won't chew over hypotheticals." Surit sounded utterly reasonable. "We're here now, and even if I was meant to die, I didn't. We still need a solution to our current problem."

Surit *wasn't* completely reasonable. There was a deep well of fear underneath—Surit's fear of becoming nothing, Surit's dread of being an unwilling pawn, his terror that everything he had built could be pulled away and every choice counted for nothing. Surit could try to keep his thoughts hidden, but his horror was so strong, Tennal heard it like a drill through a wall.

All of it Tennal's fault. He couldn't think of anything to say.

"So," Surit continued, without waiting for Tennal, "if you don't have a solution for us, we'll need something new. As Captain Halkana said, we're proceeding to the laboratory where the neuromod experiments were originally done. I don't believe Oma stripped it; I think she was only after the remnants. So, if there *is* any research there, would you be able to understand it enough to do something with it?"

"I—I suppose so?" the medic said. "Probably? It's generally a matter of programming a machine."

"Excellent," Surit said briskly, as if they were at a routine strategy meeting. "If we can find a way to deal with the brainwashing, we'll have to prioritize getting that to the rest of the army. But if the sync degrades and Captain Halkana and I don't survive the journey back, then we lose the value of his Halkana connections. We'll have to be fast. If we can take a straighter route—ah, there." His wristband pinged, and he opened it to a jump request. "Private Istara's found a route in. Tennal, they'll need you."

Tennal gave Surit an incredulous look. Somehow Surit was talking himself out of his horror with logistics.

The medic saluted. "Sir."

"Captain Halkana," Surit said politely. "The jump."

"Oh yes, the jump," Tennal said blankly. It seemed impossible to go from *my aunt tried to have you killed* to mundane piloting issues. "We'll just . . . carry on, then?"

Surit didn't quite look at him. In Tennal's head Surit's presence was a bank of heavy cloud, unnaturally still, laden with a static that had no outlet. "If you're all right."

"Brilliant, fantastic," Tennal said. "Just top form. Couldn't be any other way." It wasn't *him* who'd been in danger. His brain still struggled to process that. Tennal hadn't been thrown away, even when he'd been marched onto a ship, stripped of his communications, and chemically primed to be handed to an architect. *Surit* had been thrown away. For him. How did he make up for that? How did he deal with it? And now Surit was still in a sync, his existence irrevocably bound up with Tennal's, because Tennal's fuckups had diverted the whole course of his life.

As they left Medical, Surit bent his head to Tennal's ear. "We have to be careful," Surit said softly. "I don't want to lose myself." He wasn't so perfect at control anymore. When he spoke, fear crackled like sheet lightning.

"I know," Tennal said. "It's okay."

It sure as fuck wasn't okay.

Tennal was an accessory to murder. He couldn't even keep the whole thought in his head at the same time: it was so awful that he could only grasp the edges of it. He'd always known he made things worse for people he liked just by being around them, but he'd never imagined this.

He couldn't bear being inside his own head. He wanted to dissolve into Surit, but that wouldn't undo any of it; that would only burden Surit with Tennal's thoughts on top of his own. Tennal couldn't even leave Orshan space without dragging part of Surit's essence with him. Tennal was stuck with everything he'd ever done and everything his family had ever done, and there was nowhere to go.

Istara's request pinged on his wristband, with slightly more colorful language as they got closer to the jump.

Tennal made his way back to the bridge.

His thoughts were blank. This was the gift of the military, he realized. It made your actions automatic. He'd spent so long trying to find a way to stop thinking; who knew that all it took was to have walked down the same corridor dozens of times, to sit at a bank of desks the same as the ones you'd trained on, for your unit-mate to look up in familiar irritation and say, "*There* you are. Get your headset on. I'll get up the map." Tennal's muscles knew the drill. He didn't have to think about what he had done to Surit just by existing.

He put on his headset. He looked at the map.

It took only an instant for him to sink outside his body. It was easier every time, and this time was like water running downhill. It was as easy as blinking to draw on Surit's power now.

I'm taking us closer, Tennal said. *I can see a shortcut.* Back by his body, he could sense Istara frantically keeping the spaceship from hitting any of the near obstacles with their dual controls as Tennal ripped them all through rift after rift.

It was the same, he realized, in his dreamlike state. The contours of his mind, the storm of chaotic space, the ocean Surit saw in their heads, the fabric of space between galaxies: it was all the same. Tennal felt both unutterably expansive, as if he himself could encompass star systems, and also very small. There was so much universe. He didn't have to be a shackle around Surit's leg. He didn't even have to die. He could leave enough of himself behind, and just, and just—

Next jump is the last one for now, Surit said tersely. Tennal knew Surit could feel something was wrong but not exactly what. *That's an order.*

It made sense. Tennal could feel Surit's worry at the slow pace of galaxies, and for a single tick, Tennal felt gently regretful at how it had all turned out. But the tides of space were right there, and Tennal's mind was made for them.

He took the last jump, and let his consciousness sink into space. The last tether to his body faded away.

Time dilated.

He drifted, nameless, in the currents between the stars.

There had been concerns before, he vaguely felt, but now there was only existence. He was free, though the concept of what it meant to be *free* was rapidly unraveling.

The space cluster spun around him, spheres of rock and gas in a slow, sustained dance. He had only ever been in this space cluster, and yet somehow he had been in *every* cluster. He and his kind weren't bound by distance.

He pushed at his thoughts to try to understand that. But when he did, he found he had nothing to latch on to. All his memories were an illusion, like pushing on a door that led to thin air. Something was wrong.

It occurred to him, after another slow tick, to wonder what he was.

Halkana—Halkana! Lights, it wasn't this bad last time—where's the lieutenant? Get him here!

Something was wrong. He wasn't what he thought he was. He didn't have the right memories. He couldn't feel *horror,* not like this, but he felt a sliver of concern.

He was distracted for another tick by watching, wondering, at the slow loop of a comet.

Another distraction: a tiny packet of metal and organics. It was so close to him, it was within the area that was currently himself. He trained his attention on it. He had a vague feeling it was—had once been—important. Or was that in the future, that a speck like this would mean something?

In the tiny dollhouse rooms of the spaceship, something that had been him floated down the corridor on a gurney, a small crowd of creatures flocking urgently around the hovering stretcher. He had no names for them. That caused a moment of—wrongness. Names had been important, once. And the creature striding up front, he recognized that one. He would know them in the blackness of space. He didn't have a name for them either.

It came back to him with a lurch. Something was wrong, and it was this. He wasn't supposed to be here. He had come into being as one of that mayfly species, and now he was patched into abilities much larger than he should have. He wasn't meant for this level of consciousness.

"—nothing I've seen. You haven't broken the sync. He's just not there."

Graveyards, he thought. He could feel the echo of a graveyard in his brain. He could feel remnants of his kin on the nearest planet and on other bodies. Whole collections. And others, not yet excavated from the bones of the rock. His kin threaded through the whole sector in their graves. The remnants of their bodies had given him these abilities.

He was not really one of them. He was a mayfly who had tried to become something larger. This was not real. This was not an escape.

A set of slow ticks passed while his consciousness spun.

Back on the spaceship, the thing that had been him lay on a bed in a miniature room, with only one other creature beside it.

"Tennal," the creature said. That was it. That was his name. Surit—Surit—had his head in his hands. *"I can feel you out there. Please come back."*

The moment he let himself think the word *Tennal*, he snapped into an orbit around his body like a magnetic field.

The creature called Surit looked up, as if he'd felt something. "Tennal?" he said, and waited for a reply. When he didn't get one, he looked back at the body, like it had Tennal in it, and rested a hand on its chest. The hand shook. "Are you sure you're doing the right thing?"

Tennal had been asked that before. But this was different. He had to think like a mayfly creature again to realize why: Surit was the first person who'd said that to him expecting he might answer *yes.*

And that was when he knew, with a resignation like the weight of the ocean, that he was going to come back.

Tennal funneled himself back into his body.

Or he tried to. As he pushed into the corridors of his mind, he realized, in a panic, that he was trying to funnel a lake into a cup. His mind had lost the shape of its human brain. It had spanned stars like a nebulous cloud, and he'd *lost* parts of himself to that swirl; he'd already forgotten the parts that hadn't been important.

His lungs took a heaving breath. Surit's eyes widened, and he grabbed Tennal's wrist. The core of Tennal was suddenly present in the tiny bunk room he shared with Surit, the thin whine of ship systems in his ears, the familiar astringent smell of clean linen in his nose. He nearly choked. His tongue was thick and sandy in his mouth, the tiniest piece of organic matter, and yet these tiny movements that kept it out of his airway were all that kept this body alive. *Surit, I've lost it. I've lost*—He couldn't remember what.

He felt Surit in his mind, looking at the disordered remains of what had been *Tennal.* Tennal had expected dismay, but that wasn't what he got. Instead Surit circled thoughtfully around his mind in that quiet, determined way that said Surit thought he knew what he was doing.

Stay there, Surit said.

Tennal had forced his eyes open, but he couldn't see past the void in his mind. He was exhausted. Like a rat in a maze, you could try every Lights-lost method at your disposal to escape yourself and even make up new ones unknown to science, and you would *still* end up here, with the fractured pieces of yourself, alone, with no escape and with an even steeper hill to climb. It was staggeringly unfair.

Only, this time, he wasn't alone.

He said, *Surit, I fucked up.*

There was a thoughtful pause, and in that silence—not despairing but busy—Tennal felt like he had hit the ocean floor, and his fall was arrested.

You tried something that didn't work, Surit said at last. Tennal recognized what Surit was doing, now. He was sifting through the chaos and pulling splinters of Tennal out of his own mind, out of Tennal's mind, out of the fragmented space around them.

This is you. Surit's mental voice was strong and assured, and with it came a piece of Tennal.

Tennal saw—

In the middle of the flag chamber, among military types Surit knew well, Tennalhin Halkana sat crackling with energy like an exposed wire. Surit had met him once and now meant to ignore him, but he was impossible to ignore: a barbed comment for every argument, a knife slid into every weak point, an upturned nail in every path. Surit had tried to look away. That hadn't worked.

He saw—

Tennal, feet up on the seat opposite him, cradling Surit's stolen tea, sketching an impossible past and an impossible future like picking sweets from a tray. Surit still thought sometimes, What if we'd met in Exana? *He hadn't been able to stop.*

Tennal saw himself over and over again. He stalked down the corridors of the *Note,* lied smoothly to Oma, threw himself behind his captain's desk on the station, hung over the back of Istara's chair to argue piloting, took briefings from Basavi, wordlessly turned to Surit. In Surit's mind, Tennal was both an open flame in a fuel depot and someone Surit could rely on completely. And Surit didn't seem to see a contradiction.

Surit set the points in Tennal's mind like stars in the firmament. Tennal had no way to *argue.*

Lights. Tennal was going to have to fill in the gaps himself. He knew what he was like. He knew he was selfish. He knew he was lazy. He knew he made things worse as a defense, or a manipulation tactic, or simply because he was bored. The memories came filtering back into his head, as if he and Surit were condensing the essence of Tennal out of thin air.

Surit hesitated at the new memories. *Yes, but,* he said. And more came from him in a flood: the Tennal he had known over the past few stormy weeks, a hundred points of light. Surit wasn't even playing down the worst parts. He just somehow saw them differently.

We tried to kill you, Tennal said.

That was the legislator. You never even tried to hurt me. It wasn't excusing Tennal. It was a simple statement of fact. *There doesn't have to be a winner and a loser.*

There's always a loser, Tennal said.

Surit didn't dignify that with a response. He was having more difficulty finding the last pieces of Tennal and fitting them back together. Tennal felt Surit's spiking frustration. Tennal had some control of his own body now that his mind was rebuilding itself— not all the way, but enough for him to lift his hands and rub the base of his palms into his closed eyes.

Hey, it's all right, he said, as Surit's frustration peaked. *It's all right if I'm not salvageable. Not your fault.*

Surit paused, no less frustrated, and said, *Stop doing that.*

Tennal had to explain. He had always operated on the principle of never explaining, but in this moment, half on the ship Surit commanded and half still in the void of deep space, he owed Surit.

I'm fucked up, Tennal said, as neutrally as possible. *I blame, in no particular order: my aunt, my personality, society, my bad choices, and the inside of my own head. Oh, and being a reader, but that was never the root of the problem. Even with Orshan the way it is. Plenty of readers are well-adjusted and not complete assholes. The problem is my brain.*

Tennal could feel Surit—not rejecting that, exactly, but dissenting. Surit didn't deny that Tennal was fucked up, but Surit disagreed about the extent of the problem, and also felt things had been more unfair than Tennal had allowed.

Of course it's unfair, Tennal said impatiently. *The army was unfair on me, and it was unfair on you. The way they recruit readers is unfair on everyone. But we're talking about* me: *Tennalhin Halkana, First Family, the nephew of the legislator. I have a charmed fucking life. My aunt was ready to commit murder just to get rid of my little reading problem. And look at Zin, who had exactly the same aunt and the same reader genes. She's just fine.*

Surit took a breath.

Tennal, opening his eyes, jolted suddenly back to the physical room and became aware that Surit's hands were on his chest, unnecessarily, like Surit thought of this as mental CPR.

Surit realized it at the same time. He looked down at his hands on Tennal's tunic, then took them away. Tennal only had a moment to miss the warmth before he realized Surit was speaking, with his vocal cords and his lungs and all those other things Tennal had temporarily forgotten they both had. They must have been talking in their minds up until now. That was probably bad, given what they knew about their sync degrading.

Surit said, with finality, "Just because someone else is okay doesn't mean you had to be."

There was silence.

"I think my mind is nearly back together," Tennal said conversationally. "Don't suppose you could do me a favor and sand off the rough edges?"

Tennal could feel Surit's mind moving around him, marking out the boundaries of *Tennal* like a hundred pinpoints of stars. "No." It was a flat denial.

Tennal's eyes were dry and full of sand. He blinked too many times.

He wasn't meant to vanish into the cold void of the cosmos. He was human, and he had a body and memories. He had Surit, he had Zin, he had the person he'd been the past few weeks and the weight and shadow of the person he'd been all his life. He would have given anything to escape for so long, but he wouldn't give those up. He was back in his body, all unreliable five foot eleven of it, with his mind—flawed and erratic, but *his*—pinned to it by Surit's network of stars. He shook himself mentally until he was settled into every inch.

He sat up.

"All right," he said. "I'm here."

CHAPTER 27

Surit slept through the night in total exhaustion. He thought he felt Tennal wake up. Surit was so tired that he managed to drag his half of their shared brain back into sleep and barely even felt the separation until he woke.

There was a cup of dispenser coffee beside Surit's bunk. The smell wafted over, rich and bitter. And a foil-covered breakfast tray. Tennal had never done that before.

Surit picked up the coffee. There was a standard packet of milk powder on the tray next to it. He stared at the packet.

He'd talked about this with Tennal. One of them took their coffee with milk powder; one of them didn't. His own taste had slipped Surit's mind last time, but he'd been distracted. Now, he consciously tried to remember, but to his unease, he found the information wasn't there. His preference was just . . . gone.

It was only a cup of coffee. Surit drank it.

Tennal had left Surit alone to sleep, but he wasn't completely gone; Surit was aware of him hovering in his head, like someone constantly leaning over his shoulder. Tennal's presence felt fresh to Surit, as if a complete rebuild of his mind had just made him more himself. His newly focused emotions were as accessible to Surit as if Tennal had written them in a comms message. Tennal had let himself care when Surit put him back together. Tennal had let himself have a goal. He was afraid but determined.

I owe you, Tennal said, in a thread in Surit's head as Surit made his way up to the bridge. *Thanks.*

Surit felt a resonance behind *owe*. Surit didn't want anyone owing him, but that wasn't quite what Tennal meant. He wasn't sure what he was feeling. He sent a thread of whatever it was back and didn't even realize until Tennal responded in kind, with amusement, that it was *affection*.

A few days ago, Surit would have thought he might be in trouble. But in the chaos they were all in now, this was a drop in the bucket.

When he entered the bridge, it was business as usual. Tennal, Istara, and Basavi—technically the high command of their skeleton crew—congregated around the pilot seats, working on a map of their position.

Istara and Basavi stood and exchanged salutes with Surit. Tennal, slumped on his elbows over the map, didn't move. Instead his consciousness slipped in beside Surit's mind, still with that thread of affection, and shared Surit's eyes as Surit looked at the map over his shoulder.

There were no accurate maps of chaotic space. The three of them—*No, it was Istara and me,* Tennal commented—had drawn the worst illustration Surit had ever seen, which seemed to be their joint idea of chaotic space and the area around it. Surit could see Tennal's memories of working on it. They'd drawn dots to represent known ship positions. The misshapen doodle of a horse—*That means Cavalry,* Tennal said—was Tennal's handiwork, and Istara had put a stick figure labeled *Oma* on a ship to Orshan Central. Chaotic space was a series of carefully drawn lines and some stars for effect. The army did not like to work freehand, and it showed.

Surit examined it closely, Tennal's mind twinned quietly and attentively around his own.

They weren't fooling themselves that their mission had much of a chance. This was a coup, a hurried civil war, like Orshan had been rocked by several times before. The difference here was that Oma had capabilities beyond anyone's ability to fight. This ship, the unit, Surit and Tennal themselves: they were just after-thoughts in the larger crisis.

But if they were right and the signal was coming from the abandoned lab, something the *Fractal Note* had opened the way to, then they might find something there that could counter her brainwashing. Surit studied the red-shaded area where the pilots had guessed the lab should be. If they found some of the neuro-modification research there, they could—maybe—stop this war.

Surit was not going to be like his mother, even if she had done it for the right reasons. Surit was not going to make a last stand and get his unit killed. There had to be a better way. They had to be clever.

Marit had not had Surit's unit. She hadn't had someone like Tennal.

She didn't have someone like you, Tennal said.

They both paused. There had been uncertainty around the *you*, as if they were both losing their grip on what that meant.

A hand reached across the table. In the state they had slipped into, neither of them looked at the physical bodies around them, but their joined instincts could recognize *threat*. And they were fast. Surit seized the attacker's arm.

"Sir, Halkana isn't breathing!" Istara snapped.

Surit dropped their hand. His mind fell apart from Tennal's in shock.

Tennal's body sagged over the console, empty-eyed. Now that Surit was paying more attention, he could feel a faraway part of Tennal dying, starved of oxygen, ignored by their merged thoughts. Istara caught Tennal's arm. Surit grabbed both his shoulders instinctively and thought furiously, *Tennal! Get back in there!*

Tennal's mind spun in Surit's head, disconcerted. Then he seemed to grasp how to do it, said *oh*, and Tennal's body took a choking breath under Surit's hands.

Surit clutched Tennal's shoulders. Tennal took gulp after gulp of air, like he'd just been pulled up from drowning. When he turned his head, the skin around his lips was a dull shade of blue. "I'm fine."

Their shared mind spun with terror. Tennal had slipped into Surit's mind so completely they'd both forgotten Tennal needed to breathe with his own lungs.

"Halkana, what the fuck," Istara said. Basavi leaned over and handed Tennal a cup of water.

"It was nothing," Tennal said insistently, to Surit as much as to them. Surit could still feel him in his head, though not as close as a few seconds ago. "I just had a moment. Fell asleep. Quick nap." He pressed the tips of his fingers against the table, massaging oxygenated blood back into them. "Where were we?"

Surit took a breath. That had been a dangerous moment. Falling into someone else's body for a handful of seconds might be less terrifying than, say, seeing your soldier—your reader—your friend—spread out like a micron-thin layer of plasma across the void of the stars and disintegrate, but it wasn't *pleasant*. He tried building a wall between them again. It was harder this time, like piling up sand in a stream.

Still, Tennal felt it. *What are you doing?* Tennal said into his head, sharp and nervous.

We're still spiraling into the sync, Surit pointed out. *I'm trying to stop us.*

He felt reluctant agreement from Tennal and a spike of fear. Tennal could feel it as much as he could: the end result of whatever was happening in their heads wasn't one they'd both survive in a recognizable state. They had to keep it stable, and one thing Tennal had never managed was *stability*. And that wasn't the only thing Tennal was afraid of.

If we break this sync, you die, Tennal said.

Surit acknowledged that with a brief mental nod. He pushed

himself away from Tennal and took a seat by the console. *I'm not planning to die.*

"Show me our ship's position," Surit said aloud.

Istara and Basavi exchanged dubious glances, but Basavi laid out the map across the whole pilot's console, a light-screen that covered two terminals. "Here, Lieutenant. It's not to scale."

Tennal tapped the edge of the sloped bank of metal the screens covered. "It's changed since we were last here."

"It's *chaotic space*," Istara said. "It changes all the time. Ignore him, sir. We think we've got a rough fix on where the lab might have drifted to."

"How long?" Surit said.

"I—" Tennal hesitated and looked to Istara.

Istara traded glances with him. "Depends on the next jump," they said. They saw Surit's mild incomprehension and pointed at the part of the map that looked most like two primary school children scribbling on a wall. "Halkana's creepy ability to fling his mind into space—"

"—my *great reading skills*—"

"—combined with someone who has actual, you know, piloting education, means we can get through narrow folds of space without the ship distorting. Hopefully. The sensors found some possible ways through. It's shifting behind us as well. If one of the new passages stays open, we could get out much faster than we came in."

Movement flickered in the corner of Surit's eye: the ranker covering the comms station had just sat up straight. Comms were unpredictable in chaotic space and came in queued packets, often bundled together. A second later a ping came to the command channel.

Basavi scooped it up. "Compressed burst," she said, after a moment.

"It's either Cavalry calling us in or Oma trying to bribe me over so she can put me on more vids," Tennal said, his eyes still glued to the pilot console. "Either way, they can't make us do anything while we're in here. Can I see?"

"It's just the newslogs," Basavi reported after a moment, sounding nonplussed. "I don't recognize the name of the originating ship; it's just relaying newslogs into chaotic space. I don't know if it even knows we're in here."

At that moment, something from the same burst pinged on Surit's wristband. A transmission marked *private*.

The others didn't notice him open it. A small, personal screen appeared in front of his eyes, as if he were reading a report. On it was an image of Governor Oma.

The clip was two seconds long. Oma simply looked straight into the camera and said, "*Yeni, stop and report back.*"

What—

Surit had never before felt a compulsion settle its firm, merciless grip on his mind. He had thought he was too strong an architect for compulsions to take on him for long. Of course, Oma had put one on him when they'd first taken him to Archer Link Station, but people had tried compelling Surit before, and surely . . .

But he only had a moment to think that, and then that was it. The compulsion settled over him, and everything realigned around a sudden, certain knowledge: he had to get back to Archer Link Station. He had to get back to Oma's office. He *had* to.

His whole brain kicked into gear, synapses firing to work out how to get back as fast as possible. He had a vague sense that the crew might resist. That had to be avoided at all costs. "We need to change course," he said. "We have to get out of chaotic space. Immediately."

Basavi killed the comms screen, startled. "Yes, sir. Why . . . ?"

Tennal's head snapped up. Surit felt Tennal's presence stir awake in his mind as well, aware of the change in Surit's thoughts but not understanding it, not yet. "Surit, what the fuck?"

Tennal was his greatest threat. But Surit was a Rank One architect, and Tennal was his synced reader.

As Surit reached for the full extent of his powers, he wondered why he'd never used them much before. They came to his hand easily; they seemed stronger here, resonating with the chaos outside, with the fabric of space, with Tennal in his head. They filled his ears like a symphony.

We have to go, he said calmly. And he wrote Tennal.

Tennal's shock came off him like a wave. And, after that split second of immobility, Tennal *fought* him. He fought like a wildcat, he fought with every dirty mental trick possible, he sent stabs of phantom guilt and lances of pain into Surit's thoughts. Surit overrode all of them. He had direct access to Tennal's mind. It felt like they were two halves of the same being, but Surit was better at this. Surit was an architect with access to Tennal's thoughts, and whatever Tennal did, Surit could reach in and shape him like putty.

At his wits' end, Tennal finally recognized it was a compulsion and reached in desperation for techniques to defend himself from it. Surit hadn't realized Tennal knew those, but ultimately that didn't help him. Nobody was compelling Tennal himself so the techniques were useless. But they were irritating. Surit wrote him quiet.

Tennal's mind convulsed one final time. Then, like an exhausted animal, he went compliant.

For the first time, they were genuinely, seamlessly, one mind, and Surit had control.

"Oh," Tennal said calmly. "Yes, I see now. We have to get back, don't we? Let's take the closest route out of here."

Istara swung around as Tennal moved from his copilot chair and settled into their empty seat. Tennal's hands hesitated as he entered the instructions, but he had basic pilot training: Istara and Basavi had trained him themselves. Surit could feel him gathering confidence. *Urgent,* Surit reminded him, and Tennal sped up.

"Halkana, what are you doing?" Istara said.

Tennal was about to explain Surit's message, Surit realized, and that wouldn't do. They had to get back to Archer Link Station because Surit had to return to Oma's office, and Istara might try to stop them if they knew what Tennal was doing. "I received an urgent request for help on a private channel," Surit said. And to Tennal: *Tell them that's true.*

"He's right," Tennal said, his eyes unfocused. He wasn't quite pliable, Surit could tell. He was going to have to keep at least half his attention on keeping Tennal cooperative. The thought caused some odd dissonance. "It's an emergency. Secure crew for approach."

"Announce course change to the ship," Surit said to Basavi.

It was habit. She would have run this routine hundreds of times since training, the same as Surit had. He heard her start to mouth the standard reply then stop. Her eyes narrowed.

That sent a spike of fear into Surit. If she refused, then Istara would follow, and the crew would follow them. Surit couldn't afford that. He had to return to Archer Link Station. He took some of his attention off Tennal and wrote both of them.

It wasn't as easy as writing Tennal, but Surit was at the height of his powers. Basavi jerked on her feet slightly and said, "Yes, sir, announcing course." Surit swung around to Istara, but they were already sliding dutifully into the copilot's chair.

Switching his architect powers between three people was not easy at all. Tennal and Istara exchanged a few terse words, but they'd done this before, so Surit had no need to force them through the individual steps. Surit took hold of a safety strap and watched them, his heart beating in a terrified patter. He had to get back. His entire future narrowed to that. He had to walk through the door to Oma's office in Archer Link Station and report. That was the only thing that mattered.

Tennal shut his eyes. The ship shuddered as Istara brought it closer to distorted space. Surit recognized Tennal's wayfinding method now and was no longer afraid when Tennal's eyes turned empty and his fingers moved like a puppet, inputting information and directions to Istara.

It took minutes. The gravity fluctuated; Surit was the only one not strapped in and had to secure himself halfway through so he didn't get thrown onto the ceiling. Anything could go wrong. Surit had to force himself to breathe.

Finally the shuddering of the ship stopped, and the gravity stabilized. Surit unstrapped himself and took a stride toward Tennal and Istara in the pilots' chairs. They must be near normal space now. "Set course for—"

He was arrested by a forearm over his windpipe like a vise.

"Sir," said Basavi's voice in his ear. Her bulk behind him was immovable, pinning him to the spot in a textbook unarmed wrestling move. "I think you should go to Medical."

Surit's body moved automatically. He grabbed her wrist and threw her over his shoulder. He had taken unarmed combat classes in basic training, but so had Basavi, and Surit was used to having more of a height and weight advantage than he had here. She came flying over his shoulder but grabbed his arm on the way. Surit came down with a crash. Basavi rolled onto him and jammed her elbow into his stomach.

That moment of inattention was all Tennal needed to say, "*He's compelled*," and Istara stood from their terminal.

Surit slammed a write command into Istara, and they dropped back into their seat. But he'd taken his eyes away from Basavi, who punched him in the stomach a second time like a demolition ball. The other soldiers on the bridge started to stand and shout. Surit ignored the pain in his stomach and gathered the energy for another write command—

And then Istara shot him.

"Okay," Tennal said, with a wan attempt at a smile, "the good news is, you're not brainwashed."

He perched on a portable medical cabinet beside the bed, ignoring the perfectly good chair. Surit wasn't in Medical but instead in the dormitory he and Tennal had been sleeping in. His shirt was off, and the ship's air circulation prickled on his naked chest. Someone had slapped a transparent dressing over his collarbone. Under it was the red rash of a capper shot.

Surit said nothing.

This didn't deter Tennal. "Apparently Oma told us the truth when she said brainwashing wouldn't work on people who were synced and that she didn't try it on you." Tennal tried the awful smile again. "This was just a normal, trigger-based compulsion. Nice and straightforward."

Just a compulsion. Just a compulsion, complicated by Surit's architect powers, by the fact Surit was *a weapon of war.* By the fact Tennal had voluntarily synced with him, so Surit had a pathway into Tennal's brain. If Surit had been even slightly more subtle, even slightly better at lying, they might be on their way to Archer Link Station right now, to fall into the hands of Oma's allies.

Tennal was very pale. Surit remembered Tennal's fear, back when they'd been shut in a room for three days straight: his fear of being a puppet. His fear of being used as a tool by someone else.

Tennal had fought the write commands like he was dying. Surit hadn't given him any leeway at all, any choice. That was Tennal's worst nightmare. Surit had done it to him.

Tennal heard Surit's thought in their enmeshed minds and brushed it impatiently aside. "You didn't have a choice," Tennal said. "And this is nothing. One more incredibly dumb problem to baffle my therapist with. The important thing is, I'd be able to tell if you were brainwashed, and you're not."

Surit touched the blistered red skin on his chest. He had experienced capper shots before, during training exercises. "Istara knocked me out."

"Well, yes," Tennal said. "I offered them a commendation for shooting a senior officer, but they thought it might not look good on their record." That wasn't what Surit meant, and Tennal knew it because Tennal was in his mind. The bad smile slipped off Tennal's face. "To be honest, we should have expected this. Oma did tell us she'd put a compulsion on you. I suppose even she didn't realize it would become useful later. I didn't think compulsions would work on you; I didn't realize you were . . ."

". . . vulnerable," Surit said, completing the thought. The word felt unpleasant in his mouth. He had never been vulnerable to writing. Compulsions were more difficult than normal architect commands and even harder to make last beyond a few seconds; Surit had thought he was too defended to worry about it.

"Right." Tennal's lips quirked. "She used the remnants, didn't she? To enhance it. She must have had one on hand that we didn't see."

Surit reached back into his memory and found with a shock that it was hazy, as if his normal visualizations had been sunk into fog. She must have.

"Those remnants are a game changer," Tennal said, seeing Surit's fuzzy memory at the same time as Surit did. "Maybe the bloody Resolution is right, and they should all be locked up. Though Lights know I wouldn't trust the Resolution with them either."

Tennal was worried—no, Tennal was *terrified*. He wasn't showing it outwardly, but it was threaded like veins through his every thought, and he had no way of hiding it from Surit. He wasn't even trying.

Surit had a duty not to make it any worse. So he pulled all his own fear behind the partition he'd built. And in that small, private space, he thought: Tennal had synced with Surit to save him from Oma, and this was how Surit had repaid him.

Tennal took a breath and slid off the cabinet to his feet. "All right. The bad news is we've lost ground. We're in normal space, farther from where the lab is. But we think we've found a way back to where we were." He looked Surit straight in the eye. "I want to kill your wristband's comms function."

Surit touched his wristband. That meant he wouldn't be able to contact anyone outside the same room. He'd have to rely on the others to relay commands. "Yes."

Some of the tension left Tennal, and Surit realized he'd been expecting a fight. "That's not going to work once we head to Or-shan Central, but . . . we'll think of something."

"Yes," Surit said.

As Tennal pushed himself away from the cabinet, Surit's vision blurred. For an instant, he saw the floor by Tennal's feet through Tennal's eyes. Tennal stumbled, grabbed at the bed to steady him-self, and they fell apart.

Tennal righted himself and dusted off his sleeve, as if nothing had happened. There had been no reason for them to merge, just then. It had simply happened.

Surit said: "It's getting worse, isn't it?"

Tennal tried another forced smile. This one wasn't any better. "I told you. I trust you."

He left Surit alone.

Surit didn't know how long he sat there, his body slowly pull-ing itself out of a capper hangover while his mind spiraled into controlled fear. He still had a sliver of private space where he could hide his thoughts if he concentrated. He could feel Tennal immediately embroiled in a piloting problem as he reached the bridge.

Yesterday, Tennal had stopped breathing. He had nearly died.

That had been Surit's fault. Tennal was dissolving into the sync with Surit and neither of them could stop it. And worse—ten minutes after the breathing incident, Surit had written Tennal. He had overridden Tennal's will because Oma had put a compulsion on him.

Surit had always known other people might act unpredictably.

They might save you, or they might let you down. The one person you could always rely on to act with total predictability was yourself. Your own mind was the only thing you had total control of.

Yet he had let Oma use him to betray his unit.

Tennal had said it last night and again this morning: *I trust you*. Surit's chest twisted. What if Oma had planted more compulsions? Surit didn't remember any, but he hadn't realized this compulsion was strong enough to last for weeks. What if she had a way to make him forget?

Surit had always been the strongest architect around. He should have fought harder. He'd refused to acknowledge what he had, and it had been used against Tennal. Against his unit. He had built his entire life around being dependable, and it turned out that was only a delusion.

Surit had used Tennal like a puppet. The sync was killing him.

We have some unwelcome visitors, Tennal commented in his head, from the bridge.

Surit roused himself out of the spiral and asked for detail. This, too, was his fault. Tennal offered a mental picture of the map, now functioning since they were on the edge of normal space. A trio of Archer ships tracked slowly toward them. *I think we were supposed to run straight into their arms,* Tennal added. *They sent the clip that triggered your compulsion.*

Can we escape?

Tennal formed Surit's hand muscles into a thumbs-up. *We should be able to jump back into chaotic space without much trouble.* Surit looked down, and Tennal dropped the thumbs-up. *Sorry. Want to come to the bridge and see?*

No. Surit gave him the vague impression that he had to work on something to do with the ship. He could tell Tennal was wary of the way Surit was hiding his thoughts, fearful of what the merge was making them, but more concretely fearful of what would happen if they separated. And he still trusted Surit, even after what Surit had done to him. That hurt.

All right, Tennal said. *I'll leave you to it.*

Surit didn't get to work. Instead he let a screen hang in front of him, blank, and turned his gaze inward. Tennal trusted Surit to know the right thing to do, even if Tennal didn't know what it was. Surit had never been trusted like that before. It was humbling. Surit felt like he was piloting a tiny boat in the middle of the vast ocean, under an endless, eternal sky, and everywhere he looked, the sea echoed the stars' light.

There was a right thing to do and Surit knew what it was.

His and Tennal's minds were tangled irretrievably. But Surit knew how to recognize the parts of Tennal's presence now. He had pulled every part of it out of the void, separated it from his own mind, and helped Tennal rebuild himself like cracked pottery. The sync was a mess, but like puzzle pieces of two colors, Surit now knew which piece was which.

Tentatively at first, then with increasing momentum, he went methodically through his mind—through the ocean inside it, the submerged timbers and bits of flotsam that had once been a house—and tagged each current as *him* and *not him.* Even with Surit's new knowledge and his talent for memory, holding that many pieces of information at once stretched his abilities to the utmost. But he could do it.

He got off the bed and shrugged on his tunic. The twinge of mild pain from the capper rash wiped out a whole swathe of his mental tagging. Surit had to pause with his hand on the bunk, concentrating hard, to redo the pieces he'd lost. It felt like he was holding a stack of glass vases in his head, as if one wrong move would see them smashed on the floor.

He walked, very carefully, to their old, empty shuttle, where the retrieval tugs had once launched.

As he stepped up to the closed door of a retrieval tug, he carved off a tiny fraction of his attention to authorize the tug's departure. The alert wouldn't reach anyone: on a fully crewed ship, some bored ranker would be monitoring this, but the *Note*'s skeleton crew barely had enough people to monitor life support. The door opened. Surit climbed into the pilot's chair.

In his head, he had drawn a bright line between parts he knew as *Tennal* and parts he knew as *himself*. He wasn't interfering with them, and Tennal couldn't tell what he was doing. Keeping them all in place was like spinning a thousand plates at once. In the dark space of their minds, he could see all the parts of him and Tennal threaded through with a shining net of connective tissue, like the invisible lines of gravity that connected the stars.

Surit sealed the tug and used its systems to send an order to Basavi: *continue course*. He marked it as low priority and put it in the bottom of the command queue.

For the last time as the lieutenant of a Cavalry ship, Surit gave a console the command to launch a tug. The vacuum hissed as the corridor sealed behind him. There were no windows. The only sign he was ejecting into space was the clanking movement of the tug around him and the gentle acceleration as he eased out of the bright cocoon of the *Fractal Note* and into the cold, star-strewn dark.

Goodbye, Tennal, Surit said softly, and broke every connective tissue in the sync at once.

His head thudded back against the headrest. A searing light flashed across his eyes. His hearing cut out, as if he'd stepped on a sound grenade. He had time to think: *At least this will be quick.*

But it wasn't. The light drained away, and his vision slowly cleared. His heartbeat thundered in his ears, but Surit could see. He wanted to pass out. He clung to consciousness with a supreme effort of will.

The tug crawled slowly out from under the shade of the *Note*, into the vast emptiness. Surit's wristband was cut off from incoming comms. Somewhere, Tennal would be furious. The bridge would be in chaos. It would take them a while to realize where Surit had gone. They couldn't send anyone after him without losing them to the oncoming Archer ships.

Tennal could be as angry as he liked, but at least he would be free and alive.

Surit stared at the radar and imagined the great metal bulk of the *Note,* the scattered points of light beyond. He could feel the medic hadn't been lying: the ordered structure that held his mind together was crumbling, but it was happening so slowly. He might be conscious for hours at this rate. Maybe days. He automatically went to call up the next thing to do on his list, but, of course, it was blank. He had nothing left to do. It felt . . . peaceful.

He could sleep. He hadn't slept without a list of tasks in such a long time.

A harsh chiming woke him out of his doze. He'd drifted for hours, according to the tug's console, but its alert system was flashing a green light: the tug had been caught in a tractor beam. The system thought its occupant was being rescued. When Surit brought up the radar, he saw the hours had brought him close enough to the Archer ships that he'd been caught.

It didn't matter. His mind was a bundle of slowly fraying strings. They couldn't do anything with him. Surit Yeni was no longer a lever for someone else to use.

But as he accepted the tractor beam alert—not that he could do anything about it—he felt the echo of Tennal in his mind. It wasn't real, of course. He had no communication with Tennal, no route back to him, just the echoing husk where the presence that was *Tennal* had been.

And that phantom presence suggested: *You're free.*

Surit wasn't dead yet.

He activated the tug's comms. Possibility prickled in his veins. Tennal had never been free to do as he chose the whole time Surit knew him, and yet Tennal was the least circumscribed person Surit had ever met. Surit understood that now. The freedom to do something gloriously unwise. The freedom to be a firework in a munitions dump.

A query came over the voice channel. They hadn't expected him to activate the comms. They'd expected him to be taken prisoner.

Surit gathered the unraveling strings of his mind, concentrated to keep his thoughts together, and opened the voice channel.

"Lieutenant Surit Yeni, Cavalry Division," Surit said. "I'd like to see Governor Oma."

CHAPTER 28

—need him conscious—

—treatment half-finished, don't you dare—

—higher sedative dose, he has a tolerance—

—give him time. You're lucky he's not dead.

Tennal woke in the sterile surroundings of Medical with a hole in the fabric of himself.

It felt like he had been bleeding out for days, though he couldn't feel a wound. Surit was gone. Tennal was stuck in a bed with—he cataloged swiftly—a drip, some standard monitors, and two scanning bars in a precise tent over his head. The bars were heavy and white, like square metal arms. They gave Tennal a buzzing sensation in his back teeth.

Tennal should've probably let whatever treatment this was finish. But Tennal had gone to the ends of the earth and the far reaches of outer space to avoid being picked over by concerned people in military medic uniforms, and even when the rest of his mind was bobbing like a fishing lure in a whirlpool, he was very clear on one thing: *fuck this.*

Tennal swung the bars aside—the buzzing stopped—and sat up. He'd been on drips before after too many experiments with drugs; this one was just hydration, a preventative measure, so Tennal nicked it out and stole some tape to put pressure on the scratch. He felt Surit's absence like a wound, like someone had sliced Tennal's mind in half. But the wound had been cauterized. Tennal knew without thinking that he was going to survive—more than that, he was going to be fine, even if his brain felt like someone had freshly irradiated it. He even had Surit's old thought patterns. He didn't know what the scanner had done, but his reading abilities had desperately latched on to the vestiges of Surit and taken the dregs of his powers as Tennal's own.

The medic had told them the truth. Tennal could see how to *write* now.

Tennal knew instinctively he'd never be that good at writing because it took some sort of energy Tennal didn't have, but by the same alien instinct, he knew it was just the opposite side of the reading coin, like someone had taken his head and gently turned it around to a new angle.

To hell with that. Tennal had no desire to be an architect. He swung his legs off the edge of the bed in the empty med bay, stopped to catch his breath, and thought, *Fuck you in particular, Surit Yeni.*

There was no answer. Surit was gone.

He didn't have to wonder why Surit had done it. Tennal had lived in Surit's mind for eight days. Surit had known there was no future in the rapidly worsening sync, even before Oma's compulsion. Trust Surit to weigh up the most utilitarian outcome and decide he would be the sacrifice. Tennal was going to find him and then murder Surit himself.

If he could find him. Tennal's limbs weighed him down like lead and his head felt like someone was drilling an auger into it. But he'd started out a prisoner and now had his own ship and, technically, his own shitty side in their burgeoning civil war, so theoretically anything was possible.

Anything is possible. The words in his head felt hollow, like someone repeating an empty catechism.

He put a standard signal out to whoever was listening to messages from his wristband: *request attention.* The ship must be on its way to the lab. He should know what was going on. It was hard to care, but he was technically part of the ship's command. He had responsibilities.

Tennal stared at the ceiling. The void called to him from beyond it, no longer inviting but a great threatening storm. He thought about how the universe was mostly nothing but humans made up stories about the things that were there and pretended they were more important than the crushing weight of the nothing.

Lights, Surit would hate him thinking like that. Zin would too. Everyone Tennal loved was worse off for knowing him. He was a hole in the hull, a bug in the software.

Shit, he thought, as he heard the exact phrasing that had just gone through his head. *Was I—*

The thought was so nagging that he had to sit up and think it. *Am I in love?*

Every other thought drained out of his head—they were dull anyway; with a sudden jolt, he recognized them as things he'd thought thousands of times before. How *boring* to have the same thoughts about how you were a stain on the universe for the thousandth time. He was tired of it. Tennal was sick of being sick of himself.

He had to get up, to stand and walk across the room and be restless at this new thought, like electricity through his muscles. *Am I—*

He put on his wristband: *attention, emergency.*

Surit might've thought there was no future, but Tennal had never made a habit of agreeing with anyone unconditionally, so he didn't see why he should start with Surit's ghost. In the absence of Surit, Tennal could make a good case to be the ranking officer, if Basavi would play along. This ship was fueled to chase Surit. It was all smoke and mirrors, but this was *their* ship, and *their* smoke and mirrors.

When Basavi stumbled into the room, dragging the medic, she found Tennal disconnected from the brain scanner and examining the unit's hand-drawn map on his wristband.

The medic stopped in the doorway, clearly taken aback to find him up. "Are you—"

"I'm unsynced," Tennal said, "I'm awake, and I'm feeling particularly insufferable today."

The medic's eye twitched. "Lie down."

Tennal didn't move. He looked at Basavi. There wasn't even a hint of a smile on her blank face; in fact, Tennal had the strong impression that she was furious. Interesting. She saluted. "Captain. We're near your target. Lieutenant Yeni's whereabouts have been unknown for three days. You've been unconscious."

Three *days*. They'd lost Surit three days ago. "Why didn't we turn around?"

Basavi went even more furious. She opened her mouth, but at that point, the speakers in the room crackled. Basavi must have been allowing someone to eavesdrop through her wristband.

Istara said, through the ship's speakers, "Did you forget you had a *plan*, Halkana? Did you come up with another way to stop Oma's creepy brainwashing thing? Or can you just not hold a thought in your head for more than twenty-four hours?"

"I've been unconscious!" Tennal said to the speaker. All the rest of the crew should know was that Tennal and Surit weren't synced, not why or how parts of Surit's architect abilities had been cauterized onto Tennal. "I've had a *traumatic medical experience*, Private Istara. I need sympathy and reasonable workplace adjustments."

"Yeah, yeah." Istara paused. "Glad you're back. But we had a plan."

Basavi said, "Lieutenant Yeni sent the order to continue, before he left. We discussed it."

Basavi had clearly argued to go after Surit and had just as clearly lost. Tennal was inclined to be on her side—they had to get Surit while he was still alive and fix this somehow. Of course, Surit would still be alive. There were no other options.

"We're *at* the lab," Istara said. "Yeni wanted us to carry on, so we carried on. And I don't want that remnant-addicted fucker as legislator any more than Yeni did."

Tennal hesitated.

"What if there's nothing in that module," Basavi said, with the air of someone carrying on a three-day argument. "It was abandoned twenty years ago. What if it doesn't help us, and we still have to try and stop Governor Oma?"

"There are only three dozen of us," Tennal said. His head hurt, but it was gradually clearing enough to remember why he had the plan in the first place. "We're not an army. Without a lever, we're a joke."

"There's no way the commander's people had enough time to clear out the whole lab last time," Istara said. "The Archer troops hit us like a hammer, remember? Even if there are just some more remnants in there, maybe we can use them. And—"

"You need to lie down, Captain Halkana," the medic said to Tennal, interrupting Istara. "You need to be stable—we need to finish the treatment—"

"I don't give a shit," Tennal said. "I've never been stable. Why would I start now?"

"*What if there's nothing to find,*" Basavi snapped.

"That's what I'm trying to say!" Istara said, turning up the volume on the speakers until their voice was deafening. The rest of them went quiet. Basavi glared into empty air.

Into the silence, Istara said, "I've got a scan on the lab. It's picked up energy signatures. Someone's in there ahead of us."

The laboratory facility spun in a planet-sized lull in chaotic space. It was a ring of linked modules, ancient by the *Note*'s standards but large enough to be entirely self-sustaining. It wasn't lit; to the naked eye, it was only distinguishable by the dark void where it blocked the scattering of distorted stars. The pod's inbuilt scanners gave the image a faint wash of silver. Half the modules were gone; there were gaping wounds in others. That would have been Marit Yeni's doing. But some of the modules were still whole.

Tennal watched it approach on the screen of the tiny transfer pod and tried to put out of his mind that Surit must have felt the comforting hull of the *Note* recede behind him in the same way.

But the lab wasn't dead, not entirely. In the midst of its vast dark bulk, one small pilot light gleamed by a docking hatch.

"There's a ship," Basavi reported from the chair next to him. "Look. It's deflecting scanners."

"So we know that hatch is powered and working," Tennal said, with an entirely false confidence. "Bring us in."

"I wish we had even the faintest idea who was in there," Basavi muttered. She sent their position back to Istara on the *Note* and got an immediate acknowledgment. Istara must've been hovering over their console.

The light was so old that its blue glow flickered. A new, insistent ping came over their comm.

"That's the station alert channel," Tennal said, nonplussed, as Basavi took them into dock. "Someone wants to talk to us." He brought the screen up before she could protest. It only occurred to him afterward that maybe he should have taken it just on voice.

The visuals on the other end were blank. A voice said sharply, "Identify—" There was an intake of breath. "Sen Tennalhin."

The connection cut off. Tennal didn't even have a chance to reply.

"Who was that?" Basavi said.

"No clue."

"They knew you."

"Lots of people do," Tennal said, but that wasn't actually true. If you didn't have Surit's absurd memory, you probably wouldn't recognize him from the tiny handful of times he'd appeared in pictures with the legislator.

The hatch light turned green as Basavi approached, and they suited up. She didn't even have to request entry. The ship just docked smoothly, and the airlock opened, and cold atmosphere flooded into their pod.

As they unstrapped themselves and emerged into the docking corridor, Basavi tried to open a connection to the station alert channel again. There was no response.

"Friendly," Tennal said. It didn't make either of them feel better.

The docking corridor was dark. Low green emergency lighting ran in glowing wells at the edges of the floor. It made an eerie path stretching in front of them. For Tennal, who was born and raised planetside, the only place he'd seen this kind of scene was disaster documentaries.

Basavi didn't seem as deeply unsettled, or if she was, she hid it better. She opened comms back to Istara. "We have atmosphere and some light," she said. "Where are the people?"

"*I can't tell,*" Istara said, through Basavi's wristband. "*I think the energy the scanner picked up was just the basic life systems.*"

"All right," Basavi said. "Halkana, proceed."

She'd fallen into a position beside him, hand on her capper, that Tennal recognized from Surit: they must drill it into them in the army. She was protecting his right side and expecting him to protect her left.

Tennal glanced sideways at Basavi's complete lack of expression. This was a terrible idea, but it was *his* terrible idea. "Look, maybe you should go back," he said. "I'm aware just walking in here is probably a bad idea."

Basavi gave him a look like he'd suggested jumping out the airlock. "No," she said. "You're in my unit."

It was a bit like finding you hadn't just put your foot down on the next step but somewhere else entirely. Tennal could have pointed out he'd never volunteered to be in her unit. He could point out Surit had brought him in and Tennal had ended up syncing Surit and losing him. He didn't. He fell into step with Basavi instead.

They followed the emergency lighting. Not all the accesses were still turned on: they found unpowered doors, sullen and unlit. As they walked deeper into the station, their footsteps ringing out on the metal flooring, they passed old, discolored wall displays, blank and dead. Some of the plastic panels were cracked. In one corridor they turned into, even the emergency lights were broken, and they both stopped to listen for the awful hiss of escaping atmosphere.

"Clear," Basavi said after a moment.

"*Is* it?" Tennal muttered, which wasn't an approved military response, as they felt their way through the darkness.

They hit several dead ends. Tennal got Basavi to show him how the manual releases for doors worked and tried every single one that had atmosphere. That led them to an emergency staircase and another level.

This was supposed to be a laboratory, but the part they were in didn't look like one. A couple of the doors stood open, as if the main power had gone off unexpectedly during evacuation. Through them, Tennal could see . . . beds. Personal lockers. All abandoned.

On the third level, they heard the occupants.

Basavi and Tennal stepped out into a sudden eye-scrunching brightness. This was a working floor: doors had standard lock/unlock lights over them. There was a rumble of voices a few rooms away. As Tennal looked at the camera eyes in the ceiling, the distant conversation stopped with a suddenness that made the back of his neck prickle.

At the same moment, the door at the end of the corridor switched to UNLOCK.

"Well," Basavi said, after a moment.

"I never turn down an invitation," Tennal said. "And, coincidentally, I really don't like being played with." He strode down the corridor, ignoring the churning in his stomach, the unsteadiness of his feet, and the way his mind still felt like a viciously pruned rosebush. He was going to find out what was going on if it killed him.

The door opened into what looked like an anteroom. Tennal caught sight of a silhouette through frosted glass that sent all his false bravery scurrying back into the pit it had come from. "Basavi," he said, in a voice that sounded very strange, "could you wait out here?"

Basavi took one look at his face, nodded, and drew her capper.

Tennal stepped into the wide bay. In the middle of a nest of medical equipment, from an ambulance chair, a small silhouette of a woman looked up with a glint in her eye like the end of a burn gun.

His aunt said, "I rather thought I'd hear from Zinyary first. But I see you're the element of chaos as usual, Tennalhin."

"*Legislator Yasanin,*" Tennal said. "And here I fucking wondered where I got it from."

PART FIVE

CHAPTER 29

The legislator of the Orshan sector was not dead, but it looked like it had come pretty close.

The portable ambulance chair she sat in was within reach of a discarded IV line. She wore not her normal conservative outfits but a loose medical gown covering a bulkiness that suggested dressings on her torso underneath. She was alive. She had conscripted Tennal, planned to murder Surit, been shot by Oma, and she was alive, and Tennal should have bloody known. You didn't just lose the bane of your life as easily as that.

She tried to sit up, and her breath caught in pain.

Tennal had gone from zero to overwhelming fury in less time than it took to turn on a light, only to be hit in the chest with that.

The legislator drew a great heaving breath. "Don't even fucking think about it," she said, as she levered herself up with the arm of the chair. Tennal hadn't realized he'd started forward, his hand out. "I'm not an invalid. This will pass."

Tennal let his hand drop.

It was only then that he realized what the room was. The legislator might be in an ambulance chair, but that had been brought in here; it wasn't a medical bay. There were powered-down game boards against the wall and faded soft furnishings. It looked like the rec room on the *Fractal Note*.

It *was* a rec room. This must've been where she and her unit had lived when they'd stayed here and had their brains irradiated by remnants, some twenty years ago.

He said, "So how much of your act back on the station was fake?"

"You're going to have to be clearer than that."

"I thought you were dead." It was easier to say if he didn't look at her. "But I was just an afterthought, wasn't I? The point was to make Oma think you were dead. And now you're here. How many layers deep do your plans go, Auntie dearest? How many of us are just pieces?"

The legislator opened her mouth in the same way as when she was about to verbally annihilate a rival politician in a Convocation session. Then, for the first time Tennal could remember, she hesitated.

"I didn't see it coming," she said. Tennal felt shock prickle down his back. The legislator never admitted she was wrong. She lifted a hand and made a tired gesture at the med machines, at her own exhausted form. "I suppose I should be flattered at the thought that this was intentional, coming from you. But I've gone to ground, Tennalhin. I'm here to lick my wounds. I have a very good extraction team, and I was wearing protective armor under my clothes, and those are the reasons I'm still alive. If that shot had landed five centimeters up, I would be dead."

Tennal said nothing. Something was blocking his throat.

"I fucked up," the legislator said brutally. "I never thought Hsanan Oma would go that far, and I've paid for it, and so have troops I valued. Don't get me wrong, though—there will be a reckoning. This is a coup. We are at war." She looked at Tennal's expression and said, "Did you think I was some kind of master manipulator?"

Tennal took a breath that was, for some reason, difficult. "I think you're a politician."

Talking to his aunt had always been like a fistfight: if you didn't get your next words in quickly enough, that left you open for a counterpunch. Tennal was used to that. He wasn't used to this, where his aunt paused before she answered, as if what Tennal said deserved consideration.

"I'm a soldier, Tennalhin," his aunt said, "and Orshan has always been a battlefield."

Tennal was, he found, still furious. "No! That's no Lights-lost excuse. You can make world-weary pronouncements about the nature of power all day long; *you tried to murder Surit.*"

His aunt looked blank.

"Surit *Yeni*. Lieutenant Yeni!" He could hear his own voice raise. "Your expendable Rank One that you sent to die in space. To make me into an architect. Did you even know what you had in him?"

"Your architect," his aunt said, as if just reaching that conclusion. She didn't even have the grace to look remorseful. "Where is he?"

"He cut our sync."

The legislator paused as if she had been presented with something genuinely unexpected. "Ah."

Tennal's fury reached incandescence. "Yes, Auntie, *ah*. You tried to sacrifice him to fix me. He was your soldier!"

"And you're my family," his aunt said, with all the warmth of a granite cliff.

It took Tennal like a blow to the lungs. "Wow," he said, cresting on a wave of disbelief, "you're worse than me."

"I raised you," the legislator said brusquely. "And do you know what? From the time you were fourteen up until now, I had a front-row seat to the way you turned every single one of your destructive urges on yourself. It was brutal. It was like launching a brand-new, fresh-off-the-line warship and watching it fire all its shells at its own hull. For bloody *years*."

Tennal opened his mouth then shut it again. Then he said, "That wasn't because I was a reader."

"Maybe not all of it," the legislator said. "But it was part of the problem. You scorched the earth with all your therapists, and the civilian medics want six forms of patient consent before they do their bloody jobs. What options did I have left?"

"What options?" Tennal said. "What *options*? How many options did you go down before you picked *sacrificing a bystander*?"

She sat there with an expression like stone, unmoving and unrepentant. Tennal didn't know what he'd been expecting to get from her. He was like a child shouting at—

He swung around at a bulky form filling the door. His first, awful thought was *Surit*. His second thought was his aunt's soldiers. But it was Basavi, her capper pointed at the legislator.

Tennal's backup.

She saw it was the legislator, and her eyes widened, but her capper didn't waver. "Captain," she said, very neutrally. It was, very clearly, *I heard shouting. Do you need help?* In that moment Tennal could have signed over his firstborn to her. It wasn't just him, losing ground inch by inch to the one person who'd always been able to outflank him. He had a unit. He had people, even if those people were only helping him out of lingering loyalty to Surit.

"I'm all right," Tennal said, "but thank you." The legislator had escaped thanks to *her team,* which meant those unobtrusive bodyguards, and Tennal would bet that if Basavi didn't lower her capper in a few seconds, they would have guests. "Have you met my aunt?"

After a moment Basavi sheathed her capper and saluted. "Legislator. Sir."

"Designation?" the legislator said, her coolly interested gaze on Basavi. She seemed completely unfazed at the capper. Tennal supposed it wasn't the first time.

"Private Basavi, Cavalry Retrieval Unit Two-Eight-Seven, ranker, first-class," Basavi said, staring at the wall behind the legislator. Her capper was at her belt now, but her hand was still on it. Tennal didn't miss the implication, though it still took him some effort to get his head around it. There were two sides here, and for once, someone was on Tennal's.

"So you've brought forces," the legislator said to Tennal. Her eyes went to Tennal's torn collar, where he'd ripped off his pin. "Captain, is it?"

For the sake of Basavi, standing there with tabs she had earned over years, and Surit, who had given the ship to them and gone to die, Tennal found he couldn't say no. Instead, he said, "Captain Tennalhin Halkana. Cavalry Retrieval Unit Two-Eight-Seven, now Archer. Don't even think about retribution against my first-class rankers, *sir*."

"An Archer promotion," the legislator said contemplatively. "Lights, didn't think I'd see the day. Though you're not still working for Oma, because I know her, and she never backtracks. She found the Constellation remnants in here, so she won't be back. She thinks she's got what she needs. Why are *you* here, then, Captain Halkana and Private Basavi?"

Coming to the lab had been Tennal's idea. He had responsibilities he couldn't shake off. He had a sudden vision of how Surit would have approached this: calm and businesslike even under extreme pressure. Surit wouldn't have shouted at all.

But Tennal had his own way of doing things. "What the fuck is going on, sir?" he said. "You know Oma is brainwashing people? Using the remnants that came from here! How come we didn't know that was possible?"

"Mm, I thought so," the legislator said. "She always made such a song and dance of not caring about the research and wanting it to stay dead. I should have guessed she had her sources in the project."

"The *project*?"

"Oh, there's no conspiracy," the legislator said, then seemed to reconsider. "Well, only as much as all the research was under confidentiality seals. It was years ago." She sighed. "What do you know about the first neuromodifications?"

"The first architects and readers were made twenty years ago in a military lab," Tennal said. You couldn't go through the Orshan school system without picking that up. He glanced around. "This lab, right?" The legislator nodded, her eyes hooded. "Great. We're all on a little living history tour. How fun for us. They invented readers and architects to help defend Orshan. You were one of them; you were in the first wave. Our textbooks never said *what* they were meant to defend us from, since no other sector can invade us without breaking their Resolution treaty, but after my brief and exciting military career, I can only assume it was to give one faction an edge in the next civil war."

"Not far off," the legislator said. "Go on."

"It turned out readers were harder to control," Tennal said. "The first readers went rogue and started a coup. Marit Yeni joined them. There weren't enough architects to stop them. The divisions panicked, scaled up the production facilities, and started making architects out of all the soldiers they could fly in. Hundreds of thousands of people got turned into architects, including"—he hesitated—"my gen-parent. Your sister. And, ta-da, with all those architects, they crushed the rebellion without much problem. That's when they came up with the solution of syncing rogue readers. Oh yes, and then the Resolution noticed what we were doing, took away most of our remnants, and nearly kicked us out of the treaty on top of it."

"We were lucky with our allies in the Resolution," the legislator said shortly, "or we'd be having a different conversation right now under another sector's rule. But the official story of the reader rebellion isn't what happened."

"You *shock* me," Tennal said. "I'm floored. Stunned. Baffled." His eyes hadn't left her face. "What happened, Auntie? We found a picture of you and Oma in Marit Yeni's storage. You were all . . . here."

The legislator winced, then hesitated, then made a control gesture over her wristband. "Bring me one of the salvage cases," she said. A voice snapped an acknowledgment.

Tennal had been right. Her bodyguards were paying attention, and nothing was private here. That was fine. Basavi was listening anyway. Tennal had no secrets.

"Dodging the question?" Tennal said.

His aunt made a casually rude gesture and opened a screen. Tennal didn't realize what she was doing until an image flickered up. For one confused second, he thought it was the group shot he and Surit had found. The same faces stared back at him. His aunt, small and fierce. Oma wearing a sunny smile. Marit Yeni, looking neutral and so painfully like Surit that Tennal nearly bit his tongue. But this was new—this was a picture from his aunt's private archives. They were all in a rec room. They were all in *this room*.

"We were volunteers," the legislator said softly. "The most ambitious and reckless junior soldiers of our generation. Who else would take an experimental neuro procedure? They took the remnants, and they made us into something alien."

Tennal inhaled sharply. Thoughts he didn't want to remember came back to him. Surit had cut the sync because what they were turning into scared them both. And Tennal had almost ended the bond himself by throwing his mind into space—something that should not have been possible. Space was a physical plane, not somewhere you could extend your awareness. But if that was true, how did reader piloting work?

Space was a physical plane. Or rather: space was a physical plane for *humans*.

"You mean they turned you into architects," he said. "Or readers, some of you."

But the legislator had seen his face while he thought. "You've found out something, haven't you?" she said. "No. They used the remnants to *neuromodify* us. In the early days, that meant all of us could read and write. They weren't separate powers. But the experiment was unstable. A third of our group died. Some of the others . . ." The lines deepened at the corners of her mouth. "Thought they could run the world. Can't blame them; lots of people have thought that even without neuro powers. The divisions were saber-rattling in any case, and each of us early volunteers was a weapon. So we started the war."

"Wait," Tennal said. "So it wasn't a *reader* rebellion?"

"No. At that point, we could all do both. They stabilized us later by splitting our powers, because it turned out that human brains weren't strong enough to handle it. I saw some of the volunteers who died . . . anyway. We don't understand the remnants. I was stabilized into what we call an *architect* now, and here I am, twenty years later, so it hasn't killed me yet. But the war wasn't a reader rebellion. It was a fucking mess. The ceasefire needed a scapegoat."

"And you picked readers," Tennal said, feeling sick.

"I was twenty fucking years old and a junior lieutenant," his aunt said, with some asperity. "I didn't pick anyone."

"Don't give me that shit. *I'm* twenty."

"And you're doing so well," his aunt said. She grimaced and looked away. "They had to blame it on someone, and the Cavalry leader at the time thought readers would die out. We didn't know they'd show up in architects' kids."

"Oh, fantastic," Tennal said. "Always nice to know we're wanted. So you stopped experimenting with the remnants?"

Basavi spoke up, her voice like gravel. Her face had taken on a grayish tinge. "But they didn't," she said. "They didn't stop until General Yeni tried to blow this place up."

The legislator glanced at her, as if surprised someone other than Tennal was giving her trouble. She paused for a moment before answering, "Some of the experiments carried on. They wanted to see if they could make readers less intrusive, at first, and then they must have got onto brainwashing. The Resolution confiscated most of the remnants, but we had thousands of them. I know you want grisly details, but I don't *have* any. I was making my career in those years, not peering over the shoulder of a bunch of scientists.

Both of you are too young to know, but it was difficult enough for society to deal with suddenly having architects around—and architects are common and controllable. We don't even know how many readers are out there. There are no tests. But this was all years ago. Nobody really cares whose fault it was anymore."

"Nobody cares? Nobody cares whether readers are trustworthy? You were going to *murder Surit to make me an architect!*" Tennal said. "I bloody care. Would you go public with all this?"

The legislator snorted. "If the Convocation brings it to me to sign." *Never,* she meant.

"General Yeni rebelled," Basavi said, doggedly following a train of thought. "General Yeni knew all this."

"Marit Yeni had . . . principles," the legislator said. "I couldn't bloody stand Marit, but you couldn't accuse her of wavering. Shit went down. High command took her soldiers; she came here on a suicide mission. She blew up the lab, and we called her a rogue element." Her mouth twisted. "I didn't know they were working on brainwashing here. I became legislator much later. I interdicted the site. Then, a couple weeks ago, I finally got around to sending a fleet in to strip it of anything dangerous—that was the mission I attached you to. For all the good that did," she added. Then she called, "Come in!"

Tennal, already twitchy, spun as the door opened.

One of the unobtrusive black-suited aides—a bodyguard?—came in and gave Tennal and Basavi a hard look. She laid a case on the small table by the legislator and wordlessly checked some of the readings from the medical equipment.

"Yes, I'm fine," the legislator said to her shortly. "I'm not overexerting myself. You *have* these readings." She rested her hand on the case. Tennal was already getting the same itch in his head from the case as he had when Oma had unveiled her remnants.

"Sir," the bodyguard said. "The ship nearby won't give a name or a division."

"Captain Halkana's unit should be treated as independent allies," the legislator said briskly. "Ask the . . . what's your ship, Tennalhin?"

"The *Fractal Note*."

She raised her eyebrows. "You hijacked the ship I put you on?"

"*Hijacked* is a strong term," Tennal said, while beside him, Basavi—who had technically been the one who stole it from Archer Link Station—went even more stony-faced.

"Ask the *Fractal Note* if they need resupply or docking," the legislator said. "That will be all."

When the bodyguard had gone, the legislator put on a pair of heavy gloves and opened the case. Tennal was expecting something like Oma's case, something almost ceremonial, as if the remnants were jewels. But this case was bursting at the seams with equipment—random parts of hardware Tennal didn't recognize. It looked like the legislator's people had been stripping the lab.

Nestled in the corner was a remnant. It was small, pea-sized, and looked like a tiny piece of white coral. The legislator plucked it out and held it in the palm of her protective glove. It radiated . . . not sound, but something like it, a high-pitched feeling in Tennal's brain.

He didn't notice he had started forward until the legislator closed her fingers over the remnant and pulled it away.

Basavi's hand was on Tennal's arm, holding him back. Tennal had tried to *snatch* the remnant from his aunt. "Watch it, Captain," Basavi said neutrally. "Looks dangerous."

Tennal didn't move. "It feels like . . . mine," he said, strained. That wasn't the whole truth, but he didn't know how to articulate that it felt like part of his body, like his lungs or his inner ear. Admittedly, if someone had shown him his own inner ear, he wouldn't necessarily be lunging to wrestle it from them. Tennal wasn't even sure what that would look like; maybe nothing like the small pearlescent stone in front of him.

The legislator said nothing for a moment. Then she put her

gloved hand with the remnant back in her lap and said, "You *were* synced, weren't you?"

"Yes, but it didn't feel right," Tennal said. He shot a quick, restless glance at Basavi, who had probably guessed most of it. "We did it in a hurry, and I think we might have gone . . . too deep? Is that possible? The pilot syncs must be more sustainable. Ours felt like . . ." He stopped. When he said it out loud to his aunt, it sounded absurd.

"Go on," the legislator said, for once in her life without judgment.

"It felt like we weren't going to exist as separate halves much longer," Tennal admitted. It didn't sound any better when he verbalized it. "It felt like we were turning into something else."

"You never said that part," Basavi said.

"Surit thought it would be bad for morale."

"You could have said," Basavi said, in a slightly off-balance voice that proved Surit's morale point.

Tennal took a deep breath. "I don't know anything about remnants, except that they were made by weird aliens who don't seem to be around anymore, and the Resolution prefers to keep them in a freezer. But is it possible the remnants they used for the experiments are . . . the *body* of something?"

"That's one of the Resolution's theories," the legislator said.

"That's absurd, though," Tennal felt obliged to point out. "That's not a bone or a fossil or anything organic. That's a weird rock."

"What's a *body*?" the legislator said. "We don't have a good concept of what they considered physically a part of them. All I know is that we transferred something from the remnants when we used them, and then the same thing showed up in our kids. Maybe there's a good reason the Resolution wants to sit on these, but just because early humans didn't understand fire, it doesn't mean they didn't use it."

Tennal looked away from the remnant. A curl of horror sat in his stomach. "So what me and Surit felt was an echo of something dead," he said, trying not to listen to his own voice. "Our parents used a remnant to alter their brains, and a generation later, we can still hear it."

"I don't know why you're so squeamish," the legislator said. "We used a corpse for its materials. We eat food from the earth our ancestors rotted in. Everything goes in cycles."

Not like that, Tennal wanted to say, but he couldn't put words to what he felt. His reader powers must be the same thing: a sliver of a dead alien. And they were a part of him as much as his arms or his legs.

"You were a reader, sir," Basavi said suddenly, as if she'd been thinking about it.

The legislator gave her another of those slightly surprised looks. "Somewhat complicated, Private."

"Lights, give her a straight answer," Tennal said. Basavi deserved it if anyone did; she'd hidden her powers for years.

The legislator paused, as if editing the swear words out of her sentence. "I had reader abilities. And I came out as an architect in the split. Yes. The separation was something we invented."

"You were a reader," Basavi said, "and you still let everyone believe readers can't be trusted?"

The legislator grimaced between her and Tennal. "Society isn't something you can just snap your fingers and change," she said. "And it didn't seem wise to flag to the Resolution that we have a lot of unidentified low-level readers." Her gaze flickered to Basavi.

Tennal found, almost with relief, that he was still furious. "You could have tried. Surit would have tried. Zin, with all her lawyer stuff, is *trying right now.*" But Surit and Zin weren't the kind of personalities that made it into power, were they? To be in power, you needed to be a weasel.

"All right, maybe," his aunt said at last. "I did what I could. There's been so much to do."

Her wristband pinged, with the discreet bodyguard informing her that the *Fractal Note* was docking for resupply. Tennal and Basavi traded glances. Basavi said, "I'll go and keep an eye on them."

It was a subtle inquiry. *Are you going to be all right, or are you planning to have an emotional breakdown in front of your aunt?* But Tennal didn't have time for emotional breakdowns in front of his aunt. "Yeah," he said, "don't let Istara bleed them dry."

The legislator watched Basavi leave the room. "How many soldiers do you have?" she said. "You might as well merge them with my forces. They can stay—"

"No," Tennal said. "We're not under your command." Technically they might be, but Surit wasn't here to explain the technicalities.

"Lights fucking guide me," the legislator said. "Do you even understand we're at war, Tennalhin? Every commander Oma hasn't brainwashed is readying their soldiers for a counterattack. There will be casualties. There could be fewer if we do this right. I could use you."

There will be casualties. "I used to be unusable because I was a mess," Tennal said. "Now I've spent time as a ranker and time as an officer, and you know what? Now I'm unusable by *choice*."

"So what are you going to do?" the legislator said. The contempt Tennal remembered was back in her voice. "Take your stolen ship and run? Where do you think you're going to go?"

"Well, I have the paperwork to get through the Archer link," Tennal said, just to see his aunt's furious twitch.

"You're going to the fucking *Galactics*?" his aunt said. "You think you'll find it easier there?"

It should have been satisfying. Instead Tennal was surprised to look inside himself and find only a sober heaviness. It wasn't even a choice anymore. Zin was on this side of the link and probably always would be. Surit was somewhere in the sector and needed Tennal. And his aunt, whom he'd always thought he'd run to the end of the universe to escape, was glaring at him from six feet away, after admitting she would have murdered a stranger for him without regret—and that was something Tennal set aside to think about later, maybe after the heat death of the universe. "No," he said. "No, I'm staying. But I have to find Surit, and I don't trust you with him."

The legislator narrowed her eyes. "You can't go off on a half-assed rescue mission now," she said. "It'll take you months of treatment to finish bringing out your architect powers. You'll need the medic I gave you. It won't be comfortable, but—"

"I'm not turning into an architect," Tennal said. "I need to sync with Surit."

"You got this far," the legislator said incredulously. "You'd throw it all away to go back into a *sync*? You said yourself the sync was killing you."

Tennal didn't exactly want to either, but—"He'll die otherwise," he said. The prospect of Surit dying wasn't even concerning. It was just a terrifying blank. "If you want to keep me alive, give me a way to deal with Oma. Unless . . ." He looked her over, in some doubt for the first time. "*Are* you planning to deal with Oma? Or are you hiding out until you're healed? They got you pretty badly."

His aunt said brutishly, "If you sympathize with me, Tennalhin, I will have you court-martialed." She opened the case by her side and slipped the remnant back in it. "Of course we're here to deal with the brainwashing. I've had my people strip out what files remained in the storage systems here. There weren't many. But it's clear the brainwashing actively pulls on the energy of the remnants in a way normal powers don't. So we're back to containment."

She took a piece of equipment that looked like a half sphere of plain metal from the case, like a handheld scanner that everyone from doctors to mechanics used a version of. This one was unusual, though: the face on one side was laddered with glowing white filaments.

"Don't touch the active elements," his aunt warned. She placed the remnant on the tray. "I remember the medics using these in the lab—Lights, that was decades ago. I've seen the Resolution's people use them too."

"What do they do?" Tennal said.

In answer, the legislator passed the scanner over the remnant slowly. And although Tennal sensed nothing—no noise, no temperature change—the remnant started to turn dull. As Tennal watched, a film of ice formed on it, sending tendrils across the tray below.

The high buzzing sound in Tennal's head stopped.

As the legislator took the scanner away, the ice didn't melt, even though the tendrils were tiny and the room was reasonably warm. The remnant just sat there, no longer white and iridescent but dull as a piece of pumice. It radiated cold.

"It's nothing special. A temporary containment," the legislator said. "It lasts a few hours and it was meant for transporting remnants. But we found a half dozen of these scanners and dispatched them to our best troops. You wanted to know the plan— I've sent them to find the remnants Oma stole and deactivate them. It might disrupt the brainwashing."

"But you're not sure because you've never dealt with brainwashing before," Tennal said. "And you have no idea where her pile of remnants is, and she's probably guarding them with her life. And there are thousands of them."

"You haven't been in the army long," his aunt said dryly. "This is what we call a *stretch* operation."

"*Stretch* as in, wildly optimistic, lots of people probably die?" Tennal said. "Give me the spare scanner. Maybe I can take the remnants out of action when I find Surit."

His aunt narrowed her eyes. "No."

"Have you got another team ready to go? Oma knows me. I can get close to her."

"Not you," his aunt said flatly. "As you said many times, you're a civilian. You didn't sign up for this."

Tennal paused. There was an odd resonance in his memory as she said that. Surit had said almost the same thing.

"My esteemed colleague Basavi may listen to you," Tennal said. "Surit Yeni may have listened to you, but he's not here because of the little matter of you trying to murder him. *I*, however, don't have to listen to you at all. I'm going back to Orshan. Give me the scanner and I might be able to help you anyway."

"*Why?*" the legislator said. "Why can't I stop you from taking yourself on a solo mission where *you might die*?"

"I really have to get Surit." Tennal met her gaze and held his hand out for the scanner. There was something hard in her eyes that found an absolute mirror in his own, and Tennal thought for a moment they might be having some kind of belated connection before he realized: *Oh yes. It's that we're both stubborn assholes.* "Would a quid pro quo make you feel better?" he asked. "I want Governor Birimi restored. Exonerated. Put them back in charge of Archer Link Station."

"*Now* you want something?" the legislator said, in the voice of a woman who had gone past incredulity to whatever was on the other side. And then, blankly: "Who's Birimi? Oh—the one Oma was having trouble with." She stared into space for a moment, contemplating it. "Hah. Why not?"

"Right," Tennal said. He didn't have to explain why he'd gotten involved with the ex-governor's affairs. It was Zin's fault anyway, reader or not. "I'll have a look for your remnants and see if I can break the brainwashing link. No promises."

"Keep it quiet," the legislator said reluctantly. "Don't push her into anything drastic. Remember, if the Resolution picks up that we kept thousands of remnants and we're using them, we'll be in an entirely different sort of trouble. Even Hsanan Oma wouldn't go that far."

"Can't wait to get in whole new sorts of trouble," Tennal said lightly. "Speaking of, I should get back to my unit." He glanced over her again, her small frame supported by the ambulance chair, emerging barely alive from a situation she'd walked into herself. The cornered fox, holed up.

Tennal paused halfway through turning away. He heard himself say, "What you said earlier. About . . ." He stopped. "It didn't cross your mind to give me any advice?"

"I gave you plenty of advice," the legislator said.

"You know what I fucking mean," Tennal said. "You could have told me. That you were—" *like me,* he couldn't quite say.

A quiet intake of breath. A crack. And then, eventually: "What could I have said? 'Turn it on other people like I did'? No." She gave him something that was not a smile at all. "You and Zinyary were supposed to be better than me. You're the new generation. And, anyway, you managed to fuck up enough all by yourself."

"Yeah," Tennal said. He wasn't sure what his face was doing.

The legislator said reflectively, "You seem to have done remarkably." She paused for an instant while Tennal's whole brain went blank. "I say that in the senior officer sense of 'I have no fucking idea what you're going to do next.'"

Tennal's chest felt like it was full of blown glass, like it might crack. "I'm going to find Surit," he said. "I'll see you on Orshan Central."

CHAPTER 30

The stone spires of Exana were wreathed in flowers. Surit stood by the window in a tiny locked room on a high floor of the central barracks, looking down at the main thoroughfare as a ceremonial procession wound toward the domes of the Codifier Halls for the opening of the Convocation. The sky was a humid gray, but the politicians wore bright formal wraps, green and amber like new spring. There were no spectators except the birdlike silver flash of press drones. Governor Oma walked solemnly at the back.

Legislator Oma, now.

It didn't look much like a coup; at least not at first. There hadn't been any real coups in Surit's lifetime. The closest thing was the Reader War before he'd been born, where the media had reported on Marit as if she'd been about to land a rogue fleet on Orshan Central. His mother had never intended that. But Oma had done it.

Surit rested his forehead on the clammy glass and watched the tail end of the procession disappear into the Codifier Halls. No one even shouted. The street was deserted.

Surit had been here for four days. He could put the sequence of events together from the newslog broadcasts that made it to his throttled wristband. Everyone who had traveled with the legislator to Archer Link Station had thrown their support behind Oma. The other division chiefs, the cabinet of state advisors, the senior members of the Convocation—they all gave serious interviews about the loss of the last legislator and the *need for stability*.

The newslog anchors sounded sometimes baffled. They weren't used to consensus. Surit could spot the brainwashing.

Surit didn't see Zinyary on the broadcasts again, but from the defensive tone of the official interviews, it certainly seemed like *someone* was counter-briefing. And the lack of spectators, the Archer troops stationed around the barriers—yes. There was a war going on. Just not here, in the humid, breathless center of Exana, where they'd locked Surit in the barracks.

Surit had let himself be taken prisoner, so he couldn't complain. The Archer troops who'd picked up his tug had been understandably surprised. They'd been sent to capture Tennalhin Halkana. But Surit was also on Oma's wanted list, and they couldn't catch Tennal—something Surit could have told them a while ago—so they detached a ship to bring him home.

Home, for Surit, wasn't Exana. He'd only ever been to this glossy, flowery city on a school trip. Home was a range of green mountains and industrial sprawl three thousand miles away.

He didn't particularly want to die here.

He'd tried not to think about it on the way back. The headaches had started out short: brief flowers of pain that made him black out. He'd wake up on the floor of his cabin with time gone. For the first few days, it was only minutes at a time; then it started stretching out into hours. It took two weeks to get back to Orshan Central from that pocket of chaotic space. By the time Surit had been brought to Exana and locked in an empty barrack, he was unconscious for longer periods than he was lucid.

Surit rubbed aside the dust on the window. He wasn't normally impatient, but he didn't have much time. He was being held here until Oma could see him. She could try brainwashing him, but whether that worked or not, she wouldn't get much use out of him. Surit would get one chance at her.

And in the end, as it turned out, that wasn't enough.

As he watched the street outside clear, the Archer troops dispersing, he started to feel the prickling in the top of his spine that heralded one of the headaches. He tried to ignore it. He even got as far as sitting on the narrow bed and opening his letter to Elvi, a ten-screen attempt to explain everything to his alt-parent after Surit was gone, but within seconds the screen blurred.

This one was a bad one. The first real wave was like a pickax to the skull. Surit lost vision.

He surfaced in pieces, with a raging thirst and Archer medics leaning over the bed in worry. It took him long moments to remember how to move his limbs. That had never happened before. He didn't even really have time to process it before the headache started again.

The third time he came back to consciousness, Oma was there.

"Lieutenant Yeni," she said. "What in the paths of Guidance happened to you?"

Surit tried to lift his head from the bed, his vision swimming. He didn't waste time wondering if it was a hallucination. He didn't even waste time trying to converse.

"Oh," Oma said, disappointed. It sounded like her voice was coming through water. "You're dying."

Surit had mostly ignored his architect abilities. They weren't relevant. But they'd always been *there,* a deep well of energy in the back of his mind. He'd never thought that one day he would be too sick to use them.

"I can't influence him," he heard Oma say briefly to someone else. "He's on his way out. Shame—we're running out of accessible Rank Ones."

Surit struggled to use something—*anything*—of his power. All he got was a weak suggestion that Oma didn't even have to put in effort to brush off. She turned away. Surit's vision faded to black again.

When he woke up again, it was to the diffuse gray light of dawn. He'd lost nearly a day and night to the attacks.

I failed, Surit thought blankly.

His throat felt like sandpaper as he sat on the edge of the bed, looking up at the tiny window. His bones ached from a disappointment so bitter that it was almost grief. He'd meant to kill Oma, and he'd failed.

List: Resources.

Item: Not a reliable body. That was terrifying. He had maybe a few hours of consciousness at a time now. After one of these episodes he wouldn't wake up. It felt like that was coming soon.

Item: No unit, either. He'd made the choice to leave, and he didn't regret it; he owed them that safety. No allies at all. That was fine, though; Surit had always ultimately relied on himself. He closed his eyes and tried to shut out the nagging memory that for three short weeks he'd had *Tennal*—Tennal, a lit fuse, a hydrogen fire that had inexplicably decided to be on Surit's side—and been closer to him than anyone he'd ever known.

He had no way to contact Cavalry or his legitimate chain of command. As a prisoner in a coup, Surit had a duty to escape. But he had no way to contact them for orders.

And then, a stray thought: *Do I even want to?*

It was Retrieval Two who had gotten him off Archer station. It was Tennal who had plunged himself into the sync to protect Surit from brainwashing. All Cavalry Division had done—all his last commander had done—was order him to sync Tennal so Surit could be sacrificed. They must have been so certain that nobody in Cavalry Division would ask questions. And why would they? This was the army.

Surit might not blame Tennal for that, but he was starting to realize, like the slow shifting of continental plates, that didn't mean he wasn't angry.

Surit hadn't finished his list, so he turned his attention to that. Last item: He had receive-only comms. And that was it—no, wait, not quite. Did he have his architect powers? He poked at them experimentally and found that, yes, they still felt like a seeping wound, but while he was conscious, he could use them.

He wanted to laugh. After all this, after all the trouble his powers had gotten him into before they'd failed him—after everything, he was still an *architect*.

A distant explosion rocked the breeze-block walls of the room.

Surit was on his feet before he'd even fully processed the sound. His overstretched nerves twitched as he crossed to the tiny window and peered out.

Yesterday, this street had been deserted except for the politicians. Today, it was not. Smoke rose a few streets over from the Codifier Halls. A pair of soldiers ran across the road to disappear into a side alley, low and purposeful. The tabs on their shoulders were Cavalry red. A handful of civilians stood and muttered in front of a shop. They melted away rapidly when an Archer patrol came through.

Surit turned on the basic comms his wristband was still allowed.

BATTLEGROUND IN CODIFIER HALLS, the newslogs blared. Surit took a moment to work out what that even meant. Oma controlled the Codifier Halls right now, so *battleground* must mean the other divisions were trying to stop her. Surit's side, technically. He stared at the feed of glossy corridors with dark-uniformed soldiers running in the smoke. He was dying. Did he even care who won?

And then Surit saw a silhouette he recognized.

Everyone Surit had ever met was imprinted on his memory. Some people were good at math, some had good balance, Surit had a mental drawer full of everything he'd seen. That meant he knew the way one lone figure ran before they slipped into a side door, away from the security guards with the news drone.

Was that *Istara*?

That was impossible. Surit killed the screen and strode back to the window, craning his neck to see the Codifier Halls. They sat there as they always had, built of warm golden stone, with domes and high walls and two wings extended majestically from the entranceway, like the claws of a crab. A thin plume of smoke emanated from one roof.

And Surit stared at the grand center of power, home to Tennal but strange to him, and thought of three things. First: It was completely impossible that Istara was in there, but he'd seen them. Second: He was dying, but he was not dead.

And third: He was still, even after everything, an architect.

When the Archer guard came with his food, Surit was sitting politely on his bed.

"I would like to leave now, please," he said.

"What?" The guard seemed more confused than anything else.

The guard was by himself. That was a change from yesterday. At first, there had been three guards, all strong architects, one of whom had stayed out in the corridor—so, clearly, they knew Surit's abilities. But then they'd seen Surit sick, helpless for hours at a time, and now Oma had declared him useless. Surit could leverage that. "General Oma doesn't need me," Surit said reasonably. "I don't have long left. You don't need to hold me anymore." He had some sympathy for the guard, who was clearly just a ranker. That was why Surit stayed sitting.

The guard said shortly, "I haven't had any orders." And, as Surit rose to his feet: "Don't move. I'll get backup. I mean it."

Surit closed his eyes. As soon as he looked for it, it was there: the well of power within him that he'd ignored for so long. Surit had no time to grieve—not for himself, not for what he'd had to do—but he could still use what he had.

Surit opened his eyes. "*I would like to leave now.*"

The guard's mind folded in front of his like wet paper.

"Of course," the guard said blankly, and opened the door. He saluted as Surit went through.

Surit walked alone up the city's wide central avenue, the artery of Exana, to the Codifier Halls.

He barely thought. His mind was empty and yet, at the same time, filled to bursting with a buzzing energy. He was bigger than the fragile shell of his skin. He burned like a torch: high and bright and brief.

As he approached the halls, an Archer patrol rounded the corner and spotted him. Surit should maybe have been more concerned, but he felt power pool in his hands and didn't even slow as they cut across his path.

"Halt—" one of them said.

"*None of you are authorized to stop me,*" Surit said. There were five of them. It shouldn't be possible to control that many people at once, but he could see how to do it one after the other like a rapid pendulum, split seconds apart. His head complained, as did something in his ribs, but what did it matter if he drained himself? He wouldn't be long.

He saw sweat break out on some of their faces as they tried to fight it. Then one of them cracked, backing off and stumbling, running in the other direction. The others followed.

There were ways of dealing with strong architects, Surit knew, because he had learned them in officer academy while carefully not thinking about whether they could apply to him. The simplest was just to rush them and shoot them while they were distracted. But nobody had been expecting a Rank One to walk up.

In the back of his mind, he noted that the handful of soldiers appearing at the mouths of alleyways were armed. Surit was a clear target, outlined against the avenue.

No one shot. But before he'd gone another fifty yards, one of them broke cover.

She sprinted to him. Because she wasn't armed, Surit stopped. Her shoulder tabs were Cavalry red, and her uniform had officer's braid.

"Division?" the soldier said urgently.

Surit had to pause. *Division* seemed an overly detailed human concept to the part of his mind that was fully immersed in his powers; it was almost irrelevant. But the rest of him rebelled. This was carved into his bones. "Cavalry."

"Cavalry operations are already in progress in this area," the soldier said anxiously. "You must report to the local commander."

"I'm not going to wait," Surit said, gently moving her away with a mental push. "I need to see Governor Oma."

He didn't even watch to see if she'd followed him. He knew she hadn't.

The gates of the Codifier Halls were a huge arch of stone, garlanded in bright-silver flowers for the new legislator. It was filled in with stone blocks, and a dozen smaller arched doorways cut into that, each with its own shimmering force field. Surit stopped in front of one.

When they'd come here on his school trip, these had been open. Now there was a security interface.

A security guard—*not,* interestingly, an Archer trooper, but a civilian—flickered on-screen. "Name and business?"

Surit tried to reach out instinctively, but of course, you couldn't write someone through a screen. He had to *remind* his brain of that, as if he hadn't learned it in primary school. Some deep instinct said *space is an illusion,* but Surit hesitated and didn't quite understand.

All right, then. Surit thought back to all the times he'd been on guard duty, stared at the screen, and said nothing.

That was unusual enough behavior to get the guard to swear under her breath and dispatch her colleagues. A few minutes later, three security guards appeared on the other side of the force field, cappers drawn.

Quite sensible. One to challenge him and two to shoot if he turned out to be a threat. It wasn't as if you could expect a random visitor to be a Rank One architect.

He homed in on the closest. The others, he gave quick commands to—*sleep for a bit*—and they crumpled, cappers dropping from their hands as they fell.

"Let me in," Surit said to the last guard. Writing her took

another wave of power, more than Surit expected. He was running through his reserves. "I need to see Oma."

"Legislator Oma?" the guard said, blank-faced. "Oh. Yeah. Of course."

Surit had no sooner taken two steps past the gate, into the tiled and garlanded inner yard, than he felt the first tickle of pain in the back of his head.

Not now. Not *now*. He could have screamed in frustration.

If he collapsed here, that was it. He might not have much time before the pain fully developed—but he had to find Oma. He *had* to. Tennal would have thought of a way around it.

Surit didn't have Tennal anymore, and the hopelessness of that hit him like an unexpected blow in the ribs. He had accepted everything else. But he would have liked to see his alt-parent one more time. He would have liked to see Tennal. But all there was left was to find Oma, and Surit would do that if it killed him.

"This way, sir," the guard added, and Surit followed her mindlessly, pressing at the back of his own neck with his fingers as if he could stop the oncoming headache. He didn't think to question where they were going until the guard input her bios, and Surit realized *let me in,* in the guard's brain, had been translated into the security room. Two faces looked up at him from the desks. The occupants of the Codifier Halls security room and Surit stared at each other in mutual incomprehension. Surit recovered first.

"*Go home.*" Surit didn't know what that would translate to. He didn't care. Wherever that was for them.

This time, the effort left him panting. He braced his hands on a desk. The tingling headache was starting to spread, he could feel it.

They left him alone, grappling with the damage to his head, in the security control room of the Codifier Halls.

Surit took ten long seconds to realize what a gift this was. He had the *camera feeds.* He forced his way past the incipient headache and urgently gestured all the screens to circle him, searching for Oma's tall, angular silhouette.

The Codifier Halls were operating normally. Politicians in bright civilian patterns talked in their offices, walked through corridors, cast nervous glances at the Archer troops around them. Surit couldn't even tell who was brainwashed. Surely all the senior ones were. But how many senior people did you really need to brainwash before the rest accepted that their bosses had switched sides? Even civilians had chains of command.

He couldn't see Oma.

There were gaps in the cameras. The biggest one had to be the hall that housed the Convocation itself, where politicians met to vote. If Oma was anywhere in the Codifier Halls, it made sense that she'd be there. There were actual Archer troops stationed around the central doors, though, not just security guards. Officers. Some of them would be architects. Surit stared at them on the screens, feeling the prickling of his incipient collapse in the back of his head. He could take on a handful of unsuspecting rankers, but he couldn't take on the world.

A call came in. Surit was about to ignore it, but the alert showed a Cavalry originator.

When he picked it up, the square, florid face of Commander Vinys stared back at him. The original commander of the *Fractal Note*. The one Surit had served under who had secret orders to have Surit die. Surit's mind went blank.

He saluted out of instinct.

"Our forces surround the perimeter," Commander Vinys said without preamble. "You will open the doors—" He apparently noticed Surit was by himself and not in uniform. The commander frowned at Surit as if a recollection was just out of reach. "Who are you?"

Surit felt another spike of that new anger. *You tried to have me killed and you can't remember who I am?*

At least that got rid of any guilt Surit had for hijacking his ship. "Lieutenant Surit Yeni, sir," he said levelly, "previously of the *Fractal Note*." He had the satisfaction of seeing the commander flinch.

"Good work, soldier," the commander said, in a tone that conveyed the opposite. "I don't know how you breached the control room without orders, but well done. We're about to launch an operation to take back the Codifier Halls. Lower the force fields, let my troops into the control room, and don't make any sudden movements. This is a shoot-to-kill."

It was? Operations like this were done with incapacitation guns. The only reason to shoot to kill was if you were too afraid of what your opponents could do if they woke up.

Surit felt detached from the whole terrible idea, like a bird gliding above the water. He thought of that glimpse of Istara. "There may be Cavalry troops in here, sir."

The commander's expression didn't change. "Every soldier in these grounds is a traitor, Lieutenant."

Surit finally managed to bring up a camera view of the gates. The area in front of the gates was no longer empty: the commander led a formation of soldiers who had spread out across the entrance, covering all angles, burn guns out. The majority was Cavalry, but he had Infantry and Pilot units in there as well. Another distant explosion echoed from somewhere. The soldiers looked significantly less comfortable at the idea of attacking their own citizens than their commander did.

Surit had left two security guards down there, unconscious. One was still unconscious. The other must have woken up and objected—though that was an assumption, because all Surit could see was the burn gun mark in the chest of his corpse.

Surit gripped the edge of the desk until his knuckles were white. He said, "Sir, are you brainwashed?"

He didn't even need the commander's outraged denial. He knew he wasn't. That had been a military decision.

Surit had had a moment of hope that he didn't have to find Oma alone. If someone could have shepherded him through the next blackout headache, he could have had another chance. He felt that hope die, and in its place came a moment of crystal clarity: sometimes the universe gave you a responsibility you could not evade. He realized Marit had looked at the roads in front of her and seen only one choice.

I understand, Marit, Surit thought.

"What are you doing?" the Commander said sharply, as Surit set all the outside barriers to full lockdown. "Stop—"

"I'm going to find Oma," Surit said. "Lieutenant Yeni, signing off, sir."

He shut down comms.

Like his mother, Surit wouldn't be a tool. Like her, he would be the last explosion in the dark.

As he strode out of the security control room, several alarms blared from the lockdown he'd set. Behind him, other guards started making frantic calls to the control room, which stayed unanswered. Surit set out for the Convocation at the center of the halls.

Shadows gathered at the corners of his eyes to join the tingling in the back of his neck. He knew what would come next: faint vibrations of pain like his skull was a struck bell, then a wave of pain, then unconsciousness. He had minutes.

At first he went unnoticed, save a few suspicious looks from politicians already nervous from the alarms. Surit barely had to tap his rapidly depleting energy to make them look away. He'd never realized how *easy* it was to swing out with one write command after another, like a scythe felling wheat.

His first real obstacle was a half dozen Archer troopers at a fortified door. Surit dealt with them the same way he had with the guards outside; six unconscious bodies crumpled. Surit's head was starting to pound, his breath growing harsher. He couldn't tell if it was the oncoming blackout or the reckless way he was using his powers, but he had to be more careful. He had to make it to Oma.

A long tiled corridor. Two gorgeous sprays of flowers set up like an arch in front of a staircase. But the next set of troopers was ready for him, racing down the stairs from the floor above. A shot sizzled past Surit, and he flung himself against the wall. Another handful of troopers had knelt behind the stair railings to shoot at him.

He didn't even think about saving his powers. *This* and *this* and *this* to take out the snipers—three forms slumped behind the railings—then a capper shot grazed his shoulder.

Surit stumbled, reeling, nauseous. He couldn't get a grip on his powers. Instead he slammed his head into the nearest soldier's stomach.

They both went down. The impact forced the air from Surit's lungs. His vision tunneled down to the capper in the soldier's hand. Surit grabbed his wrist. He tried to fire off architect commands—*don't, stop, leave*—but he had no idea if they hit. A red-veined darkness clouded his eyes. His head hurt so much, he couldn't feel his limbs.

A table went flying. The great spray of flowers came down in a kaleidoscope of color, and a *crack*—the vase shattered, water flooded the tiles. Someone was bleeding. Surit thought it might be him.

He couldn't move. He stared up at the ceiling and couldn't see it.

"Get the architects," someone said urgently. "The majors—*hurry!*"

Oh yes. When Oma had said, *We're running out of accessible Rank Ones,* she hadn't meant she didn't have any. Surit was not unique. He was only stubborn and ambitious, and now he was dying.

Then, while Surit lay on his back, his vision swirling red, there was a final explosion.

This one wasn't distant. This one was real and present enough that Surit felt the percussive blow. Plaster flaked onto his face.

"Half the corridor wall around—"

"The stairs too—"

"Fucking *Cavalry*—"

Surit was no longer the biggest threat. Hands grabbed him. He couldn't force his limbs to move. He just lay there like a rag doll, *you failed* circling in his head.

He was dragged through a door, through a service corridor. His handlers didn't speak. Then the space was suddenly quiet, and someone shut the door, and a voice he recognized said, "We lost them—Guidance Lights, he looks half-dead."

Something in Surit's brain clicked. He knew the hand helping him up. He knew the crackle of energy in front of him.

"Hi," said Tennal.

Tennal, the other half of Surit.

Tennal had the temerity to grin—uncertain, wary, but triumphant. "I thought we'd screwed up rescuing you, but it looks like we're actually great at this."

The stubborn core of Surit that had always relied entirely on himself gave up its grip. And the rest of him, which had hoped beyond thought and beyond reason, took over.

"You're late," he said, and collapsed on Tennal.

CHAPTER 31

In the end, a moment was all it took.

Tennal's mind flowed into Surit's, knitting back together the indefinable wounds all at once. Their first sync had been like a tempest; this one was the confluence of two rivers. The shape of Tennal's mind around his was so familiar, Surit could have wept. It was like breathing oxygen for the first time in weeks.

The pain in his head disappeared. Surit could think and move and balance on his own feet again. He rested his hands on Tennal's shoulders to push himself upright. They were in some kind of office; Surit didn't care. Tennal stood there. *Tennal,* with his sharp eyes boring into Surit and his bony shoulders under Surit's hands, his whole body a lightning strike caught in motion, his face pale from tiredness but vital and alive. He had made it across uncounted miles of space into enemy territory to find Surit. And he'd given up his mind a second time to keep Surit alive.

Surit was struck, confounded, by the immovable way he loved him.

Like no other thought he'd had, that almost caused a rift—Tennal's mind didn't understand; it slid from the notion like oil from water. But Tennal wasn't done. He rested his forehead against Surit's, his eyes green and close and his breath on Surit's face, and said, "Hey, Surit. Don't ever do that again."

Surit kissed him.

There was no room to think. Tennal made a noise of surprise then said into his mouth, "Lights, Surit, *now*?" But before Surit could pull away, Tennal seized the back of his neck and kissed back, unexpectedly hard. If Surit had thought it would be soft, he'd been mistaken; there was no yielding, kissing Tennal—not a millimeter of leeway given or taken. It was like kissing a landslide. Some inconceivably huge space unfolded in his mind, something insupportable, something unbearable.

When they broke away, after only a couple of moments, Surit grinned fiercely. "If not now, when?"

Tennal had shut his eyes, his whole face tense. But they had no barriers between them. His exaltation rang through both their minds like a bell.

Tennal opened his eyes. "So, before you buy me dinner, you might want to know," he said, his smile intense and slightly off-key, "I'm half a dead alien."

Surit's mind went blank.

"Great news, so are you!" Tennal said. "I realize that's not what you were looking for just now. But it's probably important. Let me explain."

They were no longer having weighty emotions. That was, to the sensible part of Surit, a relief. Surit shoved the burbling river of *what he felt about Tennal* deep down to where it couldn't interfere with the mission.

"Smooth, Halkana," Basavi's familiar voice said gravely. Istara gave a gurgle of laughter.

Surit finally looked up past his laser focus on Tennal's face. "What do you mean, *alien*? How did you *get* here?"

Tennal had backup, in this small, unoccupied office: Istara lounged against the desk sporting a smart civilian wrap, an ostentatious earpiece, and six light-screens trailing behind them. Istara looked, Surit realized, like one of the many interchangeable junior politicians he'd passed in the corridor. Basavi had donned a set of maintenance overalls; her face did not invite questions about their origin. And Tennal, of course, still had the Archer tabs on his shoulders.

Tennal looked extremely pleased with himself. "My access permissions still work," he said. "I used to live in the Legislator's Residence, you know. It's all part of the same complex. Oma's been spending all her time at the halls to consolidate herself as legislator. We thought she might have been holding you somewhere here."

"She wasn't," Surit said.

"Well, you're here *now*, aren't you?"

"He sensed when you got into the building," Istara said, exchanging a glance with Basavi. Her expression softened the moment Istara looked at her. Something had changed there. "It was very weird. Like a dog with a bone. I thought you weren't synced anymore."

Basavi tore her eyes away from Istara and grunted. "Tell him your alien theory, Halkana."

Tennal's eyes clouded. "Oh yes. Well. You know remnants are technically called . . . xenotechnology or something like that?"

"Yes," Surit said. "Because they were artifacts made by nonhuman life-forms. Life-forms that died out." That was the standard answer they taught in schools; anyone who wanted to study more got a Resolution scholarship and moved out-system.

"Yes. Okay. But—Surit, they altered your genes, and we have them in our head. Do they feel like *artifacts* to you?" Tennal met his eyes. He said, without moving his lips, *Does this feel like an artifact to you?*

Surit suspected he wasn't going to like this. "Say it out loud."

"We altered ourselves beyond human, and it carried down in our genes," Tennal said, more quietly. "Not much. I think our parents would have died if they'd altered themselves much further. But the remnants are *something's body*. Can't you feel it? They're the remains of something dead. Something that didn't see the universe like humans do. And we took a shadow of a shadow of what they could do, and we split it in half, and we gave it to ourselves. We hacked our powers together out of the bones of dead aliens."

"Wish he wouldn't keep putting it like that," Basavi said. She and Istara were, for some reason, ransacking the desk drawers. Istara nodded with the air of someone who had just been in an enclosed space with Tennal for several days after he'd come up with this.

Tennal made a rude gesture vaguely in Basavi and Istara's direction. "Listen. When an architect and a reader sync, it feels like we're coming back together. But we're just the echo of a whole lifeform. We're the corpse of a dead alien."

Submersed back in the ocean of Tennal's thoughts, the constant churn of waves in his ears, Surit could feel the layer of panic under Tennal's voice. "All right."

"All *right*?" Tennal said incredulously. "How is that all *right*?"

"It doesn't matter what we are," Surit said. It would have bothered him a few days ago, but he'd given himself a mission, and right now there was no room for anything except the mission. "It matters what we do."

Tennal's eyes narrowed. "Yeah?" Surit felt him look at Surit's thoughts and take a wary mental step back.

"I want to go and find Oma," Surit said.

Tennal said, in his head, *I know.* And he did know. Their thoughts were tightly bound. Tennal might have saved Surit's life, for now, but that didn't mean their sync was any more stable than before; if anything, it was worse. Surit strongly felt they were rushing toward a waterfall together, and if so, Surit was going to bring Oma down with them.

Tennal was right up against him. At some point he had put his hand on Surit's sternum, resting over his uniform jacket. His eyes met Surit's, and it looked like he was trying to say something his thoughts hadn't yet formed.

There was a loud splintering *crack* from across the room. They both looked away.

"Well, they're not in here," Istara announced.

Basavi was standing over the remains of what had been the desk with a crowbar. The desk drawers, or parts of them, were on the floor. Istara crouched over them with a handheld scanner that glowed a bright white.

Tennal frowned. "Lights take it. I was hoping—oh, sorry," he added, at sensing Surit's confusion. He turned and dumped a bewildering package of information in Surit's mind.

Surit flinched. It was like getting thrown a ball made of sharp metal scraps. He got flashes of memory: the legislator, alive. A conversation in an abandoned space station that, in Tennal's memory, was razor-edged. A plan to tear Oma away from her remnants.

"You want to deactivate her remnants? You have no idea if that will work," Surit said out loud. "What if she only needed the remnants to *create* the brainwashing link? You have no proof that deactivating them will make any difference."

Basavi looked entirely too comfortable with the crowbar in her hand. She looked up from it, frowned, and said, "Didn't seem to be a better option, sir. And the legislator ordered it."

Surit was used to last-minute briefings scraped together with insufficient information, but this one was particularly bad. "Why do you think this is going to work? And why did you think she'd keep her remnants in *here*?"

Tennal patted him on the shoulder, his face neutral but a flash of dark amusement leaping from his thoughts to Surit's. "I'll try anything once," he said. "Breaking some remnants? Syncing? Helping out with a coup? No, sorry, all right. We're in here because this is my aunt's office." He waved a hand around the small, disused room. "Her constituency office, that is; she hasn't used it since she became legislator. Oma seems obsessed with taking over from her, so I thought this would be a neat place to hide her remnants. Oh well, they can't all be winners. Next stop—" He hesitated.

"The Legislator's Residence," Basavi said implacably. "You did say you had access. That's the other likely place."

"Yes," Tennal said, more reluctantly than Surit was used to; breaking into the Legislator's Residence was an absurd idea, and usually Tennal was on those like hungry trainees fell on dinner. "It's not like it's far." *And it's a better idea than your half-baked plan of throwing yourself at Oma like a grenade,* he thought at Surit.

The light through the windows had tilted toward sunset, a crack in the clouds. Tennal's face was shadowed, and the glass around him was a gentle reddish gold. He was also all around Surit, threaded through every one of his thoughts, eroding his walls like sand. Surit felt affection, and dread, and a bone-deep aversion to seeing his home without his aunt. That was the point at which Surit realized they were, once again, inextricable. He couldn't even start to detangle their thoughts. There had to be an end at some point.

"There has to be an end somewhere," Tennal echoed out loud, "but let's cause some trouble first." He gave Surit a half smile. "Time to go home."

CHAPTER 32

Beneath the shadow of the Codifier Halls was a tiny walled garden that held the Legislator's Residence. The back entrance was a nondescript wooden gate set between the stones in the old wall. As they approached, Tennal waved his wristband. The protective force field dissipated, and the old gate swung open for him.

When Surit stepped into the garden, it was full of shadows and sunset light. Bushes higher than his head covered crumbling walls. He stopped and listened for movement as an evening bird called softly and repetitively from a tree. The air tasted of humidity and respiring leaves and, somewhere, citrus flowers. Surit, who had only breathed the dry air of ships for years now, was sharply reminded of being ten years old in his village again.

"Are there guards?" Istara said under their breath. "This is the *Legislator's* Residence."

"I'm checking," Tennal said, just as quietly. "Give me a moment."

Tennal closed his eyes. That was unusual: Surit knew Tennal was reaching out with his reader powers, but normally Tennal was strong enough to read without making a show of it.

Tennal was too distracted to concentrate. He and Surit were merged enough that, in an instant, Surit understood the problem. It was the garden. The moment they'd stepped into it, a shiver had gone down Tennal's back that Surit had felt on his own skin. The plant scents, the hanging shadows, the outline of the house: they were all tied up with a complicated longing deep in Tennal's bones. *Home.* That was where Surit's own wistfulness was coming from. Tennal had come home.

Basavi, who had also closed her eyes, opened them and broke the silence. "Around the front."

They all stared at her. It took Tennal and Surit a moment to figure out they were using one joint pair of eyes to do that, and while they got themselves sorted out, Istara said, "Did you just—"

"Two people, I think?" Basavi said uncertainly. She touched her temple, looking faintly embarrassed. She *was* a reader, Surit remembered belatedly. She'd just used her reader senses.

"*Basavi,*" Istara said, sounding shocked and delighted.

"I don't think it's illegal if everyone else is breaking the law," Basavi said, a sentence Surit did not agree with but, under the circumstances, wasn't going to dispute.

None of them needed to be told to keep silent. Surit held aside the branch of a flowering tree as Tennal ducked under it. Istara muffled their normal careless tread. They took the stone path that wound among the shaded plants up to the back of the low villa; Surit watched Tennal slow down as he drew near to the carved door.

Tennal paused outside it. "Keep watch," he said very softly to the rest of them. "If anyone comes, yell and run."

Surit breathed in the soft, earthy evening scent of the garden where Tennal had once lived. He didn't even need to reach into Tennal's thoughts to know he was, for some reason, more afraid of this than he had been of infiltrating the Codifier Halls. This felt closer to the bone. "I'm coming in."

Surit left no room for debate, either in his tone or in their combined thoughts. Tennal hesitated, then his mouth crooked, and he said in Surit's head, *Yes, boss.*

It was smaller inside than Surit had expected. He'd always assumed the legislator lived in a palace, not a single-floor villa with narrow corridors. But it was luxurious: it gave off the heavy, hushed air of a museum, with low lighting and ceramic vases and paintings you were obviously not supposed to touch. The carpets swallowed their footsteps. Tennal unthinkingly dodged every side table and statue in a habitual pattern, while Surit followed, holding his breath so as not to knock anything over.

If Oma was in the Convocation room as they suspected, there was no one but the guard outside to worry about, but Surit kept silent anyway. Tennal glanced at a couple of doors but didn't open them.

One ahead was ajar. The room inside looked empty; no light was turned on. Surit felt a pressure in his head.

Tennal turned his head back to Surit and mouthed, *Study.* The word landed in Surit's head. *We should try there first.*

Tennal laid his hand on the door and froze.

Surit, behind him, saw what had made him stop. The light from the corridor fell on an alcove that should hold a Guidance shrine. Only, it had been dismantled: the icons lay in a facedown stack, the candleholders empty. The gaps yawned like broken teeth.

Oma had moved in recently, but a priest should have dismantled the shrine, discreetly veiled, and treated the contents with respect. Tennal's reaction to the shell of it—his family shrine— crackled with disproportionate shock in Surit's head.

But Surit had no attention to spare for that, because he knew Oma was in that room.

He knew it as surely as if he'd seen her, despite the darkness, despite the dead silence. He eased Tennal back and stepped forward. He felt *possessed,* if that was the word. Just like humans recognized other humans, the ghostly impression in his and Tennal's head recognized the traces of its own kind. And Surit, maybe because he was the child of Marit Yeni or maybe because he was himself, would use whatever weapons he had to chase the rot to its source.

Surit, Tennal said. Then, more urgently, *Surit, what are you*—He grabbed Surit's shoulder. *Guidance Lights, will you stop trying to do things alone!*

Surit had already pushed open the door. A thin shaft of light followed him in from the corridor.

In the dark, Oma looked up from the desk in the center of the room.

Her eyes were luminescent. A thin sheen of white glinted over them and disappeared, like a cat caught in a flashlight, though there was no light source on her face. Only her tall, angular form behind the desk and a case in front of her that held a pile of stone-like fragments. The remains of aliens.

The remnants were here, then, in front of Oma. Tennal's scheme to deactivate them wouldn't have worked. This close, Surit could almost see thousands of pale lines creeping from the remnants to Oma, from the case, from a cabinet next to her. He and Tennal were an abomination to the ghost inside their head, split into two, but how much *more* so was this patchwork Oma had made of herself. He took a breath and—

And Tennal waved his wristband and turned on the lights.

Harsh light flooded the room. No more than a second had passed. And now it was suddenly a human scene again.

Governor Oma—now Legislator Oma—commanded the room in a crisp neutral suit, not a civilian or military pattern. But her collar was askew, a cuff button undone. Her bare head still gleamed pristinely under the lights. She surveyed them coolly. "Problem after problem," she said. There was an exhausted undertone to her voice. "Halkana *and* Yeni, hm? I really did think you were dead."

"We just keep getting back up," Tennal said agreeably, as if this were a briefing back on Archer Link Station and Tennal were admitting to a minor fault. Under it, in their shared mind, Surit saw him replay the memory of Oma with her burn gun aimed at his aunt. "Why did you wreck my family shrine?"

Surit watched Oma like a fencer waiting for the first rush. The presence in his head recognized a more powerful opponent. It knew how to duel in a way totally alien from anything Surit did. It knew the first strike was coming.

The last thing Surit had expected from her was *confusion*. But Oma blinked, looked at the shrine, and seemed to take a while to recognize what it was. "Lights, I meant to do something about that. Meant to get someone in. Replace it the normal way." She looked at the bare wooden shelves and the carelessly stacked icons and gave a strange laugh. "Having four hundred people in your head changes a great deal." Surit caught Tennal's shocked reaction at *four hundred,* but Surit wasn't surprised. There were hundreds of key government figures who would be useful to a coup. Oma had enough remnants for it. Once you'd found something that worked, why stop?

But it was clearly getting to her. Oma stared at the empty shrine and put a finger to her temple. "I meant to . . . get a priest in, I suppose? It doesn't matter, does it? It's only more material clutter."

The sick lurch in Tennal's head surprised both of them. But Surit, watching Oma's presence build and shift like a thundercloud, had insight into why. "It's not the four hundred people," Surit said quietly. "It's the effect of the remnants, isn't it, sir? It's like four hundred syncs. You're even less human than us."

Oma stilled. "You're an expert, are you, Lieutenant?"

"*Why?*" Tennal said. "Why any of this? Guidance knows my dear darling aunt was never a paragon, but neither are you. You were one of the original neuromods. And you were already a general! You had thousands of soldiers, you were a senior officer, so why *start a coup?*"

Oma looked between them, a distant frown on her face as if she didn't understand why they didn't get it. "There's no safety unless you're in command."

"What?"

"I was on the wrong side of the first war," Oma said patiently. "The one Cavalry decided to blame on readers. I was eighteen, and my commanding officer—never mind. The point is, they nearly rounded *me* up. I was a full neuromod, back then: a reader and an architect. They wanted to try out one of the first syncs on me. My relatives had to pull every string they could to get me exonerated, to get me altered into just an architect. It was chaos back then, when the lab was operational. But *you* should really understand this," she said to Tennal. "How much did it help you, that you were a citizen, and a Cavalry dependent, and Yasanin's nephew? How much did it help when they came to conscript you?"

Surit and Tennal didn't even have to look at each other. "Funny way of dealing with it," Tennal said. "I'm personally considered a leading light in the field of maladaptive coping mechanisms, but it's amazing how I never managed to brainwash hundreds of people and take over the government."

There was something else going on. The thundercloud of Oma's presence piled up, rolling in on itself.

Oma laughed abruptly, as if she'd found that genuinely funny. She looked down at the box of remnants and casually *dug her hand* into it. Surit and Tennal flinched. "Ah, well, I suppose there's no other—"

And between one word and another, her towering alien presence attacked.

The neat study and its heavy drapes and the scented night air fell away. The attacker and the thing that was Surit-and-Tennal were ripped away with it.

A planet had layers between it and the peaceful sea of space. The three mayfly bodies—Surit, Tennal, Oma—stood in a tiny stone box in the churning troposphere, the layer that clung to the surface rock of the planet, dense and foul with air. Those tiny bodies weren't relevant anymore. Two warring consciousnesses, larger than planets themselves, shot out from the surface through heat and cold as ultraviolet rays scattered, through the plunge of the mesosphere, and through the thermosphere, where the messy planetary gravity finally released its hoarded air.

Once in true space, the planet of Orshan Central shrank into a glittering speck below. The star system unfolded around them.

The thing that had been Oma roared up opposite, as far away

as the circle of orbit. Surit—and Tennal—felt an instinctive, terrible kinship with her. Oma was an abomination, one mass of hundreds of souls patched together, but Surit and Tennal were no less strange, and they understood what she felt because the same thing echoed in their genes.

But they had been challenged. Both they and Oma had the same inherited instinct. This was a duel.

Surit and Tennal had a single, unified presence, albeit in a dimension Surit didn't understand. Out here, it was obvious that, as humans, they'd only seen a fraction of what space really was. Through the eyes of whatever they were now, there was no endless void here, no cold darkness between the stars. Space *lived*. It teemed with sleeting particles and cosmic winds. The fabric of gravity sang. A current cascaded from the sun like a river and joined the great dance between the slow planets.

They had lived like this, once. It took Surit a second to understand those weren't his own memories. Those were the memories of a ghost of a ghost, imprinted on his genes and on his mind because humans had taken the remnants and used them on themselves. Surit was, by the standards of the aliens who had become the remnants, a monster. But maybe it was worth it—maybe it was worth being a monster—for this moment of glory. Chaotic space made sense now, like pockets of riptides within the water, beautiful and exhilarating. Above it all was the great spinning majesty of the galactic link, like a whirlpool in—

—a *sea,* Surit thought.

He teetered on the edge of an understanding the same way a ship teetered on the edge of foundering.

It was the same. The fabric of space and the currents in Tennal's mind, in Surit's own mind. The beings who had become the remnants saw no difference. They had traveled through space, and they had read and written mind-to-mind, and it was all the *same*—they perceived it all along some axis humans couldn't comprehend. The reason Tennal's mind had felt like the universe was because it was.

These thoughts all felt too big for Surit. Tennal caught the edges and followed them, and they were merged; Surit had no way to hide.

And there was no reason Tennal shouldn't see it. He felt Tennal stumble and flinch as he saw Surit's conclusions: that the universe was beautiful beyond measure, that Tennal's mind was the mirrored universe itself.

There was a millisecond of silence that lasted, out here, like an eternity. Then Tennal commented, amused: *Can't believe you never took me out to dinner.*

And that was the last human thought they had for a while.

Oma struck at them like a falling star. It was obvious why she'd picked this fight: she was exponentially more powerful than them, not a sync of two but a patched-together composite of hundreds. Her presence slammed into theirs with an energy field like a blast.

The first impact nearly destroyed them. They spun dizzyingly away, their mind ringing in pain, their edges dissolving. Oma drifted away from the collision, into a cloud of rocky shrapnel and regoliths, and turned, lining her great composite presence up for another attack. They both had the impression that she expected this to be easy. She wasn't wrong.

Fuck, Tennal-Surit said, and fled.

They slid into the currents of space like a fish. The corona of the sun flared to their left, but they fled away, toward the eddies of chaotic space. Like the ghost in their mind, the presence of Surit-and-Tennal knew how these fights went, and they knew they were too small to stand a chance. *Remember at the end, when there was no room for more than one in system,* Surit thought, then wondered where that voice had come from, and if Tennal had even heard it.

Tennal didn't seem to register the words. *Let's try and get where she can't see,* he suggested. *I need your—*

Here, Surit said. He fed his architect powers to Tennal. Even now, they weren't perfectly unified: Tennal was their eyes and their movement, but their joint presence burned energy, and Tennal—the reader—had almost none, while Surit controlled a deep reserve.

They didn't have long to work it out. Oma drifted past, silent and intent, like a planet occluding the sky.

Tennal-and-Surit struck. They realized it was a mistake almost the moment they'd done it. It was like attacking a battleship with a tugboat. Surit couldn't feed Tennal energy fast enough, even doing his frantic best—Oma had *hundreds* of people to draw on. She brushed the attack off casually. Her presence paused, triangulating, then projected an aura of annihilating energy at them. It seared their presence like a third-degree burn.

Hide, Surit said grimly. Another one like that and they were dead. Tennal-Surit dove back into the eddies of chaotic space. But just as they were learning, Oma was too: she slid between the disturbed currents after them.

She's following us, Tennal said frantically. *We have to try something else.*

Surit realized what was nearby. The parent and origin of all the disturbances of chaotic space. The galactic link itself.

Oh Lights, Tennal said, in either a curse or a religious plea that echoed strangely in their alien mind. *Guide us if you ever fucking have. All right, Surit.*

Tennal-Surit jumped into the relative calm of clear space, across the interstellar winds, and into the maelstrom around the link.

The currents were shockingly strong. Tennal couldn't keep them on a straight course. Instead they had to ride the eddies, trying desperately to lose Oma. At first, neither of them remembered Archer Link Station, bobbing like a leaf in a pond on winds humans couldn't see. The horror of it hit them both at once: either they or Oma could destroy it with one careless movement. They skidded around it, traveling millions of human miles to circle around the link.

From here, they could see what the center of the link actually was. And both Tennal and Surit stopped moving altogether in stunned fascination.

To a human, the link only looked like a crackling storm. But the ghost in their minds could see the way the link led out of their sector—it was a tunnel, but not just one: it was a network, a web of them. They could both feel their minds expanding to accommodate new dimensions. Humans used one axis of the link to skip between two fixed points, like skipping a stone across the water, but that wasn't what they were for. That wasn't all they were. Surit thought of the root system of a forest, tendrils upon tendrils, every bare patch of earth connected, eventually, to everything else.

Oh shit, Tennal said suddenly. Like the whirlpool it resembled, the circling currents had sucked them closer to the vortex of the link, to those infinite fractal paths through space. Tennal threw them backward, panicking. *Let's not get sucked into that.*

The whirlpool shuddered behind them.

Oma wasn't as small and nimble as them. Instead of navigating the currents around the link, she forged her way through them. The power she was drawing on shaped the fabric of space around her. The link shivered like metal under stress.

I don't think this is good, Surit said.

No! Pretty bad, actually! Tennal said, and Surit saw what he saw: the maelstrom throwing out new tendrils as if in reaction to the disturbance, perilously close to the tiny rings of Archer Link Station.

The heart of the link pulsed behind them, with its fractal tunnels and dangerous rifts.

Surit said, *What if—*

Oh, Tennal said. *Of course.* There was no moment where he weighed the idea. It had come from Surit; it went straight to Tennal carrying it out.

Tennal hovered their presence at the edge of the portal, like a rock in the current. Surit unspooled a steady flow of energy to keep them there and fed it to Tennal. There was no question that Oma would see them. It was hard to know now what was a fight about the coup in Exana and what was an imprint of the ghosts in their minds, pacing through a puppet show of aliens who had fought for reasons too ancient to remember. Tennal, Surit, Oma—all three of them had thrown themselves into the alien patterns too deeply, too thoughtlessly. And none of them were going to come out of this alive.

Don't think that, Tennal said. *This will work. Watch.*

They floated at the edge of the portal, motionless. Oma came on, the fabric of the link shrieking around her, like a meteor.

Will it?

I'm just very good at fucking up other people's plans.

Oma hit them.

They shattered into pieces. It hurt exquisitely, it hurt on a dimensional axis Surit didn't even know *could* hurt. He—they—he nearly fell apart. They were still synced, but only because power was pouring from Surit to Tennal like blood.

In the same instant, Tennal slithered the last fragments of their presence behind the composite hundreds of Oma's, and struck.

They didn't try to do damage. They only added momentum to the trajectory.

Shock radiated from the mass of souls—denial, fury. But Oma's consciousness already had momentum, and Tennal had leverage and all of Surit's reserves. The shifting, multifaceted presence, magnificent like the sun was magnificent, plunged into one of the deep tunnels of the link.

Tennal-Surit knew what to do, how to protect their space, from some instinct deep in their ancestral memory. But Surit was almost spent. *I need more energy,* Tennal said urgently. *Please! Now!*

The fragments of Surit didn't answer. He was nearly beyond consciousness, a collection of memories and thoughts unraveling in the currents. But he still had something left. The final impact had ripped open the reservoir of his architect powers like a wound, and the last thing he did was force it wider. His powers had never been useful for much. He could use them for this.

He felt Tennal take them and seal the single tunnel, the one root among thousands that Oma had fallen through.

As the last of Surit's powers drained out, he fell away from Tennal and drifted, unmoored. He had nothing left. Surit came apart.

He lost all sense of time; the moments of his end stretched out, oddly gentle, to eternity. Tennal had not yet noticed Surit was gone. Or perhaps he had—a handful of seconds ago or a thousand years ago. The currents Surit sank into measured time in the deaths of galaxies.

As Surit bled out, exhausted, into the cosmos, the flow of time warped for him. He felt stars change and disappear. He saw the link grow out of nothing, and shrink, and stabilize. He saw other links open, like the pulse of the universe. And, in the final moments, he saw a procession of beings like him, a great congregation, vast and solemn and utterly beyond comprehension. He saw their ghosts disappear into the link: a death, a withdrawing. The same link that humanity used to go from a single point to a single point, like children skipping rocks.

Surit—Surit! Don't you fucking dare!

He knew that voice. Surit struggled to remember—humanity. Tennal. Marit.

It was over.

Blaze of glory, Surit thought at Tennal, and went dark.

Head. Check. Limbs—all there, check. Lungs and heart. Spinal cord—two? No, just one. Check.

Where the fuck was his spleen? Oh, there.

Tennal lay on the plush carpet of his aunt's office, with—against all odds—nobody inside his head but himself.

It was so quiet.

He levered himself up in the deathly hush. His limbs felt filled with sawdust. He could almost imagine he was nine and playing hide-and-seek in here with Zin, until he saw it: Oma's body, slumped forward on the antique wood of the legislator's desk. Her eyes were glassy and unseeing. She wasn't breathing.

Fuck, Tennal thought. She looked beyond help, but surely they had to try: *Medical?*

There was no echo of someone else hearing him. Tennal turned his head.

He remembered the last few moments of the fight at the same instant as he saw Surit's body crumpled in front of the desk.

As if in a dream, Tennal saw himself dropping to his knees beside Surit, grabbing his shoulders, shaking him. Tennal knew his own lungs had worked a minute ago, so why had they stopped now? He could only take short snatches of breath. *Surit*, he said. *Surit*.

No answer. Of course.

But Surit wasn't *gone*. Unlike Oma, Tennal could feel a trace of him still in there. As Tennal dived in, chasing the thread through Surit's quiescent mind, he realized Surit wasn't just in here: he was somewhere else. He was spread across the sector, drifting and dissipating. Like Tennal had done to himself before, but a thousand times farther.

If the universe wasn't going to give Surit back, Tennal would bloody well take him.

Surit had done this for him, so Tennal had some desperate idea of what to do. He had to *know* Surit, but he did, better than anyone. Tennal started out with the pieces he knew best, yanking them from the void: Surit's steadfastness, his ironclad sense of right and wrong, his quiet kindness, the lists and responsibilities and traces of guilt that tangled his every movement. Surit's feeling that he could never be *good enough*, which was much less inexplicable once you knew how much Marit Yeni's death had screwed up his thinking. Tennal picked them out of the stars. And the other parts: Surit's pigheadedness, his recalcitrant, by-the-book stubbornness when anyone tried to cross him. His hidden satisfaction when things went his way; his dogged optimism when they didn't. His pride in his unit. The horrible tea he liked. The quirk of his mouth when he was trying not to laugh.

"Don't you dare do a Marit Yeni on me, Surit, do you hear?" Tennal said grimly as he worked. His aunt had believed the next generation would be better, and Lights knew if that was true, but if Tennal had anything to do with it, then it was at least going to be different. "No heroic deaths. Don't you *dare*."

He felt Surit's mind echo, like a faint signal from an occluded satellite. He was nearly there. Something was missing. Something important, or that had been important to Surit when he fell apart.

"Guidance fucking lose us," Tennal said, realizing. *You love me too.*

Tennal's whole mind hurt as he put it in words, like someone had exploded a sparkler in the back of his head. But now that he recognized it, the final major piece that came trailing everything else, he could pick it out of the currents of the void and shove it back into Surit's mind. He was losing his grip on Surit—they weren't *synced* anymore; their presence had fallen apart in the fight. "Wake up," he said. "Wake up, boss. Lieutenant Yeni. *Surit.*"

In the hushed, still air of the legislator's study, in the warm, mild evening, with birds singing outside despite the faint sounds of fighting, Surit Yeni sat up, dry-retched, doubled over on himself, and said, "What happened?"

"Watch it, Lights, fuck," Tennal said, pressing his hand on Surit's back. He didn't have the faintest idea how to do first aid. "Breathe! Do you need a doctor? I take that back—I don't think any doctor is going to know what to do with you. You're back."

Surit took three long breaths. "I didn't know you knew me," he said quietly, wonderingly. "Not like that."

Tennal sat back on his heels. "Didn't they tell you, Lieutenant

Yeni? If you stare into the void long enough," he said, and laughed until his lungs hurt.

Surit winced, and grinned, and tried to breathe.

"We're not synced," Surit said, after a long pause. "I can't feel you."

Tennal forced himself to sober up. He wanted to go into hysterics. That seemed like a reasonable reaction, honestly; Tennal had never held back a meltdown for this long in his life. "We fell apart in that last attack," he said. "I think I put you back together separately from me. Maybe that's why—oh *shit.*"

He suddenly realized what he had missed, and at the same time, he saw Surit's face change.

"Your architect powers," Tennal said. "I forgot." Or rather, he hadn't forgotten—he hadn't *known.* Surit had used them so rarely, and they were so foreign to Tennal. Tennal couldn't go back. His own mind was as weak and wrung out as a frayed piece of string. They'd be gone by now, anyway: traces of Surit had been disappearing into the fabric of space even as Tennal had frantically pulled them out. "Lights. I'm—" *Sorry* seemed inadequate. Surit had been a Rank One architect. He could have been a general.

"No," Surit said, in a measured tone. "That's good." He was still making heavy weather of breathing, but he seemed—earnest. In one way, Tennal regretted no longer having easy access to Surit's head, but in another, he'd missed this. He'd missed the everlasting surprise of Surit never, ever reacting the way Tennal thought he would.

"Explain."

"I wrote some people on the way here," Surit said, looking down at his knees. "Took them over. It was easy. I could—I don't want to be that person." He took another slow, painful breath and looked up at Tennal. "I think I do need a doctor. What's the situation?"

For one blank moment, Tennal could only think of their moment in the Codifier Halls. *Hey, sorry you kissed me when you thought you were going to die and now we're still here. Awkward!* But Surit wasn't in his head anymore. Tennal would have to say that out loud, and he would rather be immolated in a fuel tank explosion.

And that wasn't even what Surit was asking about. "Oma's dead. Or something like it."

Surit tried to get to his feet regardless of the fact his legs weren't working. He made a last-ditch grasp at an ornamental screen, which cracked under his weight. Tennal grabbed at his arm. "You're not in any state to walk."

From his new position, Surit could see Oma's body, slumped on the desk, not breathing.

"I don't think she's dead," Surit said, after staring in silence for several seconds. "I think she's not here."

"Great!" Tennal said. "Great, fantastic, we haven't been meddling with forces we don't understand or anything, can't *wait* to explain that to the general staff. *Dear sirs, I solved your problem by shoving your rogue commander through a wormhole we didn't know existed. Her disembodied consciousness might be anywhere in the universe. You're welcome.*"

The corner of Surit's mouth twitched. Tennal had missed that.

"I don't think you had a choice," Surit said. "And wherever she is, she's not in our sector anymore." He slumped back, against the remains of the screen. His warm-chestnut eyes went to Tennal with an intensity that Tennal didn't think he'd ever get used to. "You brought me back."

It meant something, a question Tennal only half understood. He didn't know if he had an answer either—or rather he had too many answers, all of them tentative. *I think I want to be here,* Tennal didn't say. *I think I can live with myself. I'd like to believe I've finished fucking up just for the sake of it, but let's be honest, I'll probably do it again. I think I want you, Surit, after all the dust has settled. I think I can do this.*

What Tennal said was: "*Are* you going to buy me dinner?" Surit choked. Tennal said, mendaciously, "Sorry, forgot you were too sensible for that."

"I'm done being sensible," Surit said. He shifted and looked up as the door clicked.

Tennal heard a voice outside shout, "Wait, Sen—your security—!"

That and the running footsteps were all the warning Tennal got before Zinyary flung herself on his crouched back like a limpet and said, "*Tenn!*"

It wasn't a stable position for hugging. Tennal collapsed to the floor with Zin on his back. She clung with her arms around his shoulders; he clung to her wrists. Tennal's mind had been full of *Oma, Surit, fighting, survival*. Now it was blank. His eyes were prickling and painful. *Zin.*

When he was sure his voice wasn't going to crack, he rolled over—away from Surit, who had politely shifted backward—and said, "Lights, enthusiastic much? Let me breathe, sprat."

The difference in Zin hit Tennal as soon as he saw her face. Her hair was up and had been styled by a professional. She wore a formal wrap-jacket like the legislator; it made her look five years older. She was crying and wasn't admitting to it. Instead she punched him hard in the shoulder as he sat up.

"Ow," Tennal said, "I've been looking for you for weeks. Is that any way to—"

"*I've* been looking for *you!*" Zin said. "Tenn, I could kill her. I thought you were dead. I made them go through the fatality lists. Where were you?"

Tennal hadn't been expecting that, somehow, though he should have been. He stared down at her and remembered her on the opposition's propaganda broadcasts, throwing herself into their aunt's faction to try to stabilize things. He'd thought he was rescuing her. His little sister. But, of course, Zin was *his sister*. His aunt's blood. A Halkana to the bone.

And Tennal thought, *She grew up and I never saw.*

"I was trying to get back to you," Tennal said. "I got hung up. Sorry."

There was a crash as someone finally got the study door fully open. First through it were two Cavalry soldiers, obviously Zin's security. Behind them, Istara looked around the doorframe. "Cavalry division took the residence. I let your sister through. Basavi's outside with—" Their eyes landed on Oma's slumped form, followed by Surit on the ground. "Holy shit, sir."

"I'm fine, Private," Surit said. He shifted as more people flooded into the office and put out his hand for Tennal to help him up. Tennal took it. Surit put his entire weight on Tennal, as if there was no doubt Tennal could manage it. He braced his feet and did.

Zin whispered, "Leave this to me." She tried to rearrange her hair as Tennal let go of her arm, and she went over to her security first, scattering reassurances and directing the soldiers to Oma's body. The handful of rankers debated urgently over the corpse, looking over their shoulders.

Who they were waiting for became apparent a moment later, when Commander Vinys stepped through the doorway.

"Oh, wow," Tennal said under his breath. "The cherry on the cake."

The commander had caked blood and burned skin on the side of his temple and looked more furious than Tennal had ever seen him. Tennal could not summon any sympathy. "Secure the scene," he snapped. Then he spotted Surit, and Tennal beside him, and if a look could have melted someone's face off, this would have done it. "Lieutenant Yeni," he said. "So glad your outright insubordination has brought you here. There will be a court-martial. If you would like to make things less bad for yourself—"

Surit looked at him and said, "We're leaving."

"*Excuse me?*"

"I'm leaving," Surit said patiently, "with Captain Halkana. If you want to stop us, please consider I'm a Rank One architect."

Before the commander had time to shoot Surit or Tennal, Zin jumped in. "Commander Vinys," she said, with the exact same certainty in her voice as she'd had in the propaganda broadcast, "Governor Oma seems to be dead. This is my childhood home. I need some air. I'm just going to step outside, and I'll send you the Infantry and Pilot leads in a minute. Tennal and"—she hesitated—"Yeni, is it? Can I borrow you?"

Winsome, collected, sixteen-year-old Zinyary Halkana was clearly the entire opposition's mascot by this point. Tennal had to admire it. It wasn't a tactic he could have used. One soldier even offered her their water flask in sympathy. The commander couldn't reasonably deny her.

"And I'm not a captain," Tennal said. "I'm a civilian." He patted the commander's shoulder as he passed. "Great to see you again, though. Keep up the good work."

The commander needed to go down. Surit wouldn't hold a grudge, but Tennal could. Two months ago Tennal wouldn't have dreamed of ever managing to take down a senior military commander. Now, though, Tennal could see a different future. If you'd asked him what made normal people clean up their act, he wouldn't have said *spite,* but if it worked, he'd take it.

He glanced at Surit, and at Zin, and at the unthinkable traces of combat soldiers in his aunt's house. Maybe other factors had an influence as well.

When they emerged into the warm evening air of the garden, no longer quiet—some Infantry soldiers had set up a comms tent in the shrubbery—Zin said, "Tenn, I thought I was very restrained in there, but what in Lights' gaze did you do?"

"We have solved your situation for you," Tennal announced grandly.

"You haven't!" Zin said. "You absolutely haven't!"

"We have fucked up the situation," Tennal amended, just as grandly, "in a new and interesting way."

Zin finally cracked, crying and laughing at the same time. She collapsed to sit on a wall and took an enormous gulp of air. "Did you kill Governor Oma?"

"In our defense," Tennal said, "she did very much try to kill us."

"She's not dead." With Tennal's help, Surit lowered himself carefully to sit on the wall a few feet away. "Excuse me, Sen Zinyary. Her body is. But we think her mind . . . escaped somewhere. Possibly somewhere outside the sector. I hope her victims are recovering—she was brainwashing hundreds of people."

"Oh, wow, great," Zin said, in a tone of voice Tennal suspected she'd gotten from him. "Big fan of that. Well, we got a flurry of messages from her officers about ten minutes ago. Something about compulsions. Were those the victims you meant? That was how we got the intel that she was here and why the other side fell apart. Did you know our aunt's alive, by the way, Tenn? I could kill her myself."

"Yes—" Tennal started to say.

LOCATED, a voice said. It was on a frequency that set Tennal's whole nervous system on edge. It wasn't a human voice, and it didn't exactly come through his hearing. Surit flinched in shock. Zin clapped her hands over her ears.

And then others, like a clamor of discordant bells:

LOCATED.

LOCATED.

OPENING VISUAL.

There was a disturbance above the garden steps, on a level with Tennal's head. Visible currents gathered around a tiny area of empty air, coin-sized. The miniature stitch in space opened to a small, pale swirl. Like an eye.

Another one materialized and opened behind Surit's head. Then another, and another. Dozens of ghostly eyes opened and fixed themselves on Tennal and Surit and Zin. Tennal glanced hurriedly behind them and could see the eyes opening in the corridor as well, and outside, even over the roof.

LOCATED.

LOCATED.

Surit sat up straight, because you could take the soldier out of the crisis, but you couldn't take the 98 percent Crisis Response test grade out of the soldier. "What is going on?"

As if in answer, one of the eyelike swirls exploded into a round light-screen that was, under the circumstances, shockingly human. There was a person in it.

The person had the featureless, colorless eye shield that meant they were from the Resolution.

"*A xeno projection event was detected in this area,*" the person said. Their accent was one Tennal couldn't place, from some Resolution planet he had probably never even heard of. "*Remnant abuse is a violation of the Resolution treaty. Your planetary authority has been contacted. Do not attempt to leave local space.*"

"Well," Tennal said, after a moment of absolute silence. "It looks like we fucked up in an even more creative way than I thought."

CHAPTER 33

Tennal absolutely adored being decanted into a full Resolution inquest seven hours after he had stopped a civil war.

It had been deep into the night before he and Zin had managed to get away from the Legislator's Residence. One of the coin-sized eyes followed each of them, floating behind like an invisible leash. The army had admitted Surit to a hospital, where last time Tennal had seen him, he'd been looking less like a wrung-out cloth who'd bled his life force out into deep space and more like a human who needed some rehydration sachets. He had an eye hovering beside his bed as well.

Surit smiled when Tennal came in. And before that, hours ago, Surit had kissed him in an abandoned office in the Codifier Halls. Tennal still wasn't sure what to do with that.

Tennal hadn't come through all this to abandon Surit in a hospital and was considering sleeping in a chair when Surit fixed him with his most officer-type look and said, "You haven't been called until morning. The rest of our unit has lodgings. Go to bed, Tennal."

So Tennal had found a bed to go to. Zin lived in an apartment in Exana, and technically Tennal lived there too, albeit he hadn't slept in his old bedroom for nearly ten months. The Resolution eye followed him all the way to the apartment, then all the way to the door outside his old bedroom, where Tennal turned around and looked at it. "Yeah, all right," Tennal said. "I'm going to get undressed in there. Don't be weird." He made a shooing motion. His hand went straight through the eye, with no obvious physical effect, but the air folded over it to hide the white swirl like an eyelid, as if he'd embarrassed it. Tennal stared at it for a further moment then decided he was too tired for this. "You can watch the door," he said. "I'm not going anywhere." He might have felt weird, but instead he fell asleep the moment he was horizontal.

He'd had three hours of sleep and barely a shower when a flyer showed up outside Zin's apartment to take him to the halls. The eye was hovering behind his shoulder again. A ranker jumped out of the flyer and saluted him.

Tennal smiled, touched his throat briefly, and walked straight past the flyer and out onto the street.

It took him ten minutes to walk to the Codifier Halls under his own steam, the eye floating behind him. The dawn air was cool. The sky had opened into a pure blue above and a muted haze in the distance; it would be hot later. Flowers tumbled down Exana's old walls, and Tennal lingered to catch a glimpse of someone's garden through a trellis. Tennal hadn't been on a planet by himself for weeks.

He didn't think, *Why did I leave here?* That wasn't how he handled things. But he breathed deeply. His brain felt like a hundred glass pieces, all carefully and intricately slotted together, but it was all *his* brain. He had a new, fragile control. It felt good.

When he reached the Codifier Halls, he somehow wasn't surprised to see his aunt waiting for him at the arches of the entrance.

"Feeling better, were you?" Tennal said. She must have left chaotic space soon after he had. She leaned on a cane and looked irritated about the need to use it. There was an eye hovering over her shoulder as well.

He was expecting the searching, judgmental look when she saw him but not the amused twitch of her mouth. "I'm not dead. But the sooner I can get rid of the bloody cane, the better. You're late. I sent a flyer for you."

"A military flyer," Tennal said conversationally. "I'm a civilian, Auntie dearest."

"I thought Archer made you a Lights-lost captain."

"I'm demobilized," Tennal said. He moved a step closer, lowered his voice so her security couldn't hear, and said, "Aren't I? I had better be. Because if *not*, I might be the one who tells the world how you planned to murder one of your own lieutenants to help your nephew hide his reader skills."

"Is that right?" his aunt said. Tennal was expecting a flood of invective, but instead the crow's-feet around her eyes crinkled in a way he didn't recognize.

"Anyway," Tennal said, "your division still has Surit, and he's worth ten of me. Figure out how to use *him*. I'm out."

She clapped him on the shoulder. "You fucking snake," she said. "Pity—you would have gone far. Get in there. The Resolution wants you."

And with that, she was gone, the cane an irregular tap in her stride.

Tennal joined the crowd funneling into the public entrance. The Codifier Halls were humming with politicians and soldiers, most of whom had the wild-eyed look of people who had been up all night frantically scrambling to get answers for an enigmatic intergalactic body that paid no attention to time zones or logistical issues. The Resolution eye hovering behind Tennal's head got him waved through all the security checks in an instant.

The heartbeat of the inquest proceeded in the Convocation itself. The hall that housed the Convocation was a huge square room with a series of cushioned benches in concentric squares, centering on a speaker's platform that was just a sunken slab of marble. Today dozens upon dozens of the Resolution's eyes occupied one whole side of the benches. A few of them had opened into screens with Resolution staffers on them. A ragtag group of Convocation politicians and military officers sat at a wary distance; most of them seemed to have been here all night as well.

On the platform was Commander Vinys. One of the politicians seemed to be quizzing him about his operation yesterday, while the Resolution listened. Tennal was pleased to see he was sweating.

Today there was no media; instead the benches near the door were scattered with a motley assortment of people the inquest wanted to speak to. Tennal spotted Basavi and Istara sitting on a corner bench at the back.

They were holding hands. They pulled apart when Tennal slipped in next to them. Basavi looked fractionally embarrassed.

Istara did not. "We think the lieutenant's up next," they said in a whisper. "He's at the front."

"I know," Tennal said, then stopped in surprise. He did know. He was absolutely, 100 percent certain Surit was fifty yards ahead of him and a little to the left. He could have located him from a satellite.

He and Surit weren't synced anymore. Tennal had thought they were entirely separate.

When he craned his neck, he could see he was right. Surit sat, upright and serious, next to a pair of grave-looking politicians. He'd found a Cavalry uniform and looked, against all odds, like a model soldier again. There was only a tinge of gray under his eyes.

Tennal looked at the ankles of Surit's new uniform trousers, which Surit had hurriedly let down so they fit. He imagined Surit in the gray predawn light in a hospital room, waking up so he could use a travel sewing kit and make himself neat enough to testify on behalf of an army that had been happy to kill him.

Tennal had been in love before. Generally, he knew it as an adrenaline high, three days without sleep, a weeklong obsession with someone just as reckless as him. It hadn't ever been a steady, quiet pulse like this before. But it hadn't involved syncing and civil war and alien ghosts either.

Did this kind of feeling last? It might tug at Tennal like a tap on his chest every time he thought of it, but maybe Surit had forgotten already. Surit might have come to his senses the moment he had time to breathe and think.

And if not—then what? Tennal was not used to taking things slowly and sensibly. It was a terrifying idea. He'd almost rather face the Resolution.

Then he tuned in to what the commander on the speaker's platform was saying.

"—rogue architect, Yeni." The commander didn't even glance at Surit. "Yeni went over to Governor Oma's side weeks back; I assume he was coerced. Must have convinced Halkana to join him. Oma didn't have any remnants as far as I know. My soldiers searched her study when they cleaned up."

That was news to Tennal. The Resolution eyes clearly transmitted back *some* visuals. But then, it was possible some quick-thinking soldier had simply flipped the lid back on the case and it had looked like any other storage box. It might have been moved even now, while the Resolution wasn't paying attention. Just another black hole in the army's assets.

"Yes—certainly, some of us are neuromods," the commander said, in response to a question. "Some of my soldiers, yes. But you people"—a gesture toward the Resolution eyes—"agreed to the neuromods years ago. Nothing out of the ordinary."

"*And the projection event?*" one of the Resolution's staffers said from their screen. Tennal didn't think he was imagining the dry tone.

"Must have been an accident," Commander Vinys said. "A malfunction in your sensors."

There was a silence. Then the Resolution staffer said, "*No further questions.*"

Surit stood as the commander left the speaker's platform. As the commander passed him, he gave Surit a complacent nod. He'd painted Surit as incompetent but not entirely criminal. The message was clear: if Surit swallowed his pride and backed up the commander's version of events, they might all come out of this battered but unchanged.

Tennal sat forward expectantly. Beside him, Istara whispered something to Basavi.

Surit walked onto the marble slab of the speaker's platform. It was exposed: spectators on all four sides. This didn't seem to disturb him. He saluted the division commanders sitting on the side. He stood at ease. Then he turned to the Resolution's eyes. "That isn't true," Surit said, in the clear, clipped tone of a soldier making a report.

"Told you," Istara muttered, as the room started shifting and a murmur rose from the benches.

Surit seemed to take a perverse strength from that, like someone setting his face against the wind. "Oma had multiple remnants that weren't surrendered to the Resolution. She took them from an abandoned facility in chaotic space, and she used them to brainwash people. Tennalhin and I—she fought us. We were synced. She was a merge of hundreds. If you want to know how she did it, maybe the remnants will help you. I don't want anyone to have that kind of power again."

"*I see,*" the Resolution staffer said. Tennal squinted at their tiny image on the screen. The swirling eye-shield the Resolution staff wore made it difficult to get a read on them. "*We will investigate. Do you know where the remnants are?*"

"I don't," Surit said, staring expressionlessly ahead of him. He must have noticed the death glares coming his way from the line of division commanders. In fact he did, because he turned to them and said, "One more thing. Sirs. I would like to take this opportunity to resign my post. I request a discharge without honors."

"Wait," Istara said beside Tennal. "What?"

Resign? Tennal stared at Surit. This wasn't how it was supposed to go at all. Tennal was leaving the army, and Surit would stay in it and become a general or whatever. Surit was their model soldier. What about Surit's years of officer academy? What about his parent's *pension*?

There was a question the speaker's platform mic didn't pick up, but Tennal could tell what it was by the stiff line of Surit's shoulders. Tennal rose to his feet and started to push his way through the benches. "I think this *is* the time, actually, sir," Surit said up front. He was aware the mic was picking up his words, Tennal could tell. This was aimed at the whole hall. "My mother, General Yeni, fixed a great wrong when she stopped the last experiments on readers. She was smeared for it. You took a reader I respected, and you treated him like an object. You treated me like an object. And I don't mind working for the greater good, but I'm not sure I am."

Surit, for Lights' sake, Tennal thought, though of course Surit didn't hear. As Tennal pushed his way to the front, he spotted Zin. She was sitting with a group of people in the green and gray of working lawyers. That must be her law shoal. One of the senior lawyers had her hand on Zin's shoulder, as if to stop Zin from jumping up. Maybe Zin could rescue Surit after he'd stopped *accidentally digging himself into a court-martial.*

"So I resign, sir," Surit said implacably. "Effective immediately, or if there's a court-martial, after whatever term of imprisonment that panel decides."

Unbelievable. Tennal had the worst lieutenant possible. Tennal emerged from the benches, the marble slab with the division commanders on his left and the Resolution eyes and screens on his right, and said to both of them, "Excuse me. Excuse me! You're not going to jail him."

Two security guards stepped forward, glancing at each other and at Tennal, but after a fraction of a second, the person on the Resolution screen said, *"Ah. You are Tennalhin Halkana. The other neuromod at the site of the incident."* They added, *"Clear the platform for Tennalhin Halkana, please."*

Surit locked eyes with Tennal but didn't speak a word in range of the speaker's platform and its mic. But as he passed Tennal, he raised his hand and brushed his fingers against Tennal's inner elbow, a touch that probably looked like nothing to onlookers but was intimate enough to make Tennal shiver even through his clothes.

Tennal stepped onto the platform, trying desperately to get his mind back on track. This was not exactly what he had meant to do.

And it wasn't what he had to do either, because the moment he stepped onto the platform, Zin jumped from her chair like a coiled spring and followed him up.

"Hi," Zin said to the Resolution screens, shifting from foot to foot beside Tennal. She sounded bright and overstretched as a taut wire, a sign she was very nervous. "Hi, hello, I'm speaking for Tennalhin. I'm his legal representative and spokesperson under Subjects of Participating Polities: Communication codicil one-two-five A."

There was a microsecond's pause.

"*Tennalhin Halkana: confirm, please?*"

Tennal gave Zin a baffled look. "Sure. Absolutely." Why not? She clearly had something up her sleeve.

Zin swallowed. "I invoke the right to active audience."

From the Convocation on Orshan Central, there was only a faint confusion, but this meant something to the Resolution. One by one, every single coin-sized white eye opened and turned into a circular light-screen. Each floating screen showed a Resolution staffer with a swirling face-field covering their eyes. Zin's demand had clearly taken some of them by surprise: a few showed glimpses of their eyes as they hastily turned on their masks.

Zin faced them. Only Tennal could see her fingers nervously twisting together at her side. "This whole incident is based on a treaty violation," she said. "Orshan got permission for the neuro-mods, as long as they don't travel. We never told you about the syncs."

"*Syncs?*" the Resolution staffer said.

They didn't know about the syncs? Tennal was astonished for all of two seconds, then he saw his aunt pinching the bridge of her nose, and astonishment changed into a growing dark glee. *Get them, Zin.*

"The Orshan army conscripts strong readers," Zin explained. "They bind them to architects in a way we call a *sync*. It allows the architect to control the reader. The readers are supposed to be convicted criminals, but that's not true for all of them. A strong architect-reader team makes a good piloting unit. I submit that under our treaty and amendments, *all* forced military syncs are illegal, and Orshan has been systematically hiding this from the Resolution."

How long had Zin been sitting on this? Tennal glanced back at Zin's law shoal, where the senior lawyer was nodding, unsurprised. Zin had had help. Of course she had. *It's a reader rights group*, she'd said before he left, weeks ago. Tennal hadn't paid enough attention.

Nobody on the Orshan side was trying to gainsay Zin—possibly knowing it would look worse—though Zin had instantaneously blown all her goodwill with the divisions and possibly most of the planet. Tennal had forgotten that their core family trait was a willingness to break things to get what they wanted. And Zin had decided that what she wanted was to stop the syncs.

If the law shoal was involved, they must at least have judged that the Resolution wouldn't annul Orshan's treaty over this. Being outside the Resolution was unthinkable; the Resolution wouldn't do that lightly. But they could make trouble.

"*This changes things,*" one of the people on the light-screens said. Interestingly, it was a different one from the staffer who had been doing all the talking up to this point. "*They'll need an irregular audit.*"

A third staffer said acerbically, "*Because the last Orshan audit found so much, did it?*" There was a silence after that one had spoken, and from the tiny twitches of heads on the screens, Tennal got the feeling that a second, more animated argument was going on somewhere their audience couldn't hear.

A cane tapped as the legislator made her way onto the platform. "There has been a misunderstanding," she said, with all the pleasantness of a boxer starting a fight. "Orshan will be pleased to help clear it up. We came to an agreement twenty years ago. We can come to another agreement this time."

"*How many times, Orshan?*" one of the Resolution staffers said. "*Is this really in the spirit of the treaty?*"

The legislator gave a grim, crooked smile. "You've done it elsewhere," she said, "and I know we're not your most noncompliant planet. Would you like to talk about the High Chain? Or not, because half of you originate from there?"

The inaudible argument this time was more animated.

"*A gesture of goodwill would help. We'd like the neuromod*"—a slight pause—"*the 'architect' at the center of this. It would be useful if Surit Yeni could come to Resolution space for examination.*"

"What does that mean?" Zin said.

"*He will not be harmed and will be free to return when the examination is finished.*"

"Wait," Tennal said instinctively. Surit had gone still. Tennal didn't need to be in his mind to know that leaving his home sector to be poked and prodded about the neuromod powers he'd always hated was the last thing Surit wanted. "He's not even an architect anymore."

"*We will determine that.*"

Every eye in the room was on the legislator. Tennal couldn't parse her hesitation. She'd been okay with planning Surit's death. Where were her lines? Tennal was starting to suspect if you cracked open the moral center of her brain, you'd find a mesh of wires in five dimensions.

She'd put a halt to the brainwashing program when she became legislator. She hadn't investigated what it had done. She hadn't exonerated Marit Yeni's memory—but she hadn't continued the research.

The legislator said, "No."

Surit sagged in relief. But none of the Resolution screens seemed pleased. "*If Orshan intends to be obstructionist*—"

"There's an easy answer," Tennal said, loud enough to stop both them and his aunt's snapped reply. "I'll go."

He said it instinctively. He said it because Surit was afraid and tired and shouldn't be made to go, but they couldn't have the Resolution kicking them out of the treaty. But as he said it, the idea unfolded in his mind like a window opening in a small room. The universe was bigger and stranger than he'd thought. He didn't have to stay in the Orshan sector. He could go where he liked— and maybe the Resolution knew about things that were weirder and more incredible than readers and architects or whatever Surit and Tennal had become. Maybe he could find out while he was there.

"What?" his aunt said.

"I can volunteer to go and talk to the Resolution." The looks he was getting suggested this had been neither a normal instinct nor an advisable one, but Tennal felt all the adrenaline centers in his brain light up. Tennal had never considered he could stand up in the Codifier Halls, the dullest place in the entire sector, and get the familiar rush of applying a match to a fuse. "I was the other person in their *projection event*. And I'm still neuromodified. He's not."

The Resolution staffers swiftly conferred. The division chiefs on the front benches leaned forward, locked in their own muttered discussion. Even Zin whispered, "Tenn, what are you *doing*?"

But the only person Tennal looked at was Surit, several feet away on a front bench. Tennal no longer had a cell-deep awareness of

Surit's lungs, but he almost felt it as Surit inhaled sharply then let out his breath, his gaze not wavering from Tennal's eyes.

And that was all that mattered, really. Surit trusted him. Tennal stopped second-guessing his irrepressible thrill at throwing the rest of them off course and just let his face do what it wanted to. He'd once been told his smile was insufferable. He hoped it still was.

While the Resolution still conferred, the legislator took Tennal's shoulder and dragged him three steps out of the speaker's platform, shoving her cane into the ground like it had offended her. When they were out of mic range, she said, "We don't know what this means. Even if they say *unharmed,* this means we'd send you to Resolution space—with handlers, because they don't allow unsupervised neuromods to travel—for Lights know how long. Tennalhin, this is not a responsibility I can ask you to take."

"Auntie dear," Tennal said lovingly, "I don't think you can stop me. And in any case, I want to go."

His aunt closed her eyes and let his shoulder go. "I won't pretend we don't need it."

"Lucky you spent all that time hiding the syncs from the Resolution, isn't it?"

His aunt grunted. "Don't expect special treatment when you come back."

"I want a planetary medal," Tennal said. "And a new flyer. And a horse—"

She was already turning back to the platform. The Resolution seemed to have arrived at a conclusion.

"*We accept. We will now adjourn for the rest of the—morning, is it? Morning.*" Half the Resolution screens had started to close, but the spokesperson was still there. "*When we reconvene this afternoon, we will need Zinyary Halkana.*"

Zin looked terrified and exhilarated as the crowd started to dissipate. Tennal sneakily punched her as he passed, knuckling his hand into her bicep. "Can't believe you nearly got us kicked out of the Resolution because you wanted to take my side against our aunt."

"It will help other people, it was the *right thing to do*—" Zin said, in high indignation, but Tennal had already left her behind. He looked for Surit, but Surit had been pulled into a debriefing with the division commanders. Never mind. Surit would be there later. Tennal had the overwhelming urge to be outside, breathing the air of his own planet.

He quickened his stride, walking past the politicians and soldiers and aides. Past Istara—who gave him a quick thumbs-up—and Basavi. Past the last of the inquest and the anteroom outside. Tennal burst through the double doors of the Codifier Halls like a diver emerging from the sea.

He was the first out of the hall. For a moment he had the wide, shallow steps to himself.

The courtyard was fresh with the early morning air. He noticed, as if for the first time, the trees that crept along the outer walls were heavy with rose-pink blossoms—a triumphant shout of color, a jubilant scent in the air. People crossed the paths below. Flyers hovered low against the warm Exana sky. Tennal didn't know what had changed that he couldn't stop noticing things, but he drank in each movement, each touch of the breeze on his skin, each facet of light like the morning had turned him into a mirror, reflecting everything.

He told himself it was just a reaction to being back on the planet. He told himself it couldn't last, and that was true, but for once the thought didn't hurt. There would be bad times again. There would be times so dull and gray that he would claw at the walls of his own head to get out of them. But they would end—he had *proof* they would end—and it would be in the same way as this, with a raging blaze of color, with a defiant breath of air, with the restless spurring of his body onward into the city and the day.

Last time he had been in Exana, everywhere had felt like a

prison. He could pinpoint it now: the terror that everything would be dull forever. How could that be the same place?

But it was the same. Tennal breathed in and took the stairs down two at a time. The wider universe hummed with possibility, and Tennal was alive.

CHAPTER 34

Surit's dishonorable discharge paperwork came through surprisingly fast.

He was excluded from the afternoon session of the inquest, as was most of the previous audience. Surit didn't mind. He went back to the barracks and spent the afternoon signing statements and military release forms.

He didn't know where Tennal was. Before he'd left the halls, a politician's aide had delicately asked about the sync then drawn him aside and murmured, "I wouldn't contact him before he goes to the Resolution; the less neuromodified he seems, the better."

Surit had said, "Is that right?"

The rest of the day was a blur. Several officers tried to stop Surit from being discharged. Someone very senior in Cavalry Division came to glare at him and urge him to think very carefully about what he was doing. This barely registered; Surit fixed his gaze on the barracks wall behind the officer and thought about the lunch he'd missed.

He spent his spare time writing up a promotion recommendation for Basavi. He was leaving behind good people. The thought wasn't enough to stop him.

At one point his collection of forms was tagged HOLD PENDING COURT-MARTIAL, and Surit guessed it wasn't going to go through. But later on, the tag disappeared, and magically, five minutes later, his notice period was waived, and he was cleared to go.

Surit wondered whom he had to thank for that.

And without further ceremony, the barracks spat him out into the pale gold of the summer street in a set of machine-extruded civvies, the remains of his personal possessions in a bag over his back. Surit had always been a soldier, and now he wasn't.

He felt incredible.

It was early afternoon. The sun filtered through a haze in the sky. His body felt *home* in a way spacefarers only felt when they came back to the atmosphere they grew up in: the city was strange to him, but the gravity and the breeze were right. The atmospheric pressure cradled him like a cocoon. Above him there was weather, not just ventilation but the massive weight of several billion tons of air across thousands of miles of planet. The smell of fried dough wafted from a nearby food cart. The street was busy, and barely anyone was in uniform at all.

Surit wandered aimlessly down a tree-lined avenue and into a park. There was so much of the day left. For the first time in years, his mental to-do list was gloriously blank.

In the back of his mind, he was waiting.

It took him about half a lap of the park to decide that a break was pleasant, but it had gone on long enough, and to start filling his to-do list again. He didn't have a purpose. Maybe he'd never had one. But Surit could always find things to do.

Surit downloaded maps and oriented himself in this new city. After so long spaceside, he thought he could get used to sprawling, flowery, busy Exana, at least for a while. He registered himself as hunting for work. He booked a cheap hostel room and marveled at how much nicer it was than the barracks—the bed, so soft, and only one of it, racks of storage for bags Surit didn't have, even enough room to swing his arms around if he liked.

That evening, he lay on the soft, ordinary bed and made the one call he'd been dreading.

His parent Elvi answered after a delay. He was outside in the garden, his rangy form crouched over a bed of vegetables. Surit had been thinking of Elvi as tired and lined, as he'd been in his last message, but he'd forgotten his parent was more often like this: bright and vague with unfocused purpose. Elvi smiled when he saw Surit.

"Well, look who's back on-planet," Elvi said. "Thought you'd forgotten me."

Surit's heart was beating painfully for no reason. Elvi hadn't repudiated Marit, even after the false stories. There was no reason he'd be upset with Surit. "Have you seen the newslogs?"

The newslogs hadn't carried Surit's part in things. Elvi looked at Surit then laid his trowel aside and stood. The light-screen came with him. Behind Elvi, the sprawling garden disappeared into glossy-leafed trees and wilderness.

"Tell me," Elvi said.

The explanation Surit gave was neither crisp nor coherent. He had written a full, clear accounting of every action he'd taken, back when he'd thought he was going to die. He hadn't meant to go out without telling Elvi what had happened. Now, for the first time, he thought: *What would it have been like to receive that letter? What would it have been like to read that from your child?* He could barely look at the screen.

". . . and I asked to be discharged," Surit finished. He couldn't quite say, *You were right,* because he and Elvi had never had a direct conversation about it. Conversations about the army had always been mired in Surit's undirected teenage anger and a private, prickly sorrow from Elvi that Elvi, in his mild way, never talked about or explained. Surit wanted to say: *If you'd just told me.* He wanted to say: *Why didn't you explain?* But Surit wouldn't have entertained any narrative that wasn't black-and-white, not back then, and then he'd enrolled in the army, and there had been no more chances. "I'm not in the army anymore. I couldn't take it. There's no chance of Marit's pension, I think. I'm sorry."

Elvi looked surprised in a way that made Surit feel they'd been having parallel conversations.

"Whatever you want," Elvi said. "We'll manage. We've always

managed. It's been a good growing season." He smiled, standing in the shaded part of the garden that Surit suddenly missed like a hole in his chest.

They *had* always managed. Surit felt ashamed, or grateful; he couldn't tell which. "I'm coming home," he said. "Next week. I can stay for—a couple of days?"

Elvi paused then suggested, "Or longer?"

"Or longer," Surit said.

After the call, Surit didn't expect to sleep—but he did, and he woke up lighter. As he left the hostel into the morning sun, it felt like yet another weight had rolled off his back.

He didn't stop waiting.

As he waited, he looked for something to do. He didn't have any connections to call on, not after burning his bridges so spectacularly, so he applied for jobs that didn't need qualifications. After a couple of days' work hefting lost drones out of ditches and sewers, he was surprised when an interview for a desk job came through. He cleaned his shoes, did the best he could with his basic civvies, and went.

And this was all fine right up until his interviewer stepped into the room.

"Lieutenant Yeni?" she said, bewildered. "What are you doing here?"

Surit rose hastily to his feet and touched his throat. "It's just Surit, please, Sen Zinyary. I'm . . . applying for the clerical job?" *What about you?* seemed a bit rude.

Zinyary belatedly made a gesture of greeting in return. "This is . . . the rights group that my law shoal works with. You knew that, didn't you?"

Surit had known the job was with the same parent organization, but he hadn't thought he'd meet Tennal's sister. This was a little embarrassing. They'd barely spoken; he didn't want her to think he was trying to draw on a connection that didn't exist. "I didn't think you'd be involved."

"No, you didn't!" Zinyary agreed. "They only asked me to do this interview because my senior's out sick and this is an entry-level role. I'm just an apprentice!"

"They let you negotiate with the Resolution," Surit said neutrally. She might look familiar, but here was a difference: modesty was not an issue Tennal had.

"Yes, but mainly I memorized a script my senior wrote," Zinyary said. "Lieutenant Yeni—sorry, I mean, Sen Surit—" She gestured vaguely. "You do know this is a data-entry role? It's not even an apprenticeship."

"Yes," Surit said.

"Anyone could do it," Zinyary persisted. "Why did you apply for it? You were an officer!"

"I left the army." It should hurt to explain, especially to an apprentice, but Surit found he was poking a wound that had already cauterized. "I don't have any skills."

Zinyary looked at him with the same expression Tennal had when he found someone completely hopeless. "Please," she said. "Tennal told me about you. You were a lieutenant; you managed people and operations and things. You thwarted a coup! Do you think we don't need that on the civilian side? Well, maybe not the coup," she added. But then she leaned forward, bright and intent. "You *could* work for us, and not like this. Our allies need people who aren't scared of the military. You ran a whole unit—I'm sure they can find something for you."

Surit blinked. "I don't have civilian qualifi—"

"And besides!" Zinyary said, continuing like a steamroller. "You dealt with my brother for weeks without strangling him. That's as good as a certificate." Her eyes flickered over to something behind him. "And they didn't even give you *hazard pay*."

Surit remembered: Zinyary hadn't shut the door of the small office room. There was a change in the texture of the air behind him. A deep instinct pinged his mind.

Surit finally stopped waiting.

"You took your time, Tennal," he said.

"Hey," Tennal said from the doorway. He leaned against the frame with his arms crossed. Surit looked him over wordlessly, savoring the opportunity to just watch him without being in his mind. Tennal's green eyes were sharp, no longer lined with exhaustion. He moved like he occupied his own skin fully. He looked like he might leave a line of electricity in the air as he went.

Tennal's expression changed to outrage as he took in the room setup. "Wait," he said. "Your hostel said you were at a job interview. That can't be with my *sister*."

Zin bounced to her feet. "Are you saying I'm not qualified to do job interviews?" she asked combatively. Apparently modesty was only for outsiders.

"I'm saying you're not allowed to *poach Surit*!"

"Too late!" Zinyary said. "We can use him, and you were too slow!"

"You've barely met him, *Zin*," From the side, the two aquiline-nosed Halkana siblings faced each other like sniping birds of prey. Surit could appreciate Zinyary's artistry. Tennal didn't even seem to notice he was being wound up.

No point in letting it go on too long, though. "Nobody's using me," Surit said calmly. "Sen Zinyary, can you excuse us?" It was the height of irresponsibility to walk out of a job interview. Surit savored it.

Zin stopped winding Tennal up regretfully. "You don't need to withdraw, I'll tell them we rescheduled," she said. "I can at least give you my work contact." She touched her wristband and glanced at Tennal as if she were uncertain, then straight at Surit. When she was serious, she looked a lot like Tennal and a lot like the legislator. Surit didn't know which one made him warier. "Really, though, you were a lot of help to my family. If you need anything—the Halkanas are in your debt."

"Don't turn that down," Tennal muttered to Surit. "She can coax anything out of the legislator. Get her to sort out that pension."

Surit wasn't entirely sure he wanted to be more tangled up with the Halkanas—but then again, he already was, and he didn't see that ending any time soon. "Thank you," Surit said. He bowed to Zinyary and touched his throat, then let Tennal pull him outside.

On the sunbaked flagstones outside Zin's workplace, Tennal watched Surit's familiar broad shoulders and solid presence and wondered why he'd ever thought his luck was bad.

Surit shut the bronze swinging doors with meticulous care, turned around, and smiled. Even in the handful of days he'd been on-planet, he'd lost some of his space pallor. He seemed slower and a little absentminded, and—happier. Was Tennal still lucky? Well, he was here to find out.

"Hey, boss," Tennal said, by way of greeting. *Keep it casual.* Surit didn't know what was happening in his head, and right now that was a good thing. And Tennal only felt the ghost of a temptation to read him.

Surit looked Tennal over, and then he smiled again. This really wasn't fair. Surit's smile made all Tennal's trains of thought derail. Surit said, "You look good."

Tennal's mind blanked. He had come here to be *emotionally honest,* but when the chips were down, he absolutely couldn't do it. "Thank you, I know." It came out in the same breezy and superficial tone he would have used a year ago. "It's all the political infighting that does it. Gives me a beautiful glow to the skin. You haven't cut your hair in weeks, have you? It suits you."

He'd fucked up; he'd meant to say something meaningful, and he'd fucked *up.* He could feel his expression defaulting to *condescending posh twit.*

Surit laughed. It wasn't really a full laugh but a low rumble in his chest. "I'll remember that."

Maybe he hadn't fucked up completely. Tennal couldn't manage to say what he'd come to say, but he groped for a lifeline. "We said we'd go out in Exana once, remember?" He gestured to the hazy street. "Got some time?"

"Always," Surit said agreeably. He fell in beside Tennal in a way that felt natural. Surit hadn't lost his measured officer's stride, and after all those weeks, Tennal's pace was nearly the same. "You said flatbread."

"If I can find any," Tennal said. "Everything's changed since I lived here." A flock of birds darted overhead, flashes of blue and white wings against the burnished gold of the sky.

They strolled away from the new buildings of stone and glass to a district of low crumbling walls. Tennal found a cart selling drinks, and they both got flatbread and cold glasses of sugarmint, the condensation dripping off the glass and blissfully chilling Tennal's hand. The citrus taste was sharper than Tennal remembered.

They stopped under a flowering tree. Surit leaned against it, and Tennal sat on the back of a bench. He didn't even have to watch Surit anymore—he still had that sense of his presence, like a constant pulse left over from the sync—but he did anyway. Surit looked at home, Tennal thought. But of course he did; Surit looked at home in most places.

"Sorry it's been a couple of days," Tennal said. "I had to get my head sorted out."

Surit had been peering up at the sky through the tree branches in fascination, as if it had been a while since he'd seen blossoms, but at that he focused his full attention and his sober brown eyes on Tennal. "What have you sorted out?"

"I think I missed you like a normal person, these past few days," Tennal said, as if that made any sense. "Or as close to normal as I can get. It's not the sync. It's just . . . you."

Surit didn't immediately answer, his expression complicated, and Tennal felt like he'd thrown himself off a cliff.

"I missed you too," Surit said. Then, before Tennal could fully process that: "How long?"

Tennal knew what he was asking. "Six months," he said. "I've seen the agreement. The Resolution has to give back our nationals when they say they will. It's in all the treaties; Zin checked the language. Six months from now, I should be right here again."

Surit still had that distant, obscure look on his face. Tennal's heart hammered. He'd known rejection was *possible,* but he hadn't accepted that, not really. He'd never made himself this vulnerable before.

"I tried to go too," Surit said at last.

"What?"

"I asked the treaty team," Surit said. "You should have someone you know with you. But if they're assigning an escort team, they don't want architects, and they don't believe I'm not one."

"Ah," Tennal said blankly, as the colors around him became more vivid, the sun brighter, the shade deeper. Surit had asked to come with him. Even more than Surit's smile when he saw him, this made Tennal's chest feel like there was a pool of molten metal inside it. "I'm coming back," he hastened to add. "It won't be that long before I'm here again. If you . . ." He didn't know how to finish that sentence.

Surit said thoughtfully, "And when you get back? What will you do?"

"I don't know. Politics, maybe," Tennal said. It didn't sound as flippant as it should; or maybe Surit knew him too well, because that was the first thing Tennal had said that genuinely surprised him. Tennal swallowed. "Look, I don't think there are any winners from what we went through. I don't trust my aunt, and I don't think she should have everything her own way. I've concluded that I can be a nightmare *and* do something useful." He took a breath. "Being a nightmare might be helpful, in fact."

Surit's expression was now indescribable, the twitch of his mouth both familiar and totally foreign. Tennal was shocked with how much he wanted to lay his fingertips on Surit's jaw and feel the tiny shifts of the muscles. "You were never a nightmare."

Tennal looked at the corner of Surit's mouth and his warm eyes.

He thought of waking up on a Cavalry ship in chaotic space and thinking, *Do I love him?* He thought of putting Surit back together and realizing: *You love me too.* "I meant it," Tennal said, more quietly. "All of it. I don't know about you, but I meant it."

Surit made a choked noise. He turned over his hand, palm up. He reached out.

Tennal pushed himself off the bench he was leaning against and seized Surit's hand like the last tether to an airlock. He'd kissed Surit before. He didn't remember this rush like he was drowning, the last vestiges of their sync merging. Tennal closed his hand over Surit's shoulder, feeling the warm press of his skin through the rough weave of his shirt. Surit was as solid as a rooted tree, as warm as the sunlight. The kiss sent a flood of heat through Tennal's bones—but it was more than that. Tennal knew this was an orbit he could always return to.

"You said there weren't winners," Surit said against his mouth.

"You can always cheat though," Tennal said. "I was told you weren't even supposed to see me, Lieutenant Yeni. Does that count as cheating?"

"No, because it's you," Surit said. Tennal didn't have to be a reader to understand the swell of joy, because he felt it too. "I don't care about orders. It's always been you."

It was summer in Exana. And if Tennal could have read every mind in this city—in this sector—he still wouldn't have swapped with any of them in favor of being here, now, kissing Surit under the shade of a tree on this street. On this quiet afternoon, under this patchwork of shade, on this flawed, fractious planet where he was born, Tennal's own head finally felt like home.

EPILOGUE

When Tennal came to say goodbye, Surit was at the vegetable beds back home, his hands deep in the sun-drenched soil.

Surit hadn't expected it. It had been two weeks. After Exana, Tennal had disappeared off-planet for paperwork and intensive secret briefings—which must have been fun for everyone involved—and Surit had gone back to see his parent Elvi in his village. Surit had assumed that was it until Tennal left for the Resolution. Tennal didn't seem like the type for niceties like goodbyes. Surit had made his peace with that.

But here was Tennal, dusty from the dirt track, short black wisps of hair clinging to the back of his neck with sweat, clearly annoyed, clearly hadn't slept, and here in Surit's old village as out of place as a fish on a spaceship.

"Lights, it took me thirty-six hours to get here," Tennal said by way of greeting. "Have you considered moving your rustic ancestral farmstead somewhere with *any* transport links? That mountain road nearly finished me off. Is this how you thought you'd get away from me?"

And Surit noticed how the whole world was brighter and thought with resigned amusement, *Surit, you haven't made peace with anything at all.*

"You're just standing there smiling," Tennal said suspiciously.

"Yeah," Surit said. He didn't see any reason to hide it now. "You're here."

He wasn't expecting Tennal to visibly fumble for what to say next. "I didn't come here to get *clotheslined*," Tennal said with feeling. "For fuck's sake. Just act like a normal person and make fun of me for coming all this way to say goodbye, thanks." Surit was too busy dusting his hands off and smiling at him, so Tennal closed the gap and kissed him instead.

Two weeks without Tennal had done nothing for the effect he had on Surit. Surit wrapped his hand around Tennal's back to steady them both and fell into the electric warmth of Tennal's mouth on his like falling into the universe. The first time had been urgent. Surit tried to make this light and careful, a welcome kiss, but nothing with Tennal was light and careful. He laughed and bit Surit's lip. Surit fought down a surge of heat; they were outside, and surely Tennal was staying.

"So," Tennal said brightly, breaking apart as Surit was still catching his breath, "I've got fourteen hours before my absolute drop-dead leaving deadline, crawler ticket booked, Resolution ship scheduled, all that shit." He looked over Surit's shoulder at the house. "Do I get invited in?"

"Always," Surit said, and he saw Tennal lose his words again and twitch his eyebrows in annoyance. Elvi's house was low and unassuming, framed by white-leafed trailing branches. The wood smelled of dust, gently parching in the summer heat. Surit pushed open the door into the welcome shade. "I should warn you," Surit said, "I don't have any champagne."

"I crossed the planet for no champagne?"

"It got too warm and I had to throw it out," Surit said. "Standards."

Tennal laughed. "Standards, Surit Yeni? Too late." He turned around the open living space, taking in the work tools, the dried herbs, the colorful rugs Elvi collected, and Surit could feel the energy from him like a vibration in the air. "I like the house."

"Oh," Surit said, "I like my standards." This also, fascinatingly, made Tennal twitch. Surit filed that away for further exploration.

"Elvi's on a buyers' trip, by the way," Surit added. "He'll be sorry to have missed you."

Surit had once known Tennal's mood every second of every day just by the currents in his own brain. But now that he was on the outside it was a tantalizing puzzle every time. Surit enjoyed puzzles. Tennal was restless in a focused, hungry way, like a tiger stalking its prey, and what he was focused on was Surit.

"Then my timing was perfect and I'm a genius." Tennal put a hand on Surit's hip and touched the side of his face, all five fingertips resting lightly on Surit's skin like points of light. Surit held still. "What do you want from me, Surit?" Tennal said softly. "I'm going out-sector tomorrow. You can have it now."

Surit lifted his hand to Tennal's shoulder, feeling the way the muscles flexed, and closed his eyes. He savored the touch, the gift, the terrifying way Tennal just opened himself up. A couple of weeks ago Surit would have seized the offer immediately, but this was now, and right now, neither of them was going to die. Even if Tennal didn't dare to work in *futures*, Surit could at least plan out possibilities for both of them.

And here was a possibility: that there would always be time.

"I want," Surit said, "to make you some tea."

There was a pause. Tennal gave an explosive snort of laughter. "All right, fuck you," he said fondly. "Or not. Are you keeping track of my hydration levels?"

"You just told me you'd been traveling for a day and a half," Surit said mildly. That kind of distance meant Tennal had come down from low orbit as well, probably from wherever they were holding his briefings. "You told me that three minutes ago. Sit down and be a guest."

Tennal did not sit down. He did not have any tea. Instead, he tagged along into the kitchen while Surit cooked and made disparaging noises about Surit's taste in spices, then hovered over his shoulder and ate half the result while it was on the stove. Surit made him shower before they sat at the table. It was a joy, to put food in front of Tennal and watch him eat it, to listen to Tennal's bright and vicious commentary on everyone he'd met over the last two weeks, to offer up his own story of coming back to the village.

"Do you think you'll stay?" Tennal said abruptly.

Surit said, "I don't know."

"Don't you? Oh, then, I'll just have to know and you'll just have to find out," Tennal said. He maddeningly refused to elaborate. Surit patiently went through his most official debriefing checklist until both of them were laughing and they'd forgotten the question, but he didn't get any more answers.

We could be like this, Surit thought, looking at Tennal's face. It wasn't anything certain. Six months was a long time, and he knew for certain that Tennal wasn't thinking about the future. But Surit could do this again, maybe thousands of times, if Tennal and the universe let him.

And then, after they'd finished eating, Tennal said, "I didn't actually come here for the food," and they did end up in Surit's bedroom, the bed rolled out hastily on the floor and the last of the red sunset falling in a square on the foot of it. Surit's patience cracked and he pulled Tennal against him, his own skin already sensitive and wanting, and Tennal fell into the embrace hungrily. The rhythm was easy as they kissed and kissed. Surit's belt came off to Tennal's sharp tugs. Surit unbuttoned Tennal's shirt and pushed it off his shoulders to mouth at his collarbone as Tennal sprawled out underneath him. As Surit's mouth found new places on Tennal's skin, Tennal made noises he had never heard before, and every one made liquid heat pool hotter in Surit's chest. It was a relief that this wasn't a sync, was the only fleeting thing Surit remembered, because Surit couldn't have surprised Tennal in a sync. He couldn't have touched him like one person hungry for another, couldn't have had their wrists accidentally clashing as Surit finally dragged Tennal's shirt over his head, the unintentional catch of Tennal's cuff in Surit's mouth, the awkwardness and the ridiculousness and the joy of Tennal underneath him and surging up to kiss him, while Surit held them back just to savor the ache.

Tennal didn't stay underneath for long. Surit went over with him with Tennal's teeth on Surit's lip and his knee pushed firmly between Surit's thighs, and Surit held on to his defenses like ranks of soldiers surrounding the flag as one by one, in the onslaught from Tennal's hands and mouth, they fell away.

It was so much. It was so *much.* And then there was a reprieve as Tennal pushed himself up on his arms and took a breath, then resumed sweeter and much slower.

At first Surit drank that in as well; he hadn't expected *sweet* from Tennal, but he'd take it. He'd take anything Tennal wanted to give. But then he caught the moment's hesitation before Tennal kissed him again.

Hesitating wasn't like Tennal. It hadn't even been a real hesitation; Surit had no idea where it had come from, but he recognized the flash of calculation in Tennal's eyes.

Surit didn't bother forming the question. He just said, "Status?"

Tennal, stretched across Surit's body, skin hot on bare skin, looked down at Surit with an expression that had suddenly become very complicated. Then, as if he'd realized he was giving too much away, that was erased and in its place was flippancy. "Just pretending I'm the type to take it slow. Isn't that how you like it?"

In the quiet, warm night, every sense was full of Tennal, Tennal's face, Tennal's voice, his scent. It was hard for Surit to get his words in order. "I don't want you to pretend for me."

Tennal's expression did not get less complicated. He lay on Surit's chest and balanced his elbows on the bed so he could take hold of Surit's head with both his hands, fingers greedy on his face. "All right, boss, just shoot down *all* my shields."

That wasn't what Surit had meant at all. He brought up his own hand so he could rest his thumb on Tennal's chin. Tennal's eyes were like black holes. "Sorry," he murmured. "We can pretend all you like. What are we pretending?"

Tennal's kiss this time was a savage mixture of sweet and ruthless. "Normally," Tennal said, and kissed him again, "the other guy isn't in on it."

"I want to be, though."

Surit felt Tennal's helpless ripple of laughter, vicious and silent, through the shiver of his ribs. "I'm terrible," Tennal said. "I know you know that. You've been in my fucking brain."

"I like what you are," Surit said. "I like you." The whole ocean. Every vortex and riptide and drowning depth of it. Every ripple, every lightless wonder. Every tooth and bone. Surit's hands roamed over the sharpness of Tennal's hips, the sensitive skin as he moved to the front, and Tennal made a choked, swallowed noise, and held Surit down.

They woke the next morning to birdsong and Tennal's blaring alarm for his Resolution deadline. Tennal moved grudgingly, sprawled exhausted over Surit's chest.

"I didn't even need the alarm," Tennal said. "Those bloody birds woke me up. Lift your arm."

Surit reluctantly lifted his arm from over Tennal's back and released him. Tennal used his freedom of movement to scramble to his feet and incidentally flip off a bird that had landed on a tree branch outside to squawk. "Surit Yeni's rural idyll. Does it land on your shoulder to sing songs?"

"No, mainly it eats the planting seed," Surit said mildly. "Or it did when I was younger."

Tennal splashed water on his face from the basin, and unexpectedly laughed. Surit looked up as Tennal turned around; he was caught by the picture his bright face made, salt-washed with the gray dawn light even here, in a familiar place with no sea.

"It's nice here," Tennal said. "Quiet. Predictable. Heaven for a country boy, I suppose." And he added, with complete certainty, "Lucky for me, though, you'll never stay for long."

"Why?" Surit said, but he knew the answer.

"You want the universe," Tennal said. "You always have."

Wanting the universe; wanting Tennal. Surit took a quick breath and pushed himself up onto his elbows. *Yes, always.*

Tennal was right. The sun was rising. And the sky awaited.

ACKNOWLEDGMENTS

First of all, thanks go to my wonderful partner, Eleanor, for cheering on this book, putting up with me through numerous deadlines, and applying serious medical knowledge to questions like, "Is there a good biological reason to forget about your lungs if you're in someone else's brain?"

Also to the fabulous Ali Fisher, who shaped this book into what it is with her editorial insight, enthusiasm, expertise, and a terrific willingness to dive headlong into its weirdness; and to Kristin Temple, who kept the wheels on the whole project with verve.

To Tamara Kawar, World's Greatest Agent, for supporting it every step of the way, *also* fully rolling with things like "and then they both sort of mind-merge into space" and "I swear this will make sense in context."

To the team at Tor US, including the great team of Becky Yeager, Renata Sweeney, Rachel Taylor, and Caro Perny, for their enthusiasm and skill in telling as many people as possible the book exists; Megan Kiddoo, Steven Bucsok, Greg Collins, Katie Klimowicz, and Michelle Foytek for their creativity and attention to detail in making it a beautiful object in both the digital and physical worlds (and especially for allowing a heroic number of last-minute corrections; thank you!); and to Devi Pillai, Eileen Lawrence, Sarah Reidy, and Lucille Rettino. Thanks go as well to the sensitivity readers who worked on this project, including moukies, for their keen eyes and their suggestions.

To the team at Orbit UK, including my wonderful editor, Jenni Hill, and the brilliant and tireless efforts of Nazia Khatun, Nadia Saward, Madeleine Hall, Joanna Kramer, and Anna Jackson. (Due to the nature of book printing schedules, I will have missed some very talented people who worked on this book from this list, for which I apologize!)

To my family, especially Mum and Mark, who both gallantly proofread the manuscript.

To Emily Tesh, A. K. Larkwood, Megan Stannard, Ariella Bouskila, Sophia Kalman, and Maz, who convinced me not to give up several times, and who *continue* to be unfairly talented and funny, and on whom I intend to take revenge by making them finish their own books.

And lastly, to everyone who supported *Winter's Orbit* or this book—thank you.

ABOUT THE AUTHOR

Richard Wilson Photography

EVERINA MAXWELL is the author of *Winter's Orbit* and *Ocean's Echo*. She lives and works in Yorkshire, where she collects books and kills houseplants.

everinamaxwell.com
avoliot.tumblr.com
Twitter: @Av_Stories
Instagram: @everina_maxwell